QUEEN'S MATE

○

At the height of the Battle of the Atlantic in the winter of 1943, a German U boat was sunk leaving only one survivor: coxswain Ulrich Muller. Sighted and rescued by an American destroyer he masqueraded as a Norwegian seaman and under this cover was to become the key man in the Germans' boldest wartime opertion at sea: the seizure of the 81,000 ton liner Queen Mary in mid-ocean.

Ordered to strike on Voyage 97, Muller only learns when he has boarded the ship that Voyage 97 was to be important for quite a different reason. Winston Churchill is also on board, together with the top echelon of the British war leadership, on his way to the Trident Summit Conference.

Drawing on official records, ships drawings and his own extensive knowledge of the Battle of the Atlantic, Terence Hughes has pieced together the thrilling and intriguing story of what happened in those dramatic hours when the ship was sailing unescorted into danger.

Queen's Mate

Terence Hughes

CORONET BOOKS
Hodder and Stoughton

For my wife

Copyright © 1982 by Terence Hughes

First published in Great Britain 1982
by Hodder and Stoughton Ltd

Coronet edition 1984

British Library C.I.P.

Hughes, Terry
  Queen's mate.
  I. Title
  823' .914[F]   PR6058.U38

  ISBN 0-340-34909-3

Printed and bound in Great Britain for
Hodder and Stoughton Paperbacks, a
division of Hodder and Stoughton Ltd.,
Mill Road, Dunton Green, Sevenoaks,
Kent (Editorial Office: 47 Bedford
Square, London, WC1 3DP) by
Hunt Barnard Printing Ltd.,
Aylesbury, Bucks.

'We left London on the night of May 4 and went aboard the *Queen Mary* in the Clyde on the following day. The ship had been admirably fitted up to meet all our needs. The whole delegation was accommodated on the main deck, which was sealed off from the rest of the ship. Offices, conference rooms and of course the Map Room stood ready for immediate use. From the moment we got on board our work went forward ceaselessly.'

Winston Churchill
The Second World War, Vol. *IV*, *Chapter XLIII*

Chapter 1

A winter dawn broke over the fields of Brittany on the morning of 19 February 1943. A light layer of snow covered the frozen lawns and flower beds of a large country house outside the port of Lorient, the headquarters of the German Navy's U-boat arm. Inside the rambling mansion a handful of officers worked quietly at a row of desks in what had once been the owner's dining room. Some of them were drafting signals, others were engrossed in complex calculations of ships' positions and speeds. They were all young and showed little sign of fatigue, although they had been working all night.

There was a hushed atmosphere in the room, almost as if it were a library or place of learning. The lighting was subdued, except for two bright lamps which illuminated a vast map of the Atlantic ocean. It covered the whole of one wall and depicted the Atlantic from Norway to Mexico, from Greenland to the Plate. This immense sea area was divided into coded squares and dotted with coloured pins and markers, giving an up-to-date presentation of the position of the German U-boat fleet. There were large clusters of pins in the bases of Brest and Lorient, and some squares were bisected by neat fences blocking the enemy shipping routes.

The slender figure of the commander in chief, U-boats, stood thoughtfully before the chart, chin cupped in his hand. The ascetic features revealed no sign of emotion as his deep-set eyes stared fixedly at square D22, eight hundred miles south-west of the Azores. For the whole of the night D22 had been the most important area in the whole Atlantic ocean, because it was from this position only twenty hours before that U-1543 had signalled, 'Convoy sighted'.

The terse message had been followed by intense activity as orders and directives streamed out from operational HQ homing every U-boat within striking distance on to the convoy. By the time the early morning light touched the freezing Breton landscape the C in C had surrounded his target with a wolf pack of eighteen U-boats. Everyone in the room now awaited his final order for the Allied convoy to be torn to pieces.

Chief Petty Officer Ulrich Müller stood on the bridge of U-1543 and cursed the full moon. On such a clear night the low profile of an Atlantic U-boat could be spotted by enemy look-outs.

At his side the watchkeeper dropped his binoculars and looked anxiously towards him, eyes red with spray.

'Why the hell doesn't HQ give the order to attack? They'll see us in this light.'

'Don't worry. You'll get the order soon enough.' Müller turned back to the convoy. He had seen many, but this one was an impressive sight, staked out over thirty square miles of ocean. It always moved him to see the long lines of merchant-men advancing with orderly seamanlike discipline. There were tankers full of paraffin, Liberty ships packed with ammunition and freighters low in the water with K rations and Hershey Bars. From the convoy's position he guessed that it was on its way to supply General Eisenhower's armies in North Africa, and he wondered how many would reach their destination.

At twenty-five Müller was a veteran of ocean war, and U-1543 was his third boat. In a command which had lost over half its experienced men since the beginning of the war, Müller was conscious of being regarded with a degree of awe at having survived so long. Many of the young commanders and their crews had been killed or drowned, and he frequently wondered how much longer his luck would hold out. Perhaps the attack on the convoy would be his last. He pushed such thoughts from his mind. As the leading non-commissioned officer aboard, Müller knew that the young seamen, many just out of school, depended heavily on him.

As a war voyage wore on, Müller knew how quickly morale could deteriorate, and on tours of inspection through the mess decks he kept his eye open for any sullen or dejected face. Over the years he had created his own methods for distracting and occupying a fatigued crew. The most difficult moments came during raging gales which could last for days. During such times the U-boat never stopped pitching and rolling, and it became almost impossible to eat, sleep or keep dry after standing watches on the exposed bridge. Yet the bridge still had to be manned, and Müller made it his job to steady the look-outs, sometimes lashing them to the conning tower. At such times men, half-drowned by the seas sweeping over them, would turn automatically to Müller for guidance, and he came into his own as a man of the sea.

Since his earliest days he had known the feel of a keel beneath his feet, and from the age of six he had been sailing a dinghy through the hazardous waters of northern Norway, where he had been brought up. Battling across a fjord, or cruising along the rocky coastline, he had learnt how to test his nerve. His prowess had become legendary in his home town of Lavanger, near Narvik. His father, a German teacher at the local high school, preferred a book-lined study to any kind of adventure, and worried about his son, but Müller's mother was different. She never questioned her son's exploits, however bold, and throughout his childhood, when told of some ambitious plan to sail to Lofoten or into the Arctic seas, she would quietly set out seaboots, jerseys, equipment and food for him.

His thoughts were interrupted by the sound of Kapitanleutnant Fritz Thannemann clambering on to the bridge.

'I'll never understand U-Boat Command,' Thannemann complained loudly. 'There must be a huge wolf pack around this convoy by now.'

Müller felt some sympathy for him. At twenty-nine Thannemann was too old to be a U-boat commander, and would have been much happier serving out the war in the Baltic.

'This is the biggest convoy I've seen on the Atlantic, Captain,' Müller assured him. 'Once we get started we shall sink plenty of ships—and they'll have to turn out the brass band at Lorient when we return!'

Wedged against the sleeve of the periscope, Thannemann checked the port and starboard sea areas ahead, then asked:

'Which one do you fancy, Müller?'

9

Forage cap pulled down low on his head, Müller peered into the darkness. 'I can't quite read all their names in this moonlight, Captain. Although I think I can recognise one or two of the skippers.'

There was laughter from the three other watchkeepers on the bridge, though Thannemann merely smiled.

When he addressed Müller again his eyes were bright.

'What about those fat cows in the middle of the herd? You like fat ones, so I've been told.'

Müller, whose sexual prowess among the girls of Lorient was a joke aboard U-1543, looked at the tankers.

'Fat ones are more satisfying in every way, Captain.'

'Signal, Captain. From U-Boat Command.'

Everyone on U-1543's bridge strained their ears, as Eckhardt, the baby-faced first officer, climbed clumsily through the hatch from below, holding the signal log. Thannemann snatched it from him and read aloud:

'ATTACK NOW. DRIVE FORWARD RELENT-LESSLY. GOOD LUCK. C IN C.'

He grinned triumphantly. 'Let's get started.'

Below, blaring alarms transformed the crew. There was a scramble as men dodged each other and wriggled into fighting positions. They snaked through narrow hatches, crawled behind racing pistons and slammed bulkheads tight. Mess tables were bundled away; personal belongings swept into lockers. In the bow chamber men strained to haul the one-and-a-half-ton torpedoes into position.

'Full ahead both,' Thannemann ordered.

U-1543's MAN diesels surged to full power.

'I'm going for a fine bow shot. Outer group of three.'

'Yes, Captain,' Eckhardt acknowledged.

Leaning into the night, Thannemann kept his eyes on the convoy, as the first officer methodically checked the surface attack sight. Müller turned his back on the bridge to urge on the gun's crew as they scrambled on to the 'Wintergarten', behind the conning tower, and unwound the twin 20mm flak ammunition belts. At the same time, his professional eye watched the heavier-calibre 37mm cannon, situated farther astern, closed up for action.

'Where's the escort?' Thannemann barked.

'Lead destroyer holding tight to her position,' the starboard look-out reported.

'We should be all right . . .'

The captain's words were cut short. A bunch of Snowflake flares burst over the convoy, lighting the scene like a macabre gala. Then, in a wall of flame, a 'fat cow' in the heart of the convoy split apart, and 15,000 tons of ship disintegrated in a column of fire. Müller watched entranced. Whenever a ship exploded it exhilarated him, but then the sickness came to his stomach as the smoke billowed up high into the sky. He was silent as the men around him broke into a wild cheer. Thannemann jumped up and down like a schoolboy.

'Fantastic,' he shouted. 'Come on, make it snappy, Number One. There won't be anything left for us.' He turned to Eckhardt. 'We're inside their screen. Attack the first two ships in the starboard outer column. Clear tubes one, two and three for surface firing.'

In the bow chamber the torpedo-men prepared the tubes.

Müller grabbed the stopwatch dangling round his neck and took up his position behind Eckhardt. His duty would be to time the running of the torpedo to the point of impact on the target. He watched as the number one brought the thin cross-wires over the first Liberty ship, and shouted out bearings to the petty officer hunched over the Fahnrichter calculator below. Quickly the 53cm torpedoes were set.

'Angle on bow two, seven left. Range one thousand. Torpedo speed three zero, depth two metres. Follow for bearing.'

'Stand by to fire one, two and three. Bridge firing,' Thannemann ordered.

Number one's plump hand tightened on the pistol grip, compressed air hissed into the for'ard tubes and three torpedoes surged out of the U-boat's hull in a deadly fan.

'Torpedoes running!'

It was a moment of intense satisfaction. Müller's thumb pressed the stopwatch and he began to count down the seconds to target impact. It was a small ritual, like pronouncing a sentence of death on the enemy. He enjoyed it.

To improve her angle of approach, Thannemann now swung U-1543 on to a new course. This time Eckhardt wasted no time in rapping out directions for the next attack.

Müller still studied the stopwatch. Only twenty seconds to go. Apprehensively he glanced at the U-boat's boiling wake. There was a strong danger that the enemy escorts would pick it up, but speed was all that mattered.

'How much longer?' Thannemann shouted impatiently.

'Fifteen seconds, sir.'

Spray swept over the U-boat's bow and every man waited tensely.

'We've overshot,' Thannemann muttered.

Müller clicked the watch. Zero. Then it came: a sound Müller had heard often before, the hollow reverberation across the water as a torpedo found its mark.

'A hit. A hit,' Thannemann yelled.

The 37mm gun's crew hugged each other and cheering rose from below. Thannemann thumped Eckhardt on the back and promised him one of his last Havanas. Müller, however, continued to study the convoy. Snowflake flares broke over the disordered columns and the Liberty ship was belching smoke; but the Allied ships still kept formation, their masters aware that they faced a massacre if the long columns broke.

'There's absolute chaos over there, Captain,' Müller said.

Through his binoculars he could see that the freighter had taken a steep list to starboard. Tanks were rolling off her decks and into the sea. For a moment he felt for the crews, especially the stokers working half-naked in steaming engine rooms, who had little chance of escape.

'We've sunk a Liberty ship. Break out cognac all round,' Thannemann announced jubilantly to his men waiting below. But even as he said it Müller heard a rushing sound like an approaching express train. Instinctively he dived for cover behind the armoured wall of the conning tower. A fraction of a second later, a glistening tower of water soared above U-1543, then crashed down over the bridge as an enemy shell exploded twenty yards to starboard.

Water streamed from his nose and ears, and from below

12

he heard the cries of men hurled against bulkheads. Dimly Müller distinguished the stunned figure of Thannemann clinging to the periscope mast. Eckhardt was on all fours, shaking his head. One watchkeeper had disappeared, another lay moaning, both hands clutching his ribs.

The second blow fell unheralded. Blast swept the bridge. There was an agonised cry from Eckhardt as his head smashed into the compass, and the pressure hull convulsed with the shock of a direct hit.

Müller's chest ached with every breath. Only the armoured flank of the conning tower had saved him. Miraculously Thannemann stood hanging on to what was left of the WANZ radar detector.

'Hard a-port. Full ahead both. Damage control report. Fast!'

Müller struggled to his feet, and was just able to make out the tell-tale bow wave of a British escort.

'Enemy ship three thousand metres on starboard quarter, Captain. It's a corvette,' Müller said without emotion. 'We've got the edge on her. She can only do fifteen knots at best.' Then he bent over Eckhardt. There was little to be done. Blood was oozing from a gaping wound in his head. Part of his brain stuck to the deck casing.

'Casualty party up here now. Fast,' Thannemann shouted down the voice tube.

The chief engineer acknowledged the bridge and calmly launched into a damage report.

'We've been hit four metres abaft the lower bridge. Pressure hull ruptured. Severe damage to aft mess deck. Three dead, four injured. Working on alternative power circuits. Engines fully operational.'

It sounded almost comforting, but Müller knew that U-1543's position was serious. She had lost her primary defence—invisibility. With a damaged pressure hull she had to stay on the surface.

Suddenly the bridge was bathed in the harsh glare of a searchlight, and Müller saw a dark shape coming up fast.

'Destroyer, sir, on the starboard bow.'

With the convoy on his port beam and the corvette astern, Müller knew they were trapped.

'We'll have to break between them,' Thannemann declared. 'Hard a-starboard. Full speed both.'

U-1543 veered at a steep angle and almost turned in her length.

'Open fire on the searchlight. Kill it fast,' the commander shouted to the gun batteries.

Tracer ripped into the night and arched towards the destroyer. Then there was darkness, but Müller kept his eyes on the enemy bow wave.

'If it's a Hunt class destroyer she will be down our necks in a few minutes,' he said quietly, concious that Thannemann could not play off the two ships for long. But U-1543 still had a sting in her tail. The stern tubes were still loaded, and if the enemy warship came really close it might just be possible to torpedo her.

A hail of shots sprayed over Müller and struck the conning tower, and there was a cry of pain from the 20mm gun crew. The destroyer was now very close. Orange flashes spurted along her upper works as she let loose with her secondary armament.

Thannemann crouched like an animal over the night sight.

'*Now*, Müller. She's two hundred metres away. Fire tubes five and six!'

His eyes shone like black pools as the torpedoes sped towards the enemy, then U-1543 went hard over, diesels racing. Water flooded across her stern casing; a dead gunner slid into the sea.

For a moment the destroyer maintained her course, bow wave creaming and battle ensign flying. Then, sensing U-1543's dying efforts, the British commander threw his ship into a tight curve. Foam curled across the tilting deck and the destroyer's stern swung violently as a torpedo streaked below the fantail, inches from the rudder. Now the destroyer was pointing like a stake at the exposed hull of the submarine.

Müller watched the bow towering towards them. 'He's going to ram us, Captain. Will you abandon ship?'

Thannemann was silent. Fifty yards away the bow was cutting towards them at thirty knots, and the Oerlikons opened up again, but Thannemann still seemed unable to move. Müller shouldered him aside. 'Abandon ship, abandon ship!' he yelled.

There was a frantic scramble for the narrow hatches, a terrible screech of steel on steel. Sparks sprayed from the destroyer's keel as her bows reared. Müller felt the deck tilt beneath his feet. The rending and tearing was like a giant saw, and with dazed fascination he watched barnacles and ancient layers of seaweed stream from the ship's belly as it rolled over the U-boat. The conning tower plunged horizontally into the waves, and the Atlantic thundered into the crowded compartments below. Then darkness. A hand seemed to be drawing Müller down into the depths, and the steel tomb of U-1543 began to skewer gently towards the ocean floor.

Chapter 2

Mist clung to the surface of the ocean: the waters moved listlessly after the night's slaughter. A sickening stench of diesel filled Müller's nostrils as he rolled on to his back. To free his limbs he had kicked off his heavy sea boots. Only the yellow Kriegsmarine life-jacket stood between him and the bottom of the Atlantic.

It was eerily quiet, and he had lost all sense of time, but his aching chest and neck told him that he had been in the sea for several hours. He was alone. U-1543's young community of forty-six men had disappeared, their grave marked only by a tennis shoe, a battered cap and the thick film of diesel.

Oily sea slurped into his mouth and made him retch. There was no sign of the British destroyer, and he thought ironically of the Kriegsmarine's standing orders: 'Do not rescue any men . . . do not care for any boats . . . we must be hard in this war.' Now it was his turn. He had often wondered how he would face up to it, and now felt strangely inadequate.

Night had given way to a grey morning. Mist blocked out the sun and Müller was thankful for the protection it gave against the heat. Strength ebbed from his body and he could no longer feel his tired legs, but his neck muscles were gripped by an agonising pain as the life-jacket forced his chin to remain in a fixed position above water hour after hour.

Müller wondered how long he could stand the ordeal and tried not to think of the empty ocean around him. To control his fear he fought to apply a simple technique, setting himself mental problems—algebraic equations, simple codes, anything that would keep his mind from turning in upon itself—but slowly he lost concentration. Memories of sailing off North Cape drifted before him, where survival could be measured in minutes, unlike the warm waters of the mid-Atlantic where he would take days to die. Almost in a panic, Müller remembered the sharks which hunted in these latitudes. He had seen their fins from U-1543's conning tower; they appeared from nowhere, ready to scavenge anything thrown overboard, and once the whole crew had been stunned by the terrible aftermath of a shark attack on a survivor, when U-1543 came across the body of a legless seaman drifting on the current. With a conscious effort Müller closed his mind to the image and once more looked around the horizon. It seemed to be clearer now, and the mist was lightening.

Then, across the water, clear and recognisable, came a man's voice. It was shouting in English, a language Müller thanked God he had been taught at his Norwegian school.

'Ahoy! Ahoy there. Over here.'

Fifty yards away, emerging from the mist, was a ship's life-boat. An emaciated figure stood amidships waving his arms.

'Take it easy. We'll come and get you.'

Oars were thrust over the side, and the boat began to pull slowly towards him. There were long streaks of rust along her sides, and an improvised canvas awning hung across the bow for shelter, while a tatty collection of chipped mugs and enamel basins had been placed around the boat to catch rainwater.

A stocky middle-aged man was at the tiller, and from his battered cap and stained gold rings Müller recognised a first officer of the British Merchant Navy. Next to him a negro seaman sat disconsolately, wrapped in a navy blue overcoat and watching with round exhausted eyes as the other two men prepared to take Müller aboard. One of them was skinny and wore a grubby singlet, but the other seaman, clad in faded jeans and a T-shirt, had a muscular frame and was deeply tanned. When he spoke Müller immediately detected a Scandinavian accent.

'Bring her over a bit, Skipper, or we'll miss him.'

Conserving his energy, Müller paddled gently towards the boat, and when it drew alongside marshalled all his remaining strength to grip the gunwale. The two men above him leaned out and grabbed his arms. The boat rocked as Müller crashed on to the bottom boards, where he lay, panting. Water trickled out of his nose and mouth, then his stomach heaved and he threw up a mouthful of black oil.

The first officer looked down at him. The sun had broken through the mist now and picked out the grey threads in the seaman's beard. His eyes were friendly.

'You all right, mate?' he asked. 'No bones broken, nothing like that?'

Müller mustered a grin. 'I'm okay,' he replied, hoping that his English had enough of a Norwegian accent to allay suspicion.

A three-quarters-empty bottle of Martell brandy was produced, and the first officer took an enamel mug from the awning and poured a careful measure. Gently he wiped the liquorice-brown stains from Müller's mouth before pressing the brandy to his lips. Müller nodded his thanks.

'Where you from, mate?' the thin seaman asked in a flat Liverpudlian voice.

Müller hesitated, lost for a reply. To his relief the Scandinavian seaman intervened.

'Can't you see he's been in the water for hours? Give him a chance.' His blue eyes turned back to Müller, who guessed that he was Norwegian. One of the thousands serving with the Allied merchant marine.

Blood started to flow back into Müller's limbs, and he began to breathe more easily. He pulled himself up into a sitting position and studied the men around him. They were thin and worn, and when they spoke their speech seemed slurred.

The men's movements were slow and laboured, and they grouped around Müller, watching him with quiet fascination. The young seaman was paying close attention to Müller's Kriegsmarine life-jacket. His eyes suddenly narrowed in triumph.

'Look at his life-jacket—that's a Jerry design. I've seen them before, dozens of times.' A thin finger pointed at the safety instructions printed on the yellow rubber. 'That's German, ain't it?'

The first officer glared at Müller. 'Get that life-jacket off.'

They tugged the rubber vest away and the first officer handed it to the Norwegian.

'Here, Larsen, is this German? Looks it to me.'

The clear blue eyes scanned the lines, then the seaman's expression hardened and he turned to the officer.

'It's German all right, Skipper. Standard issue.'

'Come on, admit it,' the young man shouted. 'You're a bloody Jerry.'

Müller stared back, his face impassive, as he began to work out his chances. In spite of his time in the sea, he still felt able to defend himself. The negro was very weak and could be discounted, but it would be difficult to overpower the Norwegian. There was also the young Englishman to contend with, and he was carrying a narrow-bladed sheath knife on his hip. Instinctively Müller looked for a weapon, and spotted a marlin spike jammed in the gunwale five feet behind Larsen. But, whether intentionally or not, the big seaman was blocking his way, his eyes fixed intently on Müller. There seemed little alternative to persuasion. Müller cleared his throat.

'I am Obersteuermann Ulrich Müller, Deutsche Kriegsmarine. My boat, U-1543, was sunk by a British destroyer last night. I believe I am the only survivor.'

The thin young man crowed. 'Just as I said. He's a bloody Jerry . . .'

'Then you were in the battle last night,' the first officer said. 'Enough fireworks for a Brock's display. Must have

18

been seen all the way back in New York, and there we were in the middle of it. But nobody spotted us bobbing around.'

'Trust us to be missed by seventy ships,' the young man said.

'One of your lot spotted us a couple of days ago,' the skipper went on. 'Big broad fellow. Was on the bridge. A cocky bastard, I can tell you. Wouldn't help. Just said that the nearest land was hundreds of miles away.'

There was a heavy silence, and Müller knew what they were thinking. U-boats never picked up survivors; why should they make room for a German?

Müller spoke again. 'And how long have you been drifting like this?'

'Eleven days,' the skipper muttered. 'We were sunk four days out of New York. Straggling, as usual. We never could keep up even with the slowest convoys. You bastards were bound to get us sooner or later. There was a cargo of tanks on board, and she went down in minutes.'

'You didn't need to fire a torpedo. Her plates were so thin a pencil would have done the trick,' the young man said.

'There was another lifeboat, but we haven't seen her,' Larsen added, muttering quietly. 'We started out with nine in this one.'

'Skipper?' There was menace in the Merseysider's voice, and his words did not surprise Müller. 'If he's a Jerry he ought to go over the side. Back where he came from. They don't help us, we shouldn't help them. You've seen the rafts and lifeboats full of dead, even women and kids. They machine-gun us in the water.'

'That's not true!' Müller snapped.

'Don't try and tell me what's true and what's not true, you bloody Jerry murderer,' the young man shouted. His eyes blazed and he darted for the marlin spike. Müller saw it just in time as the Englishman hurled it. With an instinctive move, he rolled sideways, hearing the point splinter the woodwork behind him. The sailor's skinny frame was only a few feet away, and his eyes were blazing angrily. He was still coming at Müller, who swiftly side-stepped. As the young Englishman blundered past, he hit him expertly between the shoulder blades, as he had dealt with drunken seamen in the bars of Lorient. Moaning, the lad fell to his knees, and Müller grasped the spike, ready to finish off his assistant, but a powerful hand locked over his wrist.

'Move and you will be dead in seconds.' Larsen's eyes were expressionless; a sheath knife gleamed in his other hand. Nobody spoke. There was only the rhythmic slurp of waves on the hull. A blazing sun had cleared the mist and the Atlantic stretched away endlessly. It seemed pointless to resist; they would probably all be dead soon.

'If you want to throw me back, okay,' Müller conceded quietly. 'There's nothing I can do.'

'I don't like doing it,' the skipper said, 'but you could make all the difference between life and death. Who knows when we'll be picked up?' He paused. 'We'll give you back your life-jacket.'

Müller shook his head and laughed. 'What good will that do against the whole Atlantic Ocean? You're condemning me to death. Why don't you just kill me?' He nodded at the Norwegian, whose knife was still inches from his chest. 'I'm sure your friend here will oblige.'

The pale eyes flickered.

'You will oblige, won't you?' Müller said suddenly in Norwegian.

A look of surprise came across Larsen's face. 'Are you a Norwegian?'

'Almost. I'm German, but I've lived all my life in Norway. My father was a local schoolmaster in—'

'Then what are you doing in the German Navy?'

'I told you, I am a German,' Müller answered, still in Norwegian.

The big man's shoulders relaxed and he put down his knife, but his gaze was fixed unwaveringly on Müller.

'Well, you're still the enemy, aren't you?' he said quietly. 'Doesn't change a thing.'

'Of course not, but if you wish to commit a war crime go ahead. Push me overboard. I don't suppose anybody will ever know.'

The skipper's brow furrowed. 'What the hell are you two talking about?'

Müller answered in English. 'I said if you want to commit a war crime why don't you just go ahead? It's not very sensible though, is it?'

The first officer shifted uncomfortably, and straightened his faded cap. 'We have to take hard decisions in war . . .'

Müller glanced around the boat, then said deliberately, 'Perhaps it doesn't really matter. I don't think you'll last long anyway.'

A scowl passed over the skipper's face, and Müller, aware that the other exhausted men were listening closely, played his trump. 'Do you even know where you are, or what course you are sailing?'

'I've been laying course by the stars.'

Müller shook his head slowly. 'You will never reach land. The coast of Africa is perhaps sixteen hundred miles away. And you are drifting south.'

There was a sudden hysterical laugh from the negro, who was sitting up straight, struggling to comprehend the discussion.

'Sixteen hundred miles,' he shouted. 'Why, that ain't no distance for a boat like this. No distance at all, if we know we are going in the right direction . . .'

'Shut up, Steamboat,' the skipper said sharply.

Müller went on quickly. 'Believe it or not, I am trying to help you. Hours ago I was on the bridge of my U-boat. I know the exact position and,' he added slowly, 'a convoy is due to pass close to us in two days.'

'How do you know?' To Müller's surprise it was the young Liverpudlian speaking. He had revived, and was clutching his head.

'Intelligence reports,' Müller replied. 'We can read all your codes.'

The skipper thought for a moment, then spoke. 'All right. If you know the course, what do we steer?'

'Oh, come on, Skipper,' Larsen protested. 'You can't expect a man to tell you that and then be thrown to the sharks.'

'No, I suppose not.'

As the skipper wavered, Müller pressed on.

'I could set a course which would bring you across the

route of the next convoy, or even reach the Azores, but you would need to do something about this boat.'

He pointed towards the awning. 'You have quite a lot of canvas there. Enough for a large sail.'

Müller now had his back to the stern and the others eyed him watchfully.

'Seems he's talking sense,' the skipper concluded. Then he addressed Müller. 'If you can rig a mast and get us somewhere I'll go along with it.'

Larsen nodded in agreement.

'But wait a minute—' the young man objected.

'Shut up,' the skipper rapped. 'Just do as you're told.'

'Come on, let's get organised,' Larsen said. 'Then have as much rest as possible. We can start tomorrow morning.'

Müller leaned back wearily, his back aching from his hours in the water. His limbs felt leaden but he fought to stay awake, watching the young seaman who had withdrawn to the stern. Like a watchdog, Larsen had parked himself between the two men, determined to stop any further trouble. Müller wondered how the survivors would react when they discovered that there was no convoy. In his head he tried to work out the likely position of the wolf pack, which would be heading south-east towards a refuelling rendezvous. With luck and the right rigging the lifeboat could reach this zone in a day or so, and might be spotted by the Germans. If not, he would have to take his chance.

Next morning everyone sat shivering in the dawn, as five mugs were set out in front of the bow awning, and Larsen poured two inches of water into each. Then he levered open a tin, brought out three square biscuits from the crinkled paper and carefully split them with his sheath knife. With a grin, he reached for a large tin of Robertson's marmalade and put a sliver on each biscuit.

For Müller it seemed the best breakfast a man could possibly eat. Steamboat was suffering badly from exposure and it was only with difficulty that he could be made to take anything. Müller watched as Larsen patiently coaxed the weak man to take a morsel of biscuit.

They started work on the sail immediately after they had eaten, but it was slow going. Days of exposure had reduced their work rate to a crawl, and it took almost an hour to strip off the awning.

To his relief, nobody resented Müller giving instructions, and even his thin young enemy, whose name, Müller discovered, was Staines, threw himself into the job. But it was the quiet Norwegian who was Müller's principal workmate.

Their first task was to hack away with sheath knives to create a three-foot-long flat surface on the round haft of one of the oars, repeating the job on the second oar so that the two could slide snugly together. Then a heavy warp was tied round the join, and a sixteen-foot mast laid down the centre of the boat.

The next stage was to fit the canvas sail. The awning was a large oblong, and holes had to be punched along the leading edge to make a mainsail that could then be hitched to the mast with cord.

Stepping the mast in the tabernacle was the hardest part, but with a heave they managed to get it halfway, then with a final all-out push raised it upright. At once it creaked as it took the strain, then the sail billowed and the lifeboat began to heave. She was under way.

'Bloody good, lads,' the skipper yelled, and they passed round the Martell for a celebratory swig.

'What course can we steer now?' the skipper asked.

'Just before U-1543 went down we were eight hundred miles south-west of the Azores. I think we should make south-east.'

The boat moved clumsily but steadily south, with Müller and Larsen, the two fittest men, taking it in turns to man the sail. It was clearly going to be a race against time for Steamboat. He had begun to hallucinate and was too weak to move. Müller noticed too that the skipper had moments of depression, and would ramble on about the *Empire Rose*, the old tramp steamer that had become his home. He was an ageing first officer, who would never be given command of a ship. As he looked at him leaning on the tiller, a strip of gold braid hanging pathetically from the peak of his cap, Müller felt a touch of sadness for him, and admired the way he had held the survivors together. Now the skipper meandered on, verging on the border of dementia.

The boat seemed to be making good headway before a southerly breeze when suddenly there was a cry from Staines who now spent most of the time hunched alone in the bows. Two dorsal fins were circling some fifty yards away.

'There must have been a convoy here,' Staines remarked. 'They live on dead sailors, the fat bastards.'

'Hammerheads,' the skipper declared. 'Real man-eaters. We'll see more if we're moving south.'

Müller shivered as he watched the sharks cruising effortlessly alongside.

'You know,' he said to the skipper, 'I can never understand my luck. They never attacked me when I was in the water.'

The skipper straightened his battered cap. 'Diesel, that's why. They can't stand the stuff, and you were swimming in it.'

Müller laughed. 'Perhaps they're on Hitler's side.'

The boat scudded on; as Müller half expected, there were no signs of shipping. Steamboat had now lapsed into a coma, and Müller could see there was little they could do for him. He lay motionless on the bottom boards in the bow and Larsen, who had always been friendly to him, did his best to make him comfortable. But the negro was unable to take even a sip of water. Watching, Müller resolved to do all in his power to have the survivors taken on board if they did find a U-boat. However, it was unlikely that the commander would agree, in which case he would see to it that they were given food and water.

During the long hot hours, Müller usually sat next to the skipper, advising him on navigation, and ready to take over the tiller whenever he tired. Larsen stayed amidships, keeping an eye on Steamboat and Staines. Very few words were exchanged in the boat; everyone was intent on conserving his strength.

It was on the third day of the new course that morale touched rock bottom. Larsen tried to rouse Steamboat, but the young negro was dead. Sadly the Norwegian broke a thwart from the centre of the boat to create a makeshift bier, then the others helped to stretch out Steamboat's corpse and covered it with his old blue overcoat. Nobody spoke as they stood around the body, Staines's hollow eyes wet with tears.

It was quickly over. The skipper managed a few mumbled words from the burial service at sea, and together they pushed the body overboard. They turned away in disgust as, almost immediately, a shark surged hungrily forward. Only Staines watched, his face ashen. Suddenly he turned his emaciated frame on Müller.

'Jerry bastard! It's your fault. Steamboat would have been alive if it weren't for you. We're lost.' With a flick of his arm, Staines whipped out the thin blade from his belt. Larsen and Müller drew back cautiously before him.

Staines's voice rose out of control. 'Stay out of this, Larsen!'

Inch by inch the three men moved towards the stern, where the skipper seemed confused by the scene.

'Don't look for your knife, Larsen,' Staines shouted. 'I've got it. You're a Jerry too, Larsen. You speak like him. You're all the same.'

He leapt on to a thwart. 'Come on, Jerry, what are you waiting for?' he taunted, brandishing the knife. Müller kept his eyes fixed on Staines's contorted features, and edged backwards towards the stern. Without a weapon he was dangerously vulnerable. He threw a sidelong glance at Larsen, just as the heavy frame of the skipper pushed between the two men. Staines's wild shouting had brought him to his senses.

'Put that bloody knife down, Staines. Don't be such a fool . . .' the skipper ordered, his hand outstretched. Staines stood motionless, and the skipper took a pace towards him. Suddenly the boat rocked and he stumbled over the thwart. As he did so Larsen moved. Hoping to catch Staines off guard he had jumped towards the sailor, but the Liverpudlian was fast on his feet, and with a sideways flick of his foot kicked the Norwegian viciously in the groin. Larsen fell to his knees with a grunt and Staines turned on Müller, whose back was almost at the stern post.

Staines came at him, the blade slashing at the German's throat. A warm trickle of blood ran down Müller's forearm, and only the tiller post saved him from being pushed overboard. He could feel the post at his back and desperately pushed with all his strength to dodge the slashing blade.

Staines toppled back, then leapt on to another thwart. The boat rocked, water spilling over the gunwales. For a moment the Englishman's arms waved and a look of fear swept across his narrow features as he tried to keep his balance. It was Müller's chance—with a kick he struck Staines in the ankle. The Englishman tottered, struggled to regain his balance, then with a cry of horror fell over the side.

'Grab him! Grab him, for God's sake!' the skipper yelled.

But he was too late. A dorsal fin sliced through the water, and serrated rows of teeth tore into Staines's trunk. In a frenzy the shark lifted the bloody torso clear of the water, then dragged it triumphantly under.

Nobody could speak. Müller stared at the blood staining the sea. Larsen had come round and stood beside him. 'Is it true?' he asked in an even voice. 'Did you set out to fool us?'

Müller stared back calmly. 'I was only trying to save myself. What else did you expect? We would have landed up in the middle of a wolf pack if I had got it right.'

Larsen's jaw was set in a grim expression. 'And what would have happened to us?'

Müller shrugged. 'I don't know the answer to that. But I tell you, Larsen, I would have done what I could to save you.'

The Norwegian's hand moved towards his belt, and Müller tensed, ready for yet another attack.

'Shut up, the pair of you.'

The skipper moved unsteadily forward and pushed between them. Even though exhausted he was still strong.

'Right out here where nobody cares a sod, have we all got to go overboard just so you two can have a fight? Take a look at that lot.'

Purple clouds were piled over the western horizon, their weird shapes promising a violent storm. Pressure was dropping, and the wind began to grow rapidly.

'Get the mast down—fast!' Müller cried.

The boat shook as it butted into a huge wave. Like a whiplash, the canvas cut across the stern and billowed out to sea. Then, with a crack like a rifle shot, the mast snapped, seven feet above the deck, and careered over the side. Ahead, the Atlantic rollers advanced in mountainous ridges, and spray broke over the bows, drenching them.

Throughout the night they hung on, and Müller wondered how much pounding the boat could take. He was relieved when dawn broke and the wind began to moderate; almost as suddenly as they had arisen the waves were rolling gently against the side. For a time all three men lay exhausted. Müller was the first to revive, wiping salt from his eyes and nostrils.

The boat was in chaos. There were short spikes where the mast had stood, while mugs, tins and blankets sloshed up and down the bottom boards. Mechanically, he began to straighten out the boat. Like men in a trance the others followed suit, putting the biscuit tins back under the stern and re-rigging the blankets as temporary shelter.

Soon the sky was cloudless again and the temperature rose till the boat was like a furnace. They stripped to the waist and crawled under the blankets for shelter, but the heat was still suffocating. From time to time Müller made his way to the bows where he had carefully slung an improvised fishing line over the side, baited with ship's biscuit; but apart from some attention from flying fish it caught nothing. Occasionally a shark cruised past.

The heat began to affect the skipper, who was suffering longer and longer periods of dementia. He shouted incoherently, and tried to climb over the side, to 'go below' or 'to see the Chief'. Yet he could sound misleadingly cogent and more than once pointed confidently to 'land' on the starboard bow. When dusk came he calmed down and lost consciousness. Larsen made him as comfortable as possible, then turned his eyes on Müller. They were tired; and the Norwegian's face was burnt and lifeless.

'Where do you think we are?' he asked.

'I've been trying to guess. The storm must have blown us a hundred miles or so south-west. We could be drifting around a thousand miles off the Azores. I don't know any more.'

Larsen nodded towards the skipper. 'We'll have to take it in turn to man the tiller. I don't think he will last long.'

Two days later, with Müller speaking a half-remembered prayer in German, they buried the old man. He watched Larsen slowly put the skipper's cap and wallet in the locker under the stern sheets.

The Norwegian was becoming noticeably weak now, and had to prop himself against the side, close to the blankets.

'Have we got much water left?' he asked wearily.

Müller had no need to glance at the bottle.

'About a litre. Enough until we are rescued.'

'You're an optimist, Müller. Perhaps you've got something to look forward to? Perhaps they will give you another U-boat so that you can sink bigger and better ships. I ought to have killed you.'

The words jarred, and Müller realised how much he had developed a working relationship with Larsen, regarding him now as a shipmate.

'I'm sorry, Larsen,' he said quietly. 'Do you know what they called me on my U-boat? "Iceman." '

Larsen's lips parted in a tired smile, and slowly Müller began to tell him about the schoolboy origins of the nickname. A long time ago he had gone on a pre-war summer trip north, towards the Lofoten Isles with two Norwegian friends.

Under a threatening sky they had been forced to shelter on a lonely island when they ran their boat on to the stony beach. The place seemed dark and threatening, and Müller recalled the stories of a mad old pastor who inhabited one of the islands. But the storm was blowing up and they crawled into the warmth of their sleeping bags. Then Müller heard it. A chilling shriek. It was not the wind, nor was it human. Terrified, he had crawled outside, his friends behind him. On the skyline there stood a massive figure, grey hair streaming in the wind, his body wrapped in a black ankle-length coat.

'Get out! Intruders! This is my sanctuary.'

A gnarled hand waved a rifle and brought it up, ready to fire. Yet Müller felt strangely calm and he stepped forward, praying that his terrified friends would not panic. Slowly he walked towards the figure, hand outstretched, looking into eyes maddened by wood alcohol.

'We are only here to shelter from the storm,' Müller said quietly. 'Don't hurt us on *your* island.'

At sixteen Müller had a strong physique, but the giant towered over him, and he feared the maniac's power. Then, suddenly, the crazy eyes lost focus, and the giant stumbled away, sobbing. Müller's friends stood transfixed, then they crawled back into their sleeping bags, saying nothing. The next day they made ready to sail home, relieved but sobered by the night's experience. They looked at Müller in a new light, and by the time they reached home his achievement had earned him his nickname.

Larsen was half-conscious when Müller finished. Then his words came faintly.

'Why couldn't you Nazi bastards leave us alone? They could have been your own people.'

Müller stared at the swollen lips and remembered the exhilaration he had felt as the Germans swept into Norway. It had been a great moment in his life, although his father had loathed it. For Müller the Führer's motives had been right: the British would steal Norway if the Reich did not protect it. But how could Larsen understand that? None of the Norwegians did; they did not want to.

Müller took in Larsen's emaciated frame, the frame of a man who had once been powerfully built. His own head began to reel; he tried to think, but his brain refused to respond. It was all over for both of them, he knew that, and it was futile to think otherwise. At least Larsen seemed to bear him no grudge.

'We turn in ten minutes, then back on the home leg.'

Lieutenant Pat McLellan USN heard the slow drawl of the navigator over the intercom, then turned his eyes back to the flat ocean below. The Catalina had been flying steadily for six hours on anti-U-boat patrol from the US navy base at Norfolk, Virginia. As usual they had seen nothing, except a westbound convoy of forty ships.

McLellan yawned and took out a Panatella. The intercom spluttered.

'Skipper? Starboard waist gunner. There's something out there at ten o'clock. Looks like a boat or something.'

McLellan cut auto-pilot and swung the flying boat into an arc, throttling back to lose height, while the co-pilot swept the sea with his binoculars.

'It's a boat, all right.' It was the waist gunner again.

'Anyone in it?'

'Can't tell.'

'Okay. I'm coming down to fifty feet.'

The sea rose to meet them and raced beneath the wings. Just over a mile ahead a small black shape appeared. In seconds they were up to it, then it was gone.

There was a yell from the waist gunner.

'There's a man down there. Just one.'

'Okay,' McLellan said quietly. 'What's the fix, navigator? We'll call up Norfolk and get a rescue ship out here.'

Two hours later the escort destroyer USS *Jason Armitage* nosed alongside the battered lifeboat and a party clambered down. Gently the seamen placed the worn body in a survivor's net and winched him on board. It was virtually a skeleton; only the eyes clung to life. The skin had been burnt and blistered by the sun, giving the fair hair an eerie whiteness. Already the ship's surgeon had hustled to his side.

'Only one survivor, sir,' the ensign reported over the bridge phone. 'There must have been several others. The men are just clearing out the lifeboat. A few personal belongings, not much more.'

Orders came down the line. 'Okay. Cast off when you're ready. Prepare to sink by gunfire.'

The survivor was carefully placed on a stretcher and taken below.

It was not until the following day that he showed any sign of real awareness, peering up from the iron cot in the sick bay at the attendant, who came across to him.

'Here, man. Can you use this? Christ, that must have been some trouble you was in. Must have been in that boat a lifetime.' The attendant offered him orange juice.

The thin burnt face summoned a whisper. 'It seemed like it.'

A clipped footstep announced the captain, a short, well-built man, more like a business executive than a naval officer. He took off his cap and sat on the edge of the bed whilst the doctor hovered behind.

'Well, sailor, you had a rough time out there. What was the ship you were on?'

The man in the cot hesitated, and winced with pain.

'*Empire Rose*, sir. Five thousand GRT. Out of New York.'

'Sunk by a U-boat?'

'Yes, sir. We were lagging from one of the big convoys.'

The captain asked a few more questions before the doctor intervened. 'I think you should let him rest a bit, sir.'

'Of course.' He rose and put on his cap, then thrust his hand into his pocket. 'Here, I almost forgot this.'

With a flick of the wrist he tossed a worn identity card on to the counterpane. It was dog-eared and stained with a spidery signature. Olaf Larsen. Where the picture had been glued to the card there was only a mottled water mark.

'I must say I admire the guts of you Norwegians.'

Müller reached out a claw-like hand and took the card, murmuring his thanks.

Chapter 3

The gardens beyond the windows of Norfolk Navy Hospital, Virginia, were inviting. On his first day out of bed Müller found a quiet bench in the shade of a cypress and breathed in the rich air. His strength had returned, and for the first time since the rescue he felt fit and fully alert. To his relief everybody accepted him as Olaf Larsen, Norwegian seaman, torpedoed in the Atlantic, and the Americans went out of their way to make him feel comfortable. They brought him books, comics and candy, and fussed endlessly about his welfare; but at all times he carefully avoided their questions about his ordeal. Many of the patients, mostly merchant seamen, were eager to know what had happened to him, and tried to gossip to Müller in a friendly way, but he was naturally reticent and found it easy to shelter behind his shyness. Yet for all his outward composure he found it impossible to relax.

Once again he went over the dark memory of those last

31

days in the lifeboat, trying to distinguish fact from fantasy. Whenever he did so, he could not escape a disturbing image: Larsen's sightless eyes staring at him accusingly as he pushed the Norwegian's body over the side. Is that how he had died? Müller told himself that he would never know. Perhaps it had been exposure—even worse, perhaps he had killed the Norwegian in a half-sane moment. He tried to tell himself that it did not matter; in war there were casualties . . . To divert his mind he opened the local newspaper. He struggled to take in the long columns of print, and thought of the problems ahead. As he looked around the sunny garden it seemed strange to be sitting unsuspected in the heart of the United States.

There were few signs of war. No air raids, no black-outs, food was plentiful—all in marked contrast to the misery and rationing in Europe. Anger rose inside him at the thought of the rich Americans smugly insulated from the war, and the young faces of U-1543's crew flashed before him, and their cries as the U-boat foundered. In that moment he felt a cold hatred, and knew that he had to get back to the Kriegsmarine.

His attention drifted back to the newspaper, searching for clues on how to get away. The war was going badly. It seemed impossible that Rommel was being beaten in North Africa by the hopelessly unwarlike Americans and the washed-out British. Page two was worse, with a US Navy statement that twenty U-boats had been sunk that month. Müller swore and dismissed it all as propaganda. Instead, he turned to the local news items, the ads and photos, trying to build up a picture of the huge country outside the hospital walls.

'Good morning! How are you today?'

The young ward nurse peered over the top of his paper, her dark eyes shining.

Müller gave a slow smile. 'I'm feeling really good, nurse.'

Her oval face was framed by dark curly hair. 'You know, you are famous. Quite a few newspapermen want to come and talk to you.'

Müller's face clouded as he put down the newspaper. 'Sure, they've told me, but I don't want to talk about all that. Not yet.'

Her eyes softened. 'I understand. Anyway, you have another kind of visitor.'

'Who?'

'A Navy lieutenant.'

Müller felt alarmed. So far the Americans had not shown any trace of suspicion.

'What does he want?'

The nurse seemed amused. 'Just routine. Finding out about your personal background and experiences. They do it to everybody who comes in here.'

'You mean he's some kind of intelligence man?'

'I suppose so. It's red tape, really. He's waiting.'

Müller stared after her trim white uniform as she walked away. Perhaps the hospital had lulled him in to a false sense of security, and the American had been watching him all the time. He went over the main points of his cover story, piecing together the long rambling conversations he had had in the lifeboat with the skipper and with Larsen. He dare not make a mistake in any detail, from the name of the ship's cat to her port of registration. He pushed the fear from his mind that the Americans might have information about the *Empire Rose* or Olaf Larsen which he did not possess, and prayed that the ordeal in the lifeboat had not damaged his memory.

The lieutenant was very young, and had certainly never seen a shot fired in anger. A new cap lay ostentatiously on the table in the ward sister's office. Without more ado, he launched into a battery of questions.

'Where you from, sailor?'

'Norway.'

'Norway? That's a long way off. What part?'

'Sandefjord. A whaling town about one hundred miles outside Oslo.'

'How long have you lived there?'

The questions into Larsen's background, his parentage and career rolled on monotonously, but there were no attempts to catch him out, and Müller began to answer with confidence. The details of the *Empire Rose*, her builders, owners, displacement and cargo which the skipper had mumbled to him came back effortlessly.

Suddenly the tone of the interview altered and the lieutenant looked up from his notebook.

'Did you see the enemy at all?'

Müller paused, then answered slowly. 'Yes. He surfaced. It was a U-boat.'

'Can you describe it?'

Müller smiled inwardly at the question. 'It was long and black. Very low in the water, about eight hundred tons, with half a dozen men on the bridge. She was making a steady twelve knots, motoring on about three-quarter diesel power.'

'Armament?'

'Abaft the conning tower there was a Wintergarten with quadruple cannon 20mm.'

The lieutenant stopped writing, eyes blinking behind rimless spectacles. Müller's easy confidence and mastery of the subject seemed to disturb him.

'Wintergarten? That's a strange word for the gun emplacement. It's German, isn't it?'

Müller stared back, and knew that he had blundered. Quickly he thought out his answer.

'Yes, it's German all right,' he said. 'That's what they call the "bandstand" carrying the 20mm cannon. I heard some German prisoners talking about it when we fished them out of the sea off Newfoundland. They thought I couldn't understand them, but we Norwegian's can speak German.'

The lieutenant seemed to relax again, and Müller seized the initiative.

'I didn't see any number on the U-boat, but there was a picture on the conning tower. It was a big black cat, grinning to itself, with a row of white mice at its feet. Must have been the U-boat's victims.'

'Could be,' the lieutenant muttered. 'U-boat commanders use all kinds of mascots from horned devils to Viking ships.' Müller knew there was no grinning cat.

'Did you see any antennae? Any radar or radio masts? Anything like this?' The lieutenant pushed forward a sketch of a wire barrel atop a thin mast. Müller recognised the drawing as a crude representation of the *Hagenuk*, the Kriegsmarine's latest device for detecting enemy aircraft.

34

'No, I didn't see anything like that,' he lied.

The lieutenant persisted. 'Nothing mattress-shaped?'

'No, nothing mattress-shaped. But there was an aerial a bit like this.'

He reached forward and sketched an imaginary corkscrew mast with an elaborate array of antennae. Such a device did not exist, but the lieutenant stared at the sheet of paper and smiled. It might bring him another ring on his sleeve.

'I'll take this with me if I may, sailor. I guess you've had enough now. As soon as you are back on your feet report to the War Shipping Administration. They will issue you new papers.'

He put his pen away. 'We have to be careful, you understand. For everybody's sake.'

Two days later Müller stood in the War Shipping Administration office in downtown Norfolk, and waited while a surly female clerk went through the motions of issuing him papers in the name of Olaf Larsen.

His picture was taken staring rigidly at camera, and the fingerprint department made a mark for every finger on his right hand.

'Seems like the sea water ruined the originals,' the clerk drawled as she pasted his identity documents on to an ID card and inserted them into a leatherette wallet, adding a special certificate issued by the US Immigration Service which permitted the holder to pass in and out of the United States.

'Of course, the originals aren't here. They're back in England somewhere, in the Ministry of Shipping. Except that it's been blitzed, so truth to tell nobody knows who the hell you are!'

Outside in the afternoon sun Müller took a deep breath and relaxed. He congratulated himself that his luck was holding up incredibly well. He laughed out loud. By courtesy of the US government he now had a new identity. Tucking his documents away he crossed the road to a bar and ordered a celebratory beer.

Sitting at the window he watched the prosperous citizens of Norfolk stroll past. There were also large numbers of servicemen, mainly Navy and marines, eyeing up the pretty girls. Lumbering Oldsmobiles and Pontiacs filled the road, and blared at the huge trucks hustling through.

Müller sipped his Budweiser and pondered his next move. He was determined to get back to the Kriegsmarine. After the lifeboat rescue and the issue of the identity card it seemed his destiny to succeed. The new identity card might get him aboard an Allied ship, but it could be dangerous. There was always the chance that he might encounter somebody who knew the real Larsen. A non-belligerent ship en route for Spain or Portugal might be better, especially if he could get to South America, but if he attempted the journey, whom could he trust?

Then Müller remembered. Many years before, his father had told him of his uncle, a young businessman who had emigrated to South America, and had then moved north to Mexico. There had been little communication with the family, but Müller knew that the last letter had come from Mexico City three years before. He had never met his uncle, who may even have moved from Mexico; but he was Müller's best hope to ease the way to South America where there were many Nazi sympathisers. It would be a risk, though. Müller had no idea how his uncle would react to his arrival.

He finished his beer and decided to head south next day. Contemplating the empty glass he wondered how to fill the rest of the day, and his mind turned irresistibly to the young nurse who had been so kind to him. It had been a long time since he had entertained a woman. There was a phone booth in the bar and a few minutes later he was through to her. Her name was Laura, Müller discovered. She would be free in an hour's time, she said, and could meet him at the local swimming pool.

When Müller arrived at the rendezvous the pool was almost empty. Most of the children had obeyed their parents' instructions and gone home by four o'clock; the place would not become busy until working hours had ended. Only a few young couples were lying around or swimming, and Müller settled down on a sun bed to wait. In a few moments he had begun to doze off into a luxurious sleep.

'Hi there!'

Laura was smiling down at him, and the sight of her instantly brought Müller to his senses. She wore a lemon-coloured swimsuit and by the shade of her well-shaped legs and shoulders Müller could see that she was no stranger to the pool. She tossed back her hair and sat down on the sun bed next to him. Her brown eyes glanced over his torso.

'You're looking in better shape now than when I first saw you,' she said softly.

'Thanks to your gentle care and attention,' Müller grinned.

'So where are you going now? Not back to sea, surely?'

Müller shrugged. 'There's a war on.'

Her mouth turned down at the corners as he continued, 'I have to report back for duty.'

'Where?'

Müller had prepared the answer. 'New York.'

Her dark lashes fell for a moment. 'Damn,' she uttered softly.

Müller anticipated more questions, and got briskly to his feet.

'Well, how about a swim . . .?'

When they climbed out of the water he happily accepted Laura's invitation for a cup of tea at her nearby apartment, before she returned to duty, and soon Müller was sitting in the solitary armchair that she possessed, watching her pour tea.

'I don't really know much about you,' she said quietly, handing him a cup, her body moving lazily under a pink cotton dress. 'Only what I've read in your medical files.'

Müller feigned disapproval. 'You shouldn't do that. It's private.'

She laughed. 'Nothing is private in a hospital.'

Müller stirred his tea, carefully composing a reply, knowing that he could not avoid satisfying her curiosity.

Once again he launched into the story of Olaf Larsen. As he talked he realised that he was becoming increasingly confident in assuming Larsen's identity, so that he even added an occasional embellishment to make it more interesting.

Laura leaned forward, her chin on her palms, and when Müller finished she studied him from beneath her fine black eyebrows.

'You know, it's funny. But sometimes when you speak you don't sound like a Norwegian at all—more like a German.'

Müller put down his cup, shaken by her remark, but kept control of his feelings.

'I can assure you that I am as Norwegian as King Haakon himself—and I feel sad that you could take me for one of my country's enemies.'

Laura's mouth opened, and for a moment she looked bewildered, then she grasped Müller's hand.

'Oh, I'm so sorry, I really am . . .!'

She did not finish the words. Müller pulled her towards him and kissed her. Gently he slipped his hand inside the cool dress and caressed her breast, fondling the delicate nipple. Slowly he removed her clothes and stared at her appreciatively. It had been a long time since Lorient, and he made love to her with almost brutal intensity.

When it was over, she lay still for a while before placing her hand gently on Müller's chest.

'I don't make a habit of this with any man I happen to meet,' she whispered. 'And I don't want you to walk out of my life.'

Müller covered her hand.

'If you have to report for duty in New York,' she went on earnestly, 'we could meet there. Or maybe you could come down here. It's not that far.'

Müller sat up. 'I'd love that,' he said slowly. 'But you must understand that I might be given a ship at once.'

She too sat up and put her arms round his shoulders. 'I want to see you again. Soon. Please.'

Müller felt her cool flesh and glanced at the soft young breasts. Perhaps he should meet her in New York and forget the Kriegsmarine and the Mexico plan? But he realised that it would be dangerous. If he spent even a few days with her, his guard would be lowered—he wouldn't be able to avoid it.

'I just don't know what my orders will be until I report at

the Shipping Administration in New York. I can ring you as soon as they tell me.'

She sat on her haunches studying him.

'You must phone me. I know just the place where we can stay. I went there as a kid. A real old-style hotel right in the heart of Manhattan—the Gotham on Fifth Avenue. We'll book a luxury suite—with a very big bed.'

Müller laughed and reached for his shirt. 'Let me get there first.'

The next day Müller caught the Greyhound bus for New Orleans. Laura was still on duty and unable to bid him farewell. By the time the bus had reached the suburbs of Norfolk he had dismissed her from his mind.

Chapter 4

A chill wind blew over the grey hills of Wales as an army convoy rolled into Tregaron prisoner of war camp. Light snow covered the ground, and the troops sitting in the backs of the trucks found their weapons ice cold and painful to touch. In the warmth of the commandant's office a tall brigadier of the Cameronians watched his men drive in.

'I've brought two hundred and fifty in all. They're fit and ready for anything.'

Colonel Phelps, the commandant, drew on his pipe and nodded his thanks. He was a middle-aged man and his full head of grey hair gave him a diplomatic bearing.

'Sorry I had to call on you, but things were getting out of hand. Your chaps look as if they can do the job all right.'

'It's the first time most of them have faced the enemy, but they'll be okay. Most of them come from the Gorbals.'

Phelps smiled. Outside, the troops clambered from their trucks and began to form up in open order, then advanced to within thirty yards of the three Nissen huts already ringed by camp guards.

The commandant tapped out his pipe. 'Shall we send for von Stoltz now?'

'The sooner the better.'

A few minutes later there was a ring of boots. Colonel Friedrich von Stoltz was escorted into the office by two military policemen. He was a deep-chested man, with a formidable jaw, whose arrogant bearing had won him the hearty dislike of the British guards.

Colonel Phelps calmly studied the well-cut uniform with its Palm Tree insignia of the Afrika Korps, then nodded towards the brigadier.

'Colonel von Stoltz, may I introduce Brigadier Macdonald of the First Cameronians?'

Von Stoltz clicked his heels. 'Fine soldiers,' he said coldly. 'I have come across them before.'

'Then I hope we will not disappoint you,' the brigadier replied softly.

The commandant sat back in his chair and addressed von Stoltz like a magistrate.

'Colonel, the officers under your command in Hut Fourteen were ordered to parade for roll call at seven a.m. today. This was a perfectly reasonable order, according to the conventions governing the treatment of prisoners. Your officers did not comply. Since then they have been ordered to parade three times, but they have answered by barricading themselves inside their huts. What is the meaning of this?'

Von Stoltz airily waved his hand at the two British officers.

'The reason the order was not obeyed is perfectly clear, Herr Commandant. It is because you intend to arrest Major Preuss and we intend to prevent that.'

Phelps raised his eyebrows. 'Indeed, Colonel, you are right. It is my intention to place Major Preuss under close arrest, and I have every right to do so. I am sure you are aware that he is the ringleader of this mutiny.'

Von Stoltz regarded his two interrogators with ill-concealed contempt.

'Herr Commandant, my officers have been living in foul conditions since they came into your camp. Indeed, since they came to Britain. Even our fly-blown quarters in Tunisia were not as bad. Here we have bad food, overcrowding, poor latrines. The health of our men is at risk. It is no surprise they mutiny.'

The commandant detected a smile on Macdonald's face as he took up the challenge.

'Colonel von Stoltz, I can assure you that this camp meets the most exacting standards laid down by international conventions. Of course it is inconvient that we have had to take in very large numbers of prisoners because of our repeated successes, but I totally reject the charge that this camp is below standard.'

Von Stoltz shook his head. 'I do not condone acts of indiscipline, but I am not responsible for this situation.'

Phelps kept his temper, speaking quietly but distinctly. 'Colonel, I believe we are seeing a deliberate act of provocation on the part of certain officers, led by Preuss. For what reason I can only surmise. I am afraid you leave me with no choice other than to act with whatever force I deem necessary.'

Von Stoltz squared his shoulders. 'I warn you, Herr Commandant, if you use military force on unarmed prisoners I shall protest formally to the International Red Cross.'

The German's attitude infuriated the brigadier, who drew in his breath and marched up to him, standing only two feet away.

'Colonel von Stoltz, I want you to instruct your officers to call off this absurd gesture before matters get out of hand.'

Von Stoltz replied tartly, 'Gentlemen, unless there is anything more that we can usefully discuss, perhaps I may return to my quarters?'

The commandant sighed. 'Very well, but I am afraid I must request you to stay there until this matter is dealt with.'

He pressed a bell on his desk and the two MPs came back into the room. Von Stoltz threw a contemptuous look at his adversaries, clicked his heels and marched out. As the door closed, the brigadier exploded.

'What an arrogant bastard!'

Colonel Phelps rose quickly to his feet. 'We'll have to act fast before we have real trouble on our hands. This whole camp could explode.'

Outside, the Cameronians cheered by mugs of tea, were standing easy when the two officers walked up.

'The prisoners have been very quiet, sir,' one of Macdonald's officers said.

'Probably cooking something up,' Phelps replied. 'Well, we have something up our sleeve too.'

The commandant pointed to several telegraph poles lying on the ground. 'I thought you might find those useful.'

Macdonald grinned. 'With six men each side, they'll make damn good battering rams. Come on, let's take a look at the Hun.'

Together they walked through the cordon of camp guards towards Hut Fourteen. Macdonald looked curiously at the faces peering over the tops of the wardrobes and up-ended bedsteads that blocked the windows.

A few yards from the first window Phelps stopped and leaned on his walking stick.

'Major Preuss!' he called

Almost at once a pale young face appeared. The man's hair was so short-cropped that his head seemed like a skull. The widely-set eyes were dark and intelligent and there was a cynical twist to the man's mouth.

'*Ja*, Herr Commandant. This is Major Preuss.'

'I would like you to come out and assist us in our disciplinary enquiries.'

The German laughed. 'You mean have myself locked up.'

'As a soldier you will know the value of discipline.'

'And also comradeship. I will ask my brother officers what they think. You will give me a moment, Colonel?'

The head bobbed down and a few seconds later a loud cheer echoed from the hut. Preuss's head reappeared.

'I think you know the answer, Commandant. You will have to come and get me.'

The commandant nodded slowly, then dug his walking stick into the mud and walked away. Macdonald turned and bellowed to his men, 'Right! Let's get started.'

The camp guards, mostly older men, were pulled back

and NCOs barked orders, forming the Cameronians into close ranks. In order to avoid any accidental shooting Macdonald gave instructions for all rifles to be stacked, and his troops now stood equipped with an assortment of truncheons and batons. A captain marched along the ranks and selected twenty of the biggest men, who were divided into two squads. Each group picked up a massive telegraph pole, ready to spearhead the attack on the front and back of Hut Fourteen.

Macdonald surveyed the scene from a small rise in the ground, and nodded with approval as two army fire trucks jogged over the grass. Their steel-helmeted crews jumped down and began to uncoil the high-pressure hoses ready to train them on the huts should there by any attempt at a mass breakout.

Preuss could be seen watching the preparations from behind a barred window. Other German faces had also appeared and some prisoners began shouting abuse.

Macdonald took a last look round his dispositions then nodded curtly to a captain standing beside him. The officer raised a pistol and a red Very light soared into the air.

With a roar the brawny Cameronians charged down the slope, wielding the telegraph pole like a medieval battering ram. Hut Fourteen shook on its foundations as the pole thundered in to the front door. Almost at once another splintering crash announced that the second assault party had started to work on the rear entrance.

Again the Cameronians swept down the slope, accompanied by other troops attacking Hut Fourteen's windows. There was another colossal blow and the door split across the middle, a hinge bursting away. Shouts and the sound of breaking glass came from the sides of the hut and a Cameronian fell back from a window frame, blood streaming from his face.

The assault party went in once again, and this time broke into a cheer as the pole drove straight through the woodwork, thrusting aside the heavy table that had acted as an additional barrier.

The captain shouted and a squad of men armed with cudgels swarmed into the gap. They found the prisoners ready for them, armed with broomsticks, brush handles and chair legs. Battle was joined.

In the centre of the hut, Preuss stood on a piece of furniture looking down on the melee and shouting orders and encouragement to the Germans. When the back door finally caved in and more Scots poured in, Preuss was ready. With a few words he ordered a group of prisoners held specially in reserve to repel the intruders. They closed agressively with the enemy, who mercilessly set about the Germans with fists and truncheons. Used to the gangwars of Glasgow, the Scots lashed out brutally with studded boots and broken bottles. They worked themselves into a frenzy, ramming German heads against the walls and kicking men senseless as they lay on the floor. The prisoners fought back grimly with anything they could lay their hands on. One man swung a large kettle, knocking a Scot to the ground; another used a broomstick as a vicious lance.

Yet more Scots reinforcements poured in, and soon weight of numbers began to tell; the Germans succumbed and were hauled unceremoniously out of the hut.

Preuss himself leapt down from his perch to join in the fray. An enormous Cameronian grabbed him round the shoulders whilst another knocked him to the ground, where he was pummelled unmercifully before being dragged out by his feet.

In five minutes the skirmish was over, the hut cleared. Macdonald ordered the fire trucks to withdraw. Phelps disconsolately watched the stream of injured men staggering out of the hut, making their way to a casualty station. Many of the troops nursed injured limbs or clutched field dressings around their wounds. The prisoners had fared even worse, and over a dozen men were stretched out, badly injured or unconscious, on the grass in front of Hut Fourteen.

Macdonald strode across the miniature battlefield like a victorious monarch, comforting his injured men and determined to find the one man responsible for it all. Eventually he found Preuss sitting half-dazed among the wounded Germans, his face pale and a blood-stained bandage round his bony head. His cheek was swollen in a discoloured bruise, but his eyes blazed.

'Well, Major Preuss,' Macdonald said laconically. 'You were warned. That was almost as tough as El Alamein, wouldn't you say? And another defeat for the Wehrmacht, I'm afraid.'

Preuss glared up at the burly Scot, and when he spoke it was in excellent English. 'It's not over yet, Brigadier. Not by any means.'

It was just after seven a.m. in London, and the barrage balloons floating lazily over Westminster reflected the dazzling March sunshine. Crossing St James's Park on his way to the War Cabinet Office, Squadron Leader James Alloway enjoyed the fresh morning air. Only four hours before he had still been at work, acting as secretary to a special defence committee, and already he was returning for another spell of duty in the War Cabinet Office.

In philosophical mood he trudged across Horse Guards Parade and showed his pass to the Grenadier guardsman on duty at the high sandbag wall blocking the end of Downing Street. The squadron leader passed inside, limping awkwardly from his war wound, and bade the police constable on duty outside Number Ten a cheerful good morning. The man replied with a perfunctory salute and Alloway continued towards the large building at the end of the street, marvelling that the row of Georgian houses was still the nerve centre of the British war machine.

He soon reached the imposing edifice at the end of Downing Street which had been converted into the War Cabinet Office annexe, to house temporary staff who had been drafted into Whitehall on war duties. The lofty room on the first floor where Alloway worked was already the scene of intense activity. Personnel from all services were at their desks around the room, and civilian staff dashed to and fro with files and papers.

A young woman sat at a small typist's desk adjacent to Alloway's. She was wearing a pale green austerity dress which ended an inch above her knees, and presented an attractive sight in the morning sunlight. Alloway looked at her short blonde hair and felt lucky to have such a pretty girl working as his PA. She greeted him solemnly.

'The general has been looking for you.'

He smiled at her, thumping down his briefcase. 'Thanks, Barbara. Doesn't give a man much of a chance, does he?'

'He seemed a bit put out that you weren't to be found,' she said, her eyes sparkling behind spectacles.

'Why? What's the flap?'

'I don't know. He just seemed anxious to speak to you.' She smiled, then returned to her typewriter.

Alloway's chief, Lieutenant-General Sir Hastings Ismay, was a brilliant political soldier who had become Churchill's right-hand man in running the military machine. Shrewd and unassuming, Ismay was Military Secretary to the War Cabinet, and since Churchill had also taken over the role of Minister of Defence the general acted as the prime minister's personal chief of staff and head of the Defence Office. Alloway had heard the prime minister describe his quiet pug-faced chief as the 'head of his handling machine', and was aware that he was at Churchill's beck and call and had to endure the full range of his leader's moods and impulses. It astonished Alloway how his chief always managed to remain equable under such pressure.

Ismay had a small but powerful staff of officers to assist him, drafting papers on every conceivable subject, sifting memoranda and organising the flow of information between the military commands. They acted as a high-powered secretariat and attended any meeting of importance, serving as the general's 'eyes and ears'.

It was four months since Alloway had been recruited, and he still found it surprising to be working in such distinguished company. Now, as he made for General Ismay's office, he wondered what new problem would be thrown at him that day.

He found Sir Hastings sitting behind an oak desk that looked as if it had seen service in the Crimea. A large map of the world faced him, showing the strength of Allied forces in the various war theatres. Ismay sat squatly in his chair, his face drawn from working regularly into the small hours. But when he spoke his voice was crisp and meticulous: many men were afraid of this 'Eminence Khaki', as he was known throughout Whitehall.

'Something's come in. There's been some trouble at one of our camps in Wales. Place called Tregaron.' The general pushed over a scrap of paper.

Alloway looked down at the teleprinter report. It was a succinct account of the POW riot and the Cameronians' action.

'Seems as if twenty Germans were badly injured. One may have a fractured skull—he's on the danger list. We suffered about a dozen casualties ourselves.'

Alloway looked blankly at him. Against the background of a world war the Tregaron incident seemed a trifling event.

The general stood up, an imposing figure with his red tabs and polished Sam Browne. His next remark surprised Alloway even more.

'The prime minister is concerned.'

'But it seems hardly significant, sir.'

In reply Sir Hastings took a sheaf of papers from his desk and handed them to Alloway.

'As you'll see, there have been other similar incidents in the last three or four weeks, and they seem to follow a pattern. There's usually a group of trouble-makers, Nazis, of course, who threaten to riot until finally we are forced to bring in valuable front-line troops to maintain order. The PM is furious, and thinks there's something more calculated in it all.'

'You mean the Germans may have primed their men to act like this? I don't see how they could; there's no way they can communicate with the camps, and they know any riot is certain to be severely crushed.'

'You're right, but what really concerns the PM is the effect of a serious riot, or even a breakout, on public morale, let alone security.' The general glanced at Alloway. 'We must get to the bottom of this. Especially as we can expect large numbers of German prisoners to arrive from North Africa very soon. A special committee is being set up with General Stubbs of Home Command as chairman, and you are to minute the proceedings and draft a report. Keep me closely informed.'

'When is the first meeting, sir?'

Alloway was in for his third surprise of the morning.

'This morning. At ten-thirty. All right?'

Ismay took up another file and began glancing through it; Alloway recognised his cue. He gathered up the papers and signals and, bidding his chief good morning, left the room.

As he made his way back to his office, he reflected on the urgency with which the special committee had been set up. Only a few months earlier it would have terrified him to have been assigned to such an important job at an hour's notice, but he had grown used to working fast in Churchill's office.

It seemed such a short time since RAF surgeons had patched him up after his Mosquito had crash-landed on the Norfolk coast. With the best part of a Luftwaffe 20mm cannon shell embedded in his leg, Alloway had miraculously nursed the plane home on one engine and a policeman had pulled him from the wreck before he bled to death. He was luckier than his observer, who had died beside him. The reconnaisance flight had nearly been abortive because the Mosquito's cameras, which had filmed an enemy research station in the Baltic, had been destroyed in the crash. Only Alloway's precise operational report on the German gantries and block houses, observed on a low-level pass, managed to salvage the mission.

His account proved of such vital importance that it reached Cabinet level, and finally the prime minister himself. Churchill had been impressed as much by its economy of style as its intelligence observations, both products of Alloway's training as a lawyer. The moment he left hospital Alloway was surprised to be ordered to join the Defence Office staff in Downing Street. At first the notion of becoming an acting temporary 'Hostilities Only' civil servant had depressed him, but he had been told that his operational flying days were over; and few were brave enough to argue with Churchill. In any event, he now had to admit that he enjoyed working at the centre of power.

Shortly before ten-thirty Alloway limped up the main stairs of the War Office, some three hundred yards along Whitehall, cursing his recalcitrant right leg which always ached when he was in a hurry. Eventually he reached the conference room, overlooking Horse Guards Parade.

A group of officers including commandants from the main POW camps was already assembled. At the head of the table sat a dapper senior officer with a ginger moustache—General Stubbs. He looked pointedly at the clock as Alloway struggled into the room. To Alloway's relief it was only ten twenty-nine.

'Got the watchdogs here, have we?'

Alloway ignored Stubbs's jibe, although he knew that many officers resented the presence of an 'eavesdropper' from Downing Street.

'Morning, James,' drawled 'Dutch' Van Kleef, a tall US Marine major, the liaison officer with US Headquarters, Europe.

'So Uncle Sam is here,' Alloway replied.

'We sure are. My general got me out of bed in the middle of the night to tell me I was coming.'

Stubbs cleared his throat impatiently. Van Kleef grinned at Alloway; they both knew their man well.

'Gentlemen,' Stubbs began, glaring at the assembled commandants, 'I sometimes wonder who is running our POW camps, you or the Germans. I've been asked by the chiefs of staff to find out what the hell is going on, and that is what I intend to do. We've had several outbreaks of violence—it's absolutely appalling—and yesterday's at Tregaron is the worst yet. What on earth has been happening?' The general looked pointedly at Colonel Phelps, the CO of Tregaron, who, though tired from having driven through the night, was goaded into a sharp reply.

'We had a particularly hard bunch to deal with, sir. I seriously thought we were in danger of a mass breakout—and there are seven thousand prisoners in my camp.'

Stubbs went round the table and the other commandants told of their own difficulties. For the first time Alloway began to sense the potential dangers they were facing.

'Well, what's happening?' Stubbs snorted. 'Are the Germans getting agents into our camps?'

Phelps spoke again. 'No, not in my opinion.'

Alloway privately agreed with him. It seemed unlikely

that the Germans would waste their agents in prisoner of war camps; there were far more vital targets.

'It seems to me to be the work of a gang of ringleaders who may have been trained by the Wehrmacht to do this if ever they were captured,' Phelps went on. 'They seem to know how to work on the frustrations and grievances of imprisoned men. They are like detonators, ready to set off an explosion.

'We have a particularly nasty piece of work at Tregaron—Major Preuss, who's an out-and-out Nazi.' Phelps indicated the photograph attached to his report, a copy of which lay in front of each committee member.

'He's thirty-one and if you look at the note you'll see he has a fine war record.'

Alloway studied Preuss's ascetic features, then scanned the typesheet in the dossier, which told how the major had distinguished himself in France, Greece and Russia. He found it easy to concur with Phelps's judgment.

'But how does he keep his hold on the prisoners?' one of the other commandants asked.

'They want to follow him,' Phelps explained. 'That's partly because they're tired of being prisoners and want to kick back at us. Of course, Preuss has his own methods of dealing with people who don't toe the line. He relies on pyschological pressure rather than intimidation; any man who's awkward finds himself socially ostracised, and that's only the start. He'll then be subjected to niggling little acts designed to annoy, like having his mug or razor stolen, or being denied any reading material. Maybe he will be sent to Coventry. And so on until he cracks.'

Stubbs went round the table asking for comments and when each officer supported Phelps's observations Alloway began to sense the serious security problems building up.

It also concerned Van Kleef, who now spoke up.

'For all that Colonel Phelps has said, I don't think we should rule out the possibility of a deeper-laid plot. This country is packed with military installations, airfields, communications centres, ammo dumps—thousands of perfect targets which the Germans could attack if ever they broke out.'

'And on top of that we have to remember the effect on the civil population if even a handful of Nazis ran amok. There could be general panic,' one of the commandants added.

Stubbs reddened at the mention of panic. 'Our people would never react like that, and the Home Guard would deal with any breakout.'

Van Kleef looked sardonically at Preuss's picture staring up at him. 'Maybe they could,' he said. 'But the Germans might well send in a suicide battalion of commandos or paratroops to support a mutiny, and then there would be real trouble.'

An elderly commandant, a First World War veteran, spoke up. 'Of course, the risks of such a thing happening will get worse as more prisoners arrive in this country. The German army is very close to surrender in North Africa. Thousands might suddenly be sent here within the next few weeks.'

There was silence round the table as the officers digested this alarming information. Stubbs squared his shoulders and pushed the meeting towards a conclusion.

'Well, we can't sit here philosophising, gentlemen. What are we going to do about it? The Cabinet is waiting for our recommendations.'

Phelps was the first to speak.

'We should remove the troublemakers immediately,' he said briskly. 'If necessary, we should seek the help of the United States. It would be much easier to isolate them over there.'

Van Kleef nodded thoughtfully. 'How many men are we talking about?'

'In the first instance I would say about a thousand.'

'It sounds a sensible idea,' Van Kleef stated. 'We don't have your difficult security problems and we get very little trouble from POWs on our side of the lake. We could easily take care of the likes of Preuss.'

'In that case,' Stubbs asked, 'could you make a formal request to your C in C to see whether we can transport the hard nuts across the Atlantic as soon as possible?'

Van Kleef agreed at once, but Alloway was concerned

that Stubbs had ignored one vital question which would certainly be raised by the Defence Office—how were the prisoners going to get to America?

'If I may come in, General,' Alloway interjected. 'We are facing a desperate shortage of shipping space at the moment, and there may be difficulty in transporting large numbers of prisoners to America at short notice. There are not enough ships to move our own men.'

Stubbs looked annoyed, as if Alloway had deliberately sabotaged the whole plan.

'The Admiralty always say there's no shipping space,' he snapped. 'I know they have their problems, but they will just have to cope.'

Alloway persisted. 'There really aren't the ships, sir. Sinkings have been very heavy.' He indicated his notes. 'We can certainly ask for shipping space, but there's little hope of getting any for the next month or so.'

'But we may have thousands more Germans on our hands by then . . .'

There was an awkward silence before Van Kleef spoke.

'I think there may be a solution. Next week the *Queen Mary* is scheduled to arrive back on the North Atlantic from Australia. She's going to be used by the American Defense Department to ship over as many GIs as we damn well can for our build-up in Britain. We could use her huge lifting capacity to move Preuss & Co. to the United States under armed guard.'

Stubbs looked triumphant, as if it had been his own idea. 'An excellent suggestion, Major. Please ask whether such a solution is acceptable to your government. Mr Alloway will ensure that the recommendation is included in his report.'

The general looked at his watch. It was just after twelve. 'Thank you, gentlemen. That will be all before lunch. I am afraid I have a meeting with Chiefs of Staff and would be grateful if we could reconvene at say two-fifteen to draw up specific plans for the Defence Committee.'

Stubbs rose to his feet and marched out. Alloway picked up his papers and cursed him for recalling the meeting, but realised the scheme would never gain acceptance by the Defence Committee unless it were practical in every detail.

'He never lets up, does he?' Dutch Van Kleef had come round to Alloway's side of the table.

'He imagines he's Monty, that's all.'

'Well, I could use a drink. Why don't you join me for a quick lunch, James?'

Alloway looked doubtful.

'How about the Connaught?' Van Kleef persisted, mentioning one of the best restaurants in wartime London.

'Well, if that's the best you can do . . .'

The Connaught was an elegant Victorian hotel close to Berkeley Square, and the doorman, his steel helmet tucked just inside the entrance, greeted Van Kleef as a respected regular. The arched lobby was crowded with officers of the Allied forces in London.

As he pushed towards the restaurant, with Alloway in his wake, Van Kleef suddenly stopped. A young woman stood in his path.

'Why, Major Van Kleef. Surprise, surprise,' the woman said in a soft American accent. She was wearing a brown velvet jacket and an expensive saffron-coloured jumper. Auburn hair hung to her shoulders.

'Tracey! And what might you be doing here?'

'Just visiting. As a matter of fact I was trying to fight my way out.'

'Don't try any more. Stay and have lunch with us.' He turned back to Alloway. 'This is Squadron Leader James Alloway, a British colleague. We hold the Anglo-American alliance together. James—Tracey O'Brien.'

Alloway glanced at his new companion. She was tall, with a willowy figure and pale complexion. Her long straight nose gave her a slightly forbidding air, but she stared back at Alloway with friendly grey eyes.

'Tracey is London correspondent of the *Chicago Sentinel*,' Van Kleef went on. 'She's a very good journalist. You have been warned.'

'Oh, come on,' she protested. 'I'm not that bad, although they do say that I got Eisenhower appointed single-handed, which has led some nasty people to accuse me of being on Hitler's side.'

Van Kleef shrugged. 'See what I mean? No understanding of we poor military fellows.'

The restaurant was small and comfortable, with heavy dining chairs and dark oak panelling. It was very busy but Van Kleef had no trouble getting a table, and the restaurant manager, impressive in striped trousers and black jacket, seated them in a corner. The menu he handed them carried the heavily printed Ministry of Food warning that it was illegal to exceed a charge of five shillings per person for any meal: a most effective method of rationing restaurants. Drinks, however, fell outside the allowance. Tracey held the menu in her long fingers and started to study the wartime dishes.

'You know, these really are a tribute to the chef's powers of invention.'

'He's reported to be one of the best in London,' Alloway commented. 'De Gaulle wouldn't eat here otherwise.'

She turned her grey eyes on him. 'That's quite a recommendation.'

An elderly English waiter came to take their order. The end of his veined nose was tinged a rosy red, suggesting that he was not averse to emptying any bottles the guests might leave unfinished.

'Good morning, Cyril,' Van Kleef greeted him. 'What have you got for us today?'

With a disdainful look that implied that Americans were to be tolerated only while hostilities lasted, Cyril pointed a stubby pencil at the *plats du jour*.

'As you see, sir, we are doing our bit against the Führer. Keeping up the morale of our Allies and staying within our ration.'

'What's this specialty—Woolton Pie?' Tracey asked.

'It's made of potatoes, ma'am, with a bed of onions, two layers of mince, garlic and mushrooms.'

'They serve this at the Savoy too,' said Dutch.

Alloway saw the look of horror on the waiter's face at Van Kleef's blunder and smiled at Tracey.

'There are many variations, I think,' he said.

'Indeed, sir,' Cyril replied, having regained his poise. 'After all, the dish is named after our Minister of Food, Lord Woolton. Like Beef Wellington, sir.'

They all decided that Woolton Pie could not be resisted, and as a first course Cyril steered them to Arbroath smokies, a mousse of smoked herring.

'We have some fine Montrachet still left in our cellars, sir,' Cyril recommended confidentially as Van Kleef studied the wine list. 'May I order you a bottle?'

Van Kleef agreed immediately, with Alloway in support. As Cyril shuffled away, the major turned to their journalist companion. 'How have you been getting on over here, Tracey? What sort of stories have you been covering?'

'Don't you read the *Sentinel*, Dutch?' she said with mock disapproval.

'Not my politics, Tracey.'

She looked towards Alloway, and he noticed that she seemed tired.

'I've been up all night with your wonderful anti-aircraft crews. Quite an experience, especially as the Germans staged a raid just for me. There was one splendid great lady on the crew who kept staggering up with enormous shells. My God, I thought she was going to drop one. They called her "Boadicea". Who was she?'

Over the Arbroath smokies Alloway amused them with a colourful account of the British Queen noted for driving chariots against the Romans with sharp blades protruding from the wheel hubs.

'My God, that must have done Caesar's boys some terrible injuries,' Van Kleef said.

They were still laughing when Cyril brought the Woolton Pie, which was topped by a magnificent golden crust. He opened the Montrachet—with exaggerated care—and at a nod from Van Kleef poured it for Alloway to taste.

As he put down his glass Alloway was aware of Tracey's eyes drifting down to his RAF pilot's wings and the blue and white striped ribbon of the DFC.

'Are you still flying, James?' she asked casually.

He shook his head, and she detected his momentary discomfort.

'He's too shy to boast,' Van Kleef intervened cheerfully. 'But the Germans had to shoot him out of the sky while they had any planes left. He was too much of a nuisance.'

Alloway shook his head. 'Wrong command, Dutch. I've never flown fighters. Nothing as glamorous.'

Tracey looked at the DFC again. 'What sort of flying did you do?' she asked.

'Just photo reconnaissance. Seeing what Jerry was up to,' Alloway replied casually, and sipped his wine.

From his tone, Tracey must have known that he did not want to talk about operations, but it was too good a chance to be missed. She leaned towards him.

'I really would like to visit an RAF squadron, James. Any kind, really. Can you help me?'

He looked at her thoughtfully. 'Yes, perhaps I can.' He smiled at her earnest features. 'I know one thing: whichever squadron you visit will certainly look after you. I might even come with you myself.'

'If Mr Churchill gives you time off,' Van Kleef interjected, giving Tracey an open invitation to pursue Alloway about his work in the Defence Office. Alloway concealed his annoyance and decided to forestall any further questions.

'I have a very minor job, Tracey,' he explained. 'I'm really a chairborne warrior. Not that I like it much.'

His words did not deter her and her eyes widened. 'But you're at the centre of power? It must be fantastic working close to Churchill—and the whole war leadership. It's history. You're very privileged.'

Alloway was still not to be drawn.

'And history it will be—one day. I'll see what I can do about getting you to an RAF station, but really it's not worth talking about my job. All right?'

Tracey crossed her arms and tried to look contrite. 'Of course not.'

'And don't forget our American boys,' Van Kleef added. 'They'd love to have a write-up, even though the *Sentinel* isn't very popular with the top brass.'

Tracey turned towards him, the light glinting in her hair. 'Don't bawl me out for not reporting the joys and sadnesses of our homesick GIs. If ever I try to find them I discover that they aren't here. When are the Yanks coming?'

'What do you want, Tracey?' Van Kleef asked. 'A strategic secret? I can't tell you how many there are here, but there are a hell of a lot coming.'

'I've heard that before.'

'This time it's true.'

'Well, that's good news,' Tracey said demurely. 'Because I hear that they might be needed to fight the Germans in this country. Apparently there have been disturbances at certain POW camps.'

Alloway glanced at Van Kleef, concerned at Tracey's probing. She sat waiting for an answer.

'Well, *I* haven't heard anything about it,' Alloway said blandly.

She was still not to be put off. 'If there aren't any problems now there certainly will be if the whole of the Afrika Korps and Hitler's army start surrendering in Tunisia. Where are you going to put them all?'

Alloway leaned towards her. 'Now you know we don't tell tales. You'll have us all shot.'

'She never did like me,' Van Kleef said jokily, trying to get off the subject.

Tracey smiled gracefully. 'All right, I understand that you gentlemen cannot tell me anything.' She turned on Alloway. 'But at least, James, do just let me in on one military secret. What did Winston eat for breakfast today? My readers would love to know. Their interest in your chief is insatiable.'

Alloway shook his dark hair and grinned. 'You're impossible, Miss O'Brien.'

He pushed back his chair. It was time for him to be on his way back. Tracey looked up at him, her eyes serious as he bade his two companions goodbye.

'I hope we meet again. I promise not to try to prise any scoops out of you.'

James took her hand. 'I enjoyed it very much.'

Van Kleef offered to hail a taxi to take Tracey to the *Sentinel* bureau, which she accepted.

As Alloway rode back along Piccadilly he thought of

Tracey's auburn hair and frank eyes. Yes, he would like to see her again. If he possibly could.

Twenty minutes later, as Alloway was beginning to sort through the papers of the Stubbs committee, Tracey sat behind her Remington in the *Sentinel*'s cluttered office just off Fleet Street.

'How's your luck, Tracey?' Chuck Mason, the Bureau Chief, shouted from his own cubicle. He was a large middle-aged man, always dressed in a rumpled shirt perpetually unbuttoned behind the knot of his tie.

'Pretty good.'

Mason turned over a page of *The Times*. 'Thank goodness for that.' He bit into a Spam sandwich. 'They've been complaining that we haven't sent enough good material for syndication.'

'But last week they had three colour stories from us,' declared Tracey.

He put down the paper and looked steadily at her.

'I just told them they only wanted more material so that they could supply the neutral press with blood and guts about the war they were missing.'

He came out of his office.

'You know something? You look as pleased as Punch. All right, don't sit there like the Mona Lisa. What is it?'

'I met an absolutely delightful Englishman.'

'So? Where?'

'Over lunch at the Connaught.'

He gasped. 'The Connaught! You've had lunch at the Connaught and all I get is a Spam sandwich.' Chuck held a pudgy hand to his forehead.

'Tall, perfectly mannered, and he works at the Cabinet Office.'

Chuck whistled. 'Some contact. Close to Churchill?'

'Like all the British, he's very discreet,' she replied. 'But believe me *I'm* going to stay close to *him*.'

Chapter 5

Dramatic countryside passed the dust-caked windows. There were weird cacti and scorched rocks, and here and there white-clad labourers toiled over rows of maize. In the distance a blue range of mountains cut into a brilliant sky.

The bus bounced through a small town where two wizened old men looked on expressionlessly. The Mexican woman next to Müller pulled out a flask of mango juice and offered it to him with a beaming smile.

Müller hesitated. For the whole of the journey from the US border he had tried to seal himself off from the rest of the passengers, and had avoided any conversation, afraid that his limited Spanish and accented English might arouse suspicion. Several times he noticed the dark Mexican faces silently studying him, and two small children had stared candidly at his blond hair. But the peasant woman had a trusting face and Müller took the drink with a mumbled *Gracias*. It tasted wonderful, and when he handed back the bottle she merely smiled and his tension eased.

An increase in the number of trucks and buses showed that they were approaching Mexico City, and as the bus rounded a spur a vast shanty town opened before them, receding tier upon tier to the valley wall. They were still out in the suburbs when Müller noticed that they had turned on to the broad Avenue Insurgentes. Pulling out a guide book, he discovered that they had joined the main thoroughfare, over twenty-five kilometres long, that bisected the city. Soon the bus was rolling through dense traffic, across large piazzas, passing the bronze statues of Mexico's heroes.

When he alighted at the bus station, Müller felt stiff and tired; he started out to find a hotel. A short distance from the terminus he found himself in a shady street called Calle de Hamburgo. There were pleasant shops, and pavement cafés were crowded with Mexicans relaxing over late afternoon drinks. He felt their eyes on him as he made his way to a narrow-fronted building at the end of the street, with a filigree sign announcing Hotel Colombo.

The young desk clerk barely glanced at him. He was ushered into a tiny lift and shown a pleasant room. It had cool white walls and was sparsely furnished, with a brass bedstead dominating the room. Tall windows looked over the street below. If he had to make a quick getaway he could do so fairly easily by climbing from one narrow balcony to another. Feeling more secure, he realised that he had become desperately tired, and thankfully sprawled on the large bed.

It was eight o'clock when he awoke, and noticeably cooler. A haze hung over the city, and one or two electric signs were alight. A dazzling neon display repeatedly spelt out Coca-Cola, and in the distance the mountains had turned deep purple.

He stepped out on to the balcony. A distant murmur of traffic on the Avenue Insurgentes rose up to him, and he wondered if he would be able to find his uncle in such a crowded city.

Downstairs he found a phone box hidden behind a potted fern, and quickly searched through the tattered directories on the shelf beneath the receiver. There were five 'E. Müllers' in the book; any one of them might be his uncle. It was risky but there seemed no choice other than to ring each number in turn to try to find the right man. Müller told himself that there were many Germans settled in Mexico, and a Norwegian seaman enquiring after one of them would be unlikely to arouse suspicion. Once he had tracked down the right man, he would have to be extremely wary deciding when to reveal his true identity.

Müller dialled the first number and a surly voice came on the line. In poor English, the speaker said that his name was Ernesto, not Ernst, and he became suspicious when Müller mentioned that the man he was seeking was German.

'I don't know any Germans,' the man replied cagily. 'There's a war on, you know that?'

'Of course I know. I am a seaman but the man I am looking for has a brother in Norway, and . . .'

'Norway? That's German too, isn't it?' the voice broke

in. 'Look, Señor, I'll help you. Give me your number and I'll make some enquires and call you back . . .'

Müller put down the phone, cursing his own stupidity at sticking his head in a noose. The man might be trying to check up on him and would pass the number to the police. Thank God he had seen the danger in time.

His next call was more cautious and he quickly rang off after the voice at the other end announced himself as Enrico. The third call proved the most disconcerting. A woman's voice came on the line, speaking perfect English with a slight trace of Teutonic accent. The telephone was registered in her name, Estela Müller, and she seemed politely ready to help.

'What sort of man is this Ernst Müller?' she asked after Müller had explained the reason for his call.

'All I know is that he is a businessman who came to this country about twenty years ago,' he replied.

'And you say you are Norwegian?'

'Yes. I am in the merchant service and a friend of Ernst Müller's brother Wolfgang.'

'Wolfgang, you say?'

'Yes. Wolfgang gave me a message for his brother when I got out of Norway last year.'

'You escaped from Norway and this Wolfgang knew you were going?' she asked with a note of incredulity. Müller became wary: there was an inquisitional note in her voice. Yet something made him hang on. 'And where did you say this Ernst Müller comes from in Germany?'

He paused, before answering carefully. 'I remember Wolfgang telling me once he grew up in Duisburg.'

There was a pause and Müller heard only the static on the line before she slowly continued. 'Duisburg, you said? I think the man you might be looking for is Señor Ernst Padilla. He came from Duisburg many years ago; his name was then Müller. Like mine.'

The line went dead and for a moment Müller stood holding the receiver. The woman might have been misleading him, yet she had sounded convincing, and had seemed very familiar with the Mexican business community. Quickly he turned through the directory until he found the entry: Lic. Ernesto Padilla, 27, Calle Copernico. It was the only one.

Across the hall the desk clerk was looking at him. He had been a long time at the telephone and he sensed that every call he made would carry an increasing risk. He went to his room and changed into a dark grey suit he had purchased on the journey from the United States, and decided to make a personal call at Calle Copernico.

Twenty minutes later the taxi dropped him at the corner of a leafy street in a prosperous quarter. The houses were very large, each surrounded by iron railings for defence as much as ornamentation, and the white stucco walls of No. 27 were set well back from the road. A Buick was parked in the drive and an Alsatian sniffed its way across the gravel.

At first there was no answer to the bell, then a stocky Mexican appeared.

'*Señor Padilla, por favor,*' Muller enquired in phrase-book Spanish.

'*Quien es Usted?*' the servant asked, eyeing him suspiciously.

'A friend of Señor Padilla,' Müller replied, testing the Mexican in English.

He turned his back on Müller and went back to the house for a few minutes, finally returning to unbolt the gate. The Alsatian came bounding across and Müller fondled its neck, then followed the Mexican up the drive towards a large portico. Inside it was dark and he was left standing in an arched court lit by a solitary lamp. Beyond, he could see the fantastic shapes and savage cacti of a Mexican garden. There was the steady burble of a fountain, and the air was heavy with fragrance. In the twilight he could just make out a low terrace surrounding the garden, with shuttered windows beyond. One was open, and soft candlelight reflected on the china and silver of a table set for dinner. As he watched, a silhouette was framed in the window, and he thought he saw a woman looking towards him across the garden.

The Mexican had been gone some time, and on his mind Müller went over his plan for maintaining cover if the man he had come to see were not Ernst Müller. He began to feel conspicuous in the pool of light.

There was a footstep behind him, and Müller whirled round. A short plump man emerged from the double doors leading into the house and stood beneath the portico. His white suit and black bow tie gave him a distinguished appearance, and the lamplight reflected on his olive complexion and polished bald head. His small dark eyes inspected Müller.

'Señor Padilla?' Müller asked.

'*Sí. Le conozco?*' The man's voice was cold.

Müller was not disconcerted at being addressed in Spanish, and answered firmly in English.

'My name is Olaf Larsen; I am a seaman with the Allied merchant marine. I come from Norway.'

'So?' Padilla's eyes were still suspicious. 'What do you want with me? Why do you come here at this time?'

Padilla's shoulders were pulled back and Müller studied him for any resemblance to his father. There was a family likeness in the squat build but Müller was still uncertain that Padilla was a blood relative until the older man turned to look across the garden. The harsh lamplight suddenly revealed the contours of his face, and Müller recognised the same flat cheeks, high forehead and firm jawline of his father.

Padilla was waiting impatiently for his visitor to speak.

'Only last year,' Müller began, 'I was still living in Norway in a small town near Narvik, where I had a great friend called Wolfgang Müller, a German.'

Padilla raised his eyebrows in surprise, his face still wary. 'How close a friend were you of this Wolfgang Müller?'

'I knew him very well, because he was my teacher; I owed a lot to him.'

'But he was a German, and surely after the invasion of your country that made a big difference in your attitude towards him?'

Müller shook his head. 'Not really. Wolfgang is a very patriotic German, but he did not approve of the invasion. It upset him deeply because he understood its terrible effect on us Norwegians. He knew that I would try to escape to England, and when somebody tipped him off, just a few days before I risked the North Sea crossing in my sailing boat, he dropped in to see me. He said that he knew what a man had to endure if he loved his country, and that if I were ever to leave Norway he hoped that I would be safe and perhaps end up in America. If that happened, he asked me to try to contact his brother Ernst.'

Padilla was listening intently, hands clasped behind his back, and Müller knew that he had found his man.

'And what message were you to give this Ernst Müller?' the small man asked.

Müller paused and smiled. 'Just that Wolfgang is well; that his family is safe in Norway where they are a long way from the bombing. He said he hoped that the war would soon be over and that he was trying to keep an eye on the family business interests still in Duisburg.'

The tension eased, and Padilla frowned.

'But my name is Padilla. Why did you come here?'

Briefly Müller described his telephone search and the conversation with the woman. When he told Padilla her name he shook his head in a gesture of disbelief.

'Well, well, well.'

'She seemed to know you very well,' Müller said.

Padilla laughed. 'She should. You were talking to my former wife.'

Müller was surprised, but he was swept by a feeling of elation when Padilla announced in clipped tones:

'Well, you have found Ernst Müller, I am Wolfgang's brother.' Gripping Müller's arm, he led his young visitor into the house, saying, 'Let's go to my study where we can talk. You must tell me everything about Wolfgang.'

In spite of his relief at finding his uncle Müller noticed that a look of suspicion remained on Padilla's face. He was still under observation.

'You realise that I am a Mexican citizen now,' Padilla said as they entered the large hall. 'My business interests here are very great and I changed my name to that of my second wife's some years ago. And to think we are now at war with Germany. Do you know, if poor Wolfgang were here he would be my enemy? I would have to turn him over to the police.'

The grip on Müller's arm suddenly felt like that of a gaoler, and he was relieved that he had kept up his cover. He had not expected this. Their footsteps rang on the tessellated paving of the hall: Padilla was clearly a wealthy man. One wall was adorned with a seventeenth-century tapestry depicting the landing of Cortes in 1519, and a marble staircase swept to the gallery above.

A tall woman in a black evening gown advanced towards them. Her raven hair set off her aristocratic Spanish features. There was a hint of disdain in her eyes as they surveyed Müller's unsophisticated suit.

'Mr Larsen, this is my wife Carmen,' Padilla announced. He turned towards her. 'He is a friend of Wolfgang.'

She seemed startled. 'Wolfgang?'

'Yes, my brother in Norway. He has brought a message for us.'

Padilla and his wife exchanged glances, and he had a hurried private word with her in Spanish. She smiled at Müller.

'Please excuse me, Mr Larsen, but I have work to do. I hope we meet again before you leave.'

She walked away, and Padilla took Müller towards a long corridor leading to the rooms overlooking the garden. Solid wooden doors opened each side of them, and they passed the dining room which Müller had seen from across the garden. He began to feel uneasy, and instinctively glanced over his shoulder. At the far end of the corridor, Padilla's Mexican servant was silently watching.

Padilla threw open the door of his study, one wall of which was covered with bookshelves and a large number of leather-bound volumes. A fireplace stood at the far end with two ancient figurines at each side. They wore bland expressions on their oval faces and sat with small hands clasped over pot bellies.

'Mayan,' Padilla said, as Müller went over to admire them. 'Probably thirteenth century; from Yucatan in the south.'

'You seem to be an expert.'

Padilla sat down behind his mahogany desk. 'In a way, but this is the one you should see.'

With a flick he illuminated the cruel features of an Aztec god on the wall behind Müller. Its eyes were dark slits and the arched mouth expressed a sadistic pleasure.

Across its throat there was a plumed serpent. Müller found it disturbing.

'It's from a sacrificial altar.'

There was a coldness in Padilla's voice which made Müller swing round. His uncle was standing impassively behind his desk, a gun in his hand.

'Sit down,' he ordered, waving towards a high-backed chair before the desk. 'You should know I am also an expert with one of these and I can kill you in two seconds.'

Müller felt bewildered and gripped the arms of the chair. Deftly his uncle swung the beam of a desk lamp into his eyes.

'Now, Mr Larsen, you know that I am Ernst Müller. It was clever of you to find me, but I can't believe that foolish story about Wolfgang. Who are you? What have you really come for?'

Müller kept control of himself. 'I have told you, I am a Norwegian. Here is my identification card, courtesy US War Shipping Administration and Immigration.'

With the gun trained on his chest, he pulled out the identity wallet and tossed it at Padilla.

'Anybody can fabricate an identity card.'

'Then why not check it with the Americans?'

'It is too late for that. The office will be closed.' A thin smile crossed Padilla's face. 'Now let's look a little more closely at your famous friendship with Wolfgang, shall we?'

Quickly Padilla launched into a cross-examination, asking about Müller's father and mother, the family home and small details about life in Norway. By now Müller was deeply disturbed about his uncle's intentions and was careful to volunteer only the sort of knowledge a friend of the family would possess. There was something expert about Padilla's technique of interrogation and Müller thought of the Mexican strong-arm man, no doubt standing guard outside the door. For the first time he began to wonder whether his uncle enjoyed intelligence connections outside the world of finance, perhaps maintaining close relations with the British and American secret agencies.

Müller found the bright light trying, and was only dimly aware of Padilla's pudgy face as he began to probe his cover.

'Now our friend Wolfgang limped, didn't he?'

'Yes,' Müller answered.

'He limped from a wound in his right leg, which he received at the battle of the Somme.'

'No, it was his left leg and it was injured at the battle of Verdun.'

'Very good,' Padilla said softly, but the gun remained pointing at his chest. 'And how many children did Wolfgang have?'

'Just one son as far as I know.'

'Name?'

'Ulrich.'

'And what is he doing?'

'He's in the Kriegsmarine. Last heard of in the U-boat service.'

Padilla nodded. 'Then at least he is doing his duty, isn't he?'

Fury was mounting inside Müller and he reached behind his chair searching for the cable connected to the desk lamp. If his fingers could find it he might be able to pull it over and disorient Padilla long enough to attack him. The Mexican would dash into the room if he heard any rumpus, but by that time Müller might be able to grab the gun. It was risky, but better than a prison camp.

Padilla's voice was sharp. 'There is one way in which you can prove that you really know Wolfgang Müller. Any friend of his would know. My brother always wore something on his person. What was it?'

Müller knew exactly what Padilla had in mind. 'Wolfgang always wore a small gold locket attached to his watch chain,' he replied. 'It was an antique that belonged to his great-grandfather, and had been worn smooth over the years.'

'Yes, but what was inside it?' Padilla asked quietly.

Known only to members of the family, Wolfgang's locket concealed a small scrap of paper, on which was printed a metallurgical formula from seventy years before. It had been an important professional secret for Müller's great-grandfather, and, although now outdated, it still had a strong mystique as a family heirloom.

Padilla was trying to set a trap. The eldest son always inherited it and passed it on intact to his heir. Müller realised that if he did not know the right answer he would either be killed or handed over to the police. But if he knew the locket's contents his cover would be blown. There was no choice; Müller chose his words carefully.

'There is something special about the locket. It contains a scrap of paper.' He described the family custom and Padilla turned down the beam of the lamp.

'There is only one man of your generation who would know that about the Müller family,' he said softly.

'Yes, your nephew Ulrich.'

Padilla still kept the gun pointing at Müller, but sat back in his chair. He was about to speak when there was a tap at the door and Carmen Padilla entered. Glancing at Müller, she placed a brown manilla envelope before her husband. Quickly he pulled out a page of press clippings, and a look of triumph came across his face. Both of them regarded Müller intently, before Padilla said, 'Welcome, Ulrich.'

He held up a page from *Signal*, the Nazi propaganda magazine. Most of the spread was taken up with a colour photograph of a man standing unshaven and swigging beer on the bridge of a U-boat. Müller was looking at his own picture.

Padilla put down the gun, but kept it within easy reach.

'Carmen,' he said, 'I think we could all do with a drink.'

She walked over to a cabinet and Müller gratefully accepted a Scotch. With light gleaming on his bald head Padilla's expression had become more friendly.

'Well, well, well,' he said through the smoke of a Havana. 'It's hard to believe you are in Mexico. How did you get here?'

Müller told him of his rescue and the acquisition of his false identity. There was no point concealing anything and he wanted to get his uncle's full co-operation in his escape plans; but he was still uncertain of his attitude.

'I need your help,' Müller said. 'I must get back to Germany. I know that it is a risk for you, but perhaps you could give me a few contacts, or at least help me reach the border.'

Padilla drew on his cigar. 'You are aware that if I am caught it could bring a charge of treason? I have enough

68

enemies here who would make sure that I would face a firing squad.'

Müller coldly decided to act alone. He would not allow even his blood relative to stand in his way. He edged closer to the lamp stand and when Padilla reached for his drink he made a lightning move for it. But his uncle was quicker. With a crash he smashed the gun barrel down on Müller's wrist. It felt as if his hand had been severed.

'You fool, Ulrich. What are you trying to do? I would have killed other men.'

Carmen was white-faced. 'What are we going to do with him, Ernst?' she asked.

The gun was only inches from Müller's temple as Padilla spoke.

'You are not going back to Germany, Ulrich. I admire your motives and they are very praiseworthy, but you are needed here.'

Müller clenched his teeth with the pain. 'But all I ask is help in getting back to the Reich. That's all, and you are my father's brother. You are really going to kill one of your own flesh and blood?'

To his surprise Padilla laughed. 'Perhaps I should introduce myself in my official capacity.' He straightened his shoulders and clicked his heels. 'Korvetten Kaptain Ernst Müller, German Naval Intelligence. Station Nine, Mexico and Caribbean. Heil Hitler!'

Müller was stunned, then recovered his senses. 'And how do I know that?'

'I can prove it, don't worry, but we have had enough vetting for one day.' He went on briskly, 'You must move out of your hotel at once. I want you here. Luis will fetch your luggage. I do not want you seen at all.'

Müller began to feel more confident. 'I understand. But when can I expect to be on my way home? They desperately need experienced U-boat men. It's my duty.'

Padilla shook his head. 'Please get this into your head, Ulrich. You are not going back.'

'I do not intend to stay here. You'll have to kill me,' Müller protested.

Padilla's face was set like a mask. 'But I am ordering you

to remain until I have referred your presence to higher authority. Understand that the Americans played right into our hands. They have given you perfect cover. You can travel anywhere inside the United States, sail on any Allied ship, get into any theatre of war.'

As Padilla's words sank in, Müller shook his head in disbelief. 'But I'm a seaman.'

Without replying, Padilla picked up the telephone and spoke rapidly in Spanish. When he put the receiver down he stroked his bald head.

'Tomorrow you will be moving out of here,' he instructed. 'I am sending you to a country estate we have. They will teach you a few things there which will be very useful. If you think you are tough now wait until you come out of our hacienda. You are more useful to the Reich now, Ulrich, than a whole wolf pack.'

Chapter 6

Kapitanleutnant Werner Hartstein lit another cigar and watched the foam break gently over the bow of U-1264. Savouring the rich Havana, he leaned over the bridge parapet and grinned at the off-duty seamen bathing on the foc'sle below. Shouting like schoolboys, they dived over the side and splashed around in the ocean while some of their comrades stretched out on the hot deck to soak up the sun. Hartstein knew that all U-boat crews on the South Atlantic station looked forward to enjoying the sea and sun once they were outside the range of enemy air patrols, and when U-1264 reached a point in the empty ocean five hundred miles south-west of Freetown he had given permission for the men to take recreation on deck. Lines had been rigged for swimmers and a special look-out posted to watch for sharks.

Hartstein could tell from his crew's faces that morale was sky-high. It would stand them in good stead on the two-thousand-mile-long voyage ahead to the unprotected shipping lanes of the Indian Ocean. So far the cruise had proved very successful for Hartstein. Off Freetown he had sent three British freighters to the bottom. When the attack had been broken off Hartstein was down to just two torpedoes and U-Boat Command had ordered him to replenish his fuel and ammunition from a supply ship at a mid-ocean rendezvous before continuing the voyage south.

He crossed over to the starboard side of the conning tower and looked down at the coxswain dangling over the sea in a chair, paint brush in hand. He had decided to take advantage of the lull to touch up U-1264's famous insignia—a scarlet Valkyrie.

'How's it coming along, Rembrandt?'

The burly coxswain beamed up at his commander. 'All right, sir. The next ship we sink will feel privileged!'

Hartstein turned to Leutnant Fritz Bode, his number one, a gangling young officer of twenty-five who had served with him on three oceans. Despite his youth Bode had a quiet authority, and seemed to spend his spare time reading philosophy. Hartstein scratched his blond, month-old beard.

'You have to admit, Bode, it's better than the North Atlantic.'

The number one nodded. 'Perhaps we could land on one of those African beaches and steal a few girls,' he said wistfully.

Hartstein assumed an air of mock disapproval.

'For a doctor of philosophy, Bode, you shock me. This is *not* a holiday cruise.'

He pushed his battered white cap on to the back of his head and leaned against the periscope. He looked fit and relaxed but never forgot his professional duty.

'If we can meet the supply ship tonight we shall have to catch up on lost time. It's another four days' sailing to the Cape and another week into the Indian Ocean!'

Already Hartstein was one of Germany's top U-boat aces.

Only two commanders had sunk more ships, and he fully intended to become the Reich's Number One. Hartstein threw his cigar stub overboard and was about to go below when a look-out, wearing a solar topee to protect him from sunstroke, stirred behind him.

'Ship on the starboard bow, sir.'

Hartstein dashed to the parapet. At first he saw nothing. Then, as he methodically swept the sea with his binoculars, he picked up a small smudge at what must have been over thirty kilometres' distance.

'Sound stations, Number One,' he commanded, and the klaxon blared.

The bathers scrambled out of the sea, and the coxswain was hauled on board.

'What's her bearing?' Hartstein asked.

'Two nought seven degrees, sir.'

He quickly ordered U-1264 to swing several points westward, to converge with the approaching ship. There was little chance of her look-outs sighting U-1264 for at least twenty minutes, and so Hartstein resolved to stay on the surface to maintain a higher speed.

The South Atlantic spray swept the bridge, and the U-boat's hull shuddered with the power of the diesels, pushing her forward at seventeen knots. Below, the crew were busy stowing gear and checking equipment and weapons. The ship was now a growing shape on the horizon.

'I think we can safely stay on the surface a little longer,' Hartstein confided to Bode.

'She's making another turn, sir,' the watchkeeper reported.

'She's on a zig-zag course,' Hartstein murmured, his hopes rising. She must almost certainly be a capital ship—a carrier or a battleship—and within striking distance . . .

The ship's upperworks were now clearly visible through the bridge binoculars, and as she turned Hartstein saw the sun shining on the massive wall of her bridge. Then he observed one—two—three raked funnels. He let out a gasp of amazement as he recognised the unmistakable profile.

'My God, it's the *Queen Mary*.'

'It's her all right,' his number one echoed. 'And she's sailing right at us.'

For a moment the watch seemed spellbound by the huge bows and by the superstructure, as tall as a block of flats.

'What speed is she making?' Hartstein demanded.

'Could be twenty-eight knots, sir. Very fast.' It was the coxswain who answered.

Hartstein cursed. 'She won't be easy to hit. And we have only two torpedoes left, damn it! Send a signal.' He spoke quickly to his number one. 'U-1264 to U-Boat Command. Have sighted British liner *Queen Mary* in block DE nine eight. Am proceeding to attack. Hartstein.'

He grinned. 'That should wake them up at Headquarters, Bode.'

He went over to the voice tube; although he could not see them he felt the crew listening below with rapt attention. 'This is Kapitan Leutnant Hartstein. We have sighted the *Queen Mary*, the world's most famous liner.'

There was no reaction for a second or two, then wild cheering broke out as the news sank in. Hartstein let it die down.

'My plan is to attack with all weapons. We will have only one chance. Everybody must be on their toes. But believe me, at one stroke we can strike a colossal blow for the Reich. We are going to sink the *Queen Mary*. Heil Hitler!'

He made a final check of the liner's position, then nodded to his number one.

'All right. Dive.'

The alarm sounded through the narrow hull, watertight doors were slammed, the hydroplane operators glued their eyes to the depth gauge and the chief threw open U-1264's sea valves. Water surged into her tanks, swept over the bow, and swirled around the conning tower. Like a team of acrobats the watch slid down the vertical ladder into the control room, and U-1264 slid beneath the waves. In just thirty seconds she had disappeared.

Hartstein coolly waited for U-1264 to reach periscope depth, then quickly ordered the periscope to be raised. The *Queen Mary* was still holding the same position.

He drew away from the eyepiece and snapped out an order. With a hiss, the steel tube sank back into its well.

Even though the *Queen Mary* was at the very edge of his torpedo range he did not want to risk the thin wake of the periscope being spotted.

In the hot control room the depth gauge needles hovered at fifteen metres, the hydroplanes were in trim, and in the bows the torpedoes were primed: it would take the destructive power of both of them to have any chance of sinking the *Queen Mary*.

Hartstein admitted to himself that he would be very lucky to sink the liner with his two remaining torpedoes, but he could at least severely damage her and slow her down. Then if HQ had received his message it would be up to them to home other U-boats on to the target. Gently he nursed U-1264 on her battery power.

'Two points to starboard.'

He strode over to the soundproof booth where the hydrophone operator was straining to hear the reverberations of the liner's four propellers through the layers of water. Leaning over him he took in the young rating's strained face. 'Well? Where is she now?'

'She's turned again, Captain.'

'What?'

'Another leg of the zig-zag. She's going away from us.'

Hartstein could have sworn out loud, but controlled his frustration in front of the crew.

'Range?' he asked.

'Seventeen thousand metres.'

The operator pressed his earphones closer. 'Twenty thousand metres . . . twenty-three thousand metres . . .'

The steady throb of the screws was fading. Hartstein clenched his fist, furious. His number one waited expectantly while he looked through the periscope; it should be safe now to check the *Queen*'s position visually. Suddenly, however, the operator shouted:

'She's turning, sir! She's making a new leg!'

The whisper of the liner's screws was growing louder, and the operator's face was tense with concentration.

'She's coming this way, Captain. Twenty thousand metres.' The operator began to call off the diminishing range, but Hartstein still had to close the angle and ordered full ahead on all battery power. Silently U-1264 began to nose into position.

'Sixteen thousand metres and closing,' the hydrophone operator continued.

Harstein grinned at Bode.

'She might turn on a zig-zag at any moment.' Bode cautioned.

'We'll just have to risk the attack now'—Hartstein retorted impatiently.

He signalled Bode to take over in the control room and climbed the ladder to the small cubicle in the conning tower which housed the attack periscope. A petty officer clambered after him and took up a position on the Fahnrichter calculator to feed guidance instructions to the torpedoes.

Hartstein threw his legs astride the triangular saddle on the periscope column.

'Up periscope!' he snapped.

Before the lens had broken surface his eye was pressed to the viewfinder, and as the lens cleared he drew in his breath sharply. Across the shimmering water Hartstein saw the most impressive sight of his career, the *Queen Mary* bearing down at full speed, bow wave arching gracefully and the ocean coursing past her grey sides. Even at a range of two thousand metres the commander could see figures on her deck. He switched the periscope lens to close-up so that he could make out the delicate array of the *Queen Mary*'s antennae. She seemed as well equipped as any warship, and for a moment he stood admiring her elegant lines. Then, with a feeling of jubilation, he brought the cross-wires to meet over the middle of her hull, carefully estimating the point of impact four metres below the surface. In a flat voice he read out the digits marked on the viewfinder.

'Range seventeen hundred metres. Bearing two two one degrees. Speed twenty-nine point two five knots.'

Behind him, the petty officer deftly clicked the dials of the Fahnrichter.

Hartstein gripped the periscope handles, his palms sweating, as the *Queen Mary* approached to just over 1,500 metres. Every man on board was waiting for the next command.

'Stand by, Number One and Two tubes.'

There was a gruff acknowledgment over the voice tube and Hartstein paused, savouring the drama of the moment. Then he spoke.

'Fire One and Two tubes!'

U-1264 shuddered as the two torpedoes surged from the hull and nosed towards their target.

At once the coxswain's voice rang out mechanically from below, calling out the time to impact. There was nothing Hartstein could do except wait for the metallic thud of a torpedo striking home.

'Down periscope,' he ordered sharply, then forced himself to relax as the tube slid back into its well. However much he wanted to observe the final run of the salvo, Hartstein knew he dare not risk being spotted at such a crucial stage of the attack. He grinned at the petty officer and considered his next moves. For a moment he tried to envisage what would happen when the mammoth hull was ruptured. Perhaps the liner would roll over and sink in just a few minutes? Far more likely it would slowly settle, like the *Titanic*. Whatever happened there would be heavy loss of life, because the *Queen Mary* was so far from the British convoy routes that even if many of the passengers and crew got away, they would never be picked up, and large-scale rescue at such a range was unthinkable. And if she remained afloat it would only be a matter of time before a wolf pack gathered to finish the job.

Hartstein resolved to have a record made of the momentous event. Every U-boat carried a trained photographer equipped with the latest Leica, and he shouted to Bode down the voice tube, 'Number One. Have the photographer stand by. As soon as we surface I want him on the bridge taking pictures. It should be quite a sight.'

In the bow chamber the torpedo-men crouched next to the empty tubes, straining to hear the first tell-tale noise of a strike.

Hartstein pressed his forehead against the cold steel of the periscope column and decided to wait no longer. The temptation was too great.

Eagerly he grabbed the handles each side of the viewfinder. 'Fifteen . . . fourteen . . . thirteen . . .'

He could not see the tracks of the torpedoes but he realised immediately that the ship had changed position. She was no longer three-quarter profile, but was turning hard to port, moving on to a new leg of her zig-zag run.

'Run, you bastards, run.'

The steel rim of the periscope bit into Hartstein's cheek. Behind him he heard the coxswain's final count-down.

'Three . . . two . . . one . . . Time of impact!'

Five seconds passed. Ten. Only the gentle hum of the ventilators and the faint rumble of the battery-powered motors broke the silence as every man in U-1264 waited for the explosion, the tearing, breaking sounds of a ship disintegrating.

Bode glanced anxiously at the coxswain, who stared ahead impassively. A hydroplane operator coughed nervously, while the photographer who now stood ready next to Bode started to polish his Leica lens. Everyone hung on the commander's words as he sat astride the attack periscope. Hartstein's eyes were smarting and his head ached. The great ship was listing under the momentum of her engines as they drove her hard to port, the wake boiling over her screws. Her funnels stepped into new alignment and the *Queen Mary*'s profile narrowed as she sped safely north.

Kapitan zur See Max Boehm sat in his office in Berlin Naval Headquarters and studied the signals received from U-1264. He lit a cigarette and pronounced his verdict to the attentive staff of junior officers of Seekriegsleitung 111, a branch of naval intelligence.

'Well, that was a major cock-up, gentlemen. Hartstein missed a sitter.'

'Not the great Hartstein?' a young lieutenant asked mockingly.

'The very man. And not just him, but the entire U-boat fleet.'

Boehm had spent the whole morning analysing U-1264's abortive attempt to sink the *Queen Mary*. From the moment Hartstein's first message had been received all hell had broken loose in the Headquarters on Tirpitzufer. When U-1264 had failed to hit the liner, U-boats had been regrouped and thrown out in patrol lines to trap her; but the effort had been in vain.

'Where is she now?' another man asked.

'I wish I knew. But we'll find her,' Boehm promised.

The other men returned to their work. They were a mixed bunch drawn from business, the professions and universities, whose job was to detect enemy shipping movements from agents' reports, air reconnaissance and even newspapers.

The phone rang on Boehm's desk. It was a call he was expecting and he recognised the deep voice of Admiral Steinfort, Director of Naval Intelligence.

'Boehm, have you done the analysis of the *Queen Mary* business? And could you come in for a moment?'

The captain picked up the report he had prepared for the admiral, and walked the few yards down the corridor to Steinfort's office. The admiral's secretary immediately ushered Boehm into his chief's room, where the admiral sat with his back to the window.

Steinfort was the epitome of a Prussian officer with his cropped hair and starched collar. He was also one of the shrewdest brains in German Intelligence. Boehm, a journalist in civilian life, suffered the admiral's faint look of disapproval at his dishevelled appearance, but knew that Steinfort respected his nose for intelligence.

Boehm put the folder on Steinfort's desk.

It took only a few moments for the senior officer to skim through it before he commented.

'So. We were one step behind all the way. Hartstein should have sunk her in the first place, even if he did have only two torpedoes. But why have the British rushed her back from Australia? It's far more dangerous for a ship like her in the Atlantic.'

Boehm knew the answer. 'It's the beginning of the mass build-up of American forces in Britain; and we know what that means . . .'

'Doesn't surprise me,' the admiral scoffed. 'After Stalingrad, the Wehrmacht will have its hands full holding the Eastern Front. We shall see the British and Americans trying to get into Europe this year.'

Boehm shook his head. 'I doubt if they can find the

shipping to build up their armies that quickly. And they have had some heavy losses. We still have a powerful U-boat fleet.'

Steinfort stiffened and regarded the captain coldly. 'I wish it were that easy.' He lowered his voice. 'Even the Grossadmiral—and here I speak in absolute confidence—has been worried by the huge increase in Anglo-American naval forces and by their anti-submarine technology.'

Boehm knew only too well that new radar, longer-range aircraft and stronger surface forces were making it harder for U-boats to operate.

Steinfort paused before continuing in a more confidential voice. 'In my view, this war will be won or lost within the next few months. The only action we can take is to sever the convoy routes once and for all. But whether we can do it I do not know.'

'You mean you doubt it?'

Steinfort's hard grey eyes glanced quickly at Boehm. 'What we desperately need now is a victory. A victory at sea. We need to inflict a spectacular and bloody defeat on the British and Americans to raise our own morale. Recently I've been on inspections to the U-boat bases in France and Norway. I can assure you the strain is beginning to tell on the crews.' The admiral drew out a silver box and offered Boehm a cigarette. 'It's also absolutely vital that we convince the Führer that the sea war is decisive. When the Grossadmiral came back from the Führer Conference this morning he was furious. I've rarely seen him so angry.'

Boehm was surprised; the Grossadmiral's tight self-control was well known.

'He was furious,' Steinfort continued, 'because Goering and Himmler have accused the Navy of incompetence for the way the *Queen Mary* slipped through. Even worse, they are pointing the finger at us in SKL111.'

'That's absurd,' Boehm protested. 'How can they blame us when almost all our agents have been rounded up and we get no help from the Abwehr or the SS on any intelligence matter?'

'Their game is obvious,' Steinfort answered contemptuously. 'Goering wants to discredit us—he wants our steel and

79

skilled workers for the Luftwaffe—and Himmler wants them for the SS. They cannot stand the Grossadmiral's influence with the Führer.'

Boehm had never heard the admiral speak so frankly. Steinfort was now leaning towards him confidentially.

'We *must* get the Führer to underwrite a naval strategy against the British and Americans. It's our only chance. The Wehrmacht can hold the Red Army, but not if the British and Americans invade the West. Only the Kriegsmarine can stop that, by severing the lifeline. Time is desperately short.'

'But it's short for the enemy too, Admiral,' Boehm replied. 'No doubt Churchill and Roosevelt are worried about Comrade Stalin; he could make a separate peace. After all, it's his men who are dying. They're desperate to start moving men and material into Britain. And that's why they've brought the *Queen Mary* and doubtless other liners back to the Atlantic.'

There was a silence before Boehm ventured, 'So it is obvious what our little Trafalgar must be. We must sink the *Queen Mary*.'

Steinfort stared at him as the captain pressed on.

'She is capable of carrying a whole division of troops at a time, no less than fifteen thousand men. If she were sunk it would drastically cut the speed of the American build-up, and her loss would have a terrible effect on British morale. She's Britain's best-loved ship.'

Steinfort thought a moment, then said appreciatively, 'The *Queen Mary* could be the perfect target. But it won't be easy. She's fast, faster than some of our torpedoes, and you know that the British Admiralty constantly changes her course while she is at sea, so that it's very difficult to predict her position.'

Boehm sensed Steinfort wavering.

'I agree she's a difficult target, but we just have to think of the right way to attack her.'

Steinfort leaned down and opened a deep drawer in the side of his desk. His gold-braided sleeve dipped inside and he drew out a bottle of whisky, pouring out two glasses. When he spoke again his square Prussian features were grave.

'We can't make another mistake, Boehm. We have enemies at court. For some time I have been quietly gathering evidence that Himmler's Reichsicherheitsamt VI are determined to absorb OKM Intelligence into the SS machine.'

At the mention of RSHA even Boehm, a hard-boiled journalist who had covered Nazi rallies and anti-Jewish pogroms, felt a tremor of fear. The RSHA was Himmler's own massive terror apparatus, with bureaux, agents and special squads wherever the swastika held sway. It employed thousands of officials and technicians and an army of secret policemen. Boehm knew the likely fate of anyone who stood in the way of this formidable machine.

'RSHA VI claims that SKL Intelligence has been weak, and that the British would be in far more trouble at sea if only we had been more effective,' Steinfort added.

'But the Grossadmiral would never allow them to get their hands on the Navy,' Boehm answered.

'Indeed, Max, I know the Grossadmiral well. He is a man of integrity and loyalty. But, make no mistake, his aim is to protect the Navy at whatever cost, and that depends on keeping the ear of Hitler. If anything threatens that confidence the Grossadmiral will act decisively—in any way he thinks fit. If he found me in any way an embarrassment, even against a trumped-up charge, I would be dropped like a stone.'

Boehm drew slowly on his cigarette. From the admiral's words there was clearly little time before Himmler's men manufactured another charge against SKL 111. When he spoke, his voice was firm.

'We have no choice, Admiral. If we are to safeguard SKL 111 we must move fast. The Grossadmiral's position must be strengthened through a naval victory.' He paused, then continued with emphasis, 'And it has to be *our* idea, *our* plan.'

The admiral listened intently as Boehm warmed to his theme. 'Our target must be the *Queen Mary*; but I need the men to help me destroy her. Experts who know the ship, her design and layout. And I need them as soon as they can be found.'

The room darkened as Steinfort rose to his feet, then walked over to a large map of the Western hemisphere,

81

above a chart cabinet at the far end of the room. Quickly he pushed it aside to reveal a gleaming wall safe. The admiral's fingers twirled the combination lock then pulled open the door. Inside Boehm saw a buff folder which the admiral drew out and brought over to his desk. He fingered the folder thoughtfully. 'Yes, Boehm, the *Queen Mary* will be our target, and I will get you the shipping experts you need. But nothing must be left to chance. Special operations demand special men.' He smiled.

'I think I have the man you need.'

He handed Boehm the dossier. On the cover there was one word: 'Iceman'. Inside was a picture of a young Kriegsmarine petty officer. The man's eyes gazed confidently at the world. An Iron Cross hung round his neck. Beneath were the typewritten words: KM 0775843 Coxswain Ulrich Müller.

Chapter 7

It was bitterly cold in the narrow cockpit, and the pilot moved awkwardly in his heated flying suit. He pushed the joystick and the Junkers 86 reconnaissance plane banked gently, streaming a white vapour trail high over Glasgow. Far below, the shipyards of Govan slipped past the port wing and the river Clyde began to broaden into an estuary. Then he saw her—two miles off the coast, the unmistakable shape of the *Queen Mary*.

A bevy of small craft churned the waters around her, their wakes criss-crossing on the sparkling sea. The pilot leaned forward, to switch on the cameras in the aircraft's belly . . .

It was early evening in London, and the black-out curtains had been drawn in the Defence Office. They hung behind the blast-proof windows and sealed off noise from the street outside. It was peaceful in the large room now that the clatter of typewriters had subsided, and men and women on the night shift began to plan their work for the hours ahead.

Alloway stretched and eased the stiffness in his leg. Stubbs's meeting had not broken up until four and he had started work on a comprehensive report as soon as he had reached the office. His desk was strewn with loading schedules, statistics and other details sent round by the Ministry of War Transport. The ship's owners had also supplied plans of the changes that were to be made to the ship in New York so that she could carry 15,000 Americans, four times the liner's peacetime capacity.

Alloway finished the last paragraph of the report and sat back satisfied at having compressed the material into two pages and four supporting appendices. He knew that the prime minister might well be scanning the document later that night and that he hated verbose, abstruse or badly thought-out statements. Sub-standard work was invariably returned with scrawled remarks like, 'It is slothful not to compress your thoughts'.

Barbara put a mug of tea in front of him. 'I hope it's not too strong.'

'Perfect,' Alloway replied cheerfully, passing her the last page to type. She glanced at the clock. In fifteen minutes he had to see General Ismay. Churchill was on a tour of East Anglia bomber bases and not expected back until late, but even then he would start work drafting letters and minutes. His energy was astounding, and important meetings often extended into the early hours of the morning, when Ismay and his staff were still expected to be at hand.

'Working late again?' Barbara asked.

She seemed too young to worry about his long hours, which he thoroughly enjoyed. Being near the centre of power, observing the subtleties of government, fascinated Alloway. He passionately loved flying, but seeing Britain's war leadership at work absorbed him and submerged his bitterness about being taken off operations.

'I don't think there's anything on early this evening,' he answered. 'No Defence Committee, no Cabinet meeting. Of course, the general may want me to be on hand in case the Stubbs Committee report comes up with the PM, but it won't be until late. I want to nip out to a cocktail party about eight.'

'Cocktail party?' Barbara echoed enviously.

'Oh, come on, I haven't been to a binge for weeks. And you know how reserved I am,' Alloway countered.

She looked disapproving. 'Of course, if you had to take a young woman with you to this party . . .'

'There's nobody I would like to take more than you, Barbara, but unfortunately it's a lady who has invited *me*.' Alloway's mind turned to Tracey, who had rung him the previous day with the invitation. Barbara shrugged her shoulders.

'All right, I understand. But promise to take me to the next one—even though it won't be until next year, at this rate.'

'Promise. Scout's honour,' Alloway declared. It was time to go, and with a wave to Barbara he hurried off through the maze of corridors to his meeting.

Ismay was deep in conversation with one of his senior staff officers when Alloway entered his room, and it was some minutes before he looked round.

'Have you finished the Stubbs report?' he asked.

Alloway handed him the papers. 'I'm afraid it's going to be quite an operation, sir.'

'Well,' the general commented as he scanned the report, 'the Americans have agreed to take a first batch of one thousand POWs, and the Ministry of War Transport have agreed that you can have the *Queen Mary*, which is what the Stubbs's Committee asked for. When can we start moving these devils?'

'Unfortunately not until the beginning of May at the earliest; about three weeks' time.'

The general's brow puckered and he swung round in his chair.

'Why?'

Alloway referred to the detailed schedule of the *Queen*

Mary's movements. 'The ship leaves for New York today, sir, where she should arrive on tenth April, dependent on weather and routing.'

'Well, that's pretty quick.'

'Yes, but once she's in New York we have to face a delay of ten days while the Americans carry out repair work and modify her to carry their own men. She won't sail on the homeward leg until about twenty-second April, and could be off the Clyde by the twenty-sixth.'

'Can't the Americans cut down on the alterations?'

Alloway shook his head. 'No. We've asked them, and they claim the work has already been cut to the absolute minimum. The yards are on standby waiting to start as soon as she arrives.'

'I see,' the general said quietly. 'It would really put their backs up if we started to interfere with things. But Stubbs had better make sure that he starts moving these men by May. If not, I can assure you that the prime minister will not be amused—and you know what that means. Angry memos, sharp words, and perhaps a few sackings *pour encourager les autres*.'

The general tapped the report. 'Thank you for this. You've given me a very clear picture. What worries me is that the situation in the camps is still serious.'

Alloway agreed, adding, 'I think they are under control now, and Colonel Phelps has done good work. He's isolated the hardliners in a special compound. General Stubbs is making an inspection next Wednesday to see the situation for himself.'

The general relaxed. 'I expect you to be on that trip. I want a complete picture of what's going on.'

Alloway rose to leave, but the general stopped him.

'Get this Stubbs thing out of the way as fast as you can, Alloway. There's something important brewing and I want you to work on it. Very soon the whole of North Africa will be ours, and we shall face a major decision on future strategy. The prime minister is very concerned about the American attitude.'

Alloway was surprised by Ismay's candour; it had been only just over two months since Churchill and Roosevelt

85

had met in a summit conference at Casablanca, where major strategy had been laid down for the rest of the year.

Ismay answered his thoughts. 'You see, there are some major differences between ourselves and Washington about where the main Allied effort should be directed. The prime minister and chiefs of staff want to exploit our gains in the Mediterranean and drive on into Southern Europe, but the Americans are keen to attack across the English Channel once we've mopped up in Africa. A summit between the president and prime minister may be called at any moment, and it's vital that we win the argument. The PM will want to take the largest and most powerful delegation to Washington, and I want you to start making contingency plans immediately. Start collecting position papers and duplicates of key files to accompany the party. Report to me daily.'

Alloway felt flattered by this new responsibility. 'Is there any likely date for the meeting, sir?'

The general shook his head. 'None at all. Let's just say that it can't be delayed very long. I've detected the signs of restlessness in the prime minister; he's anxious to sort this matter out.'

Ismay looked at his watch; it was time to move. As Alloway left he thought how typical it was of Churchill to order the most thorough preparations for his key meeting with the Americans. The prime minister hated to be beaten in any arguments on strategy. And for Alloway there was the chance of a trip to America—a release from the drab environment of wartime London.

Driving across the blacked-out city, the taxi driver unerringly found the block of flats in St John's Wood where Tracey lived. As Alloway came out of the lift the noise of the party was unmistakable.

He rang the bell and his hostess stood before him, her eyes shining. She was wearing a black dress which clung to her breasts and outlined the curve of her hips. The light behind her seemed to halo her auburn hair.

'Hello, James. It's wonderful to see you.' She brushed his cheek with a kiss. 'I thought you were too busy winning the war to be able to come. There are lots of people dying to meet you.'

She led him into her crowded flat where there was a tremendous din of conversation in several languages. Everywhere there were uniforms, insignia, badges. There must have been over forty officers in the room, and a large number of the women present were also in uniform. Several of the guests were war correspondents from the American press and radio in London, and one of their number, a dumpy brunette, was holding forth to a circle of French and Polish officers.

Van Kleef stood chatting in a group by the fireplace. Alloway spotted other familiar faces as Tracey guided him to the bar. It was far better stocked than any British equivalent, with several bottles of the finest Scotch malt and a selection of American bourbons.

'It's all right, James. I'm not in the black market,' Tracey said, reading his thoughts. 'Colonel Hall over there raided the Grosvenor Square PX for me.'

A grey-haired colonel acknowledged their glance as Alloway asked for a Jack Daniels. A plump man whose bulging collar was turning up at the points stood at Alloway's shoulder.

'James, meet Chuck Mason, my boss,' Tracey announced. Alloway shook the bureau chief's pudgy hand.

'Pleased to make your acquaintance,' Mason beamed, then jerked his head towards the crowd behind him.

'It's an impressive turnout. So far I've counted at least two generals and an admiral.'

'He's only a vice-admiral,' Tracey corrected.

Mason grinned at Alloway. 'There's one thing about this lady,' he declared. 'She's very popular with the military, and that's a valuable asset for a journalist in wartime.'

Tracey wrinkled her nose with mock disapproval. 'I'm not sure that I like your insinuations, Chuck.' She quickly addressed Alloway. 'I don't really seduce every general I meet, James. There are other ways of getting a story.'

Alloway laughed as Tracey excused herself and went off to look after her guests.

The two men watched her go. 'Tracey is an excellent journalist,' Mason remarked, a bead of perspiration on his brow. 'One of the best I've ever had working for me.' He pulled a packet of Chesterfields from his pocket and offered one to Alloway, who declined. 'I've been over here for nearly ten years,' he continued, 'and the toughest part of the job is understanding the British. Tracey seems to have done that very well.'

'Surely we aren't that difficult?' Alloway protested mildly.

Mason blew out a cloud of tobacco smoke, and emphasised his point with a raised finger. 'Squadron Leader, this is one of the hardest countries on earth to crack a story. The Establishment is extremely experienced at closing its doors and protecting its own. That famous British reserve is used most effectively to kill off embarrassing reports.'

Alloway sipped his drink. 'But now we are both fighting in the same alliance, surely you find things a little easier? I had the impression that thousands of Americans are successfully melting our famous reserve. In fact we shall never be the same again.'

'There's a lot of truth in what you say, but you British still feel that you are God's own gift to the human race, and from what my military friends tell me you regard yourselves as the senior members of the alliance.'

'Well, we have been fighting Hitler a little longer than you,' Alloway commented, beginning to be a trifle exasperated by Mason.

The journalist's eyes darted across the room to where two or three officers were grouped around Tracey. 'You've been in the war far longer, but there's a resentment about certain British attitudes. I'm always being bombarded with enquiries from my head office in Chicago for information about supposed rows between London and Washington.'

'Such as?' Alloway asked, concerned to discover any information Mason might have unearthed.

The American took a step closer. 'It's well known that the US Navy wants Roosevelt to concentrate our war effort in the Pacific, and Churchill is opposing this tooth and nail.'

Alloway was concerned. What Mason was saying was true and he was not happy that such information had leaked out.

Mason continued, 'The pressure is on Washington for results, and there's a feeling that the British have been dragging their feet about invading Europe.'

Alloway shrugged. 'That sounds like typical newspaper speculation.'

Mason gulped his gin and tonic, then said quietly, 'I can see that you're not the man to gossip about such matters. Anyway, if you ask me, I think there is no problem in this war that can't be solved by Churchill and Roosevelt after a chat together. In fact I hope that there's a summit meeting coming up—it might stop some of the rumours.'

Alloway did not rise to the bait. Instead he rejoined politely, 'You know that if I answer your questions, Mr Mason, I shall probably end up in the Tower.'

As he spoke he felt a hand grip his arm. Tracey stood by his side. 'I hope you haven't been upsetting my friend by asking questions,' she said teasingly to Mason. 'Like all English people he's very well mannered, but he could probably have you deported.'

Mason downed his glass. 'No offence, Tracey,' he muttered sheepishly, and sidled off.

Dutch Van Kleef, who had overheard the end of the conversation, joined them. 'You should have punched him on the nose,' he advised. 'That's the trouble with you upper-class Brits. Too damned reserved.'

Alloway swallowed his bourbon. 'Remember, Dutch, I also happen to be a lawyer, and I've been conditioned not to take things into my own hands, even in wartime.'

Tracey turned to Van Kleef. 'By the way,' she began purposefully, 'last time we spoke I said I wanted to do a story on our boys in Britain, but I've been trying to find them ever since. I know we have the mighty Eighth Air Force over here, but do we have any GIs? I can't find any.'

Van Kleef guffawed. 'They're not leprechauns, you know. There are plenty of GIs if you know where to look. And there're going to be an awful lot more soon.'

'You mean Washington is going to start shipping them in? It's about time, I must say.'

Alloway watched Tracey's long fingers play gently round the lip of her glass as Van Kleef blustered, 'Look, I'll fix things for you when the time comes. Okay?'

She nodded. 'Just think of those moms and girlfriends back home wondering what their GI Joe is up to.'

Alloway decided to join in. 'Well, I think they might be a little upset if you told them everything they got up to. All the pubs . . .'

'And brothels?' Tracey added demurely.

Alloway smiled. 'Unlike the Italians we don't supply them officially.'

Suddenly she became serious. 'Say, there haven't been any more of those prisoner of war stories lately, have there? It worries me, all those highly-trained enemy soldiers, some out-and-out Nazis, running amok. They would be a terrible problem if they started rioting.'

'We could mow them all down in a few minutes easily enough,' Dutch said gruffly.

'How do you know? Have you done so already?' she asked.

'Of course not,' Alloway interjected, beginning to feel angry. 'And I don't know where you get such fairy stories.'

'But surely you aren't denying that there is a problem. Nor that it will get worse, the more German prisoners arrive here?'

'There is no problem,' Van Kleef declared. 'We can ship them out before their feet touch the ground. A whole camp at a time if need be.'

'Surely that's unlikely with every ship being used to move troops around?'

Van Kleef looked superior. 'We do have some very big ships, Tracey,' he said. 'Capable of moving thousands of men on a single trip.'

'If you mean you're going to use luxury liners to move Germans and Italians, the American public won't like that. The enemy travelling in comfort!'

'It won't be the case,' Van Kleef rejoined. 'Have you been aboard the *Queen Mary* since she was adapted for war service?'

'So you *are* going to use the *Queen Mary*,' Tracey concluded triumphantly.

A look of annoyance crossed Van Kleef's face. 'You must draw your own conclusions, Tracey. But don't forget that there is an official censor.'

Next morning a rich aroma of cigar smoke greeted Tracey as she walked into the *Sentinel* office. Chuck Mason was already at work, reading through the overnight news copy.

'Hi, Tracey,' he said. 'Swell party last night.'

'Glad you enjoyed it,' she replied, and slipped off her coat. 'You were having a long chat with James Alloway. What did you make of him?'

Chuck scratched his chin. 'I liked him, but he'll never give you a story. Much too cautious—and if you ask me he doesn't have a high regard for the press. Except you, of course.'

'I hope you're right. But perhaps he won't be so fond of me when he discovers who my father is.'

She had been determined to meet James again, but had worried about his reaction to the news that her father was one of the leading isolationists in the United States. As owner of the *Sentinel* newspaper group he wielded great power, and had fought hard to keep his country out of the war. This had earned him the enmity of Churchill and the British government. She wondered now whether she should have told James of her background.

Chuck blew out a cloud of smoke and tried to reassure her.

'Listen, Tracey. Your father is a true patriot, and nobody can fault him since we entered the war. I wouldn't worry too much about it. Anyway, Alloway is interested in you, not your father.'

She gave a thin smile as Chuck added, 'If he's as fond of you as I think he is he won't give up easily.'

She smiled again and Chuck changed the subject.

'And if you want me to stay fond of you *please* write me a story before head office starts nagging. It's already late.'

Tracey wound a sheet of paper into her typewriter. 'All right. I think I have something for you.'

She quickly typed:

As the Axis collapse continues in North Africa the Allied armies are taking so many prisoners that the British are likely to be faced with a serious security problem. Already there are rumours of attempted break-outs by fanatical Nazis. To prevent future trouble large numbers of POWs will be moved to the US and Canada. The 81,000-ton Cunarder *Queen Mary* will be used to ferry them across the Atlantic. Allied authorities say that they will not provide the enemy with luxury conditions enjoyed by pre-war passengers; if necessary every inch of space will be used to shift whole camps at a time.

As she finished Chuck peered over her shoulder. 'Come on, Tracey, you can't file that.'

'Why not?'

'It's a breach of security. The Germans read our newspapers just like everybody else, and you're telling them that the *Queen Mary* is in British waters and that the British have a POW problem.'

'I think that the government censors will be delighted to see us print the story. If the story breaks now it may actually protect the *Queen*, and other liners. After all, the Germans are not going to drown their own men.'

Chuck frowned. 'I wish I could believe you. Sorry, Tracey, but we can't print that. You'll have us closed down.'

She sighed with resignation. 'Okay, you're the boss.'

Chuck's tone softened. 'Why don't you write something on British society? Some colour story?'

'What about a piece on austerity cooking? I've had some recent experience of it, after all.'

Chuck thought a moment, drawing on his cigar. 'Sure,' he said. 'That sounds great. It will amuse the folks back home.'

Tracey wound the paper into her typewriter, unenthusiastic at first. Then she thought carefully and began typing.

Lunch at the Connaught

If ever you've wondered what happened to those swish London hotels now that there is a war on, I can assure you that they are still thriving, although wartime austerity and rationing have forced them to make some remarkable adaptations. Take the Connaught. Only a few days ago I was taken to its oak-panelled restaurant by two charming officers, one British, one American. It was an excellent lunch served with a fine bottle of Montrachet. By government order the menu was based entirely on simple ingredients—potatoes, onions, greens and the *pièce de résistance*, a strange dish called 'Woolton Pie', named appropriately after Britain's Food Minister . . .

Chapter 8

Captain Boehm's staff Mercedes came to a halt in front of an ornate villa in the Berlin suburb of Wannsee. Immediately two armed petty officers moved forward to inspect his identity card before the car was allowed to make its way through the wrought iron gates and up the gravel drive. Yet another check took place before the large oak doors of the villa were finally swung open, and Boehm stepped inside the headquarters of Operation Iceman.

The house was magnificent. It had been built in the 1880s for a wealthy Berlin banker determined to make his mark on society. Glittering chandeliers hung in the downstairs rooms and the windows were framed by deep velvet curtains.

The captain walked across the highly-polished wooden floor and entered a large drawing room, where half a dozen naval officers and two civilians were working at a walnut veneer table. In a corner, junior officers were manning the teleprinters and telephones which linked the house with Naval Headquarters and SKL 111 stations in occupied Europe.

Steinfort had insisted that the planning group for Operation Iceman should be set up outside Naval Headquarters so that maximum security be maintained. The admiral had been as good as his word and had secured the experts Boehm needed. Arthur Hansen, grey-haired and professional, had arrived at the villa prepared for a long stay. He had been a senior manager of the Hamburg-Amerika line, and knew every detail about operating a transatlantic liner: sailing schedules, timetables and the effects of weather were engraved on his mind.

A cheerful, well-dressed man had arrived soon after Hansen and introduced himself as Dr Merker, a leading member of the design staff of the crack German liner *Europa*. One of Germany's most distinguished naval architects, his knowledge of the *Queen Mary*'s design and structure was impressive. On Boehm's orders he had begun to collect professional articles and specialist papers from marine institutes in order to bring their knowledge of the ship up to date.

A young lieutenant approached Boehm as he entered.

'Oslo station have checked everything they can about Larsen—family, friends, women, employers.' The officer gave Boehm a green file. 'It seems Larsen left for England almost three years ago, on twenty-first July. We don't know whether he sailed on a fishing boat or crossed the frontier into Sweden but that's the last anybody heard of him in Norway. Or so they say.'

'Was he going to join the Norwegian Resistance?'

'Everybody thought he was, but from what we know it seems he never enrolled with King Haakon's forces, and we don't believe he was the type to be infiltrated back into Norway as an agent—he was too independent for such disciplined service and preferred to serve as a merchant seaman. No doubt the British were pleased to have him.'

'He sounds quite a character,' Boehm commented, then pointed to a photograph extracted from the Norwegian Passport Office files. 'This him?'

The young officer glanced at the photograph and nodded. Boehm studied Larsen's strong face a moment, noticing a strange likeness to Müller.

'I trust you've left nothing to chance?' he asked. 'What have Oslo station done with Larsen's family?'

'The father and mother have been arrested. We've concocted a charge of resistance activities against them,' the lieutenant continued in a matter-of-fact voice. 'They're both very old and will be sent to a concentration camp. As for the two brothers, they have also been arrested and are in Narvik, charged with suspected smuggling of arms for the Resistance. Oslo have made sure that plenty of weapons have been found aboard their vessel.'

'Very good. Did Larsen have any close friends? Any women?'

'Yes. A girlfriend, Ingrid. She lived in the same village and they were lovers before he left for England. She was very attached to him, according to Oslo's investigations.' He smiled coldly. 'We are sending her to Germany, where she will be put to work in a Bremen factory making batteries for U-boats. Just the right job, don't you think, sir?'

Boehm lit a cigarette and nodded agreement. 'Keep a close watch on her.'

He dismissed the lieutenant, exchanged a few words with the communications officer, who had reserved special frequencies for coded signals to Mexico and other overseas stations, then sat down behind an escritoire. An older officer brought him the latest reconnaissance photographs.

'They've just arrived, Captain. Taken five hours ago.'

The prints felt damp. Boehm drew a magnifying glass from the desk. The broad estuary of the Clyde curled through the frame and dark hills thrust up from the sea. There were several ships making for Glasgow and the *Queen Mary*'s refuelling tanker was clearly visible; but Boehm suddenly sat bolt upright—the liner's great hull had gone.

Boehm checked the time code along the bottom of the picture and saw that it had been taken at 7.21 a.m., twelve hours after the preceding reconnaissance flight. He thought it unlikely that the liner would leave in the dark; in Boehm's estimation the ship had sailed only hours before. She should be in New York within four days: 13 April. He strode over to the communication officer.

'I want to signal Station Mexico. Code Kondor B. At once.'

Bullets hummed over Müller's head and ricocheted from the rocks behind him. Padilla's men took their job seriously, and they had no hesitation in using live ammunition. Ahead he could see the target he had been given, a small stone bridge thrown across the dried-up riverbed. Inch by inch he eased round the side of a boulder. Somewhere on the bank opposite two of his instructors were hidden, ready to open fire as soon as he showed himself.

For three weeks he had been trained in the techniques of espionage and clandestine war at the remote hacienda, an old colonial house in wild landscape. Every minute of the day had been carefully planned by his instructor. He was a middle-aged, wiry man with hollow cheeks who had quickly discerned that Müller was excellent material. After a gruelling assault course or unarmed combat session he would put his lean face close to his pupil's and tell him, 'Remember: in danger you are an animal. Every man is an animal, but you are lucky, because you can keep your savagery under control. Fear and terror clear your mind.'

Müller understood the truth of these words. Until now he had been a member of a crew, the key man in a unit, and had come to understand other men's fears and emotions, especially in danger; but since the sinking of U-1543 he had been alone and had begun to learn how to depend totally on his own resources.

The present exercise had been deliberately designed to test such powers. Hours before he had been dropped in the mountains and told to make his way to the bridge, using only a hand compass. Men had been placed at various points, but Müller's training made him a formidable prey. His senses had become so acute that he easily detected the tell-tale signs of a lurking enemy. He had crept round the hidden position of one of the men sent to trap him, and silently attacked another from behind, leaving him dazed and bound in the burning sun.

Müller studied the bridge for a moment, working out the best point to place his explosives, then slithering on his belly he dragged himself to the next boulder and with a quick move darted into the shadow of a buttress. For a moment he paused to gather his wits, and checked that nobody had seen him. Then he reached inside the small haversack he was carrying and drew out a slab of plastic explosive. Its soft, toffee-like texture fascinated him: it was quite different to the explosives he had been trained to handle at sea. Carefully he dipped his hand into his hip pocket and took out a small detonator, jabbing it into the plastic. Then he moulded the charge expertly into a crevice at the top of the buttress that held up the bridge and set the fuse, driving a lizard from its home. Bent double, he raced back along the gully, almost falling on the uneven ground before throwing himself behind a boulder. The ground shook and stones rained down like shrapnel. Then he looked up, and grinned with satisfaction as the bridge collapsed in a cloud of dust.

His instructor appeared at the end of the gully where he had been observing him from behind the shelter of a massive rock.

'Well, you found the target and destroyed it, but you were lucky not to have your head blown off. You were in my sights when you ducked away—just in time.'

Müller followed his instructor back up the gully to the hacienda. It was cool inside the house. He went straight to his room and quickly showered, the water soothing his cuts and bruises. He changed into an embroidered Mexican shirt and light denim trousers before going downstairs for breakfast.

It was a meal to which he particularly looked forward, and was served in the beamed kitchen at the rear of the hacienda where a farmhouse table was laden with hotly spiced-eggs, ham, re-fried beans, tortillas and fresh orange juice. His instructors, drawn from the German community in Mexico, always joined him, and they discussed a wide range of subjects over the meal—American politics, trade unions, seamen's clubs. They never called him Müller, only Larsen. Their purpose, he knew, was to make him think and act like the Norwegian. One of them gave him a special intelligence file on Larsen. It contained family photographs going back two generations, and the stern Puritanical faces of Larsen's father and grandfather soon became printed on his mind. Larsen's mother seemed a gentler personality, while the Norwegian's two brothers were large and un-assuming men. The photograph which intrigued him most of all, however, was of a fair-haired girl with clear, trusting eyes. He studied the candid expression and felt that he understood her. Several of her letters to her lover were in the SKL file, and Müller was touched by her adolescent sentiments. When he read Larsen's replies with their unaffected descriptions of the exotic places he was visiting, of his ships and shipmates, Müller discovered a tenderness in the formidable Norwegian which he had only half-suspected.

He had just finished a final cup of coffee when a well-built man in a dark suit entered the room. Müller recognised him immediately as the chief instructor's personal aide, a quiet, businesslike man with thinning hair, his handsome features marred only by a pinkish scar on his left cheek. He addressed Müller with politeness.

'The chief instructor wants to see you right away, Mr Larsen.'

Müller eyed him silently; the chief instructor had never sent for him like this before. Curious, he followed the man out of the breakfast room and across the hall. Müller was puzzled when, instead of turning towards the chief instructor's office, the aide went to a small door at the end of the hall. It opened on stairs to the cellar. Müller hesitated, but the aide spoke with exasperation in his voice.

'The chief instructor has a special conference room down here. He ordered me to bring you there.'

Müller shrugged and followed him down to a narrow corridor below. They continued along it for some yards, between walls constructed of breeze blocks, until eventually the aide stopped before a solid oak door which he opened. As he did so he turned and, grabbing hold of Müller, pulled him roughly across the threshold. Müller tried indignantly to shake the bodyguard off, but stopped at the sight of the room before him. It was a small airless cell, lit by a solitary electric lamp from beyond the doorway. The rooms and walls were painted black, while the only piece of furniture was a monstrous chair, high-backed, with a coat of arms on its headboard like the great chairs of medieval prelates that Müller had seen in paintings. One detail struck him: the iron tubes at the ends of each arm. They were only four inches long, and quite narrow: he was looking at a set of manacles. They were bolted to the chair, with a neat lock on each. At its far side he made out the lean shape of his instructor, his sunken cheeks half-illuminated by the beam of light.

At once the instructor spoke.

'We are almost at the end of the course. However, there is one more test you must undergo. Please sit in this chair.'

Despite his apprehension, Müller sat down. The seat was hard and his spine felt uncomfortable against the tall back. The bodyguard took hold of his wrists and Müller winced as they were pushed through the rough manacles, his skin being torn painfully away. As the small key was turned, the blood drained from his hands. His wrists were now clamped firmly to the chair.

'How long will I be here?' he demanded.

'For as long as it takes,' came the sharp answer from the instructor, who without another word turned on his heel and left the room.

For a moment the bodyguard lingered to make sure Müller could not move, a wry grin on his disfigured face. Then the door slammed and there was total darkness. Müller instinctively shut his eyes to steady himself. When he opened them he felt strangely disorientated, as if floating in space. He told himself that it was only a ploy to break him down, and tried to listen for the steps of his interrogators. They never came. The only sound was the thump of his heart and his own rapid breathing. Time passed. His limbs grew stiff, and he had no way of knowing how long he had been sitting in the darkness.

He guessed that several hours must have passed because his bladder began to ache and his stomach was cramped with hunger. His tutor seemed to be taking things much too far. Angrily, he shouted out for attention but there was no answer. Eventually he could restrain himself no longer and urinated where he sat, swept by feelings of anger and humiliation. He swore aloud at the men running the hacienda.

He could hardly move his wrists now, and his fingers seemed to have floated from his hands. The constant darkness began to play on his mind, and his sense of proportion seemed to be deserting him. A void appeared to be opening beneath his feet.

He shut his eyes, but sleep was impossible because he dreaded waking up again in such total darkness. His mind continued to turn in upon itself and once more he was back in the lifeboat, back staring into the sightless eyes of the dead Norwegian . . .

He did not hear them enter. Only when the dazzling beam brought pain to his eyes did Müller realise his inquisitors had arrived. A harsh voice sounded in the darkness from behind his shoulder. He had never heard it before, and was surprised that it was an American who was speaking.

'Who are you and where are you from?'

He was ready, having rehearsed the reply in his mind a thousand times.

'My name is Olaf Larsen. I am Norwegian—'

'Don't give me that bullshit. Who are you and where do you come from?'

Müller coolly repeated the answer, the beam of light still hurting his eyes. Now another voice came from over Müller's shoulder. It too was American, but possessed none of the harshness of the first. The tones were reasoned and enunciated in a soft nasal accent.

'I do hope you can help us. Because we have to establish your true identity, see. It will be very serious for you if you don't tell us: we might even have to kill you. You've been well trained, that's obvious, but there's nobody left in the hacienda now. They pulled out and left you.'

Müller found the statement ludicrous, and even managed a hoarse laugh.

'Very convincing,' he retorted. 'You can't fool me. I tell you my name is Olaf Larsen and I am Norwegian . . .' His head sagged, and he realised that he was speaking to a void. The light had gone out. His interrogators had left.

Müller pondered the identity of the two men, and why they had even mentioned death to him. If they were from his own side, surely they wouldn't threaten to kill him? It was just a threat. But time dragged by, and still nobody came. He tried to rationalise his position. What were they trying to do to him? He recalled that his instructors had been ready to use live ammunition when tracking him, and had almost killed him. Was the organisation testing him to the point of destruction? If he died it was better for the hacienda to have wasted only a few weeks' training than to have an eventual failure on their hands . . . but where had the Americans come from? He realised that he knew nothing of the background of the hacienda or its operations. Nothing at all.

Whether his interrogators were away for hours or minutes Müller did not know, and his head was beginning to swim with lack of food and water. The fierce beam of light told him of their return.

'Let's start again, shall we?'

It was the quiet American who was speaking, this time from what seemed only a foot in front of him; but he couldn't see clearly in the blinding beam.

'All of this will stop, you know, if you just tell us who you are. You say you are Olaf Larsen?' the man said pleasantly.

'Olaf Larsen,' Müller sighed.

'Then tell us about your family in Norway.'

Step by step, the interrogator went over the details of Larsen's life, sometimes back-tracking, or asking for more information. The reasoned questions continued and Müller began to feel confident that it would soon end. At last his interrogator stopped. Then came the harsh voice of the other American.

'You're lying. We shall find out who you are.'

The next moment Müller felt his head jerk back as he received a fierce blow to the left of his jaw. His assailant was using a hard metal object, he knew, because he felt his bones crack under the impact. He had hardly recovered when the American screamed only inches from his left ear.

'*You're German, aren't you? A bloody German.*'

Müller turned his head and tried to see the face which he sensed was very close. Furious, he spat in its direction. Perhaps he landed accurately, for immediately the interrogator hit him again, harder.

'I want a drink,' Müller panted. 'Give me a drink, whoever you are.'

'When you've given us the information,' his assailant

replied. 'We're going to leave you now. Soon we shall be back. Next time you must tell us the truth.'

The light went out. At first Müller was deeply relieved, but then the darkness began to prey on him again. He could taste blood in his mouth. It seemed lunacy, but he began to fear that perhaps they would destroy him. Perhaps they really were enemy agents. He remembered Padilla's ambivalent attitude in Mexico City, how his gun had been pointed at Müller's chest, even though he was his blood relative. And Padilla was a Mexican now . . . Perhaps he was not working for the Reich.

Slowly Müller sank into unconsciousness, confused and bewildered over how to cope, should they torture him again. Then they were back. In the darkness he could feel their presence, hear their breathing. He knew one of the Americans was very close to him before he spoke. Very softly.

'You will remain here in the darkness forever unless you tell us who you are.'

Müller felt a stab of fear, but answered mechanically, 'My name is Olaf Larsen. My ship is the *Empire Rose*.'

The other American voice sounded brutal and impatient. 'You can't be Larsen. He went down with his ship. You're a German and you are being trained in Mexico. We know this—admit it. This is not an exercise. Why not tell us who you really are—Ulrich Müller?'

The sudden use of his name jarred, and Müller was confused. Were they offering him a deal? Was it a trap? He was having difficulty in keeping his head up, but he made one last attempt to marshal his thoughts.

'We've had you under surveillance from the moment you entered Mexico. We got on to you after that phoney ID card was issued at the War Shipping Administration. That's why we've cleared out this hacienda. You see, you are the big prize.'

Müller was perplexed. Where was Padilla? His instructors? If they were still there they wouldn't tolerate this brutal treatment, surely.

As if reading his mind the American went on. 'Of course, we have Germans working for us in Mexico, and I don't

102

blame you for thinking that your uncle would help you. But what do you know about double agents—you, just a simple seaman?'

Müller could hardly speak. 'Water,' he whispered.

The light came on and once more blazed into his eyes. He almost fainted with relief when his lips touched the cold mouth of a bottle. Lovingly he washed the water into his mouth, bringing his tongue back to life. A faint smell of cognac drifted into his nostrils: the bottle must previously have held brandy. The taste brought vivid memories . . .

Sun gleamed on the Martell bottle in Larsen's lap. Müller was back in the lifeboat staring at the last inch of water. Opposite him, Larsen was watching with listless eyes, his skin taut over his skull. The big man was dying, but Müller knew that if he could just wet his tongue and rinse his mouth he would survive. He needed that water. All of it. He could still feel the rocking of the boat as he crossed over to Larsen and without regret put his hands round the other man's throat. The Norwegian barely offered any resistance. There was no hatred: it was just that there was not enough for two men to survive. There in that black cell Müller acknowledged his first act of murder; he knew that he had killed a fellow seaman without remorse, he had broken any moral restraints just to survive. And he would survive again . . .

He did not hear the American when he spoke; all he could think of were Larsen's sightless eyes. Yet he was curiously unmoved, elated even.

'. . . you are?'

The hard voice was insistent, but Müller managed a faint grin. They knew nothing.

'My name is Olaf Larsen,' he replied, half expecting another savage blow. It never came. Instead there was silence. He closed his eyes, then he felt strong hands seize him. There was the click of a lock, and a searing pain in his wrists as the iron manacles were loosened and pulled away. It was over. He had won.

When Müller came round he found himself in the luxury of clean sheets. His bed was in a bright sunny room at the top of the hacienda and the smell of bougainvillaea wafted through the open windows. He felt much better. Stiffness had left his limbs but his wrists felt bulky with bandages, and a dripfeed was attached to his arm. When he turned his head a wad of dressing pressed against his face, where the injury to his jaw had been dressed. After about twenty minutes a doctor in a white coat came in and looked him over, and to his relief removed the drip-feed. Shortly after, the chief instructor arrived. He stood erect, looking down at Müller with appraising eyes.

'My interrogators were rough on you, but it's all part of the game.' There was no trace of sympathy in his voice.

Müller gave a resigned look. 'It seems crazy to train me, then undo all the good work.'

The instructor was unmoved. 'Yes, it might look that way to you, but we have to make sure that you can stand up to anything the British or Americans may throw at you, and they have some very unpleasant methods. All the same, you did well; those two men were experts—former FBI agents.'

Müller recalled the voices in the darkness, but did not feel angry at the way they had treated him.

'How come they're working for you?'

'They had a little trouble, I don't remember the details, and had to leave the Service. They have been very useful to us.'

'But they knew all about me. Who told them?'

For the first time the chief instructor gave a hint of a smile.

'We did. But don't worry, they won't be able to tell anybody else about you.'

Müller was shaken by the inference. He studied the chief inspector's bony face and short grey hair and wondered whether he would really have let his pupil die in the cellar. Jerking his head at the bandages, he said,

'I hope they can rid me of these things. And please, warn the kitchen that I shall be down for dinner—for the biggest meal ever served in this place.'

The instructor relaxed. 'All right. I'll order the cook to kill a horse.' Then he became serious again. 'But I want you on your feet tomorrow. The games are over.'

Müller *was* on his feet—although his wrists were still bandaged—when an orderly came to collect him two days later. He was led downstairs to the large bare room used by the chief instructor. It had just one picture on the wall and there was a long, polished table at one end with brass candelabra in the centre. Leaning against it, his back to the shutters, Müller was surprised to see the plump figure of Padilla. The only other person in the room was the chief instructor, who stood with his canvas shoes apart, studying him.

Müller smiled at Padilla's familiar olive-skinned face. He had never seen him at the hacienda before, and thought that only a matter of real importance could have brought him the long journey from Mexico City. His uncle's expression was friendly but his greeting formal. His eyes flicked to the bandage on Müller's wrists and the ugly mark on his jaw. Turning to the chief instructor he asked, 'I hope you haven't been so ruthless in your training that you have knocked the guts out of him?'

The chief instructor solemnly shook his head. 'No; he's a tough character.'

Padilla smiled. 'They breed them that way in the U-boats. Isn't that so?'

Müller responded to Padilla's avuncular mood with a grin. Then his uncle's expression changed. With a curt nod he dismissed the instructor and waved a small hand towards a chair. He himself remained on his feet.

'We've given you all the training we can in the time available. From the reports sent to me I am confident that you will make a first-class agent.' Müller felt Padilla's eyes assessing him as he went on. 'You are to go on your first mission. Orders have arrived from Berlin. Two days from now you will leave for New York by bus and train. Once there, you will communicate with us by prearranged code.'

Müller studied his uncle standing motionless in front of him and felt a rising excitement that at last his rigorous training was about to be tested by a real enemy.

'What's my assignment?'

Padilla pulled back his broad shoulders. 'I can't tell you that. You have been ordered to New York and will receive instructions when you are there.'

'Am I to take any special equipment?' Müller asked.

Padilla chuckled. 'You're keen to try your luck, aren't you? You can select your own automatic and you will be taking a radio set: one that can easily be concealed in a suitcase. But you're not to use it until ordered to do so. We will also supply you with twenty thousand dollars. You will be fully briefed later.'

Müller sat silently as Padilla made for the door. Before he opened it he looked back at his nephew. For a moment Müller waited expectantly for a few words of family affection, but his uncle simply stood there, the small gimlet eyes staring at him intently. Then he spoke.

'Ulrich Müller has ceased to exist. You realise that. Good luck.'

Then the door closed behind him.

Three days later the express clanged over the points and nosed into Pennsylvania Station. Its passengers got to their feet and scrambled for the corridor. Müller let them go before carefully taking down his two suitcases. One was smaller, though heavier than the other, and contained the radio set. The terminus smelt of steam and carbon. Müller climbed the iron staircase to the concourse. Businessmen dashed past on their way home, young women in crisp cotton dresses walked snappily by and on all sides there was the navy blue and brown of service uniforms. This was New York, and although he had read much about it its furious energy took Müller by surprise.

'Excuse me, Mister.'

A hand gripped his arm and his thoughts went to the suitcase at his feet. Two white-capped military policemen stood behind him; one wore sergeant's stripes.

'Can we see your ID card?' the sergeant asked gruffly.

Müller quickly recovered and reached inside his jacket. His snub-nosed automatic was within easy reach, in its neat compartment above his groin.

The sergeant eyed his rumpled suit. 'Where you from?'

'Just come up from the south. Had a few days' vacation in New Orleans, all round there.'

'Oh yeah?' the second soldier said sardonically. Müller

was conscious of his own accent and of the MP's hostility. 'All right for some, I guess,' the soldier continued. 'Don't you know there's a war on, mister? Can't take too many vacations in wartime.'

It was the chance Müller wanted. 'I know,' he said, offering his ID card. 'I've been torpedoed three times already.'

The sergeant was silent. 'Norwegian, huh? Going back to sea?'

'On my way right now.'

The MP returned the card. 'On your way then. Best of luck. I guess you need it with those U-boats.'

Müller had passed his first test, and he began to relax. It was late afternoon and the offices were beginning to turn out. His uncle had given him the addresses of several small unobtrusive hotels, and it was up to him to pick his own, moving on as often as possible. The radio set was not to be used except in emergencies or on specific orders. Contact could be maintained through the Western Union office, which Müller was to visit regularly for post restant cables.

The first hotel on the list, the Cumberland, turned out to be a crumbling edifice on West 54th Street. A middle-aged woman in carpet slippers came out of a back room, a cigarette hanging from the corner of her mouth. She wore an apple-green cotton dress and a necklace of jet beads. Stroking her tired grey hair, she scrutinised Müller through a haze of cigarette smoke.

'You lookin' for a room?'

'Yes, Ma'am.'

She pulled out a blue leather-bound register from under the counter and opened it. There were half a dozen names scrawled untidily across the ruled page, mostly from the east coast, and Müller noticed there were no foreigners. He signed himself in, putting his home address as 'Norfolk, Virginia'. When he entered his nationality as Norwegian she looked at him with watery eyes.

'You ain't American, then?'

'No, Ma'am.'

'Norway's a long way off. But you're fighting on our side, ain't you?'

'We are indeed, Ma'am.'

'In that case I'll take a dollar off the bill.'

She came round from behind the counter and walked towards the stairs which led out of the narrow hallway.

'Come on, I'll show you to your room,' she wheezed, a cloud of tobacco smoke following her small frame.

She showed him to a small room with garishly flowered wallpaper and sky-blue paintwork, but it did have the luxury of a shower. For a few minutes the landlady hung about, chattering idly, and only when Müller began to unfasten his tie and turn on the shower did she leave.

Once her footsteps had faded away he unfastened the locks and leather straps of the larger of his two suitcases. His hands probed beneath shirts and jerseys to produce three cigar boxes. A rich smell of Havana rose when he broke the first seal and took out a handful of choice cigars. He stripped back the silver paper on which they had been packed, revealing a row of new hundred-dollar bills.

The smaller suitcase carried other personal belongings to conceal the dials and amplifiers of the radio set. Everything had been thought of, down to spare valves and two aerials. For a moment he felt uneasy. The transmitter was devastating evidence of his intentions and could easily be discovered by a prying landlady. A more secure hiding place was essential. He decided to put it in a luggage locker at a railway station. Grand Central was quite close; he would conceal it there.

It was early evening, and although he had travelled thousands of miles he felt strangely elated. After a quick shower he changed into a fresh suit, folded several hundred-dollar bills into his wallet and went down to the lobby. The landlady was enjoying a cigarette behind the reception desk, ready to embark on a long conversation, but Müller tactfully bade her good evening and went out. There were few people on West 54th. A young negro ran down the opposite side of the road with a bundle of newspapers; a policeman idly patrolled the sidewalk.

Crowds of shoppers were milling along Fifth Avenue; they paid no attention to Müller. He stopped for a moment and looked into the bright shop windows. America's prosperity impressed him and he was fascinated by the stores. He stopped by a photography shop, gazing at the latest Kodak cameras. Next to it was a shoe shop displaying the current fashions and he was tempted to spend some of Padilla's dollars on a pair of snakeskin shoes; but with a twinge of regret he moved on.

He found Grand Central Station and went down the broad steps into the vaulted concourse, threading his way to the luggage lockers at the far end. Blessing his good luck he found an empty compartment at ground level. The case fitted inside easily; he slammed the door and pocketed the key.

For a few minutes Müller leaned on a coffee stand, watching Americans surge past, before he made off towards the Western Union Office. A clerk stood idly at the counter reading a newspaper.

'Have you messages for me? My name is Larsen.'

'Identification?'

Müller showed his ID card and the clerk sauntered to a row of pigeon holes.

'Nope. There's no message.'

Müller scribbled on a cable form and handed it to the clerk. It read:

'To Fergus Bros Mexico City. For Collection.
Arrived safe and well. Ready for contract completion.
Lars.'

Chapter 9

'Thank God I was never in the bloody infantry,' Alloway declared, trudging unhappily through the pouring rain at Tregaron POW camp. The wind buffeted his large Whitehall umbrella, bringing a laugh from Dutch Van Kleef walking next to him, who peered out from under his sodden cap at the surrounding Welsh hills.

'You know, James,' he said, 'it would be nice country if it wasn't so damn wet.'

Ahead of them General Stubbs, accompanied by Colonel Phelps and an interpreter sergeant, marched steadily forward on his inspection; four disconsolate guards shouldering Lee-Enfields brought up the rear.

To Alloway's disgust Stubbs seemed to be treating his visit to Tregaron as some form of virility test. Since starting just after dawn the general had only stopped for a mug of tea and a five-minute pep talk to Phelps's staff, and now seemed determined to complete his inspection at lightning speed.

The sergeant rapped on the first hut and threw the door open. There was a scuffle of boots inside as Germans drew themselves to attention, more out of habit than respect. Most of the officers were from the German Army but there were also one or two Luftwaffe and Kriegsmarine uniforms.

Colonel Phelps introduced the general, adding, 'This is just a routine inspection. If you have any complaints the general will be interested to hear them.'

A young major was hut commander. With a click of his heels he invited the party to follow him. 'I shall be pleased to show you round our quarters,' he said, in faultless English.

The inspection began with the German leading the two senior British officers, accompanied by the camp sergeant, along the lines of bunks. Alloway and Van Kleef followed, the four armed guards bringing up the rear.

Conditions in the hut were poor. Thirty or forty men were packed into a space normally allocated to half that number, and several men had to sleep on the floor. The faces surrounding Alloway were hardly those of men who had been defeated, and his sympathies were muted. They were the enemy, after all, and there were far more justifiable demands to be met from Britain's strained resources than to cater for those who wanted to destroy her. The prisoners would have to wait. He followed the general and commandant round the hut, looking at leaks, broken furniture, jammed windows and cracked lavatory bowls.

At the end of the inspection the young major spoke up.

'Herr General, you have heard my brother officers' complaints—poor accommodation, poor food. Perhaps we will

110

find it necessary to complain to the International Red Cross if nothing is done.'

General Stubbs bristled. 'The commandant has taken a detailed account of your grievances. If there are any others, please inform him, and don't waste our time. You will be getting new accommodation shortly and, like all prisoners, you will be expected to work for your keep. Good day.'

Slightly to his surprise, Alloway found himself thoroughly approving of Stubbs's forthright attitude. It would have been fatal to weaken before an orchestrated barrage of grumbles, some of which he thought absurdly trivial. He suspected they had been well rehearsed in order to embarrass the British.

Watching Colonel Phelps as he continued to listen patiently to the Germans, Alloway began to sympathise with him. The camp was tense, yet he coped with the problems in an admirably civilised way, referring matters for attention to his accompanying NCO. In contrast, Stubbs had by now lost his early enthusiasm, and stood tapping his baton impatiently against his palm.

They went from hut to hut in the pouring rain until at last they approached the final one. The guards instinctively closed up behind the party, and after a few hurried words with the sergeant the colonel held up his arm.

'Gentlemen,' he said smoothly, 'this is Hut Fourteen. It has given us a great deal of trouble in the past. I should warn you that there are some hard nuts in here, but their bark is considerably worse than their bite.'

The general stiffened in expectation and he signalled the sergeant to open the door. Once again the Germans rose to their feet, but here the atmosphere was different. Some prisoners leaned against their beds, others lounged against the bunks and furniture, hands in pockets, but all watched the British party with a deliberate show of contempt. Again a hut commander greeted them and led them through the hut, but this time he was far more obviously intent on embarrassing his captors. Each time he stopped in front of a prisoner he introduced him formally with his name and rank and then added a record of his victories against the British.

'Lieutenant Hans Klinge. 206 Panzer Grenadiers. 21st

Panzer Division, Iron Cross Second Class,' he said before one young lieutenant. 'Four British tanks knocked out at Tobruk.'

The general cut him short. 'Any complaints?' he asked.

'My bunk is collapsing. I need a new one. There is no room to sleep properly. It is against all regulations and most unhealthy.'

'Really?' Stubbs remarked. 'How distressing for you. Commandant, are all these bunks constructed according to the general agreements about the welfare of prisoners?'

'Yes, sir. Regulation amount of air and the best conditions we can provide in the emergency. Not ideal, I am sure, but as we British say, "Don't you know there's a war on?" I'm sure they have endured far harder conditions than this.'

The party passed to the next man who virtually repeated the same grievance. This time Stubbs answered abruptly.

'Do you think you could arrange to have this hut kept a little neater? I'm rather surprised at the sloppy attitudes. Not quite what I would expect from German officers.'

The German remained silent but Phelps glanced round and commented drily, 'I agree, sir.' He turned to the hut commander. 'It is surprising to see this mess after the conditions in the other huts.' Then, raising his voice, he added, 'If our "guests" won't co-operate we shall have to think of alternative accommodation which will not be as pleasant.'

Alloway followed the inspecting party to the end of the building where Stubbs stopped to admire a painting by a middle-aged prisoner. He was a small man with the lively eyes and broad features of a Swabian, and had set up a makeshift studio by his bed. A Guinness bottle and an enamel jug stood on a battered biscuit tin as a subject for a half-finished still life. Alloway admired the man's ingenuity: his easel was made from the crude frame of an egg crate, and he had stretched a piece of sacking across it as a rudimentary canvas. A chair-back provided the support, and one or two precious tubes of paint were laid out on the seat. What struck Alloway most was the skill with which the German had created a palette from a broken Worcester dinner plate, its rim covered with bright dabs of paint. A single hog's-hair brush and watercolour sable lay on the chair seat.

The painting seemed to impress the general too.

'You could have an art gallery in this camp with chaps like this,' he declared.

'I think the captain has other galleries in mind,' the commandant replied, speaking almost as much to the prisoner as to the general.

'*Ja*, Herr Commandant,' the German said jovially. 'In Berlin. Do you know it is impossible to get paint here?'

'Oh, we shall have to do something about that,' Stubbs said airily.

'I am sure we can rely on you, sir,' said Phelps.

As they talked Alloway's attention wandered and he surveyed the hut. Half the prisoners, perhaps twenty men in all, were massed a few yards away.

In contrast to their earlier attitudes the Germans who were looking on now seemed subdued, but their sullen faces made Alloway uneasy, and his suspicions began to grow when he noticed that one ox-like member of the *Herrenvolk* glanced repeatedly at a young lieutenant ostensibly tidying up a top bunk, halfway down the hut. The officer regularly scanned the whole interior from his vantage point, and Alloway began to wonder if he had uncovered some private communication system. Instinctively, he looked for the guards, and spotted two of them standing idly on the far side of the crowd of prisoners, apparently unconcerned.

He debated whether to share his fears with the commandant's sergeant standing nearby, but thought otherwise. It might be regarded as paranoic, and he would be laughed at later; a typical Whitehall wallah who knew nothing. Anyway, the commandant seemed to prefer an informal style with the prisoners, which was perhaps his own way of defusing the situation. Alloway kept his counsel. Stubbs had now moved a few paces farther on, and had stopped by an ornate washstand, next to the artist's makeshift easel. A gaunt young man had turned it into a rudimentary desk, and an open exercise book lay on its china surface.

'Quite a cultural centre, isn't it?' the general remarked with heavy humour. The prisoner stood up from his work and turned towards them. His face was intense, his cropped hair giving him the look of a monk. For a moment his dark eyes mockingly surveyed the British party, dwelling momentarily on Alloway's umbrella: nobody could miss the SS insignia sewn on his khaki tunic.

'Major Preuss,' the commandant announced in a flat voice.

'No longer in solitary confinement, I see,' the general commented smoothly. 'I expect you are pleased about that.'

A look of contrived patience passed over Preuss's pale features. 'It is irrelevant what I feel, General, because it is not my intention to remain a prisoner much longer.'

'So you think you are going to escape?' the general mocked. 'You'll have a terrible job surviving round here.'

'It is an officer's duty to escape, is it not? In any event the question is academic. The war will soon be over, and we shall all be released. As the Führer promised.'

'Yes, you may be right. Once the Red Army start their next offensive . . .' the general began.

'Herr General,' Preuss went on, as if talking to a child. 'You don't expect me to believe the propaganda of your Bolshevik comrades.'

Colonel Phelps broke in. 'We are not here to discuss the future course of the war, interesting though that might be, but to inspect the prisoners' conditions.'

The skull-like head turned towards the colonel. 'Of course, Herr Commandant. I have a long list of grievances.' He nodded towards his notebook open on the table.

The sergeant interpreter was still at the far end of the hut making notes, so Stubbs addressed Alloway.

'Mr Alloway, you're a literary sort of chap, judging by all the reports you write, and you can understand German. Could you tell us what kind of book the major is writing?'

Alloway limped over to the washstand and picked up the exercise book. Aware that Preuss was watching him, he slowly turned the pages, and saw that they were covered with ordered rows of neat handwriting. It was difficult for him to understand, as the writing seemed to be in some sort of personal shorthand, but he made out a day and date posted on every entry.

'It seems to be some kind of log or diary,' Alloway declared. 'I think it would take time to decipher.'

There was a sarcastic laugh from Preuss. 'You don't have to rely on your Mr Alloway, General, to know what is in the diary. I will tell you. It is an account of camp life, including the behaviour of the commandant's men towards us. It may be of interest to the Red Cross, and certainly to the German authorities when the guilty come to be punished. I can promise you that some of you British will be strung up from the nearest lamp-post.'

There was a snigger from the artist POW who was standing next to his easel watching the proceedings with folded arms.

Alloway kept his temper and blandly addressed Stubbs. 'On second thoughts, sir, I think the major's work may be a work of fiction. Quite a dull read, though.'

The senior officer smiled, but Preuss glared at Alloway. Dark eyes burned in the drawn face. 'No, my clever friend. Fact.'

The SS man glanced quickly along the hut to the young lieutenant who was now kneeling on his bunk. Alloway followed his gaze—the prisoners were clearly waiting for a signal. Standing with their backs to the twenty or so Germans, the general's group were unaware of their vulnerability. There seemed to be no emergency door and Alloway realised he could not even see the sergeant interpreter, while the two soldiers on the far side of the crowd had been cleverly masked by the Germans; no doubt they would be overwhelmed by the rest of the prisoners once the signal came.

He moved quickly. Before Preuss could act he thrust the senior officers aside, stepped towards the easel and grabbed the Guinness bottle from the still-life arrangement. With one decisive movement he smashed it against the chair-back, then, with the jagged black glass in his hand, he turned on Preuss. Yelling to Van Kleef to cover him he hurled himself across the room and bowled Preuss to the floor, the kitchen table crashing over as they fell. An agonising pain shot through Alloway's legs as the German hacked at him with his boots, and Alloway was dimly aware of Van Kleef flailing at the mob of prisoners above him with what looked like his own umbrella. Eyes fixed on the jagged edges of the broken bottle, Preuss rolled on to Alloway's right arm, trying to pin it beneath him, but Alloway brought his free hand down brutally on the German's neck. Blood drained from Preuss's face and his head lolled. In a split second Alloway pressed the broken glass against the German's jugular, ready to plunge the bottle into the Nazi without a qualm. He could hear the sound of scuffling above him, but suddenly the general's parade-ground voice rang out.

'All prisoners get back. Get back. Now. Or Major Preuss will be killed.'

The Germans stopped as they were gathering to rush Van Kleef and the sergeant beyond him. From Alloway's determined expression they knew that their countryman would be dead within seconds unless they obeyed. One by one they moved back, watched by Van Kleef, holding the umbrella like a bayonet.

There was a sudden commotion, and a squad of armed infantry pushed belatedly through the prisoners, quickly forming a cordon around the general's party.

Whilst the general and Colonel Phelps were escorted out of the hut, an officer from the camp garrison drew his revolver and placed it against Preuss's head. Alloway took the jagged bottle away and stood up with relief. The German was allowed to sit up, mopping the blood from his face where it had been torn on the floorboards.

There was a cough from behind them.

'Maybe you'd like this returned to you?' Van Kleef held up Alloway's umbrella. Its point dangled limply. 'I'm afraid it met a German belly,' he explained.

Together they walked out of the hut to join the general in the main building. When they reached the headquarters an irate General Stubbs was banging his baton against his thigh; the commandant hovered by uncomfortably. Alloway detected that the first explosion of the general's wrath was over, and now there was only a strained silence. Stubbs could only be aware that his public-relations venture had nearly turned into disaster, and he could imagine the reactions at the War Office had he been taken a hostage. The general strode across the room.

'Well done, Alloway. Great initiative. At least you could see what the devils were up to. Must be all that Whitehall training. My God, you can't take any chances with men like Preuss. Perhaps we should have got rid of him altogether while we had the chance.'

'I shall put him back in solitary, General,' the commandant stated. 'And, of course, there will be an enquiry as to how it could possibly have happened.'

Stubbs pulled on his trench coat and buttoned the collar. He drew himself to his full height and addressed Phelps as if dismissing the painful affair once and for all.

'I want you to have a thousand prisoners ready to move from this camp in a week from now. We shall send them in the first possible shipment aboard the *Queen Mary*. I will leave the selection to you, but Major Preuss and the whole of that hut should be among them. Understood? And I hope it's a bloody rough crossing.'

Chapter 10

All was quiet in the Wannsee villa as the special unit toiled over every minute detail of the giant liner's design and structure. Sitting at his antique writing desk, Boehm drew a green manilla folder marked 'Operation Iceman' towards him. Inside there was a news clipping from the *Chicago Sentinel* dated 8 April with a short memo pinned to it which read:

'Received SKL Stockholm Station. 1117 hours 12 April 1943. Decoded immediately.'

The article was headed 'Lunch at the Connaught', the bye-line 'Tracey O'Brien'. Boehm quickly skimmed through the story but the account of austerity eating in London restaurants was not the real value of the clipping; Tracey O'Brien's racy style contained a coded message. A typed sheet beneath the article provided the translation:

'Mandrake to OKM. Queen Mary to ship American troops east, German prisoners west, in next weeks.'

Boehm studied the signal. Suddenly to receive information from Mandrake, a London source who had been silent for some months was a surprise, especially as it vitally affected the Iceman plans. For a moment he wondered whether the signal was a British ploy, whether perhaps they might not be working the London agent back to the Germans. But SKL 111's experts had judged the message totally reliable, according to a built-in identification code.

Boehm rose and walked into the dining room. Merker and Hansen were bent over their work, but both men looked up as they heard his approach.

'Gentlemen, I need some facts as soon as I can get them.' He turned towards the old Hamburg-Amerika representative. 'Herr Hansen, as you know the *Queen Mary* is at present sailing from Scotland to New York, where we know that she will pick up a load of American troops. She will then sail east, presumably back to her Scottish base at Gourock. How long will it take her to turn around?'

Hansen thought for a moment. 'Passengers can only leave or board the liner off the Scottish coast by using tenders, and I would estimate that each one would take about forty minutes to come alongside, load and return to the shore. Judged by pre-war schedules, including refuelling and loading stores, the whole turn-around at Gourock should take about seventy-two hours.'

'And how long will the crossing take—westbound?'

Hansen took off his spectacles before answering. 'At this time of the year, and allowing for anti-U-boat diversion, I would say four days.'

Hansen followed Boehm over to a large wall chart of the Atlantic, with its concentric rings marking the limits of Allied air patrols radiating from bases on both sides of the ocean. Between them there was a shaded area known as the 'Black Gap', where Allied ships passed beyond the range of air cover. It was here that the wolf packs destroyed their victims. Boehm picked up a crayon from a shelf beneath the chart and drew a line through the Black Gap. He indicated a point just outside the limit of the Iceland patrols.

'How long will it take for the *Queen Mary*, sailing westbound, to reach this point?' he demanded.

'I would say about fifty hours. To this I would add a few more hours for zig-zag and diversion—say sixty hours in all.'

Boehm placed a faint cross on the position and turned to Merker, who sat at his drawing board, listening attentively.

'My big problem is how to slow her down. She's almost unsinkable. If she steams at twenty-eight to thirty knots it's almost impossible for a U-boat to hit her.'

'It would take four torpedoes at least to sink her, Captain,' Merker replied. 'One would be a flea bite.'

'Then we have to slow her down by some other method. Which means sabotage.'

Merker nodded in agreement. 'I have been working on that assumption—and that any explosives to be used would be limited to about five kilos, the maximum amount an agent can be expected to carry. It's been difficult to find the exact point where such a small amount could have a decisive effect.'

Merker indicated a large line-drawing of the ship. The *Queen Mary*'s twelve decks were clearly marked from the Sun Deck with its badminton courts to H Deck 150 feet below. Every cabin was shown, and the main restaurant which stretched from one side of the ship to the other, rising through three decks. Five cavernous boiler-rooms occupied the space between the keel and the accommodation area above. The ship had been drawn in such loving detail that even the nurseries and a compound for pets were indicated.

Merker pointed with his pencil to a small housing on the main deck aft. A thin series of lines descended from it through a narrow well to the keel, where they linked with the ship's steering rods.

'This is the main steering electro hydraulic gear. It controls the links to the rudder. At its heart there is a complex valve and control bar, a fine piece of design. A five-kilo charge placed inside it would blow it apart.'

'And what would be the effect on the ship?'

Merker indicated the bottom of the *Queen Mary*'s hull. 'Power could not be transmitted to the rods and rudder, and the ship would have to heave-to while repairs were carried out. Otherwise, with damaged steering, she might just sail round in circles.'

Boehm grunted. 'Provide me with detailed drawings of the assembly and how such an operation could be carried out. I need the information today.'

The captain considered that he now had a clear enough picture to present an operational plan to the C in C. He returned to the salon and picked up a telephone.

It was dusk when Boehm, his tunic straightened for the vital meeting with the C in C, mounted the steps of Naval Headquarters in Tirpitzufer. In his briefcase he carried the detailed plans from Wannsee.

As he waited in the Grossadmiral's anteroom he felt a quickening of his pulse and quickly went over the salient points of his presentation.

Within two minutes of his arrival the connecting door into the C in C's office opened and an aide entered.

'The Grossadmiral will see you now,' he announced, and ushered Boehm into the room beyond. The C in C sat at a long table, flanked by Steinfort and two other senior members of the naval staff. His bony shoulders were erect, and his cold blue eyes appraised Boehm expectantly.

'We have little time, Captain. Please come straight to the point,' he said in a dry voice.

Boehm walked up to the assembled staff and unrolled Merker's drawing of the *Queen Mary* on the table before them.

'For some time SKL 111 has been observing the movements of the liner *Queen Mary* since her arrival in British waters. I can now report that she is on her way to New York.'

The Grossadmiral listened unimpressed.

'We have received valuable information from one of our most trusted agents in Britain that the *Queen Mary* is to play a key part in a massive movement of American troops to Britain.'

The C in C sighed. 'That surely is no surprise,' he said at last.

'Perhaps, sir,' Boehm continued. 'But we believe that the liner's arrival on the North Atlantic signals a turning point in Anglo-American strategy. She will be used to carry an unprecedented number of troops, perhaps as many as twenty thousand men. She will be joined later by the *Queen Elizabeth*, and both ships could move over one million men in a year. This could mean an invasion of Western Europe well before our Atlantic defences are completed.'

'So, if your intelligence is correct, what is SKL 111 proposing?'

'We must deprive the British and Americans of this huge lifting capacity. We *must* destroy the *Queen Mary*.'

The Grossadmiral was irritated. 'We have tried to sink the *Queen Mary* before. She has been a major target. But as SKL 111 knows better than anyone else she is a very difficult target.'

Boehm replied confidently, 'Sir, I am not proposing that the *Queen Mary* be sunk.'

The Grossadmiral raised his eyebrows.

'I am proposing she should be captured.'

'Captured!' The Grossadmiral leaned back for the first time, surprised. 'How on earth could you do that?'

'According to our intelligence, when the *Queen Mary* leaves Britain for North America she will be carrying German prisoners of war, some taken during the recent North African fighting.'

It was now quiet in the room and Boehm seized his chance.

'These prisoners are some of the Reich's best fighting men. We do not know exactly how many there will be but there is certain to be a substantial number; otherwise the British would not employ the *Queen Mary*. If these men can be organised and led in an operation to seize the liner when she is outside the range of Allied air cover the *Queen Mary* could be sailed directly to St Nazaire, thus depriving the enemy of his most important ship.'

A faint smile crossed the Grossadmiral's lips.

'A brilliant idea. But just how do you propose to organise

the German Army in mid-ocean? Surely there will be a strong garrison on board?'

Boehm quickly described the plans for Operation Iceman and the extraordinary chain of events which had enabled SKL 111 to plant Müller in New York.

'Our agent will be ordered to infiltrate the *Queen Mary*,' he continued. 'And will be briefed to knock out the ship's communications and lead the prisoners in seizing the ship.'

'You seem to be placing a very heavy burden on this man.'

'We are asking him to do a great deal, sir, I agree. But our plan has been drawn up after intensive study, and we have isolated just one or two key operations that can be executed by one man. Although the ship is very big, she is surprisingly vulnerable.'

'And the agent is first class,' Steinfort added in Boehm's support. 'He is a U-boat Obersteuermann who has been thoroughly trained by our people in Mexico.'

The Grossadmiral smiled. 'I'm surprised. An Obersteuermann?'

'A first-rate Petty Officer, sir,' Boehm added, 'who was rescued by an American ship. His name is Ulrich Müller. They call him "The Iceman".'

The Grossadmiral seemed satisfied with their joint answers. It was now the operations chief next to him who intervened.

'But the enemy will not sit by and twiddle his thumbs, will he?'

'Indeed not,' Boehm replied. 'If we are to succeed in capturing the ship much will depend on the British speed of reaction, and that will depend in turn on how soon the Admiralty is informed. If our agent can immobilise the ship's communications precious hours will be gained. Only a sighting from the air or sea would tell the enemy what was happening. By that time the ship would be rapidly approaching the French Atlantic coast. The main danger would come from air attack, but we could throw a fighter umbrella over her as soon as she entered range, and that would place the onus on the British of bombing their own ship.'

'Churchill would do that. He's ruthless,' the Grossadmiral said.

'But surely the Royal Navy would attempt to intercept first?' an older staff officer asked.

Boehm was ready with the answer. 'The size and speed of the *Queen Mary* would be her protection, and turn events to our advantage.'

He indicated the Atlantic map and drew two long lines across it. 'If we placed two battle groups of six U-boats in patrol lines across the *Queen Mary*'s course they could ambush enemy forces racing to intercept the liner.'

The Grossadmiral quietly nodded. 'Congratulations, Captain, on a highly imaginative plan. If it works we shall either steal the liner or the British will be forced to sink her. There is, however, one other consideration. What if your agent fails to seize control of the ship?'

'He will sabotage the ship's steering to slow her down, so that we can bring up the U-boat battle groups and sink the *Queen Mary* in mid-ocean.'

There was a long silence as the C in C pondered the ramifications. It was now beyond Boehm. Orders would have to be sent to the U-boats at sea, crews briefed and a vast operation set in motion. They also knew that the C in C would have to justify any action to the Führer.

The pale blue eyes flickered, and the Grossadmiral gave his decision: 'All right. Two U-boat groups will be assigned to the operation at once. They are to use the new acoustic torpedo, the Zauenkönig. And perhaps, at last, we shall sink her.'

Chapter 11

'You are checking out, Mr Larsen?'

Müller stood in the tiny lobby of the Cumberland, wearing a lightweight fawn suit and fedora.

'I guess so,' he answered. 'Urgent work.'

The landlady fluttered about, searching for his bill.

'I'm truly sorry I have to leave,' he whispered confidentially, 'but it's the War Department. I've been assigned to a special mission, and would be grateful if you would never tell anybody I've been here.'

She looked wide-eyed. 'You can rely on me, Mr Larsen. We all have our little troubles. Don't give it another thought.'

It was a warm morning, but he felt far from carefree. He had already formulated his plans. The two cases would be deposited at Grand Central, then he would visit the Western Union Office and report to Padilla.

It was just after eight when he arrived on the concourse, and quickly found a spare locker. He decided to wait until mid-morning for any messages from Mexico, and meanwhile looked for a barber's shop. A change of appearance might help his cover.

He found a barber's in the concourse, and as the cold steel of the clippers moved across Müller's neck the barber rattled off a lightning bulletin of New York news—ball games, murders, accidents, thefts, the incomprehensible deeds of City Hall.

He jerked the German's head up to finish the sideburns, and Müller saw his new image in the mirror. The blond hair had been cropped into a crew out, accentuating his forehead and stern jaw line. He could have passed for an American seaman.

It was almost ten o'clock when he made his way to the Western Union Office. Padilla had already replied.

'STAY IN NEW YORK. CONTACT BRIDGES. OFFER NEW TUNGSTEN DEAL.'

Müller had to find somewhere quickly where he could safely decode the message. This time he wanted to choose a place free of prying landladies. With the 20,000 dollars stored in the luggage locker he realised that the Reich had made him a rich man, and he could afford a good hotel. He glanced admiringly at an attractive young woman who passed him wrapped in a fur coat. Perhaps he should spend the cash while he had the chance. Nobody would know. At that moment he felt an ache for the nurse he had met in Norfolk, and even toyed with the idea of sending for her to join him. But he rejected the thought as foolhardy. Nevertheless, he decided that he would stay at the hotel she had suggested, the Gotham.

He found the hotel just off Fifth Avenue, and took a fourth-floor room. Sitting in an armchair he decoded Padilla's orders in fifteen minutes. The simple message read:

'*QUEEN MARY* DUE NEW YORK. SIGN AS CREW. FURTHER ORDERS TO FOLLOW.'

The directive took him by surprise, and he gazed out at the skyscrapers of Manhattan wondering why he was being placed in the world's most famous ship. If he could get aboard unscathed, was he going to sail to Britain? That must be it! He pulled himself to his feet, elated at his assignment.

Soon a taxi was dropping him at the Shipping Administration Office, on the West side, where Allied merchant seamen signed on for new vessels. Inside, a few seamen were sitting around, some reading newspapers, others in quiet conversation. Behind them a blackboard showed crew vacancies: three deckhands were wanted for the *Mapleleaf*, a steward and third cook for the *Bengal*.

Müller slowly walked the length of the board, but there was no list for the *Queen Mary*. He joined the small queue in front of the woman clerk who was interviewing applicants, and when he reached her he placed his ID card and Discharge Book on the counter.

Her features were homely and attractive, in spite of a severe hair style and neat tortoiseshell spectacles.

'I'm sorry, we have no places aboard the *Queen Mary*,' she replied in answer to his question, and gave him a strange look. 'Are you British?'

'Norwegian. But I have been serving on British ships.'

She looked doubtful. 'Cunard only take British subjects. It's security, and they're very strict about it. I can offer you another ship . . .'

Müller had not expected this, but quietly asked, 'If they're short of men, surely they'll take me?'

'I'm sorry.'

Müller leaned forward and lowered his voice to a whisper. 'Look, I have to get back to Britain. My wife is in Glasgow and expecting a child. I have reports that they've been bombed. I must get back. Surely you understand?'

A look of sympathy came into the woman's eyes. The light reflected on her spectacles, and she thought for a moment.

'Well, it's a bit irregular. I can give you a pass to see the staff captain—he might be able to help. The *Queen Mary* is at Pier Ninety.'

'Thank you. Believe me, I am really grateful.'

She blushed. 'I'm pleased to help.' She gave him back his papers.

Müller crossed under the elevated railway and walked the short distance to Pier 90, showing his pass to the police officer at the gate, who yawned and waved him on. Huge stacks of crates were piled on the quay, ready for loading aboard the liner, and from their stencilled War Department markings Müller guessed that they contained weapons for the American Army in Britain. A stream of heavy lorries rumbled continuously into the dock area with more cargo, and Müller chose to walk down a narrow lane between the piles of crates. He emerged at the edge of the quay and found himself beneath the *Queen Mary*'s bows. She was a breath-taking sight, her sharp prow rising over fifty feet. Massive ropes as thick as a man's trunk secured her to the shore, and Müller wondered how the longshoremen ever managed to coil them round the cast-iron bollards in front of him.

The liner's hull stretched away for a thousand feet along the pier. The way to board her appeared to be across one of the covered gangways some forty feet long which ran between the ship and the terminal alongside. There were four of them, and each seemed to be a busy thoroughfare for officers, crew and stevedores, humping stores aboard.

Müller crossed to the terminal entrance where a dock policeman checked his pass and allowed him to enter the draughty departure hall. It was full of service personnel and stevedores, a very different scene to pre-war days, although Müller noticed that the signs indicating Customs, Immigration and other services were still in place.

'Just follow those guys,' the policeman shouted, pointing to three men heading for an elevator halfway along the hall which would take them up to the level of the gangways. From their blue jerseys and jackets Müller recognised them to be members of the *Queen Mary*'s crew, and he gave them a friendly nod as he entered the lift. When it halted he made sure he was last to leave and followed them across the floor to the gangway entrance. A group of American and British officers were checking everyone's passes before allowing them to cross through the long canvas tunnel into the ship. The three seamen passed through quickly, and a moment later a British lieutenant was looking at Müller.

'Okay, let's see your papers.'

He reached inside his jacket and fished out the ID card and Shipping Federation documents, aware that an American lieutenant stood close by, clipboard held officiously under his arm.

'All right,' the Englishman said. 'Report to the staff captain. Main Deck. The corporal will take you up.'

He turned and shouted to a soldier to act as escort.

With a sense of triumph Müller stepped aboard the ship, to find himself in what seemed to be a small concourse from which long passageways ran to right and left. Before he could study the layout further the corporal made an abrupt turn towards a stairway in the middle of the concourse and began to climb up it. Müller realised they must be using one of the ship's main companionways, as a constant stream of stewards, seamen and workmen passed them. At first there were few signs that the *Queen Mary* had ever been a luxury liner—her fine veneered walls had been covered with plywood as a protection against her military passengers—but when they turned off the stairs on to the Main Deck her appearance changed. Spacious staterooms opened off the broad corridors which appeared to have retained some of their peacetime decor. At the far end of the corridor they reached the staff captain's office. With a polite tap on the door the corporal ushered Müller inside.

It was a small, neat room, in the middle of which a staff

captain sat behind a polished teak desk. He was a tall man with grey hair and a disdainful expression. He took Müller's ID card and Shipping Federation papers without a word.

Then: 'I see you are Norwegian. You know that we only take British crew members. That's a company rule.'

'But I have served all the time on British ships—the *Empire Rose* and before that the *Sirius*. Both were sunk.'

'I see,' the staff captain said. His face was expressionless. 'Well, there's little I can do about it. A rule is a rule.'

Müller tried again. 'But I have to get back to Glasgow. I have a wife expecting a baby any day now. If I can join the ship's company then I can make it in time.'

The staff captain surveyed him. 'Can't you find another ship?'

'Not in time. My last ship was torpedoed, and my wife is desperately worried. I know she'll become ill if I am not there.'

The officer looked down at the papers again, and Müller sensed he was wavering.

'It's no good,' he said finally. 'I'm sorry, but I can't break the security rules. Why don't you go back to the Shipping Federation and see what they can recommend? There will be other ships; they can get you there just as fast.'

Müller realised it was futile to argue. He would just have to find another way of getting aboard. He was escorted back to the gangway. At an elevator farther along heavy crates of weapons and ammunition were being loaded, and on the last big lift a truck was drawn up with a team of men unloading timber. A tough-looking man on top seemed to be in charge, shouting where to place the new load. Everything was moving with great efficiency, and he jumped down, mopping his brow.

'Some load,' Müller said.

'Sure is, buddy. About the tenth I've brought here since she docked.'

It occurred to Müller that if he could get a job with the timber firm he might somehow get aboard.

'Lot of work going on, then?'

'You can say that again.' The foreman turned to yell

instructions to one of his men. 'Especially if you know anything about woodwork.'

Müller was immediately interested. After having worked for a year with a small boat-building company near Bergen, he was sure he could cope with anything on board the liner.

'Do you know if there's likely to be any work aboard?'

Sweat glistened on the foreman's brow. 'There's work, all right. About a dozen guys in there already, and they're crying out for more.'

As he was talking, Müller took in the company name on the side of the truck. Somehow he knew that he would have to talk his way into a job if he was going to get aboard.

'Could they use more labour? I've worked aboard ship and have a lot of experience. Woodwork's no problem for me.'

The thick-set foreman threw him a sidelong look and seemed to approve of Müller's capable appearance. 'If you can work with timber reckon they'd jump at you, mister. They've been working themselves into the ground, and there's been all kinds of labour problems. Man to see is Murphy. Big guy. Done a bit of boxing.'

'Where do I find him?'

'Right now, in that café over there. De Marco's. Just through the dock gate.'

Müller thanked him and set off for Pier 90's entrance. A striped awning was just visible across the road. Two huge military trucks passed and he crossed the road. As he approached Müller could hear the noise of radio music. The café was packed with longshoremen, crane drivers, dock workers and seamen. They sat at check-clothed tables, eating huge plates of food. Laughter and loud-mouthed jokes filled the air.

A counter ran along one side of the café, behind which a couple whom Müller took to be the Italian proprietor and his wife toiled away beneath an imitation vine. On the wall opposite was a large map of Italy, advertising the wine-producing regions. Müller found a table and ordered lasagne with a carafe of Valpolicella, then turned to survey the clientele.

A burly man was holding forth in the corner, his glass

carefully replenished by his workmates. When he looked across, Müller recognised the battered features and flat nose of a one-time prize-fighter.

A girl brought the lasagne and Müller eyed her appreciatively. 'Is that Murphy?' He pointed to the boxer.

She nodded. 'That's him. Comes in most days.'

'Thanks.'

As he ate the steaming pasta Müller continued to watch the small group. Then, draining his glass, he moved across to Murphy's table.

'Mr Murphy?'

The ex-fighter looked up through eyes made puffy by old boxing injuries. 'That's me. What d'you want?'

'Just wondered if you had any work, that's all.'

'What kind of work you after?'

'Carpentry. Working with timber.'

Murphy's eyes were bloodshot. 'Who gave you my name?'

'The foreman on your truck over there. I'm looking for a job.'

'So you've worked as a carpenter, have you?'

Müller nodded. 'In Norfolk, Virginia, and at sea.'

Murphy's eyes lit up. 'Well maybe I could use you. Can you start right away?'

'Sure thing.'

Murphy sat back grandly. 'Okay then, I'll fix you up. We need help aboard the *Queen Mary*.'

Müller was delighted and looked suitably grateful. 'Can I fix you a drink, Mr Murphy?'

'Now that's the kind of fellow I like.'

When they had finished the bottle, Murphy stood up.

'Just follow me. I'll get you fixed up with a pass at the Dock Labour Office later, but I want you working as soon as possible. Where you from?'

'Norway.'

'Gee. That's a long way,' Murphy commented.

They walked together back to Pier 90. The guard seemed to know Murphy so well he didn't bother to stop them. They took the crew elevator to the first level, and from there Murphy led the way to the crew gangway. Unlike the other passenger gangways it was uncovered and much wider.

Stevedores were hustling backwards and forwards, loading sides of meat and other supplies, but there was still a group of guards carefully checking everybody's credentials.

A British corporal stepped across, his eyes on Müller. It almost seemed for a moment that he had recognised him for some reason, but Müller pushed the fear to the back of his mind.

'All right, Murphy, who's this chap?'

'He's working for me.'

'What kind of security has he got?'

'He's okay. Got an ID card, and he's a registered seaman.'

Müller reached inside his jacket and took out his card. The corporal studied it, then approached an officious American captain standing on the other side of the gangway entrance.

'Is this all right, sir?' he asked.

Murphy let out an exasperated sigh. 'We've got work to do if this ship is to sail. I'll vouch for him. He ain't no Nazi spy.'

The four men all looked at Müller until the lieutenant laughed, wrote down Larsen's name and waved them into the ship.

The liner's public areas seemed to be milling with dock workers and crew. Everywhere work was in hand. Stewards with armfuls of blankets almost bundled Müller off his feet, and further down the passageway they edged past a team of electricians working on ladders. Several times they passed groups of army officers studying plans of the deck layout. Murphy strode on down several flights of steps until they reached a seemingly endless corridor with small tourist-class cabins on each side. The noise of hammering came from where Murphy's men were labouring furiously to install tiers of crude bunks. Some worked at makeshift benches, others set up the long rails forming the structure of the bunks.

'This is where you'll be working,' Murphy said and shouted to a small wiry man who was sawing a long plank. The man's face was brown and wizened, and he had the gnarled hands of a craftsman. There was a trace of humour in his gimlet eyes as he surveyed Müller and proceeded to roll a cigarette between his fingers.

131

'Hank, this is Olaf Larsen. Knows his way round ships. Won't fall on his ass down the stokehold.'

'Okay. Over here.' Hank led the way to the end of the compartment and assigned Müller to work next to a middle-aged man who was screwing supports for the rails into the ship's side.

'Sure glad you've arrived,' the man drawled in a heavy American accent. 'Too much to do here and not enough time.'

Müller was given no chance to find his bearings but was immediately pitched into the job. Hank fixed him up with tools and overalls until he could purchase his own. Compared to the skills needed in boatbuilding the job was simple and consisted mainly of screwing in the steel frames of fold-away bunks. Hank went ahead marking the positions of each steel assembly and Müller followed, setting up the basic framework. Other men worked close behind, strengthening the supports and slotting in the bedsteads. The efficiency was impressive.

It was six o'clock when Müller finished and took off his overalls. He decided he would buy a tool-kit next morning.

When he got back to the Gotham Müller collected his key and took the elevator to the fourth floor, walking along the carpeted corridor to his room; at least he had enjoyed some brief luxury at Padilla's expense, but he knew that he would have to leave to avoid suspicion. When he entered his room everything seemed to be in order, and minutes later he was wallowing in the luxury of a hot bath, the stiffness seeping out of his aching limbs. Then he quickly dressed and headed for the Western Union Office. He did not expect any signals, but instead scribbled out a simple message of his own:

'ABOARD.'

Chapter 12

The Greyhound bus pulled into the station at Norfolk, Virginia, and a young, dark-haired girl climbed down on to the tarmac. She gripped a red leather suitcase, and looked round anxiously for the information desk, which she found next to the waiting room. The elderly clerk watched her approach and listened patiently to her quiet request for directions to the Naval Hospital.

It turned out to be a ten-minute walk. The weather was humid, and she began to feel the effects of her long journey from New York. However, as soon as she glimpsed the hospital's iron gates at the end of a leafy avenue her pace quickened. On reaching the entrance she fumbled a moment in her handbag, then pulled out a scrap of paper with the words 'Ward C' typed on it. With the help of a porter she found her way across the lawns to the relevant building, ignoring the wolf-whistles of the convalescent seamen relaxing in the sun.

Inside the wards a young sun-tanned staff nurse occupied a small office. She was busy making up medical records and did not notice the visitor until she spoke.

'Good afternoon. My name is Anna Rabin. I wonder if you could help me?'

Laura looked up from her papers and smiled. 'What can I do for you?'

'I'm looking for somebody.'

'A relative? Husband? Father?'

'No, not a relative. A close friend.' The girl hesitated. 'The father of my child.'

'You're pregnant?' Laura's oval face was sympathetic.

'Yes,' Anna replied in a whisper. 'He was a seaman and we were going to get married. Now he's missing. He might be dead—I don't know. I haven't heard from him, and I have to find out what's happened to him.'

'It's highly irregular for us to give the details of any patient other than a close relative. I'm sorry.'

Anna began to cry and Laura felt uncomfortable. She jumped up and offered a handkerchief.

'Please don't upset yourself. I'll fix you a coffee. What was your man's name?'

'Olaf Larsen,' Anna mumbled. Laura blinked. 'Olaf Larsen,' she repeated. Her mind went back to the quiet Norwegian and the hot afternoon they had spent together, and the way he had made love to her. Where was he? What had happened to him? He had never written.

'Who told you to come here?' she asked coolly.

'The Norwegian authorities.'

'In Washington?'

'No, in New York. They look after merchant seamen there.'

'You've come all the way from New York?'

'That's where I work.' Anna gave a faded smile. 'They told me a man called Larsen had been rescued from a lifeboat after his ship had been sunk, and he was supposed to be in the recovery ward at Norfolk Naval Hospital.'

Laura felt a wave of sympathy for the girl. It did not surprise her that Larsen had failed to make contact, especially if he knew she was pregnant. There was something calculating about him, even about his love-making, as if he coldly planned every move. No doubt he had decided to seduce her the moment he had seen her in the ward. She had written him off now—even though she knew she would probably change her mind if he should suddenly walk through the door.

She looked at Anna's tearful face. The girl seemed so vulnerable. Laura suddenly began to feel anger rising within her. No doubt Larsen was somewhere bedding another unsuspecting girl. Why should he escape Anna as he had escaped her?

She lowered her voice. 'Look, I shouldn't tell you, but we did have a man called Larsen in here until about four weeks ago. Tall, fair-haired, and yes, he was a Norwegian.'

Anna's face brightened. 'If he was here, where did he go? Why didn't he contact me?' The words tumbled out. 'Was he injured? Fit? I just can't understand why he never wrote. We were so close.'

The nurse suppressed a smile. 'When he left this hospital he was fit for duty. I think he went to New York looking for a ship.'

'New York,' Anna said in a pained voice, 'and he didn't contact me?'

'Well, it may not be the same man.' She put a hand on Anna's arm. 'Look, maybe the War Shipping Administration can help you. They have a bureau here in Norfolk, and I'm sure he'd have reported there. All merchant seamen have to. They may even have an address for him.'

'Did he ever mention an address in New York?'

Laura's mouth suddenly tightened.

'Yes. You might just try the Gotham,' she said.

'The Gotham?'

'I think he intended meeting somebody there . . .' She turned away as if to consult a file and said over her shoulder, 'I'll give you the address of the War Shipping Administration.'

Once outside, clutching the scrap of paper with the address, Anna felt unsure of herself. She had got this far and it frightened her to think what she might discover. For weeks she had lived in the hope that Larsen was still alive, but the story about the Gotham disturbed her, and she tried to dismiss it from her mind. Olaf was not the kind of man who used such hotels. She knew she had to find him. He was the closest person to her, and she longed for his company.

When Anna reached the War Shipping Administration she was attended to by a female clerk of about fifty, a heavily-built woman who stared at her through thick lenses. She listened indifferently to the younger woman's request for information and, when she had finished, merely pouted.

'We aren't allowed to give away anybody's details.'

'*Please* help. This man is very special to me, and I have to see him. The Norwegian people in New York were helpful. Surely you could just tell me where I might look for him?'

The clerk shook her head. 'Maybe you should just go back to New York and ask the Norwegians again.'

135

'Of course I'll ask them officially if they can tell me where he is: perhaps they will pass on a letter to him. But now that I've come all this way, couldn't you just tell me if it was the same man who came in here about four weeks ago?'

The woman sighed, then rummaged among the card indexes and files behind her desk, eventually returning with a large buff card and folder.

'I'm not supposed to do this, but is this him?'

Anna looked at the photograph on the card. The short hair, the cheekbones, the eyes and nose were not the features of Olaf Larsen; yet the details on the card said otherwise.

'I don't understand,' she said. 'The name's right, the ship's right, but that's not his face.'

The clerk frowned and inspected the card. 'Oh yes, I remember the guy. Well, maybe there were two Larsens off the same ship. It's a fairly common name up in Norway, isn't it?'

'I suppose it's possible that there are two. But if so, where's mine?'

'Well, honey, maybe he went down with the ship. I'm sorry.' She scooped up the cards. 'I think if you want to take it any farther you better go through the Norwegian authorities in New York again.' She brightened. 'Look, maybe the guy's gone missing. Men do, you know. Perhaps he's in England or some place. It will take a bit of checking.'

Anna felt a flush of anger. 'He wasn't the kind of man to do that.'

'Sure, I know how you feel,' the clerk commiserated. 'But men can be right bastards, you know.'

There was little more Anna could do. She thanked the woman and began to walk back to the bus station. The sun was beginning to set and the air was growing cooler, but she hardly noticed.

'Larsen, I want you on B Deck right away. Finish up here and come with me.'

Hank stood looking down at Müller, as he finished securing the post of a bunk, his eyes watering in a cloud of tobacco fumes. Gratefully, Müller put down his screwdriver and rubbed his wrist. The pace of work on board the ship had picked up so much that he found himself struggling to stay ahead of the joiners toiling behind him.

'What's up on B Deck?' he asked Hank as he gathered up his tools.

The foreman puffed at his cigarette. 'You'll find out soon enough.'

As soon as Müller was ready Hank led the way through the for'ard part of the ship where the decks were a honeycomb of cramped Third-Class accommodation.

'No room to swing a cat,' Hank commented drily, as he noticed Müller peeking into a tiny cabin.

'Do you know that they're going to pack six GIs into those kennels? Those dogfaces sleep in shifts.'

They approached B Deck up a broad, well-lit staircase, which suggested to Müller a higher standard of comfort than on the decks below. His expectations proved right when Hank stopped in front of one of the large cabin doors and threw it open to reveal a large, empty lounge from which all furniture had been removed. Bright sunlight flooded through the portholes, revealing the marks on the floor where the carpet had been. The suite had clearly been used by wealthier travellers, and a mural on the right-hand wall depicting the English countryside caught Müller's attention.

'The *Queen Mary*'s passengers treated themselves royally, didn't they?' he said.

'You haven't seen it all yet,' Hank replied, and moved off towards an adjoining door. The sound of sawing came from the other side. Hank opened the door, and Müller saw a bedroom dominated by a very large bed with an inlaid mahogany headboard. A thickset man was working at the side of it, cutting through a long piece of timber. He wore a red chequered shirt and Müller was struck by his mop of unruly black hair. Pushing it out of his eyes he nodded at the visitors but continued with his work, a massive hand holding the baulk of his wood and his knee pinning it to the carpenter's horse, as the saw slid smoothly back and forth. At last he straightened up, pulling back bear-like shoulders and thumping the timber on to a pile of expertly-cut sections. For a man of such powerful build Müller noticed that he moved lightly on his feet, wearing a pair of stained blue tennis shoes.

'This is Nat Jacobsen. He's one of our top guys round here,' Hank announced.

'He tells that to everybody,' Jacobsen boomed. 'But he never pays me any more dough.'

'Money, money, Nat. That's all you Jewish guys think about,' Hank rétorted with a laugh, and went on to introduce Müller. 'A Norwegian, you say?' Jacobsen remarked, his dark eyes taking in the blond hair and sculpted Teutonic features. For the first time since arriving in New York Müller felt vulnerable, but to his relief Jacobsen's face broke into a friendly grin.

'Welcome aboard, Larsen. It'll be a pleasure to work with you.'

Müller politely acknowledged him; he had survived an unexpected test. Hank walked over and sat on the edge of the bed, unfolding a set of drawings.

'I've got news for you guys. This lovely bed has got to come out. It has to be dismantled and piled in the corner, to await disposal—though God knows where! When it's down you've got to build ten bunks in here, and another twelve in the lounge.'

They studied the plans for a few moments, then Hank got to his feet.

'You had better work in the bedroom, Larsen; you can get going in the lounge, Jacobsen,' he said, then gave instructions where they were to find timber and supplies. He took a last look round the empty suite and said finally, 'I reckon this ship will be sailing in about forty-eight hours. We want the whole show ready by then. Don't let me down, boys.'

The door slammed. Jacobsen turned to Müller.

'I just hope to hell they don't expect me to do any overtime. I have a woman to meet tonight and, boy, is she something! I'm not wasting that chance, buddy.'

Müller humped his toolbag into the bedroom. 'I agree. You mustn't let the war interfere with your love life.'

Privately he hoped Jacobsen heeded his words, because there was a great deal he wished to do once his workmate was out of the way.

In the remaining hours of the afternoon Müller laboured at dismantling the bed, which was a much tougher proposition than he had thought. It had a very heavy frame, while its legs were bolted to the floor. Sweat poured off him as he fought to loosen them. At last, with a final tap of his hammer, the iron frame came away from the solid footboard. Then he worked through the same procedure with the massive headboard, calling on Jacobsen to help him.

Most of the time the two men worked separately, too occupied to talk, but every so often Jacobsen would throw out a few words of friendly conversation from the adjoining room. On these occasions Müller affected to be too busy to indulge in chat, which might still be dangerous. Jacobsen seemed to accept his silence.

Müller preferred the occasions when Jacobsen left him completely alone in the suite, while he went below in search of timber supplies. This gave him an opportunity to make a quick recce of B Deck, but Müller decided to wait until Jacobsen knocked off for the night before having a thorough look round.

It was six o'clock and Müller had stacked the dismantled bed against the wall, ready for removal, when the carpenter appeared in the bedroom doorway.

With a sigh the big man folded his rule into the breast pocket of his shirt and announced apologetically, 'I'm sorry I can't stay any longer, but you know how it is with a woman.'

Müller threw him a knowing look. 'You make me envious. Give her one for me.'

Jacobsen guffawed, taking off his carpenter's apron. 'If I get the chance. Don't work all night.'

The door closed after him, and Müller continued working for several minutes until he felt sure that Jacobsen had gone. Then he went to his tool bag, and after lifting out one or two tools took out a small cigar box. It had originally contained Padilla's money, but now held an assortment of screws. Müller emptied them on to the floor. Lining the bottom of the box was a sheet of paper—a sketch plan of the *Queen Mary*. He had prepared it from his own researches in the

New York Public Library, where he had gone after work, from articles in newspapers and illustrated magazines. On it he had marked a small chamber in the bows on G Deck, five levels below. He stuffed the drawing into his jeans pocket and picked up his tool bag, having memorised the route through ladders and companionways, but before he left the stateroom his eyes fell on a carpenter's apron rolled up in the corner. It must belong to Jacobsen. Quickly he tied it round his waist so that everybody would recognise him as a chippie. Then he left the suite and made his way for'ard, passing several stewards and other members of the crew. Nobody paid him any attention. He noticed that everyone was going about their own work with much greater urgency; the deadline for departure was drawing near.

The farther for'ard he moved the more the ship's interior changed. Staterooms and lounges were left behind, and he entered the working parts of the ship. He passed the mail room to find himself in the crew's quarters, a series of large cabins, each housing half a dozen men.

A burly seaman came out of one of them and almost collided with him. He seemed suspicious at first, but seeing the apron and tools walked on with a friendly nod.

Beyond the crew's quarters Müller found the stairs he was looking for, and began to descend through five decks, hauling his tool bag after him. Stairs gave way to iron ladders, and he was panting by the time he arrived in the large cargo space on F Deck. The dimly-lit area was packed with bags of potatoes, flour and other dry goods; the muffled sound of men working came from ahead. A gang of stevedores were unloading crates from a lift. Cautiously Müller retraced his steps until he discovered a narrow gap between the stacks of tea chests, just wide enough for him to squeeze through, which took him past the stevedores into the dim light beyond. He clambered through the watertight door at the end of the cargo hold and to his surprise saw three studded doors on his right. From their eye-level observation grilles he recognised them as cells. He pushed the first one and found it was open. Inside, it was small and airless, and without natural light. A hard shelf, obviously used as a bed, protruded from the wall, and there was a tap in the corner. It was a grim place, a brief reminder of his imprisonment at the hacienda, and Müller was relieved to step back outside.

From his memory of the sketch map he knew he was almost in the bows, close to the small chamber he was seeking, but before he could continue he heard footsteps ringing on the metal deck-casing a few yards ahead and the sound of voices. Whoever was approaching would find it strange confronting a carpenter in the bows of the ship where there was very little wooden construction. There was no time to retreat to the cargo hold, and as the footsteps drew nearer there was obviously more than one man. There was no other choice—Müller darted back into the cell, pulling the door gently to behind him.

The two men came closer and the footsteps stopped directly outside the cell. Instinctively Müller put his hand in the tool bag and gripped a hammer, trying to breathe softly. His heart pumped against his ribs as he heard a man's gruff voice.

'We'll have to have these cells looked at before sailing. One of the locks is very stiff. They had a great job getting the prisoner out when they docked.'

A second man, whom Müller imagined to be a maintenance worker, answered, 'With all those Yanks coming on board they're bound to need the cells again. There'll be some right villains. We'd better take a look. Which cell is it?'

Müller's mind raced for an alibi if they discovered him, but it was the door of the next cell that creaked on its hinges, and he heard the two men moving around on the other side of the wall. For some time they discussed the lock and hinges, then he heard the door close and their footsteps recede.

Sweat poured off Müller's forehead as he emerged. It was clear he would have to find another route to the bow chamber: the cells would almost certainly be in use on the voyage. He turned left along a narrow passage and at the end found another ladder, by which he descended to G Deck. The atmosphere was dank and heavy with the smell of the ship's bilges, and the area seemed to be used for storing ropes and seamen's stores. In the darkness at the far end Müller found the hatch he was looking for. Dumping his tool bag, he threw his weight against the massive door lever and felt it move. He heaved it back and crawled inside. It was pitch dark, and he shivered in the cold, sensing the sea only a few feet away on the other side of the steel hull. He fumbled for a torch and shone its beam around the chamber. There seemed very little height, and the two walls came together at the far end, making the area triangular in shape. He was in the very bows of the liner; but he had found his hiding-place.

Chapter 13

Anna Rabin pushed away a half-eaten pastrami sandwich. She sat in the small delicatessen feeling slightly sick. Since arriving back from Norfolk, Virginia, she seemed to have walked across the whole of New York City and for the first time had begun to feel afraid that she might have over-exerted herself and harmed her baby.

She had patiently checked possible addresses where Larsen might be found, trusting vaguely that he would somehow miraculously appear. She had plucked up courage to call on seamen's clubs in rougher parts of the West Side, and had visited the War Shipping Administration, only to be told bluntly by the supervisor that postings of merchant seamen were secret, and she could well end up being investigated by the FBI if she persisted with her questioning.

Those words had defeated her, and she realised in despair that she might never be able to trace her own lover, or even his mysterious namesake. Once again she thought of the strange likeness between the two men, and recalled the photo on the file in Norfolk. There was something about the eyes—confident but also hard, almost unfeeling—and it worried her.

She sipped her lukewarm coffee and stared out of the

window at the large building opposite. It would be her last call of the day. After that she would return to her job in a Madison Avenue store and try to forget Olaf Larsen.

She paid her bill and crossed the road to the Gotham. The desk clerk watched her push through the swing doors and walk uncertainly towards him.

'Can I help you, miss?'

Anna smiled at him, but it was not acknowledged. 'I'm looking for a Mr Olaf Larsen who might be staying here.'

The clerk pulled the thick leather-bound register towards him and began flicking over the pages.

'A Mr Larsen you say?'

The clerk shook his head, running down the different signatures with his finger.

'We did have a Mr Larsen, but I have a feeling that he checked out . . .'

Anna's grip tightened on her handbag.

'Wait a minute, there *is* a Mr Olaf Larsen. Norwegian nationality. Room six twenty-five.' The clerk looked over the top of his glasses at the row of keys behind him. 'He's out at the moment.'

Anna stood staring at him, the blood drained from her face.

'Would you like to leave a message for Mr Larsen?'

At last she found her voice. 'Perhaps I could wait for him?'

The clerk shrugged his shoulders and pointed to a leather armchair on the other side of the foyer.

Several blocks away Müller strode into the Western Union Office on Broadway.

'Seems your company are forgetting you, sir,' the man behind the counter said when he saw him.

Müller looked disappointed.

'Why don't you make the most of it and have a nice evening in town?' the clerk said reassuringly.

'You're sure there's no message?' Müller insisted.

'Nothing at all.'

Müller looked at his watch. In a few hours the *Queen Mary* would be sailing, and if there were no instructions by then he would have to make his own decision whether or not to sail with her. It would be risky to stow away, and Padilla would be unable to reach him at sea; but what else could he do? If he didn't join the ship now it might be impossible to get through the liner's security screen a second time.

Müller picked up a pad and quickly drafted a message informing Padilla that the *Queen Mary* was expected to leave harbour within hours, and requesting urgent instructions. Then he walked out into the evening air.

He moved through the Broadway crowds, trying to work out his next step, wondering once more why Padilla had not contacted him. Perhaps something had gone seriously wrong and the FBI had intercepted his coded messages? He glanced round instinctively. If that were the case they would be shadowing him.

For a few moments he stopped and looked into a radio shop, using the reflection in the window to check the street behind him, but he could see nothing suspicious.

He walked on and passed an array of photos outside a cinema showing Bette Davis and Paul Henreid in *Now Voyager*. For a moment he almost yielded to the temptation to buy a ticket, but decided instead to head back to the Gotham to settle his bill and start packing.

When he pushed his way through the hotel's swing doors he did not notice the young woman until he heard a quiet voice at his shoulder.

'Excuse me. May I introduce myself?'

He swivelled round to look into the wide brown eyes of a young woman in her early twenties. She stood uncertainly before him, her skin so pale it seemed almost translucent. Straight dark hair fell to her shoulders and her wide generous mouth was trembling, for all her obvious efforts at control. She spoke again.

'I'm Anna Rabin, and I think we have a mutual friend.'

The words startled Müller. He was sure he had never set eyes on her before.

'A mutual friend?' he asked courteously.

Her face was serious when she answered. 'Olaf Larsen.'

Müller stared at her incredulously as she continued, 'I

144

hope you don't think I'm rude approaching you like this, but your name *is* Olaf Larsen, isn't it?'

'That's my name. How did you know?'

'Are you Norwegian?'

He paused, his feeling of surprise turning to alarm.

'As a matter of fact I am. But why all these questions?'

He nodded towards the hotel bar at the back of the foyer where one or two people were lingering over their early evening drinks.

'Why not join me for a drink and tell me all about this in comfort?'

He escorted her to an empty stool at the far end of the bar, out of earshot of the other drinkers, and summoned the bartender. Anna ordered a Coke. Müller asked for a Scotch on the rocks, conscious of her eyes appraising him.

He turned squarely to face her. 'Now tell me. How can we have a mutual friend?'

'Well, the man I was going to marry is called Olaf Larsen and, like you, he served on the *Empire Rose*. So surely you must have known him.'

Müller's thoughts were racing. So this was Larsen's girl. Or one of them. Not the fair-haired Norwegian he had seen in the German Intelligence files at the hacienda, but a woman Larsen had never mentioned, even in the lifeboat. Where had she come from, and how on earth had she found out about him and the *Empire Rose*?

The bartender brought the drinks and Anna gave an uncertain smile.

'It's all right,' she said. 'I'm not from the FBI or anything. The hospital at Norfolk told me about you.'

Immediately Müller knew how she had tracked him down. That damned bitch of a nurse at the Naval Hospital. She had wanted to get her claws into him. She had certainly pulled a neat trick, but she didn't know what she was dealing with.

Anna continued to look at him with wide eyes, and spoke over the top of her glass.

'I'm sorry to keep staring at you like this, but you see you are so like Olaf. When you walked into the hotel I could hardly move at first, it was such a shock.'

Müller smiled at her and instinctively patted her hand. She

145

was obviously an ingenuous girl, deeply upset by the loss of her lover, and had stumbled on Müller's deception without being at all aware of its true significance. He decided that his main mission must be to play along with her, to discover how much she knew.

'Well, what a fantastic coincidence,' he said warmly. 'Of course I remember Olaf; you must be the girl he was always talking about. He never mentioned your name, but he often said how pretty you were. I can see he was right.'

Anna's eyes registered his flattery and Müller continued. 'It was something of a joke aboard the *Empire Rose* that two of us had the same name. It's a common enough name back home, but it amused the British crew.' He grinned. 'They called me Little Olaf—your man was Big Olaf.'

She seemed to accept what he said and Müller recalled once more the information on the secret file at the hacienda, using it as he spoke of the Norwegian's exploits. Only when he had finished talking did her mood change.

She touched her glass nervously, then asked, 'Where is Olaf? Please tell me.'

It was the question Müller had been waiting for. Gently he put a hand on her arm. 'I'm sorry, Anna. He went down with the *Empire Rose*.'

'Are you sure?' she asked sadly.

'Pretty sure. He wasn't in my lifeboat. Of course, there's a slender chance that he might have got away on a raft, but there's been no news of anyone else being rescued. You've got to accept that he went down with the ship. I'm sorry.'

For a moment he thought she was going to cry. When finally she spoke it was in a whisper. 'Yes, I understand. I've been thinking about it for weeks. Ever since he stopped writing to me.'

She was staring into her glass on the bar counter, and suddenly seemed very defenceless. In the soft light Müller could just discern the curl of her eyelashes and the faint purple under her eyes which betrayed her tiredness.

'There's a lot about Olaf you don't know,' he declared cheerfully. 'He was a great character. Very much liked on board.'

Anna perked up and listened intently as Müller expanded on what he knew about Larsen. Most of it he was able to invent convincingly but he also recalled several anecdotes the big Norwegian had told him during their long hours in the lifeboat. By the time he finished there was a new light in her eyes. It was time to make his next move.

'There's still a lot to tell about Olaf. Can't we have supper somewhere?'

She seemed taken aback by his suggestion. For a moment she hesitated, wrestling with some internal doubts, then smiled.

'Thank you, but it's rather late and I have a strict landlady.' She slipped off her stool and pulled her white raincoat around her shoulders.

Müller concealed his annoyance.

'Why not tomorrow, then? I would love to see you again. I could pick you up.'

She gave him a wan smile.

'All right. Tomorrow.'

'About seven?'

She agreed and fumbled in her handbag for a diary. Opening it, she jotted down her address and phone number, then tore out the page and gave it to Müller. One or two drinkers watched them as they left. Müller escorted her to the entrance. Outside she stopped on the pavement. 'Thank you so much for everything,' she whispered, then turned on her heel and hurried away. He watched her dark hair until it disappeared from view. Somehow he would have to act fast. She was an attractive young woman and it would be sad to kill her. But he had killed before; and if he had to, he would again.

He went back into the hotel, hoping that the clerk had not been too observant, and asked for his key, telling him that he would be checking out in the morning.

The lift hauled Müller slowly to the sixth floor and he stepped out into the dimly-lit passage. His feet scarcely made a sound on the thick carpet as he headed for his room at the far end.

Outside his door he paused for a moment, thinking that he detected a faint noise from inside. He held his breath as he listened intently, but there was only silence as he carefully unlocked the door and stepped inside.

He did not turn on the light, but stood a moment in the darkness listening. Then, using the shadows, he edged into the large lounge.

Suddenly a light blazed and he swung round like a cat.

'I thought you would never come.' The voice was instantly recognisable. Sitting in the armchair opposite, his hand on the switch of the table lamp, was Padilla.

'What are you doing here?' Müller asked in astonishment.

'Looking for you.' Padilla swept his hand round at the room. 'I see that you prefer to live in style.' He indicated the large chesterfield in front of the fireplace, and the expensive Louis Quinze furniture, tastefully illuminated by two standard lamps.

'Fix me a drink. A Scotch—courtesy of the Reich.'

Müller poured two Johnny Walkers and brought one over to Padilla.

'Isn't it dangerous for you to be here?' he asked. Padilla laughed. 'I'm a Mexican, and Mexico is an ally of the United States. Also, you forget I am a respected businessman. The Americans don't want any diplomatic embarrassment by having me interrogated or anything dramatic like that.'

He drew out a Havana.

'It's best to be completely ostentatious. At least for the few hours that I am here.'

He indicated a chair opposite, and Müller sat down. His uncle slowly lit the cigar. The flame danced in his expressionless eyes, and Müller recalled their equivocal first meeting. The hotel suite, his uncle's relaxed attitude—it all seemed strange. He began to feel apprehensive.

'I know that my presence here must surprise you,' said Padilla, exhaling a cloud of smoke. 'Especially as there are risks involved. But I have been ordered to come to New York by higher authorities. In fact, you could say the highest authority.'

Müller waited for the next words.

'I have orders to brief you personally,' Padilla went on. 'But first I must know exactly whether you can move easily

148

around the *Queen Mary*. Can you get your radio set on board without unnecessary risks?'

Müller at last felt on firmer ground, and quickly explained how he was working aboard the liner and how much longer he expected to be there. He spoke of the conditions and atmosphere on board, and told of the hideout he had discovered in the liner's bows.

When Müller finished there was a silence, and he wondered what Padilla was thinking as he sat with his plump chin cushioned against his chest. Then his head rose and he spoke.

'You have already fulfilled the first part of the operation successfully by getting aboard. You must stay on board at all costs, and sail with the ship. If necessary you must stow away.'

His uncle's small eyes shone. 'I want you to understand that you have been selected to strike an immense blow for the Reich. On orders sanctioned by the Führer himself, you are to seize the *Queen Mary* and bring her under cover of German sea and air forces to St Nazaire.'

In spite of his training Müller was so stunned that he wondered whether Padilla was play-acting. So this was what he had been trained for—an impossible operation! Everybody knew the immense size of the ship, and there would be thousands of enemy troops on board. Padilla's orders seemed totally impossible, and he would even have laughed at their preposterous nature had not the serious expression on Padilla's face stopped him.

'But how can *I* capture the *Queen Mary*?' he asked, still mystified. 'She will have over ten thousand men on board; it takes ten minutes to walk from one end of the ship to the other—'

'You will not be attempting the operation on your own. We know that a thousand German troops will be sailing in her—prisoners of war shipped from Scotland to the United States. They are all highly trained men, mostly captured in the North African campaign. You are to mobilise them and spearhead an attack on the ship from within.'

'But surely they will be under heavy guard. And how will I be able to organise and direct them?'

Padilla's voice was icy. 'You will be following a plan worked out in the greatest detail by fifty top experts of SKL 111 in Berlin.'

Step by step Padilla explained the SKL plan, and as he did so Müller's scepticism receded. By the time his uncle had finished speaking he was beginning to feel excited at the audacity of the scheme.

'When am I to put the plan into effect?'

'On the next voyage from Gourock to New York. Voyage ninety-three.'

Müller finished his whisky before posing his next question. 'What if the plan fails and I can't take over the ship?'

His uncle rose from his chair and walked silently across the thick carpet. He stopped in front of a battered suitcase which Müller for the first time realised had been placed in a far corner of the room.

He carried it across into the light and opened it. Müller saw a row of books packed neatly inside. Their covers were garish and they were mostly popular novels. Padilla took one out and opened it, then turned the first pages to reveal a hollow: the book was a neatly disguised box. A yellowish slab filled the cavity, and Müller recognised the soft toffee-like substance of plastic explosive.

Padilla was speaking again. 'If you cannot seize the ship you are to sabotage her. The precise point and the exact method you are to use has been carefully worked out. If you follow your instructions the ship will at the very least be slowed down, in all probability forced to a dead stop. Then she will be a perfect target for our U-boats. The *Queen Mary* will be sent to the bottom of the Atlantic Ocean.'

Müller stared at him. 'But what about the German prisoners on board?'

'They will have to take their chance.'

'But they will never get off. There aren't enough lifeboats even if the prisoners could reach the boat deck, which is extremely unlikely.'

'Then they will go down with the ship.'

In three years of bitter warfare Müller had never been asked to sacrifice his own comrades, yet Padilla's orders called for just that. He knew too that he himself would almost certainly never get off the ship.

Padilla took a step towards him, his eyes narrowing.

'You have your orders. You are to obey them to the letter. What do you think you have been trained for? Remember, there are two kinds of war: one is fought according to chivalry, rules, codes of honour, the Geneva Convention. The other is secret, undercover, vicious. In both, however, the objective is the same. Victory.'

He turned and clicked the suitcase shut. 'You will take this with you. How you smuggle it on board is your problem, but you seem to have had no difficulties with the security checks so far. Nobody suspects you?'

'No.'

'Your cover is safe?'

Müller hesitated. 'It was until a few hours ago.'

A shadow crossed Padilla's face as Müller launched straight into an account of how Anna Rabin had approached him. By the time he ended the story he was uncomfortably aware of how dangerous Anna could be to the entire SKL operation.

Padilla's face was like a mask.

'What I find strange is that you say you have never set eyes on this woman before, and that Larsen never mentioned her, even in his meanderings in the lifeboat. This woman may well be a plant.'

Müller shook his head. 'I doubt it. I know that how she found me seems the strangest coincidence, but I think she's too naive to draw any conclusions about my photograph being on file in Norfolk when Larsen's wasn't. I think I can control her.'

Padilla thought a moment, then cleared his throat.

'It's too risky. You are not to get involved with her any more.'

'I planned to meet her tomorrow night. She gave me her address.'

'Give the details to me.'

Müller drew out his wallet and handed Padilla the slip of paper on which Anna had scribbled her address. His uncle put it carefully into his pocket.

'This particular lady, I think, you can leave safely to me.'

Chapter 14

Alloway leaned on the balcony of Tracey O'Brien's flat and watched a double decker bus crawl towards Camden Town, its lights dimmed and the windows pasted over with lace netting as a protection against bomb blast. Below, the trees of Regent's Park stretched away towards the blacked-out city, where only an hour previously he had sat next to Tracey in the Wigmore Hall, enthralled by the strains of Mozart's 41st Symphony. It was the first concert he had been to for months and, staring into the night, he realised how much his mind had become geared to the tension of working almost round the clock to meet the incessant demands of the War Cabinet Office.

He congratulated himself on getting two tickets for the concert, through a brother officer, and had been delighted when he found that Tracey was free to come with him.

He thought again of the moment when he had set eyes on her in the vestibule that evening. She wore a tailored black dress which accentuated her figure and which had drawn sidelong glances from many of the men in the audience. She wore no jewellery except for a solitary ring on her right hand. It was encrusted with diamonds, but they appeared commonplace next to the lustrous emerald in the ring's centre.

By the time they left the concert hall a few hours still remained before Alloway had to return to the underground command centre, so Tracey asked him back for supper.

It had been an intimate dinner with just the two of them. They had eaten a delicious baked Virginia ham, coated with honey, followed by a piquant American cheese. During the meal she was more relaxed and talkative than ever before, and her grey eyes had sparkled as she told him about her work, her experience, her love of England. Then he had been packed off to the balcony while she made fresh coffee and cleared away.

There was a rustle behind him, and Tracey stepped out on to the balcony, pulling the curtains closed behind her.

'I don't want to be had up for breaking the black-out regulations.' She walked across to him, a glass in her hand. 'It's bourbon. Hope you like it. The coffee's inside.'

He thanked her and took the whisky.

'That was a very good idea, Squadron Leader Alloway, taking me to the Wigmore Hall. It was a marvellous concert.'

He could smell the fragrance of her perfume in the darkness.

'One of the advantages of wartime London,' he explained. 'The place is overflowing with exiled musicians on the run from Hitler.'

Tracey spoke quietly. 'I often come out here and wonder what the view will be like in peacetime, with the lights shining across the park. It must be enchanting. But I suppose it will be years before that happens.'

Alloway had been working on strategic papers for the Military Secretary earlier that day, studying the possible outcome of decisive military campaigns in the years ahead, but he found it hard to think about such matters with Tracey beside him. Even so, he said, 'It may not be that long, Tracey.'

'I hope you're right. But for years there's been talk of a landing in Europe which would finish Germany off, yet still there's no sign of it. Will it ever come?'

'What an inquisitive lady you are. My lips are sealed, as they say in Whitehall.'

She seemed to realise that she had pushed him too far and whispered, 'It's cold out here. Let's go inside.' She smiled. 'Besides, I have something I want you to look at.'

'Not your etchings?'

Tracey put on a mock-serious expression.

'Wait and see, Squadron Leader.'

She led the way back into the lounge. It was a comfortable room, dominated now by the flickering fire. A small table stood in front of the window, with a Remington portable and a vase of spring flowers on its surface. Armchairs were

153

ranged each side of the fireplace. One of them had a footstool and a pile of women's magazines before it. Light from the fire picked out the spines of modern novels and reference books in a well-stacked bookcase.

Tracey busied herself with the coffee whilst Alloway sank into one of the armchairs, leaving the other with its footstool for his hostess. She brought him a cup of steaming coffee and he watched as she bent over and reached for something beneath the work table. When she turned round Alloway saw that she was holding a pile of magazines.

'I thought you might like to see these.'

To his surprise, he was handed copies of *Signal* and *Die Wehrmacht*, the Nazi propaganda magazines circulated throughout the Reich. As he began to leaf through them Tracey drew over the footstool and sat down on it close to him. The magazines were riveting, and the Nazi war machine paraded through their pages. Luftwaffe pilots, U-boat crews, tank commanders, Hitler Youth . . . their faces all sculpted in arrogant self-confidence, an expression Alloway remembered from the Tregaron prisoner of war camp.

'Where on earth did you get these?' he asked.

'It's all right, you don't have to be so suspicious. They were sent through the American Embassy here in London. They're from my father who has asked my opinion of them. He wants to use their techniques to produce a series of magazines for our own side.'

Alloway glanced across at Tracey. She was sitting with her arms round her knees, gazing up at him.

'Your father is a journalist too?'

She burst into laughter. 'Of course he is. He *owns* the Sentinel.'

Alloway reproached himself. He should have guessed that with her name and working on the *Sentinel* Tracey must have been related to Henry O'Brien, one of the most powerful newspaper magnates in America. O'Brien was celebrated on both sides of the Atlantic for his considerable political muscle and brilliant journalistic flair. But Alloway also knew that he was thoroughly disliked in Britain for his pronounced isolationist views, views which had made him a dangerous man during the perilous years when Britain had stood alone against Germany. O'Brien had openly used his influence in attempts to dissuade President Roosevelt from sending arms to Britain.

'I'm sorry to be so ignorant. I should have known. Your father is a very powerful man.' Alloway's tone was guarded.

Tracey put her chin on her knees.

'I know he's unpopular over here. I just hope that they understand that he did what he thought was right for his country.'

Alloway chose his words carefully, not wishing to set up barriers between them. 'I can understand that. But many people here don't see it that way. Certainly not the press.'

Her grey eyes blazed. 'If they're saying that he's a Nazi sympathiser they couldn't be more wrong. If you knew him you'd know that was impossible. He's difficult— opinionated—but he's a marvellously understanding man.'

She stared into the fire, and spoke as if she were seeking his understanding.

'I'm his only child—he looked after me after my mother died when I was very young—and we're very close. My father brought me up to be a chip off the old block. He always liked to have me with him, especially at his office. Before I'd left high school he had made sure that I'd been initiated into the arts of sub-editing, compositing and, of course, reporting.'

She looked at him with a half smile. 'By the time I was fifteen I could write a banner headline in my sleep and lay out a whole front page.'

Alloway listened as she told him how her father had taken her to innumerable social events, and also insisted she accompany him on many of his foreign trips, visiting some of the most important men in the world.

'When I finished at Vassar it was natural that I should go straight on to the paper, as a correspondent.'

'And are you happy working on the *Sentinel* now?' Alloway murmured.

'Love it. And I have a sneaking suspicion that I shall end up as the proprietor one day. So you'd better watch out!'

'I think you'll be the most popular newspaper proprietor in the United States. Certainly the most attractive '

Tracey trained her eyes on him.

'What you're *really* saying is that I'll be a right bitch.'

He grinned. 'I didn't say that, but I think you could be difficult at times, yes. I've no doubt that you'll be adored by all those cunning politicians in Washington. You'll never be short of a story.'

'I suppose you will be going back into the law, defending all those glamorous divorcees. I'm sure you'll be a great success,' she said fondly.

'No such luck. I specialise in crime. Serious stuff. Murder, rape, that sort of thing.'

'You make it sound very matter of fact.'

He moved closer. 'In a way it is.'

'It must be worrying when people's lives depend on you—on your powers of persuasion. That would frighten me.'

'If it's any comfort, the system may seem to work in a completely incomprehensible way but the guilty generally get their just desserts. You can usually tell whether a person is guilty or not.'

She rose to her knees, and smiled slowly at him.

'All right, Mr Attorney. Take me, for instance. Could I commit a murder?'

He could just make out the darker gold of freckles across her cheeks.

'Yes, you could commit a murder. Most people could under pressure, provocation or orders. Especially orders. But you would do it for something else. For passion. You would do anything for a cause. The stuff martyrs are made of. Very Irish.'

At first, as he leaned forward and kissed her, she did not move. Then he felt her lips part as she responded. Awkwardly, he slipped out of the chair and knelt on the rug, his fingers moving to her dress. She did not take his hand away. A great tension which had built up through the rigours of the war coiled inside him, and suddenly he was kissing her throat, her shoulders and breasts.

Tracey drew off her black dress, revealing the soft white thighs above her silk stockings, and Alloway gently unfastened her suspender belt. She pulled him to her, helping him too to undress. When at last they both were naked, he remembered the humiliation of his wounds, the unsightly scars on his upper thighs. Following his eye, for a moment Tracey paused, then bent down to kiss the lacerations. Then slowly, still smiling, she closed her eyes and leaned back on to the rug.

It was shortly before nine p.m. when Alloway left the flat. For a moment he stood on the pavement, staring up at the window where he could just distinguish Tracey's figure watching him leave. Then he climbed into the waiting taxi and told the driver to take him to Downing Street.

Safe within the darkness of the cab he reflected on his evening. Alloway had known many other women, from the vacuous county girls his mother tried to foist on him to the WAAF at his RAF station, with whom he had had a tempestuous affair. Somehow Tracey was different. She had the forbidding self-assurance of a first-rate journalist but had also revealed herself as an intensely passionate young woman who wanted to be taken for herself and not a pushing news reporter—nor the daughter of the *Sentinel*'s proprietor. It was inevitable that he would see her and make love to her again, but as he sat alone in the back of the taxi a doubt began to grow in his mind. In his eagerness he had swept aside any anxiety about the damage her father might do to him. Whatever his current enthusiasms might be, O'Brien thoroughly deserved to be loathed. If he had succeeded in frustrating Roosevelt a Nazi victory would have been certain. Alloway was well aware that the British Establishment would never forgive the American, and that Churchill himself had dismissed him in scathing terms. Nor had he any illusions about what the Military Secretary's attitude might be towards his liaison with Tracey . . .

Yet how unfair it seemed! Tracey could hardly be blamed for her father's views, however close she was to him. He was sure she was no security risk. But as the taxi crossed Trafalgar Square, the doubts came back at him again. He recalled that Tracey had not told him her father's identity until he had become very close to her, perhaps too close to hold back. It could have been a totally innocent action on her part, but she must also have been aware of the highly sensitive nature of his work, in a war administration where even an indirect connection with O'Brien might be seen as damning.

Alloway almost swore aloud. His mind had been trained to make decisions according to evidence, but now he was behaving like a third-rate investigator. The insane inverted values of war were taking their toll and making him distrustful of the woman he loved.

'We're here, sir,' the cabbie shouted. The driver had been waiting for some time for his passenger to get out. Fumbling for his money Alloway made his decision. He would go on seeing Tracey—and brave the fury of his chiefs if ever they found out.

Chapter 15

Müller stepped out of the crew lift in the Cunard Terminal on Pier 90, arms straining with the weight of his tool bag. He had risen early and taken the radio transmitter out of its case, dismantling its condensers and amplifiers so that they could be concealed beneath his carpenter's tools. Only a thorough search of the bag could reveal them, and any of the ship's guards would have to be a radio expert to appreciate the significance of the equipment.

Hiding the radio had taken only a short time, however, compared to the problem of concealing the plastic explosives. Standing in front of the wardrobe mirror he had awkwardly wound adhesive plaster round the four packages, and after pulling on his jersey had checked that any bulge in his midriff would only seem a typical beer belly.

He turned on to the gangway which stretched forty yards to the shell doors opening into the ship's side. A group of guards were on duty at the far end, and he cursed the distance he had to walk while they watched him. He tried to ignore the rising tension in his chest and began to sweat with the extra weight he was carrying. His body felt hot and he began to fear that the perspiration might weaken the adhesive.

It was an hour before the day shift and he cursed inwardly again, this time at the fact that there were no other men crossing the gangway. He had almost reached the ship when he noticed one of the guards stare at him, then cross over to exchange words with his colleagues on the other side of the entrance. Müller tensed and waited for their reaction, feeling the small group's eyes on him. At the end of the gangway one of the guards, a brawny military policeman, put out his hand for Müller's ID card.

'You'd better watch your weight, Larsen, or you'll end up like Two-Ton Tony.' The other men guffawed at the un-flattering comparison of Müller with one of the New York stevedores, famous for his colossal thirst and potbelly. The MP moved to prod Müller playfully in the stomach, but he swerved neatly away.

'Not bad for a fatso,' the guard shouted, and Müller grinned back, then made his way unhurriedly on to the ship.

He made for the hiding-place in the bows. It was hard going through the narrow passageways and corridors, and it was with relief that he finally reached the compartment. He carefully pulled back the hatch, then climbed laboriously inside, lugging the heavy tool bag behind him.

The chamber was in the apex of the liner's bows, trian-gular in shape, running some ten feet at its widest, and narrowing to a point. It was so cramped that he was forced to crouch, and even then moved with his head bowed. The stale oily smell turned his stomach.

He knelt down and hauled out the amplifier and conden-ser, both of which he placed on a ledge between the casing and the ship's side. In the far corner of the compartment where the two walls met at the bow stem Müller spotted a piece of oily sacking which he spread over the components.

Next he tugged off his jersey, shivering in the dank atmosphere, before reaching almost to his spine with his right hand. His fingers touched the dog-eared end of the adhesive tape which secured two packets of plastic to his stomach and another pair to his back. With his left palm he held the two packets on his back steady, tearing away the plaster with his free hand.

His skin felt raw as the tape came free and he moved his right elbow to trap the loosened packages in his midriff, easing them gently until eventually all four packets had come away. With a sigh of relief he hid them beneath the sacking.

After a check of the hideout to ensure that the sacking would not raise any suspicions should somebody check the compartment, he slammed the door and began the journey back.

By the time Müller arrived in the stateroom, Jacobsen was there taking off his coat. He shouted a cheery good morning, to which Müller grunted an acknowledgment and began to unpack his tools.

'We'd better get a move on,' Jacobsen declared, setting to work on the last tier of bunks. 'I reckon she'll be sailing tonight.'

Müller threw him an anxious glance. So far he had only managed to get half the components of the radio aboard, and Padilla's plan called for another four packets of explosive. If Jacobsen were right only a few hours remained to complete the job. He also faced the problem of deciding the exact moment when to stow away. It would have to be in the last hour before the *Queen Mary* sailed; otherwise Jacobsen might think his absence suspicious.

He was turning these difficulties over in his mind when Hank's spare figure appeared in the doorway. The foreman stepped lightly over the piles of timber and shavings.

'All right, you two. I've got something to tell you.' Both men put down their tools. 'We've had a request from the Navy. They want urgent alterations done aboard, and they have to be ready by the time the ship reaches England. That's in about a week's time.'

Müller threw Jacobsen a glance. 'What kind of urgent work?'

'Alterations to the big drawing room on the main deck. They want to turn it into a conference area for the military.' Hank took in the large disorganised figure of Jacobsen and the lean body of Müller before continuing. 'Since you two are pretty good workers and you're both single I wondered if you might like a trip to England? Who knows, you might even get a few days ashore once you're over there.'

Müller could have burst into jubilant laughter. The little American had unwittingly come up with the answer to his most worrying problem. But he was careful not to react too enthusiastically.

'Why can't the ship's carpenters do the job?'

'Too much on their hands. That's what they say, anyway.'

'How much extra will Murphy pay? I reckon we should be in for danger money.'

Jacobsen was looking hesitant too. 'Sure thing. There're supposed to be plenty of Germans out there.'

'My God,' Hank said drily. 'Haven't you guys ever heard of patriotism? All right, I'll speak to Murphy and see if I can get you an extra fifty cents an hour. That satisfy you?'

'Okay by me,' Müller replied. Jacobsen nodded assent.

'You'll both be fixed up with accommodation in the crew's quarters,' Hank growled. 'It's the only place, unless you want to sleep on deck with the GIs, poor bastards. Report to the bosun as soon as you can, and get your things. You sail tonight.'

Hank stubbed out his cigarette and left. Müller threw Jacobsen a glance, then sat down on the frame of the half-completed bunks.

'Quite a little adventure, Nat. But you don't seem too happy.'

Jacobsen buried his fingers in his shock of hair, his bright eyes surveying the work they had completed in the stateroom so far.

'I always did want a trip on the *Queen Mary*—and just think of the money.'

'And the U-boats,' Müller added quietly.

The bulk of the *Queen Mary*'s bosun filled the doorway as he swept his arm round the room.

'This is where you'll be quartered,' he said. Müller put down his suitcase and peered at the crew cabin. It was lit by two large portholes, and fitted with a pair of bunks on each wall, with another two in the middle. There was nobody in the cabin except a small-boned man in his forties, perched on one of the central bunks, writing a letter. He had a skeletal face and the pallid complexion of someone perpetually undernourished.

'Which bunk can we have, Nobby?' the bosun asked.

Nobby put down his pen. 'That one in the bottom corner, I reckon,' he said in a cheerful Cockney voice. 'Poor old Thomas won't be back awhile.'

Müller gave the bunk a dubious look, but the bosun's bulldog features crossed in a smile. 'Don't worry, he didn't have the plague or anything.'

The bosun took a final imperious look around and left. It was cramped down near the cabin floor, with only a small locker for each person's belongings. Müller hauled his suitcase over to the spare bunk. The explosives and radio parts hidden inside would have to be stowed in the secret bow chamber. Müller looked up to see Nobby watching him.

'I'll just take this gear up to the main deck where we'll be working,' he said quickly. 'I've got a lot of tools here, and they'll only clutter the place. I won't have room to sleep.'

'Okay, mate,' Nobby replied absent-mindedly. 'By the way, you want to know anything, just ask. We'll have a pint in the Pig and Whistle later—that's our own boozer on board, just for the crew.'

Müller stopped in the doorway. 'Excuse me, but where's my mate Jacobsen? A big guy, lots of black hair?'

'Oh, they've put him in another cabin. Wasn't room here,' Nobby replied.

Müller was delighted. It was his second great stroke of luck. Jacobsen was an amiable enough character, but he seemed far too observant for Müller's comfort, and there was no way of telling how his curiosity might develop.

By now Müller was very familiar with the route to the small chamber in the bows and it took him only a short time to lug his suitcase below and conceal the explosives and radio components. When he finally arrived at the stateroom he found Jacobsen complaining bitterly to Hank about his quarters.

'Oh, stop squawking, Nat,' Hank declared. 'Come on, I'll show you both where you've got to work.'

Müller clapped the big man's shoulder and said with a grin, 'Don't worry, Nat. You should see my room. Six other guys and a load of stinking feet.'

The two men followed Hank up the for'ard staircase to the Promenade Deck. The long enclosed walk ran the whole length of the superstructure. A moment later Hank slid open a door and led the way into a large and sumptuous drawing room.

'Some place!' Jacobsen exclaimed, coming up behind him and looking around, impressed. 'Don't say we have to tear it apart.'

Hank stood in the middle of the lush carpet and looked round at the War Ministry issue of tubular tables and armchairs, placed about incongruously.

'Seems as if they've been using this as an officers' mess or something,' he said. 'All you guys have to do is turn the place into a swish conference room fit for the top brass.'

Hank walked over to the coffee table and unfolded a plan he'd been holding. Müller followed him and, studying it, saw that a large board table would have to be erected, one capable of seating thirty people. They were also to put up a series of display panels—no doubt for maps and visual aids. A space was marked on the far wall for a film projector, and on the facing wall for a screen.

'You sure we've only got five days to get through all this?' Jacobsen growled.

'That's all,' Hank replied. 'The military can be very demanding.'

'So what's it all for, chief?' Müller asked.

The foreman sighed. 'Now, you know better than to ask a stupid question like that. Just get on with it.' Müller detected the ghost of a smile on Hank's face as he said, 'Don't let me down, boys. And give my love to all those Limeys over there, especially the girls.'

For the rest of the morning the two men moved boards and timber from C Deck to the drawing room. It was not until late afternoon that they finished, and Müller immediately made for his cabin. Other seamen were in there, one dozing on a bunk, another reading a comic.

Nobby had finished his watch and gave a friendly wave.

'Been working already?' he asked with a faint air of disapproval.

'No time to hang about,' Müller muttered, and stripped off his shirt for a shower.

His new friend chuckled. 'When you're ready we'll go and have a pint. Then we can watch the show.'

'Show?'

'You'll see soon enough. Better than Hollywood,' Nobby added enigmatically.

The Pig and Whistle was crowded with seamen, greasers, cooks and stewards, all quaffing vast quantities of beer. Jet-black Guinness seemed to be the favourite drink, especially with the bosun, who dominated one corner of the bar, flanked by two equally massive bosun's mates.

On Nobby's instructions the barman set up two glasses of Newcastle Brown, and Nobby watched with amusement as Müller laboriously swallowed the treacly ale.

'Not your type of drink, eh?'

'It's fine,' Müller lied.

'Your first time aboard, then?'

'Yes.' Müller put down his glass. 'I've always wanted to sail on the *Queen Mary*.'

Nobby nodded approvingly. 'Finest ship in the world. I've been on her five years.'

'It must take that long to get to know her.'

'There are some places even I don't know, and probably never will,' Nobby philosophised. Müller wondered whether he ever inspected the bow chamber. 'What are you blokes up to?'

'Alterations on the Promenade Deck. We've got to build a conference centre by the time we reach England.'

Nobby took a swig at his beer. 'That will be for the top brass,' he commented knowledgeably. 'We carry a lot of VIPs. They feel safe on a ship this size.'

Nobby glanced at Müller enquiringly.

'Have you been to sea before, mate?'

'For many years,' Müller replied confidently. 'Carpentry is just a job I got into. My last ship was torpedoed.'

'What was her name?'

'The *Empire Rose*. She was sunk four days out of New York.'

'Rotten luck,' Nobby commiserated. 'Why, there's a bloke who works in the kitchen, one of the cooks, who was on her too. At least, I think it was the *Empire Rose*.'

Instinctively Müller tightened his grip on the glass he was holding. Surely there had been no survivors from the *Empire Rose*? That was what US Intelligence officers had told him in Norfolk. The lifeboat survivors had also been convinced that their shipmates had drowned . . .

'In fact that's him over there,' Nobby said, nodding towards a short, plump man in white overalls in the far corner. He was drinking with several other men dressed in cooks' overalls, his dark hair slicked well back, his bulbous nose stuck into a pint glass.

'Remember him?' Nobby asked.

'Can't place him exactly,' Müller answered uncertainly, then dropped his voice. 'Look, I know this sounds strange, but I want to forget the *Empire Rose*. It was a bad experience.'

The Englishman's eyes were sympathetic. 'I understand, mate. Must be terrible, having to go through all that. All the same, if you want to meet him any time I'll arrange a drink.'

Müller thanked him and memorised the cook's face. The last thing he wanted was to meet the man at close quarters.

Nobby gulped down the rest of his beer. 'Come on, let's go and watch the show,' he said and led the way out on to the deck.

Pier 90 was bustling with activity. Large cranes were still swinging crates on board, while longshoremen hustled energetically up and down the gangways. The lights of New York were reflected on the dark waters of the Hudson, and on the quay the instruments of an army brass band shone in the floodlights.

'Now, bring on the band!' Nobby shouted.

There was a hoot, and a multi-decked ferry nosed her way into the pierhead, running at right angles to the *Queen Mary*'s bows. She had crossed from New Jersey, her decks packed with soldiers. As the ramp dropped, the band took its cue and broke into the 'Stars and Stripes'. Led by a party bearing regimental colours, the first GIs marched down the gangway and on to the quay. They were in full kit, helmets gleaming. On they came, in broad columns which split and converged on each gangway, like a parade-ground display.

They were men of all ages and sizes, each laden with bulging kitbag, cape and gas mask. Rifles were slung over their shoulders, and bayonets, mugs and ammunition clinked as they marched. Each GI had a number chalked on his helmet, designating his quarters on board, and soon they were packed into every conceivable space that could hold a sleeping man. The lucky ones got bunks, where they were allocated a specified eight-hour sleeping period before a comrade took over. Even the ship's swimming pool had been emptied and converted into a dormitory.

Hour after hour the troops marched aboard, over 10,000 men, a full infantry division. As soon as one ferry disembarked another tied up, and yet another could be seen on its way. All the time the band played away, marches from Souza to Irving Berlin.

It was after ten o'clock when the music faded and the last infantryman was checked aboard. The cranes rolled back and longshoremen stood ready to cast off the nine-inch ropes from the bollards. Six tugs had secured lines on the *Queen Mary*'s bows, ready to pull her away, like a team of shire horses. Another three were butting up to her stern.

The deck crew calmly took the ropes inboard, watched by GIs lining the ship's sides in their thousands.

Orders were shouted from the *Queen Mary*'s flying bridge as the last ropes snaked through the air. Almost imperceptibly the great hull began to move, the bows inched out into the Hudson, and a widening stretch of black water appeared between the wall of the ship's side and the quay. When she was well out into the river Müller felt the shudder from the liner's engines and stood enthralled as the jagged skyline of Manhattan slid past. For the first time in many weeks he felt confident and at ease.

Dawn rose over the Biscay port of Lorient, tinting the sky a flaming red. In the half light U-1264 slid out of her concrete pen, past the bomb-shattered quays. Her tanks were full of diesel and she had enough supplies aboard for a six-week war cruise. On her bridge Kapitanleutnant Werner Hartstein shouted out orders to bring the U-boat's bows towards the harbour entrance and the ocean beyond. A minesweeper led the way, winking her signal lamp, and a flight of long-range Ju 88's roared overhead to provide air cover.

Hartstein grinned a welcome at the aircraft, and pushed his battered white cap to the back of his head. His face was still sun-tanned. Only a few days before, the boat had arrived home to the welcome of a brass band and popping of champagne corks after a victorious cruise off the Cape. Hartstein's sinkings had been recorded in a fresh row of white ships painted on the conning tower, and he was proud of the tally, which had made him the second top-scoring U-boat ace.

But the celebrations had not lasted long before orders arrived from U-Boat Command that U-1264 was to be turned round immediately for a special mission on the North Atlantic.

Hartstein had given his men just a few hours on land, enough time to get around the bistros and brothels before coming back to face the northern ocean. While the crew were ashore the captain had been delighted to receive a special message of personal commendation from the C in C of the Kriegsmarine, together with the news that he was to command his own group of six U-boats on the mysterious operation ahead. Hartstein had wondered what the mission entailed, and he had been intrigued when a despatch rider delivered sealed orders issued by Naval Headquarters, which were only to be opened on transmission of a coded signal direct from Berlin.

Shortly afterwards three trucks from the Torpedo Experimental Institute arrived under heavy guard, and when their doors swung back Hartstein had been delighted to see a gleaming row of new Zauenkönig acoustic torpedoes. Specialists had come aboard to instruct the crew in the handling of these latest weapons, which had the eerie capability of hunting a ship like a bloodhound, by homing on to the sound of her screws. Watching the snub-nosed Zauenkönigs being loaded in to U-1264, Hartstein had felt proud that his group had been entrusted to use them on their first operational firing.

The wind freshened as U-1264's bows swung round towards the harbour entrance, and Hartstein looked with satisfaction at the five other boats astern. The deck began to pitch beneath his feet as the U-boat passed beyond the mole, and he turned up the collar of his reefer jacket, anticipating the ocean ahead. Then he shouted for the telegraphist, and commanded him to transmit the first coded signal. Group Hartstein was at sea.

Chapter 16

Late afternoon sun poured into the Downing Street Annexe, dusty shafts beaming through the anti-blast tape on the tall windows and projecting a criss-cross pattern on to Alloway's desk. He looked up from his papers and glanced at the big clock on the wall. It was nearly five, and the pace of work in the large office had quickened perceptibly. Officers from all services were busy preparing reports and papers for the various evening committees. In the far corner Alloway could see three army officers holding an intensive discussion over a study for the Chiefs of Staff, at the desk next to him a naval commander imperturbably compiled a vast abstract of shipping statistics, while beyond the desks at the far end of the room a bevy of typists hammered away at their machines.

Alloway paid scant attention to this hectic activity and instead concentrated on the document before him, the final plans for moving the German prisoners to the Clyde. There would be just over a thousand in all, the large bulk of them coming from Tregaron, but several hard cases from other camps were also to be sent to America. Military convoys would move the POWs from their camps to railway stations, where special trains would ferry them north. Every detail had been taken into account: the number of prisoners per carriage, the kit they were to carry, even the meal breaks en route. Armed troops would cordon every station and each train would be continuously patrolled by camp guards and military police.

The Germans would arrive in Gourock on 29 April and a Clyde steamer would carry them to the *Queen Mary*. Alloway got up and crossed to Barbara's desk just a few feet away. She was wearing a pretty new flowered dress, and the tiredness of previous weeks had disappeared from her face: he hadn't realised before how much the spring sun lifted her spirits.

'Can I have the rest of the Stubbs Committee file?' he asked.

Barbara reached for the buff-coloured folder on her desk.

'Most of it seems to be one great railway timetable,' she said. 'Absolutely amazing.'

'The man who drew it up must have organised the bank holiday trains from Victoria,' Alloway replied, grinning. 'We'll see what the general thinks of it. There's bound to be something . . .'

It was shortly after five when Alloway knocked on the general's door. As he entered the comfortable office the military secretary cheerfully waved him to a chair, then continued to initial the sheet of minutes in front of him. Finally he tossed them into his out tray and lifted his thick eyebrows questioningly.

'I've got the final plans for moving the POWs, sir,' Alloway announced, placing a folder on the polished surface of the desk.

For a few seconds he watched the general's eyes flick from line to line, registering each point. Once or twice he asked a question, but seemed only half interested in the answer. Eventually he came to the schedule of transport movements. Reckoning it would take too much time for him to absorb everything in detail, Alloway gave a quick résumé of the plans that had been made. The general held up his hand.

'That's all right, Alloway. It seems a pretty thorough job to me.' There was a slight smile on his face as he added, 'General Stubbs is a great man for detail. Everything will work like clockwork, I'm sure. But forget that for a moment.

169

There's something else I want you to look into. In a way it's connected with all this.'

Alloway put down his file.

'We've had a request from the Americans via the Combined Chiefs asking whether we would agree to some press coverage of the arrival of their troops in Britain.'

The news came as no surprise. The request was typical of many that came from Washington, only to be refused by the security-conscious British.

'Do they want to cover the men who are arriving aboard the *Queen Mary*?' Alloway asked.

'Yes. Apparently they felt that a news story would do a lot of good for morale on both sides of the Atlantic. No doubt it would give the British the feeling that Uncle Sam was here at last, while it would tell the Americans that big events are in the offing. Whether they are or not is, of course, another matter.'

'What about the security problem? We don't want to advertise the position of the *Queen Mary*, do we, sir?'

'That's been a major consideration with the Chiefs of Staff, but the PM is very keen on some form of coverage, and thinks the security aspect can be taken care of.' A wry smile crossed the general's features. 'Don't forget that at one time in his career he was a journalist.'

'Over ten thousand Americans are arriving next week, sir, on twenty-ninth April,' Alloway declared. 'That would be an ideal event to cover.'

The general nodded. 'I don't see why we shouldn't agree to the American request. A carefully selected group of journalists could go up to the Clyde, and I'm sure the Americans will look after them very well. The story will have to be held until we give permission for it to be printed, but I'm certain that's not beyond the censors. Also, any photographs or film will have to be carefully checked for security in the usual way.'

He studied Alloway for a moment, then added, 'Anyway, the Germans have been sending regular reconnaissance flights over the Clyde, and it's only a matter of time before they discover that the *Queen Mary* is back. Please let the Americans know that we agree to their request on the strict conditions I mentioned. I'll drop a memo to their theatre commander in Europe. But if you want to pass the message now I've no objection. At least they can't accuse us of stone-walling this time.'

The general stood up and tucked a file under his arm ready for the next meeting, and Alloway made his way back to his own office.

Barbara looked up at him enquiringly as he came in.

'What's the big news?'

'Oh, just that the Americans want to cover the arrival of their troops in Gourock, and we've agreed.'

'Wonders will never cease.'

'Maybe. But just get me Major Van Kleef.'

It took a few moments for her call to be passed through three Allied switchboards before Van Kleef came on the line.

'Hi, James.' Dutch's voice was as cheerful as ever.

'I've got news for you. My general says that there's no objection to press coverage of the arrival of your troops in Britain. The PM thinks it will be good for morale, although I don't think the Admiralty are very keen.'

'Well, that's a surprise,' Van Kleef exclaimed. 'I thought they'd block that one.'

'There are conditions,' Alloway warned. He went over the general's points. 'I mentioned the arrival of the *Queen Mary* on twenty-ninth April as an ideal occasion to do this, and he said that there'd be no objection to coverage, but the port of arrival, date and time must be kept secret.'

'The censor can look after that. I'll tell our information boys. They can start organising a press trip right away.' Van Kleef's voice became less official. 'What about a drink—say in an hour's time?'

Alloway glanced at his watch. 'All right. But it has to be a quickie. The night stretches endlessly ahead.'

They agreed to meet in St Stephen's Tavern opposite Big Ben, which was a favourite haunt of MPs, civil servants and the Parliamentary lobby. By the time Alloway arrived, shortly before seven, the downstairs bar was packed: civilians in drab wartime suits and officers of every rank milled around the cellar. Alloway spotted Van Kleef through the melee, sitting across the bar with a glass of whisky in front of him.

'Hi, James. What will you have?'

'A pint of bitter would be fine.'

Clutching their drinks they left the bar and made for a quiet corner. Van Kleef offered Alloway a Camel, then lit one for himself.

'Well, I hope you're pleased with our conversion to the virtues of publicity,' Alloway said.

'We certainly are. Mind you, I still don't believe it.'

'Oh, it'll happen—so long as the rules are kept.'

Van Kleef sipped his whisky and leaned back in his seat. It struck Alloway as extraordinary that the American never looked tired. Even though well over thirty, Van Kleef had the healthy complexion of a much younger man, and his crew cut gave the impression that he was just out of college: Yet Alloway knew from his own experience that Dutch had a shrewd and experienced mind.

'I don't know how the press party is going to be made up, James,' said Van Kleef, interrupting his thoughts, 'but I have a feeling that one of your playmates isn't going to be around for the next few days.'

Alloway knew that Dutch was referring to Tracey, who would certainly be requesting a press pass to visit Gourock.

'That's the trouble when you're friendly with journalists,' he retorted. 'Difficult to deny them favours, especially when they're pretty.'

'You're a brave man,' Van Kleef laughed. 'But I hear you two get on like a house on fire.'

'You could say that.'

'Well, she's attractive all right.'

'It sounds as if you envy me.'

'Any sane man would. I've known her for some time, you know.' Van Kleef cast a steady glance at Alloway. 'Of course, you realise who her father is?'

'She told me. But if you're casting some sort of doubt on Tracey's loyalties I don't think you're justified. After all, your president seems happy to use O'Brien's talents.'

'O'Brien's done well by his daughter. As any father should. He put her into the business and then gave her this plum job in London. She can look forward to a top-class career.' Van Kleef leaned forward. 'Ever since she left college he's sent her around various bureaux abroad.' He paused a moment, then added, 'In 1940, for example, she was in Berlin. Did you know that?'

Van Kleef's words were worrying. Alloway had to admit that Tracey had not told him of her spell in Berlin, where, as a top journalist, she would have had access to senior people in the Nazi hierarchy. And the *Sentinel* was hardly an anti-Nazi newspaper at the time . . .

Alloway fingered his glass thoughtfully, trying to conceal his embarrassment. Was Tracey a danger to him? Even if she was, how could he abandon her? There was no evidence of any kind that she would breach Allied security. He caught Dutch's eyes studying him from across the table.

'So she's worked in Berlin. So did many people, but that doesn't make them traitors.'

Van Kleef chuckled. 'Traitors? Of course it doesn't. If you were in Berlin or in any part of Germany that wouldn't make you a traitor. But you have to admit that you could fall victim to temptations. Especially an attractive woman.'

Alloway angrily put down his drink, his chin set.

Van Kleef spoke in an urgent whisper. 'Sorry, James. I'm not getting at you—or Tracey. There's nothing wrong with the girl. Not that we know of.'

His last words were like an alarm bell. Who were 'we'? Had Van Kleef been sent by American Intelligence, to warn him, or was the major stepping out of line to alert Alloway that he might attract the attention of the security service? It was certain that the Americans would pass any information they had on Tracey to MI5. Alloway pushed his glass away.

'Sorry, Dutch. I'm due back for an early meeting.'

'Haven't you time for another?'

'Next time.' Alloway looked at the marine's sympathetic face. 'Thanks.'

'Don't mention it.'

It was dark outside and Alloway made his way back along the pavement and across the shaded traffic lights at the bottom of Whitehall. He walked towards Storey's Gate where the Defence Committee was to be held in the underground command headquarters. As he crossed Parliament Square he turned Van Kleef's words over in his mind, wondering whether he should go to see the general and tell him of his friendship with Tracey. He still couldn't believe that she was a security risk. It seemed wildly improbable, but if her connection with him became known she could be deported to the United States, and that would be the end of his career as well as the affair. The press visit to Gourock had come as a godsend: it would take her out of London for a few days and give him time to think.

He reached the sandbagged entrance to the underground HQ and made his way down the narrow concrete steps.

Churchill's war headquarters were established in a warren of reinforced chambers scooped out of the London clay deep below Whitehall. At its centre a communications room maintained contact with Washington and British forces throughout the world. A map room close by kept an up-to-the-minute display of the war situation, for immediate use by the prime minister and Chiefs of Staff. Churchill also had his own small cubicle close to the Cabinet Room where a BBC microphone had been installed ready for an immediate broadcast to the nation. On the concrete walls above the cot-like bed hung two simple illustrations, a constant reminder of crucial considerations in Britain's defence. The first, a hand-drawn chart, showed the state of play in the battle of Britain's life-lines. Black bars, representing sinkings month by month, often surged alarmingly ahead of parallel yellow columns of new launchings. Pinned next to it, a coloured schoolroom map of the United Kingdom showed the availability of forces to resist an invasion. Bright red lines ran from East Anglia, across the Thames Estuary and along the Kent and Sussex coast. Even in 1943 there were still some dangerous gaps.

Alloway strode through the long corridors, passing dimly-lit chambers where committees were already in session. Eventually he reached a small utility office a short distance from the main Cabinet Room. It was one used by more junior members of the Defence Office whilst waiting to be summoned to the various committees, and on this occasion it had only one occupant, a middle-aged naval

174

commander, working frantically on a detailed table of shipping statistics. These were usually the first item on the Defence Committee agenda, and Churchill was known to study them closely.

Alloway's desk was at the end of a row of three, against the bare wall of the chamber. It was only four feet across, and sparsely equipped with a utility blotter and black Ministry telephone. The Stubbs Committee's file had been sent over in a locked box by Barbara. Other staff papers Alloway was working on were locked in an iron trunk next to his desk. He opened the lid of the trunk and drew out a file on the Mediterranean strategy: his next task was to complete an analysis of Allied strategy, a job which absorbed him. Drawing on British and American staff papers, as well as decisions made at summit meetings, Alloway had to set out the latest arguments for landings in either Sicily, Greece or the South of France. He had just drafted the introduction when the commander hustled away in the direction of the emergency Cabinet Room, armed with his tables, to return thirty minutes later looking careworn and fatigued.

'You must have had a grilling,' Alloway said sympathetically.

The commander nodded. 'There's been a big convoy battle south of the Azores. Losses have been heavy. Between you and me, it's shaken the PM. But there's not a lot you can do against forty U-boats.'

'Forty? Can they concentrate that many?'

'Afraid so,' the commander replied grimly, packing his papers into a battered black briefcase. 'Well, I'll be off to the Annexe. I've got masses of work piled up there, and it all has to be done by morning. Ah well, when the war ends I hope that one of the fruits of victory will be a bloody good sleep.'

Alone in the room, Alloway yawned and was wondering whether he too would be needed when an ATS lieutenant put her head round the door. She was a skinny woman with grey frizzled hair and a face devoid of make-up. She would have made an excellent headmistress, Alloway thought.

'Mr Alloway?'

'Yes, Lieutenant.'

'General Ismay wishes to see you.'

Under her eagle eye Alloway swept up his papers and locked them into the trunk, then followed her down the corridor. Soon they were at the outer office of the Cabinet Room.

The general was standing in the middle of the long windowless chamber studying a sheet of paper. Two junior officers from the Defence Office hovered round his desk, a mahogany monument borrowed from the India Office.

Without a word Alloway's chief thrust the sheet of paper towards him. It was in the prime minister's own scrawling hand and contained a simple message to President Roosevelt:

> *Former Naval Person to President*
> *It seems most necessary that we meet together at the earliest possible moment to settle the question of Sicily and the exploitation of our Mediterranean victory. The Burma campaign too needs our joint decisions, and I am deeply concerned about the shipping stringency. There are many questions for us to decide. I can be with you within two weeks. Please say whether you would like this.*

The general spoke quietly, the weariness in his voice unmistakable. 'The PM has just decided he wants to see the president urgently. I want you to get this telegram away through the communications room at once. One-Time Pad.'

'I'll take it up to the cipher room now, sir.'

The general nodded and rubbed his eyes. 'We shan't be needing the POW report tonight. The PM is quite happy with our arrangements.' He smiled. 'It seems as if the Nazi POWs won't be the only ones crossing the Atlantic next week.'

Chapter 17

The *Queen Mary* rolled majestically in the Atlantic swell. A steady easterly wind was strengthening, and spray broke intermittently over the ship's bows and sheeted across the bridge.

In the wheelhouse an eight-man watch kept a steady eye on the advancing rollers, while on the exposed decks the anti-aircraft gunners sat huddled in their oilskins. In spite of the wind they consoled themselves that it was better to be in the open than crowded on the decks below, where thousands of troops were suffering from the incessant pitching and rolling. The lavatories could hardly cope, and the lower decks had the nauseous odour of an enormous sickroom.

In the drawing room on Promenade Deck Müller sweated as he drove a four-inch screw into the main support for the conference table. A rich smell of resin and sawdust filled the air: the large table was almost finished. It had been hard work, and each night Müller had fallen into an aching sleep almost as soon as he turned in. He was thankful that he had been able to reconnoitre the ship whilst she was at Pier 90, but he still had a few areas to cover, and they could only be visited at times when neither Jacobsen nor anybody else would notice. At least, carrying a tool bag, he found that he could pass without any questions being asked.

Jacobsen still worried Müller. He was a hard worker and usually seemed absorbed in what he was doing, but Jacobsen still seemed to feel that his fellow chippie was not pulling his weight. When he slipped out for some tools, or for fresh supplies of timber, Jacobsen would somehow lift his head, or make a sarcastic comment about Müller 'dodging the column'. He was reaching the conclusion that Jacobsen's inquisitiveness was becoming dangerous. Once or twice he suspected Jacobsen of following him, and had lain in wait for him in one of the darker passageways, listening for the soft tread of Jacobsen's rubber soles; but the carpenter never appeared. All the same, Müller believed that it was only a matter of time before his workmate became more curious still and then might shadow him in earnest.

He picked up another 1½-inch screw and began to turn it into the soft underside of the table. As he did so he went over SKL's plan in his mind to check every vital detail. In his briefing Padilla had continually underlined the specific objectives to be seized and the order in which they were to be taken. He had already reconnoitred the lower decks where the prisoners were likely to be placed, and had tried to guess where the key British units would be positioned. Moving round the liner, he had familiarised himself with the position of the stairs and companionways, which it would be essential to control once the operation was under way.

The first priority on SKL's list was control of the ship's wireless room and bridge; this was vital to prevent any distress calls which might mobilise the Allied navies. By pretending to be on another errand, Müller had managed to get on to the sports deck where the radio-receiving room was housed. Boldly he had put his head round the door and asked for directions to the gym, at the same time taking in the rows of dials and amplifiers, and the six operators.

He was pleased to have succeeded so easily, but it was too dangerous for him to carry out the same procedure on the bridge where access was strictly forbidden to all except the watch. Instead, he listened to the gossip of the men who manned the bridge, especially the quartermasters responsible for steering the liner. In this way he built up a mental picture of the layout of the ship's nerve centre. At the same time he sought any clue in the men's idle conversation as to the whereabouts of any arms and ammunition. The take-over plan called for arming the prisoners at the earliest possible moment, but so far Müller had failed to detect the location of any armoury. He had begun to grow anxious, but there was little he could do except keep his eyes and ears open and bide his time.

The remaining objective which had to be seized was the engine room. On the first evening out from New York he had gone down into the heart of the ship where he discovered a narrow door into the for'ard engine room. He opened it gingerly and peered into the vaulted chamber. The great turbines thundered their power to the four screws while a white-overalled engineer officer watched the gauges on the control platform and the two greasers patrolled the catwalks. Müller stared fascinated, the heat and smell of the engine room bringing back his days in U-1543.

'Interested, mate?' a voice said over his shoulder, and he turned to face a burly engineer in his late thirties.

'Just wanted to see this wonderful machinery of yours. Sorry if I've caused any bother.'

The look of suspicion on the engineer's face faded.

'Why, you keen on marine engineering?' he asked in a strong Welsh accent.

'I am, yes. I want to qualify one day.'

'Fine thing. Follow me and I'll show you round.'

Müller duly climbed down the steep ladder after him to the control console, and was given a tour of the engine room and the vast power unit, the Welshman totally unaware that he was lecturing an experienced member of the German Navy.

An hour later, back in his work-place again, Müller turned the last screw and massaged his wrist as he crawled from under the table. Jacobsen was taking a breather, sitting on the edge of the table. He seemed in a relaxed mood.

'If you've finished let's go and have a beer,' he said cheerfully. 'I reckon we deserve it.'

'Okay, Nat,' Müller agreed, wiping sweat off his forehead, and soon they were making their way towards the Pig and Whistle. Soldiers were lounging about everywhere, especially in the gangways, their kit piled up as pillows, and some complained bitterly as they moved to allow Müller and Jacobsen to pass.

Many GIs were in a bad way, suffering from sea sickness. The odour of cigarette smoke mixed with the familiar stench of vomit turned Müller's stomach. Even U-boats had not been this bad.

The bar was full of old North Atlantic hands, and he felt relieved to escape the hospital ship atmosphere.

'Don't tell me you've finished?' It was Nobby, his face registering mock surprise.

'Almost,' Jacobsen replied.

'Let's hope it stands up in this weather,' Nobby joked, before shouting across the bar, 'Hear that, Bosun? They've almost finished. Seems as if they're planning to put their feet up.' He looked scathingly at Jacobsen's tennis shoes.

'We'll soon see about that,' the bear-like figure growled. 'There's always plenty of work for chippies.'

'I hope you've done a good job on that conference room,' Nobby jibed. 'You never know who might use it.'

Müller was keen to know the answer himself, but instead he shrugged casually and replied, 'It may not be the most beautiful room in the world, but it's so well built even the king would be happy to use it.'

Nobby gave him a sharp nudge.

'Here, gone to sleep or something? 'Bout time you bought a round. And while you're at it buy one for this bloke too. He was a shipmate of yours.'

Müller swung round to see the urbane face of Williams, the cook from the *Empire Rose*. His cheeks were marked with the broken veins of a heavy drinker, his eyes listless and tired from long shifts in the ship's kitchen.

'I'm Bill Williams. Funny, I don't remember you aboard the *Rosie*.'

'I only sailed on her last voyage. That's my kind of luck,' Müller answered cautiously.

'That was the one trip I missed, thank God. The only one in about four years—wasn't well.' His face grew sad. 'It was tragic the way she went, though. I could have sworn that ship would come through the war. The number of times Jerry had a go at her . . .'

Müller nodded, and felt his apprehension grow. Williams shifted his bulk.

'A great shame that Duffy and MacKendrick were lost. Remember them?'

Müller had never heard of either man.

'Nice boys, weren't they?' Williams prompted.

Müller had to respond. 'Sure.'

'What did you make of Benbow then? He was a right character, wasn't he? I trained him, you know.'

This time Müller managed to identify one of the cook's mates from a rambling chat he'd had with Larsen. 'Don't think I ever saw him sober,' he replied with confidence.

Standing four-square in front of Müller, Williams continued to reminisce. At regular intervals he would raise his arm to gulp from his pint glass, seemingly intent on moving one by one through the tramp steamer's entire company. Some names Müller recognised, but most he had never heard of, and his mind raced furiously over every scrap of information he could recall from the lifeboat—off-hand remarks by Larsen, the rambling words of the skipper, even the demented rantings of Staines.

The cook plodded on, and Müller left all the talking to him, relieved that the other drinkers seemed bored.

'Whereabouts are you working on board, Bill?' he asked politely, trying to change the subject as the cook swallowed another mouthful.

'In the kitchen. Where I've always worked.'

'It must be tough down there with thousands of extra mouths to feed,' Müller added quickly, feeling slightly stupid.

'It's murder. I'm in charge of the meat, and the Americans eat all the bloody time. You try and feed over ten thousand men twice a day on rump steak—it's a hell of a job. Plenty of big joints and steamed puddings, that's all they're getting. And eggs boiled by the case.'

As he listened Müller felt the bar tilt behind his back: the ship was breasting a massive Atlantic roller. Glasses clattered along the counter, but Williams held his ground firmly.

'She doesn't roll well, this one,' the cook declared. 'Not like the old *Rosie*, eh Larsen? Tell me, what did you think of the skipper's technique when she got into a real gale?'

Müller hesitated. He felt awkward, not knowing what to answer. Nobby, and most of the other drinkers appeared to be listening now, particularly Jacobsen, who was standing by Nobby's shoulder.

'Come on, Larsen,' the carpenter crowed. 'Don't keep us in suspense.'

Müller picked up his glass and slowly swallowed a mouthful of beer, praying that Williams would be unable to contain himself from supplying his own answer. Sure enough the temptation to tell a good story proved too much for the cook.

'Captain Matthews used to shut down both engines to half ahead,' Williams went on. 'Then he'd off-load number one hold, if he could. Even threw a couple of steamrollers overboard once!'

There was a roar of laughter, in which Müller gratefully joined. 'Thank God he didn't have to do that while I was on board,' he said.

'I must admit it's a wonder she stayed afloat,' said Williams. He turned to the others. 'Still Tiger—that was the ship's cat—he always knew what was going on. He used to hide in my galley. It's a shame about him.'

'Yes.' Müller added fondly, 'He was a nice cat.'

Williams stopped laughing, a puzzled look on his face.

'You must be thinking of another ship, mate. Tiger died on my last voyage, the one before the *Rosie* caught it. The whole crew mourned him. They reckoned it was an omen.'

Müller felt the momentary silence, the faces watching him, and he was aware of Jacobsen leaning forward attentively.

'Of course I am,' Müller declared breezily. 'She also had a cat called Tiger.'

Jacobsen raised his thick eyebrows. 'Which ship was that?'

'A Norwegian coaster. She went down in the North Sea, second year of the war.'

Jacobsen's broad face was close to Müller's now, and his breath smelt of drink. 'That's interesting. I didn't know you'd been sunk twice. You've never mentioned it before.'

Müller's mind went back to the sinking. He could still see the defenceless coaster where she had been struck from a torpedo from his U-boat. It had taken only two minutes for her to disappear, the only trace left on the surface a dead cabin boy, and an oil-stained lifebelt marked . . .

'She was called the *Kristina*,' Müller said quietly. 'Not a very big ship. You can look up her details in Lloyd's register if you're that keen.'

Jacobsen stood uncertainly for a moment. His eyes seemed to clear.

'Just interested to know,' he muttered. 'After all, you meet all kinds of people aboard a ship. They've all had different experiences.'

The cook nodded sagely and Müller saw his chance. 'There are some experiences we all want to forget,' he spat out, and the other seamen murmured their assent. Jacobsen stretched out his palms in a placating gesture.

'Okay, I understand,' he said.

'Do you, mate?' Nobby cut in. 'Do you really understand? You ain't ever been to sea before. You're a chippie, aren't you? Well, you ought to learn that there are some things we don't talk about. Being sunk is one of them. Why don't you leave us and go and have something to eat, mate? The grub's served by now.'

Jacobsen stared at Müller. He seemed to be embarrassed, searching for words. Finally he banged down his glass and pushed his way out of the bar.

Müller continued drinking for the rest of the evening in the Pig and Whistle, and turned in early. He lay in the darkness of the crew cabin, listening to the regular breathing around him. As the liner smashed through another wave his bunk lurched and the sleeping seamen rolled instinctively to avoid being thrown out of their bunks on to the floor. For a moment Müller recalled how he had stood shackled to the conning tower of U-1543 in such storms, and wondered how he had ever survived the freezing seas which had smothered him and left him gasping for air.

His mind came back to the *Queen Mary*. According to his calculations she was now approaching the coast of Ireland. It was vital he checked that the radio and explosives were still secure and in such heavy weather there would be few men around to notice him making his way to the lower decks. He swung his legs over the side of his bunk and wriggled his feet into his canvas shoes. Like most men on the Atlantic Müller slept in his clothes and had only to pull on his heavy seaman's jersey to be fully dressed.

He slid open the cabin door and went out into the

passageway, steadying himself against the pitch of the deck. Quickly he made his way down the companionways and staircases, several times stopping and waiting in the shadows to make sure that he was not being followed. The ship's lighting at these levels was dim, and he had to think hard to find the exact position of the hideout. The further forward he went the more difficult it became to keep his footing, and several times he needed all his seaman's experience to stop himself being smashed against the steel sides of the passageway. Each time, as the giant bows rose and the 80,000-ton hull breasted another roller, Müller felt that he was being taken aloft in a monstrous lift, only to have his stomach heave as the bows crashed sixty feet down again. When he reached the bow chamber door, he threw his weight against the handle. Judging the movement of the ship, he yanked it open, falling inside.

On all fours he crawled across the fetid chamber, and reached the niche where the radio was hidden. Expectantly, he put his hand down into the gap between the edge of the deck casing and the wall. To his relief his fingers touched the sacking: the explosives were still firmly in place. For a moment he rested to regain his strength, breathing deeply, then crawled back through the hatch.

He climbed up the ladders and stairways and cut through D Deck, which contained food storage rooms and freezers for the ship's kitchens. Müller had begun to move swiftly past the long row of refrigerator doors when a dumpy silhouette appeared at the end of the passageway. Anxious to take no chances, he pressed himself into the doorway, breathing evenly. The man's footsteps drew nearer, then stopped a short distance away. Müller peered out. Just ten feet in front of him a squat figure in chequered trousers and stained white overalls stood reading a notice on one of the cold stores. A shaft of light illuminated his features and Müller recognised the ruddy complexion of Williams, the cook from the *Empire Rose*. Williams stopped reading and, with some effort, pulled open the freezer door and stepped inside. On tiptoe, Müller made his way across and slowly put his head round the open door. Inside were row upon row of frozen lamb carcasses hanging from meat-hooks.

They glistened in the electric light, and at the back of the freezer there were mammoth hunks of beef. Williams's breath hung upon the air as he scrutinised the first row of meat. With a heave he unhooked a carcase of lamb and dumped it against the left-hand wall, as if it were a frozen log. As Müller watched, the cook disappeared behind the line of frozen flesh to inspect the next row. Müller stood silently listening to Williams humming, and to the crunch of crystallised ice on the refrigerator floor. There was a numbness in Müller's cheeks and he could no longer feel his chin at all. No man could stand such cold for long. Soon the cook would have finished choosing the meat for the next day's meal, and would be leaving.

His battered black shoes moved towards the end of the row, and Müller remembered how his idle questions had almost exposed him. For a fleeting moment it seemed wrong to kill such a kindly man. He had done nothing to deserve it, any more than Larsen had. But Müller had to survive . . . Slowly he reached out and pushed the door shut. He could no longer hear the cheerful humming as he swung the steel lever across. Locked inside, Williams would not last long. In his flimsy kitchen clothes the cold would soon bite into him. Nor could any cry be heard from behind the thick insulated door. From his experience of the Arctic, Müller knew exactly how long he had to wait before the freezer had done its work. After ten minutes he pushed back the steel lever and cautiously wiped the handle to remove any fingerprints. Then he walked back to his cabin and was soon nestling in the warm cocoon of his bunk.

Sun broke through the woolly clouds, towering high over the ocean, and brightened the flecked sea. The wind had dropped, and the morale of the GIs began in turn to rise, as stomachs recovered now that the worst rocking and heaving of the ship had stopped. The *Queen Mary* throbbed forward at a steady twenty-nine knots and men began to emerge from their makeshift bunks, going out on deck to enjoy the air and sunshine. The luckiest GIs found themselves sheltered patches of warmth behind ventilators and lifeboat stanchions, whilst others lined the rail gazing at the broad wake furrowing the Atlantic.

At mid-morning the drone of engines heralded the arrival of an RAF Sunderland flying boat, sent to warn off marauding U-boats. She lumbered past, winking a signal. Land was only two hundred miles away.

Müller breathed in the exhilarating air to clear his head of sleep, then went to the crew's mess for breakfast. The narrow table was crowded with seamen. He took a covered plate of bacon and eggs and went to sit next to Nobby, who grunted a curt acknowledgment. Most of the crew were eating heartily, washing their meal down with mugs of strong black tea. Across the table a bleary-eyed Jacobsen gave Müller a thin smile. He had been suffering from a hangover but now showed signs of appetite. He extended a large hand and picked up the bottle of tomato ketchup, pouring it liberally over a plateful of scrambled eggs.

'How much longer before we reach Scotland?' he asked.

'Maybe first thing tomorrow morning,' said Nobby, pouring himself some tea. 'Depends on whether the Navy has diverted us to avoid any U-boats.'

Jacobsen emptied his mug and slammed it down on the table. 'I'm looking forward to some shore leave.'

'Shore leave? You'll be lucky.' One of the ABs laughed. 'We turn round in about forty-eight hours, and all the space in the tenders and ferries will be needed. There won't be any joy rides.'

'I'll ask all the same,' Jacobsen replied.

Nobby was wiping his plate clean with a piece of freshly baked bread. He looked at Müller.

'Heard the news?'

Müller looked back quizzically.

'Old Williams,' Nobby went on. 'They found him frozen to death in the meat store this morning.'

Jacobsen stopped eating.

'God! How the hell did that happen?'

'Nobody knows. An accident. The door wasn't locked or anything. He must have fainted or had a heart attack.'

'Those sides of beef can be very heavy,' a brawny seaman at the end of the table interjected. 'He might have overdone it. He wasn't a young man. But a nasty way to go.'

Müller spooned sugar into his tea and stirred it thoughtfully. 'That's really bad,' he said.

'He was stiff as a board when they found him,' Nobby elaborated. 'His face was pressed against the foot of the door, and the poor bastard's body was actually stuck to the floor.'

Müller listened silently, but he couldn't feel any great sorrow now for the man who had unwittingly become such a threat to him.

'God!' he exclaimed.

Jacobsen shook his mop of hair, his eyes sad. 'I still can't believe it. Who's to know it was an accident?'

Müller's hand instinctively tightened on his table knife as he sliced through a piece of bacon.

'Nonsense,' Nobby exploded. 'Who the hell would want to kill Williams? He'd never hurt anybody. As long as I've been on this ship I've never known anybody murdered. None of the crew anyway. Some dowager got shoved out of a porthole a few years back, but none of the crew.'

'Well, there'll be an investigation,' the burly seaman explained. 'The staff captain has handed it over to the American security people. They'll soon be nosing into everything. There might be some criminal types among those Yanks— gangsters, Chicago types.'

Müller shook his head sadly.

'But who'd knock off old Williams, and what for? An extra steak or something? Be serious.'

Nobby rolled a cigarette into a neat tube. 'I don't think there'll be much of an enquiry. Not if they're satisfied it was an accident.'

Müller thought quickly. If they questioned him his alibi was sound. He had been asleep at the time, and there was nobody to say otherwise.

Chapter 18

It was after midnight, and a deceptive calm had settled over Churchill's underground headquarters. In the communications room the duty sergeant sat with his feet propped against a filing cabinet, gently dozing over a *Times* crossword. The clatter of a machine brought him to his feet, and he hurried over to the teleprinter concerned, one of three lining the right-hand wall. It was still humming and displayed a sheet with the stark heading 'Top Secret'. From its coding and time of arrival the sergeant recognised it as a message to be deciphered and conveyed to the prime minister's staff as soon as possible.

Ten minutes later the message had reached Alloway's desk, placed there by a tired Signals major. The soldier peered down through owlish glasses and announced, 'One-Time Pad. Came in at 09 hours.'

Alloway glanced at the clock. They certainly hadn't dawdled.

'It's from the president,' the Major explained, reminding Alloway of some testy Latin master. Nodding his thanks, he quickly scanned the deciphered words.

The general, as Military Secretary of the War Cabinet, was insistent that he should be shown all messages from Washington at once. Alloway got to his feet as the major, muttering words about 'passing over responsibility', left the office. A moment later he was in the outer office of the Cabinet Room. As he expected, General Ismay was still cloistered with the Defence Committee. A young assistant in the Cabinet Office, the general's aide, shrugged his shoulders helplessly.

'They may be hours yet. If it's urgent you have to go in and brave the great man's wrath.'

Alloway nodded. He knew only too well that the PM

could become irritated with people distracting his meetings—especially junior staff. He crossed the anteroom and, throwing his weight on to his uninjured leg, carefully slid the door aside, praying that he was not creating any disturbance. A pall of tobacco smoke greeted him. About twenty men were sitting round a hollow square made up from iron-legged War Department tables. They carried utility pencils and note pads, and there were a number of water flasks and glasses dotted around. Alloway spotted a few half-empty whisky bottles.

The Chief of Air Staff was addressing the meeting, standing next to an easel which displayed a target map of Germany. Alloway suffered his bleak stare a moment, then heard him continue with a rundown on squadron readiness and bomb loads. Trying not to disturb the ministers, he made for General Ismay, whom he saw at the far table. Everyone in the room seemed tired, and the First Sea Lord dozed, chin in hand. Next to him the Chief of the Imperial General Staff languidly pencilled a few notes, his eyes darting from side to side whenever a telling point was made. Alloway cautiously went on past the massive back of Lord Cherwell, the prime minister's scientific adviser, keeping an anxious watch on the man who dominated the room, Winston Churchill.

Hunched in a blue siren suit open at the neck, Churchill was wide awake, busily pondering the elegant arguments of the Air Staff. A massive Havana was clasped in one of his small hands, and his brow was creased in concentration. Alloway finally negotiated the corner of the table where the prime minister was sitting, and felt suddenly nervous as Churchill's famous pale blue eyes cut uncomfortably through him. For a dreadful moment he thought that the prime minister would dress him down like some clumsy schoolboy, and was relieved when Churchill switched his attention elsewhere.

The general saw Alloway and leaned forward to take the slip of paper.

'Received twelve minutes ago, sir. From the president,' Alloway whispered, and saw Churchill glance towards him, having obviously overheard.

189

'Well? What is it?' he growled.

The Chief of Air Staff stopped, then asked, with a touch of acerbity, 'Shall I go on, Prime Minister?'

Churchill waved his cigar. 'Hold on a moment. Let's sort this thing out.'

He grabbed the slip of paper and scanned it through the spectacles perched on his snub nose. A slow smile crept across his face, and in his deep voice he rumbled, 'I think the Cabinet and Chiefs of Staff will be interested in this message I have just received from the president.'

As if quoting from the Bible Churchill majestically read out Roosevelt's words:

'Washington. *To Former Naval Person.*
I agree we have much to talk about. Now is the critical moment. We shall be delighted to see you and your staff in Washington by May. President.'

'Gentlemen,' Churchill added, 'the next meeting with the president may be the most important of the war. We have to decide where the Alliance is going. Have no doubts there will be strong American pressure for a cross-Channel assault at the earliest possible moment. However, we must consider every alternative, especially the immense advantages of pushing forward immediately against the enemy's soft underbelly, Sicily, then on to Italy herself.'

There was a silence as his words were digested.

'It will not be an easy session,' he continued, 'and I shall be taking the Chiefs of Staff, the Foreign Secretary and a powerful delegation with me.'

He turned to Ismay.

'It is imperative that we leave at the earliest possible moment. I want to be with the president by eleventh May. The timing is crucial.'

Alloway hovered in the background, waiting for instructions, but his chief was too absorbed in what the prime minister was saying to notice.

'How are we going to cross the Atlantic?' Churchill asked.

'Prime Minister, I have spoken to the Minister of War Transport and he suggests that we should sail aboard the

Queen Mary. It is in fact the only way available if you are to meet your eleventh May deadline.'

Alloway detected a puckish smile on the prime minister's face as he commented cheerfully, 'An excellent suggestion. I think we are entitled to a little comfort. By all means let's take the *Queen Mary*—unless, of course, we fly.'

At once the Chief of the Imperial Staff intervened. 'I don't think that is a good idea, Prime Minister.'

'Why not? We've done it before.'

'I know, sir, but if you remember it was extremely hazardous and you ended up over the air defences of Brest, which are formidable, to say the least.'

'I totally agree,' the Air Chief Marshal declared.

The First Sea Lord had roused himself and saw an opportunity to protect his capital ships from being used to ferry VIPs.

'The *Queen Mary* is definitely the best answer,' he interjected. 'And she is due here any day. We just cannot spare a capital ship at this time. We are completely stretched and besides, the liner is as fast as any battleship, and she can outrun the U-boats. She can be given an escort for a large part of the way and then rely on speed.'

'She'll be safe, so long as she doesn't run into the *Tirpitz*,' the Chief of Air Staff commented quietly.

'We are on the watch for the *Tirpitz* day and night, as the Chief of Air Staff knows full well,' the admiral retorted.

'Personally, I hope she does come out,' the prime minister added. 'We shall soon deal with her. Indeed, we might sail the *Queen Mary* to the north as a decoy.'

The Chief of the Imperial General Staff sighed. 'I think not, Prime Minister.' Alloway admired his tact as he added disarmingly, 'It will interfere with your schedule in Washington. If you want to be there by eleventh May.'

Alloway began to feel uncomfortable. He was totally ignored, and so listened closely to the discussion. Some of the problems would almost certainly involve him, especially Stubbs's plan to move the German prisoners. The same thought had occurred to the general, who now addressed the prime minister.

191

'There is just one problem we have to face, if we take the *Queen Mary*.'

Churchill's brow puckered. 'Problem? What problem? The ship is available, surely?'

'She is indeed. In fact she's due to disembark the best part of an American division at Gourock in the next forty-eight hours. But on her return trip she is scheduled to carry a thousand German prisoners of war to America. And they are nearly all battle-hardened men.'

There was silence round the table and Alloway wondered how the prime minister would react. It was the Chief of the Imperial General Staff who broke the ice.

'That really is a major security problem, isn't it?'

Churchill moved heavily in his chair, his mouth stubborn.

'Why should it be? We can load as many guards on board the ship as we need, and we will have the Royal Marines with us. The Americans have made arrangements to take these prisoners into their hands, and we want to get shot of them. The Germans will sail on the *Queen Mary* and so shall we. Please look into this by the morning, Mr Secretary. Now let's get on with the agenda.'

Alloway half-anticipated the general's words when he wheeled round to face him.

'Get in touch with the relevant ministries,' he said quickly. 'I want their plans by ten o'clock tomorrow morning. But get the security people; they must meet at eight a.m.'

Alloway edged round the room and left through the steel door. As he closed it he was already drawing up a mental list of all those to be telephoned. There would be no sleep for him that night.

Chapter 19

Müller leaned on the starboard rail of the *Queen Mary*'s main deck and watched the gulls wheeling round the ship as she steamed majestically up the Firth of Clyde. Birds dived screaming on the liner's wake, scavenging among the discarded cigarette packets, candy wrappers and other refuse tossed overboard. A tramp steamer passed downstream, her crew staring in awe at the great hull packed with troops. Beyond the small freighter Müller could make out the hills of Scotland slipping past, and knew that very shortly the *Queen Mary* would be in harbour.

The morning sun warmed him and he enjoyed having time to spare. Only the night before he and Jacobsen had put the final touches to the conference room. It seemed ironic to have performed such good work for the enemy.

On the deck around him the American troops were preparing to disembark. Orders streamed over the tannoy and long lines of men sweated on to the deck loaded with weapons and kit. For many it was their first time out of the USA, and Müller overheard a young lieutenant briefing his unit on how to treat the natives.

A gangly GI, still in his teens, came and stood next to Müller and moodily watched the distant hills. He spoke in a thick southern drawl, and at first Müller had difficulty in understanding him.

'I guess it's okay for you, buddy,' the GI said. 'You'll be seeing your own home quicker than we will.' The American was obviously taking him for a member of the crew.

'Maybe, but we have to cross that damned ocean dozens of times a year. You wouldn't like that, would you?'

The GI shrugged his shoulders and Müller felt gratified that his cover was working perfectly. He realised how fluent he had become in the enemy's language. The anxiety that he might bring suspicion on himself with a false word or by incomplete understanding of English seldom worried him now. Nobody appeared to suspect him and, by keeping close to Nobby, he felt able to discover most of what happened on board.

The only man who still worried him was Jacobsen, but in just three or four days' time, he consoled himself, it would be different: once he took over the ship he could deal with the likes of Jacobsen.

The slate roofs of Gourock had come into view, two miles off the starboard bow. It looked an inhospitable place, yet it held a fascination as the land of the enemy. He might get a few hours' shore leave, despite what some of the crew were saying. It would interest him to see the faces of the people, and he wondered whether they would have the pale, demoralised look of the citizens of Brest or Lorient or even of Germany herself.

With a thunderous blast the *Queen Mary* announced her arrival and, far away across the choppy water, Müller could see the first vessel in a small fleet of auxiliaries butting towards them. Then he heard a rumble from the bows where massive anchors plunged into the sea. Doors in the ship's side were flung open, and the crew expertly rigged a gangway to a pontoon manoeuvred into position by a tug.

As ever, the Americans could not go anywhere without music, and Müller heard the strains of a large brass band on the foredeck. Turning back to look over the side he saw that the first auxiliary, a Clyde paddle steamer, had come alongside. A stained brass plate on her upperworks read *Queen of the Firth*. Two seamen secured the steamer's raked bow to the pontoon and, encouraged by a ragged cheer from the crowded decks, the first GIs began to file down the swaying gangway. It seemed only minutes before the *Queen of the Firth*'s decks were packed with troops and she cast off, swinging back towards Gourock; the next ship was already nosing in to take her place.

Suddenly a hand clapped Müller's shoulder and he turned, instinctively alert. Jacobsen stood before him, his black hair ruffled by the wind.

'Bosun wants to see us in his office right away.'

'What for?'

Jacobsen shrugged, and began to push his way through the milling troops. Müller followed, stepping over kitbags and weapons until they reached the bosun's cabin on the main deck.

The burly figure was sitting behind a small desk. To his left Müller recognised the ship's chief carpenter, an unassuming man who supervised the team of carpenters on board. His bald head was bowed over a set of drawings.

After a sharp look of appraisal, the bosun spoke.

'You two must have worked hard to finish off the new conference area.'

'We sure have,' Jacobsen replied.

'I suppose you're looking forward to a hard-earned rest,' the bosun said with a touch of irony, placing his large knuckles on the table. 'But before you put your feet up we've got some special work to be completed.'

'What special work?' Müller asked, immediately interested.

The ship's carpenter unrolled the plans across the desk. 'We've had a message, telling us to install five ramps in different parts of the ship and to put up a number of notice boards.'

The instructions sounded odd, almost eccentric, and Müller leaned over the drawings with interest. From the elevations drawn by the carpenter he saw that the ramps were to be quite strong, and broad enough to take a bed or trolley.

'Most of them are to be built on the Main Deck,' the chippy explained; 'they are to link the staterooms with the small dining room, crossing the aft staircase, and the for'ard companionway to the bridge.'

It struck Müller as strange that the bridge figured in the plans.

'I've only got enough men for three of these jobs,' the chippy said apologetically. 'I wonder if you chaps could handle the ramp aft, and the one into the dining room?'

Keen to find out more about the strange new plans Müller agreed at once, while Jacobsen reluctantly concurred. The carpenter handed them the plans.

'How long have we got?' Müller asked.

The bosun checked his schedule. 'We sail for New York again on Saturday. Three days—a bit less.'

'We should manage that all right,' Jacobsen muttered.

The carpenter went on to tell them what timber to use and where they could draw supplies. When he had finished Müller casually asked, 'I see that these two ramps have got to be pretty strong. What are they for?'

The chippy shook his head. 'They don't tell us things like that.'

'I reckon they're for some VIP,' the bosun broke in. 'Perhaps an injured general, some high-up like that.'

Müller looked at the chippy and tried another tack. 'You also mentioned notice boards?'

'That's right,' he answered. 'There's about a dozen to be put up, but I think my blokes can cope with that. Although the lettering is a bit odd.'

'How do you mean?'

'Well, the words are in Dutch.'

'Dutch?' Müller wondered whether the carpenter could be mistaken, and consulted the paper the chippy gave him. Dutch words were very similar to German, and he could guess the sense. There were different messages for different notice boards. Some gave directions on how to reach the dining room, others the lounge or Promenade Deck. But they all possessed one expression in common: every one was formally addressed to 'Your Majesty'. Müller smiled and looked round at the inquisitive faces.

'If you ask me I think we are going to have the honour of carrying royalty—the Queen of the Netherlands.'

He glanced at Jacobsen, who was standing moodily beside the drawings.

'Come on,' he said cheerfully. 'Let's get started.'

Tracey O'Brien stood in the bows of the press launch, her khaki-clad legs splayed out against the pitching of the deck. She pulled at her war correspondent's cap and watched the grey steel wall of the *Queen Mary* tower before her. The liner's size was astonishing; the other ships around her seemed like bathtub steamers.

The urbane, middle-aged Public Affairs major in charge of the press party began to hustle the reporters and cameramen on to the well deck, ready to leap on to the pontoon. A newsreel cameraman swore as he staggered forward with his camera, the GIs lining the ship's side watching with amusement as the journalists prepared to come aboard. Eve Kirby, a reporter from the *New Yorker* and the only other woman in the party, stood next to Tracey, enjoying the men's attention. She was a slim thirty-five-year-old, whose short black hair complimented her lean and bony features.

'Christ, there're an awful lot of men up there, Tracey,' she said, with ill-concealed delight.

Tracey pulled the cap tighter. 'Sure are.'

'How do you feel about meeting a few thousand love-hungry GIs?'

'Just my scene,' Tracey retorted, and although she felt distinctly nervous she raised her arm in a friendly wave at the faces above.

Eve turned to the PA major. 'How many men on that ship?'

He screwed up his face, trying to make some calculation, then mumbled, 'Sorry, that's a secret.'

'Well, a lot. You'd agree about that?'

'It's still a secret.'

The photographers were yelling for the launch to be held steady, and Tracey was almost knocked off her feet by one of the cameramen trying to get a shot. For a moment she felt like kicking back, but thought better of it. There was a thud of fenders and engines spluttered, then she felt the PA major propel her forward. Trying not to look at the sea, she jumped for the tilting stage, and two tough seamen eagerly grabbed her like a child. The rest of the party clambered after her, and the major led the climb up the swaying steps to the square entry into the hull. An immaculately groomed young officer in a well-pressed uniform and new cap stood waiting for them. Tracey regarded him as a typical draftee from Madison Avenue; he cast a long, ingratiating look at her.

'Welcome aboard, ladies and gentlemen of the press.' His teeth gleamed like a toothpaste advertisement. 'I'm sure you could all use some coffee, and while you are being refreshed

I can give you our itinerary and the plans we have made for your visit.'

They were led along the busy deck, the men goggling when they saw Tracey and Eve.

'Now I know what it's like to be Betty Grable,' said Tracey.

She could smell the aroma of fresh coffee wafting from one of the staterooms, where a three-star general, commander of the division, stood waiting for them. He had short bow legs and sharp eyes, which glowed when he saw the two female correspondents. Tracey categorised him as the kind of man whose career had been rescued by the war. With ten thousand men under his command he believed that he was on a dazzling path to glory.

He addressed them in a gravelly voice. 'Gather round. I just want to tell you that the Sixty-first is proud to be one of the first fighting divisions of the US Army to land here in the battle zone. We're going to kick shit out of the Germans. All my boys want is a chance to get at them.'

Tracey thought of the young faces lining the rail and wondered if they agreed.

When the speech eventually finished the PA officer eagerly took the stage, clip-board in hand. With a brisk show of efficiency he ticked off the arrangements for the visit while the journalists helped themselves to drinks. The general came over to Tracey and exchanged a few words before stamping out to the click of heels.

'I didn't know we had any Prussians on our side,' Eve commented drily.

They followed their PA officer below and Tracey was impressed by the huge terraces of bunks and the cavernous restaurant. They were led into the kitchens, which seemed even more remarkable. The gleaming ranges which had once provided gourmet menus of duck, lobster and caviar now worked flat out to provide basic meals for ten thousand men.

The bridge was the next stopping point, and on the way Tracey was keen to inspect the staterooms and cabins lining the main deck, hoping to find some pre-war luxury; but only the occasional piece of polished furniture or a few exquisitely veneered panels had been left in place. Bedrooms and suites designed for kings, film stars and millionaires had become spartan offices and orderly rooms. Tracey found one exception. At the very end of the Main Deck, as the rest of the party moved towards the bridge, she peeked through an open door into a large stateroom. Eve had also seen the room, which they found to be unchanged. A large mahogany bed dominated the bed chamber, with built-in wardrobes of immaculate walnut, while, in the lounge, a thick Persian carpet stretched from wall to wall. Eve who had opened the door had been visibly impressed and whistled at the splendour.

They caught up with the journalist's party on the ship's bridge. It seemed an Olympian place. The sun was streaming through the tall windows, sparkling on the brass binnacle and engine room telegraphs. Several immaculately turned-out officers of the watch stood ready to answer the journalists' questions, but everybody stopped when after a few moments the PA lieutenant announced the arrival of the *Queen Mary*'s captain.

The ship's master was a squarely built man in his early fifties. Although he was short in stature an immense natural authority emanated from him, which Tracey assumed came from his total mastery of seamanship. He had a large beak-like nose and his shrewd eyes wandered over the journalists. When he spoke it was with a clear strong voice.

'Welcome aboard, ladies and gentlemen. I hope you enjoyed your little Cook's Tour and that you've got some idea of all the changes and refits we've had to make to carry our wartime passengers.'

Standing with his feet apart, one hand in his pocket, he held an impromptu press conference. One lanky reporter from the *Baltimore Sun* pressed the captain on the *Queen Mary*'s ability to withstand a torpedo attack.

'You must remember that the Germans have to catch us first,' the captain declared.

The reporter seemed unconvinced. 'But if you were hit, would you get all the men off? They would take a long time to evacuate, surely?'

The captain shot a dark glance at the American, and

Tracey imagined that he would have rather thrown him overboard.

'Normally I do not answer hypothetical questions, but on this occasion I will make an exception. Of course we would get every man away.'

'But you haven't enough boats,' Eve interjected.

The captain turned on her, his eyes glowering. 'Madam, I have said: we would get every man away.'

At this point the lieutenant stepped in and fulsomely thanked the captain, happy the interview was over. The captain coolly bade everyone farewell and returned to his cabin.

'Let's go and talk to the boys now,' the lieutenant suggested. It was part of the trip which interested Tracey most because she knew that the American families back home would be passionately interested in how their menfolk were faring.

The lieutenant led them down the broad companionway to C Deck where a group of about twenty soldiers had been assembled in the middle of the public foyer. In peacetime it was a shopping centre, fringed by boutiques and kiosks. Now the signs of jewellers and couturiers had been replaced with the information boards of medical sections, accommodation units and regimental offices for the administration of the troops on board. At the far end of the row there was even an office for the production of a shipboard newspaper, with typewriters and a rotary press.

The soldiers radiated fitness; all of them seemed very young. Immediately the journalists began to fire off questions at them, but most of them gravitated towards Eve and Tracey. 'Give the ladies room to breathe, you men,' a tough sergeant shouted.

The GIs stood back respectfully. Tracey had attracted about six of them, most of whom towered over her, except for a small Italian with slicked-down hair, which had somehow evaded the army barber. He immediately emerged as the regimental jester when she asked, 'What sort of trip did you have?'

'Terrible,' he answered in a thick Brooklyn accent. 'They're going to give me the Purple Star, it was so terrible.

My Momma would have died if she had known what I was going through. Worse than the Germans.' There was a gust of laughter from the GIs.

'You should have seen the waves. They were as high as the Statue of Liberty,' he continued.

'Really?' Tracey said sceptically. 'That's hard to believe.'

'You mean you ain't going to print my story?'

'I'll think about it.'

'Don't listen to him, lady; he was asleep below,' another soldier interjected. 'I saw him. Worse than Rip van Winkle.'

Tracey began to ask about their homes and jobs, jotting down names, home towns, streets and farms, aware of the importance people attached to having their relatives named in the paper. The soldiers' attitudes differed from the general's. Training had been horrible, and every man had been delighted to be going aboard a ship as famous as the *Queen Mary*, where they had innocently expected luxury treatment.

They were even ready to fight, but they didn't relish running into one of Adolf's panzer divisions. Above all, they looked forward to getting home.

Tracey soon had a notebook filled with copy and a comfortable feeling that she had a good story. She had been so busy talking to the men that she had scarcely noticed that the other journalists had started back to the boat.

The PA lieutenant bustled up.

'Come on now, Miss O'Brien. You don't want to stay aboard, do you?'

'Hey, that would be swell,' the little Italian shouted.

Tracey smiled broadly before following the PA lieutenant along the passage.

'Thanks for the help,' she said to the officer as they headed towards bright patches of sunlight marking the entrance in the ship's hold. 'I'm sorry I held you up.'

The soldier seemed flattered and gave her a warm smile. 'Don't worry. I know you have your job to do.'

'There's an awful lot of work going on aboard this ship,' she commented innocently.

'There sure is. Usually we are on our way to New York by now, but there's a whole team of workmen beavering away on the Main Deck, making it ready for a top-level delegation. It must be very special.'

Tracey immediately smelt a story, but saw that they were drawing near the doors in the ship's side.

'What are they doing up there?'

'Installing office equipment. Some of them are building ramps across the stairs and passageways.'

'Ramps?' Tracey echoed. 'Surely those are to handle wounded men? Maybe this liner is to become a hospital ship.' They were almost at the entrance now, and Tracey could feel the fresh air on her cheeks.

'If you ask me', the lieutenant remarked quietly, '—but please don't repeat it—we will be carrying a very distinguished person, a man who cannot walk, because the ramps are just wide enough to take a wheelchair.'

Tracey stopped in her tracks, intense grey eyes on the lieutenant.

'There's only one crippled man in the world for whom they would delay such an important ship—Franklin Roosevelt, President of the United States.'

The officer looked over his shoulder. 'You said it, not me. But I wouldn't be surprised to see half the US government over here by the end of May. Now, if you'll excuse me, I'll see if the boat is still there.'

He strode past her out on to the gangway, while Tracey waited inside, excited at her discovery. She felt certain that the other journalists had not uncovered the story. The smell of the sea wafted through the open doors, and Tracey detected another unmistakable odour—that of fresh paint. A few yards from the entrance a white-overalled signwriter was working carefully on a large notice. To Tracey's surprise the lettering was in a foreign language. She walked towards it.

'Who's the message for?' she asked cheerfully. The signwriter put down his brush for a moment, and perused a scrap of paper in his hands, with a copy scrawled on it.

'They say it's for Queen Wilhelmina. Queen of the Netherlands. It's Dutch anyhow, I know that.'

'The queen's coming on board then?' Tracey suggested knowingly.

'She must be, but don't say anything or you'll get me shot.'

The PA lieutenant reappeared before Tracey could ask any more questions. 'Please come along, Miss O'Brien, or the boat will go without you. I just managed to hold it.'

Tracey apologised and stepped out on to the gangway. The journalists glared up at her impatiently from the launch below, and she quickly descended to the boat, which pulled away as soon as she was aboard.

She climbed unsteadily into the stern, where she collapsed, breathlessly, next to the imposing figure of Eve.

'That was some trip,' Eve said. 'I've got one or two nice stories—let's call them "vignettes of my countrymen preparing for war". How about you?'

Tracey fastened the top button of her khaki jacket, thinking of her conversation with the lieutenant and the painter's remarks about the Queen of the Netherlands. The signwriter's words did not make sense. Queen Wilhelmina was an active woman, not someone bound to a wheelchair. It was clear to Tracey that she was being used as a cover for the much bigger story: the story of Roosevelt coming to Britain.

Tracey realised with a start that Eve was waiting for her reply, and gave her a wistful smile.

'No,' she murmured. 'I don't think I got much out of the trip.'

Chapter 20

It was late evening in London on 4 May when a fleet of ministerial limousines pulled out of Downing Street under police escort. Alloway sat between two of his colleagues in the back of the last Humber saloon. The leading car in the column swung through the masked traffic lights into

Trafalgar Square, and he caught a brief glimpse of the prime minister, his pale blue eyes gazing abstractedly into the distance. The rest of the convoy followed, carrying cabinet ministers, senior military commanders and the top-level advisers accompanying the prime minister across the Atlantic.

The past twenty-four hours had been a frantic scramble in Whitehall, as the Ministry of War Transport had hastily drawn up passenger lists, issued passes and requisitioned an express train to take the hundred-strong party to Scotland. On General Ismay's instructions Alloway had supervised the packing of two hundred top-secret files, all of which had already been shipped to the waiting train.

Many junior staff, typists, telegraphists and cipher officers had been ordered to join the train independently, and Alloway considered himself fortunate to have been given a seat in the prime minister's convoy; General Ismay liked to keep his assistants close at hand.

It was a tight squeeze in the back of the car. On Alloway's left an owlish staff major stared gloomily out of the window at the clubs in Pall Mall. On his other side sat the avuncular naval commander, the one who had presented shipping statistics to the cabinet. The front seat too was occupied, by a lieutenant from the Defence Office. The driver, an attractive girl from the government motor pool, swung the car west through Knightsbridge towards the little-used railway siding at Addison Road, where the special train was waiting.

The major shifted his weight, pushing a sharp elbow into Alloway's ribs. 'With such a large party going to Washington,' he muttered, 'it makes you wonder whether there's anybody left in Downing Street to run the place.'

The naval commander added, 'It'll be a nice break to get away from that damned bunker.'

'Don't tell me the Navy's going soft,' said the major.

'I think we've thoroughly deserved our little trip. I can't wait to see the lights of Broadway.'

Privately Alloway agreed with him. Ever since Ismay had ordered him to join the Washington team he had been delighted at the prospect of his first visit to the States. His instinct had been to ring Tracey to tell her the good news, but Van Kleef's words were still in his mind. Even so, he felt that he could not go away without leaving some word, so he had scribbled a short note, merely saying that he would be busy for a week or so, and unable to see her because of 'war duties'. Even the most suspicious mind in MI5 could hardly find that objectionable.

The cavalcade drove through the heavily guarded entrance of the Addison Road siding. As the limousine slowed to a halt the major withdrew his elbow and climbed out on to the pavement. Alloway followed. Churchill stood some distance away, surrounded by a knot of welcoming officials. For a minute he chatted to them amicably, hands thrust deep into the hip pockets of his short overcoat, a Trinity House cap set at a rakish angle. Then he turned and marched resolutely away towards his carriage, followed by his detectives, advisers and personal valet. Surrounded by a gaggle of aides and secretaries, Alloway trailed after him feeling very much a camp follower.

The procession was ushered into labelled carriages. In Alloway's First Class compartment two army captains from the Joint Planning Staff were already sitting at each side of the window. Both gave him a casual, impersonal nod as if he were joining some exclusive club.

Outside, the platform bustled with activity. Three smart Wrens, part of the twenty-strong cipher team, marched past, caps squarely on their heads. The Royal Marines who would be guarding the party seemed everywhere and, on board, stewards and orderlies sought to make their distinguished passengers as comfortable as possible.

Alloway waited for several minutes until the train had settled down, then left his compartment to report to General Ismay. On reaching his compartment he saw that it had already been turned into a makeshift office. Briefcases and folders were stacked on the seats, while Ismay himself was busy giving dictation to a young lieutenant. The general waved at Alloway to take a seat, and after some minutes' further dictation dismissed his aide and glanced across at his young subordinate.

'The files you requested, sir, are in our top-security trunks in the luggage van,' Alloway began. 'If you require them for the trip . . .'

The general smiled.

His hand moved to an Agatha Christie paperback. 'Excuse me, Alloway, but I have a little reading to catch up on . . .'

Müller sweated up the aft stairway, the long planks of wood cutting into his shoulder. It was the final load of timber to be brought up for the construction of the ramps. With relief he dumped it in a passage off the main deck, where Jacobsen had set up a temporary workshop. Amid stacks of planks and battens the carpenter finished sawing through a nine-inch plank and straightened his back.

'Okay, that's enough timber. Give me a hand here.'

Müller was becoming increasingly irritated by Jacobsen's tendency to hand out instructions, but concealed his feelings, knowing it was vital they keep on reasonable terms. He walked over to the plans pinned to the passage wall. The ramp they were building was wide enough to carry a wheel-chair or trolley, and ran for three decks down the side of the aft stairway, an ornate structure descending to the lower passenger accommodation. Müller could see that they would be lucky to finish the job before the ship sailed.

'I'll give you a hand with the sides,' he said, pointing to the two long shafts, each almost fifteen feet long, which would form the main supports of the ramp, from the Promenade Deck to the landing below.

Jacobsen wiped his brow with a chequered shirt sleeve. 'Yeah, that would help.' His dark eyes appraised the long timber planks. 'Tell you one thing, the Queen of the Netherlands must be one hell of a lady to have all this work done for her.'

'And just for one trip,' Müller added.

He walked to the far end of the stairway and gripped the rough wood. Together they lifted the plank and manoeuvred the long section out of the passageway, then round the balustrade of the staircase. Gingerly Müller edged backwards down the stairs, supporting the weight of the timber, while Jacobsen swung his arm round. It was an awkward move, and Müller was carefully maintaining his balance when he heard a cry from his workmate. The full weight of the timber thrust into his stomach, forcing breath from his lungs. On the stairs above him Jacobsen had slipped and was struggling to maintain his balance. But Müller could hold the load no longer: his foot trod air, staggered and toppled backwards, crashing down the stairs, the wood hurtling past his head like a battering ram. Jacobsen stood dumbly at the top watching as he scrambled angrily to his feet. For a moment Müller was back on the bridge of U-1543, bawling out a stupid recruit.

'You could have smashed my skull, you clumsy bastard,' he shouted.

His words visibly stung the carpenter. 'You think I planned that, or something?' he yelled back.

'You're not fucking competent enough,' Müller spat out. 'There's only one place for people like you.' There was nothing he wanted more, at that moment, than to throw Jacobsen behind barbed wire, along with the rest of the Jews.

The look of concern on Jacobsen's face changed to one of fury. His eyes blazed beneath the black hair.

'Why don't you tell me where you would like to put me? In a concentration camp? Is that right? Is it, Larsen?'

Müller glared back, his hand ready to reach out for any weapon, but his mind was clear and he was conscious that another unguarded statement could blow his cover.

'I'm sorry,' Müller blustered. 'But you could have damn well killed me. I didn't mean anything . . .'

'Okay, okay,' Jacobsen interjected, his face a mask. 'I know we Jews can sometimes be stupid. What do the Nazis call us . . . *Untermensch?*'

Müller returned Jacobsen's stare. 'That's enough, Jacobsen,' he said sharply. 'Don't start accusing me of sympathising with Jew-baiters. I've been torpedoed by them.'

The reference back to the *Empire Rose* seemed to work, and Jacobsen appeared to calm down. Stepping back he picked up the wood. Müller took up the other end and together they moved it into position. They worked in an uneasy silence, and eventually Jacobsen ventured a few words of conversation, to which Müller was careful to react in a friendly way.

For all Jacobsen's words, however, Müller felt certain that

his workmate deeply distrusted him. The expression in Jacobsen's eyes had been unmistakable: an instinctive recognition that Müller was something other than a casual woodworker.

He was convinced that he had to get rid of Jacobsen, and began to turn the problem over in his mind. He remembered that Jacobsen had often talked loudly about wanting to go ashore when the *Queen Mary* arrived in Britain. It had become something of a joke in the crew's quarters, especially when he had threatened to jump ship if his request were not granted. Those words would give Müller his alibi; all he wanted now was opportunity.

It took them the best part of the morning to complete the first stage of the ramp, and Jacobsen leaned back wearily against the wooden frame.

'I guess I'll take an early lunch,' he said.

'Okay, I'll clear up here,' Müller answered, indicating the confusion of tools, timber and shavings on the floor.

Privately, Müller was delighted to be left alone so that he could check on what was happening in other parts of the ship. If Padilla was right, the German prisoners should be arriving on board at any time.

Once Jacobsen had gone, he quickly swept the area around the ramp and piled up the tools before making for the Main Deck. Now that the Americans had left, the liner was strangely empty, even though one or two civilian passengers, no doubt government officials, had come aboard. He turned from the stairway on to the Main Deck.

'All right, hold it there!' Three men in British khaki blocked his way. They looked tough and well trained; Sten guns swung expertly on their bodies. With some apprehension Müller noticed that they were all wearing green berets and bore the shoulder flash of Royal Marine Commandos.

They had secured a thick rope cordon across the passageway. A lieutenant stood behind them, chatting to a tall major whose back was turned.

'You can't go any further,' the marine who had addressed him, his beret pulled down almost to his eyebrows, continued. 'Not unless you've got a pass.'

'Pass? What pass?'

'Special security pass. You've got to have one.'

'Since when?' Müller asked. 'And how am I to get to my work?'

The major sauntered across to them. He was tall and angular; in his early thirties. A revolver was strapped to his thigh. A neat moustache covered his upper lip.

'And who might you be?' he asked querulously, a trace of contempt in his expression.

'Olaf Larsen, sir. I'm a carpenter. I shipped aboard in New York.'

'But you're not American.'

'No, Norwegian.'

The major moved closer. 'And what have you been doing on board?'

'Working with a mate, sir. Doing conversion work.'

'Conversion work?'

'Making a conference room, and now we're building a lot of ramps.'

'Ramps? Who are they for?'

'I don't know, sir. It could be for anybody.'

There was a slight hint of a smile on the marine's face and Müller felt the urge to lash out at the major, but it would have been pointless.

'Well, it seems our security is working better than usual. Now run along, like a good chap.' He turned, leaving the lieutenant to continue.

'This deck is closed. Nobody is allowed through the Main Deck until further orders unless they have a pass. Is that understood? You can use the lower decks to get to wherever you're going.'

Müller turned away, but before he did so he noticed that there was a scene of intense activity farther along the Main Deck. Phones, telexes and cables were being installed by military engineers and filing cabinets wheeled into one of the larger staterooms.

'The lieutenant said you can use the lower deck,' one of the marines repeated pointedly to Müller.

'Of course,' Müller said affably and hurried off in the direction of the stairway. He felt bewildered by this new turn of events. The unexpected arrival of the marines alarmed him. There was no doubt that they were efficient fighting troops. Perhaps they had been sent to guard Queen Wilhelmina? But Müller doubted that the British would spare first-rate troops for that purpose alone.

The Royal Marine cordon on the Main Deck meant that he would have to approach the crew canteen along C Deck, past the open doors in the ship's side. It took several minutes to reach the entrance, and when he drew near Müller made out a mass of soldiers standing like a line of policemen each side of the opening. He was wondering who they were waiting for when he heard the distant sound of men's voices singing a song he had heard often in the U-boat training flotilla, Brittany rest camps and the bars of Lorient:

> *Gib mir deine Hand, deine weisse Hand,*
> *Lebe wohl, mein Schatz, lebe wohl*
> *Denn wir fahren, denn wir fahren*
> *Gegen England.*

It was a favourite German marching song.

With a surge of excitement he moved forward to the entrance and hovered behind the armed British guards who, he noticed, were not commandos but regular troops. Müller peered between their shoulders and saw below the *Queen of the Firth* wallowing at the pontoon, her decks a mass of field grey. Padilla had been right. Müller found himself staring down on hundreds of German soldiers. Their uniforms were faded, and they carried coloured POW identification patches. They also seemed to be carrying all their worldly possessions. Some bore kitbags, others haversacks, even paper parcels. One skinny young soldier was holding a violin case, another a small birdcage.

A British colonel, the prisoners' commandant on board, quietly supervised the arrival of his charges and gave a quick nod of welcome to the first German officer who stomped off the gangway. Müller watched as the officer clicked his heels then marched away in the direction indicated by the commandant. The German's staff followed in his wake and the rest of the prisoners began to file into the ship.

The guards directed the prisoners for'ard, giving each a

label. Müller observed that most of the Germans were sent to the lower D and E Decks, while a chosen few were lucky enough to be put into the more comfortable cabins on C Deck.

A slim and erect figure appeared silhouetted against the sun in the open doors, and Müller thought he detected a rise in tension among the British. He looked closer as the POW stepped inside and saw that the man's short hair and round head gave him a skeletal appearance. His dark eyes stared balefully around at his guards. For a moment they alighted on Müller and there seemed to be a flicker of recognition before he heard the British commandant's clear voice.

'Your accommodation has been specially selected, Major Preuss. I am sure you will enjoy it.'

The German gave a faint smile. 'I trust it is the best on the ship, Colonel.'

'Indeed. For you.' He turned to an NCO and rapped out, 'Escort Major Preuss to the swimming pool, Sergeant.'

Preuss casually strode away, a handful of officers in his wake. Müller watched them go. He felt his spirits rise.

Chapter 21

Alloway stared across the wake of the prime minister's launch at the slate roofs of Gourock receding astern. Over his shoulder a roar of laughter brought his attention back to the well of the boat, where Churchill stood like a dumpy chieftain at the head of his warlords. Somebody had cracked a joke and the prime minister seemed to be enjoying it immensely.

Everywhere Alloway looked there were famous faces, the sun glinting on gold braid and polished leather. Close to the prime minister, Admirals Pound and Somerville stood like two silent sentinels eyeing the launch as it closed with the *Queen Mary*. Next to them General Wavell was holding an animated conversation with the headmasterly General Sir Alan Brooke, Chief of General Staff, and in the stern only a few feet from Alloway stood Lord Cherwell, brooding and detached. It struck Alloway that if the launch were to hit a mine Britain would be robbed of virtually her entire leadership.

The prime minister's voice rose above the roar of marine engines and the hubbub of conversation.

'Take a look at her, gentlemen. A queen indeed.'

The whole company fell silent and watched the side of the liner approach. The monstrous steel plates fascinated Alloway, seamed together by millions of rivets, each rivet driven home by the muscle of a Clydeside shipworker. High above, the neat portholes and square windows of the superstructure resembled the edifice of a London hotel. Only the lifeboats and raked funnels destroyed the illusion, while the sea had washed along the liner's waterline, revealing vivid green algae and rust-coloured barnacles.

Strangely there seemed few signs of life on board, with only a handful of sailors manning the deck. Apart from this small group the only other men visible were soldiers, spaced at regular intervals along the rail above, each armed with a sub-machine gun.

With a firm swing of his boat hook the seaman in the launch's bows gave an elegant salute and the boat nosed gently alongside. Another sailor leapt on to the pontoon and quickly made fast. Before he had finished the prime minister advanced with short, determined steps and jumped on to the pontoon, brushing aside any offers of help. He set off up the gangway, followed by Pound and Somerville. At the ship's entrance Churchill paused for breath, then stepped aboard, touching his cap in a casual salute to Major Summers, the tall, angular commander of the Royal Marine escort, who was supervising the embarkation.

The *Queen Mary*'s captain stood at his side.

'Welcome aboard, Prime Minister. I'm afraid the ship is rather quiet at the moment. It's the security arrangements.'

Churchill shook his hand and muttered something about

'not being able to go anywhere in peace', then marched off with the captain and the chief steward into the ship's interior.

Alloway waited for some minutes until the senior party had cleared the launch, then climbed the gangway himself. When he reached the shelter of the hull the gaunt face of Summers scrutinised him. For a few moments the marine's unblinking grey eyes seemed to look straight through Alloway before giving a glimmer of recognition.

'Welcome aboard,' the major said peremptorily, and briefly consulted a list he held in his hand. 'Your accommodation is on B Deck, Mr Alloway. There's no room on the Main Deck: that's for senior staff.'

Alloway paused.

'Major Summers, you are aware that the mission documents are in the launch immediately behind us. Could you please tell me where they are to be placed on board?'

There was a hint of impatience in Summers's eyes. 'My orders are that the document trunks are to be put in a special registry in the conference area on the Promenade Deck.'

'Good,' Alloway declared. 'Of course they have been under strict guard so far and I assume that will continue, even on board.'

'I think you can leave such matters to me,' Summers retorted.

Alloway gave a thin smile. 'It's just that General Ismay is bound to ask.'

He turned on his heel, happy to have deflated Summers, who seemed to have cast himself as captain of the palace guard.

Alloway followed a marine along several passageways, stopping occasionally to appreciate the ship's architecture, even though much of it had been covered over. Several other passengers, almost all of whom were civilians, were being shown to their accommodation, and Alloway passed one silver-haired gentleman whom he recognised as a very senior government economist, no doubt on his way to an important conference in Washington. There were also small family groups of women and children being shown to their cabins, whom Alloway imagined to be refugees, or the families of diplomats.

B Deck itself was lined with cabin doors, and at one of them his guide halted. A little further on Alloway noticed a glass sign with the lettering 'Cocktail Bar'.

'It seems we have every comfort on board,' he beamed at the marine.

The soldier shook his head. 'No such luck, sir. It's not a bar any more. They've turned it into an armoury. There are enough guns in there for a division.'

'Well, at least I shall be well protected.'

The marine grinned. 'You never know, sir. We have a thousand Jerries on board.'

He threw the door open and Alloway stepped into a small cabin. It looked comfortable, and was furnished in rosewood veneer. Miraculously his luggage had already arrived. He thanked the marine and hefted his main case on to his bed.

There was just enough time for a shower before a five o'clock meeting, called by General Ismay, to organise work on board. Downing Street was at sea.

Müller sat on his bunk in the crew cabin, sipping a mug of tea. Doors had been shut to control movement between decks, and all scuttles, with their thick layer of camouflage paint, had been slammed tight following an announcement over the ship's tannoy ordering everyone except selected deck crew to return to their quarters. Anybody caught trying to observe who was coming on board faced immediate arrest. Müller had considered hiding in one of the ship's boats or behind a ventilator on the Sports Deck to try to see what was happening, but he soon dismissed the idea. Royal Marine guards were everywhere.

In the meantime he listened to the endless speculation of the seamen around him on the reasons for the curfew, until there was a click from the tannoy speaker outside the crew cabin, and immediately the seamen stopped talking. A few seconds later a voice boomed, 'All members of the crew resume normal duties. All members of the crew resume normal duties. Decks upwards of Main Deck will remain sealed to all except pass holders until further notice. By order of the captain.'

The men on the bunks got to their feet and Müller slid

down to the floor, glad to be leaving the stuffy atmosphere. Jacobsen would be expecting him back to finish off the work on the staircase, but first he was determined to discover the reason for the security measures. He made his way to the Pig and Whistle, to find the one man who could tell him— Nobby.

The little Cockney had been one of the hand-picked crew of seamen ordered to stay on deck, and Müller knew that he would never be able to contain himself over such a secret. He was on his second beer when a smug-looking Nobby arrived. Immediately Müller set him up with a pint, and waited until the glass had been half emptied before looking expectantly at the Englishman.

'Well?'

Nobby shook his head mysteriously, making Müller wait before answering. Then he said conspiratorially, 'Security? Never seen anything like it. I was up on the foc'sle and saw them come aboard. Troops all along the side. Fully armed. And that marine major was in charge of it all—said he would shoot anybody doing anything suspicious. I was confined to the foredeck.'

'Sounds incredible. But what was it for?'

'You'll get me shot if I tell you.'

'It'll soon be news all round the ship,' Müller replied caustically.

Nobby looked over his shoulder, then, reassured, leaned forward. 'I saw them come aboard. A whole launch full, just about anybody who's anybody except the king.'

'*Who?*' Muller said quietly.

'General Brooke—he was there. Pound and Portal, and Wavell of course. I recognised them from the newspapers.'

Müller knew the names of the British military leaders, but he was not prepared for Nobby's next revelation.

'And of course the old man himself. Plain as a pikestaff, standing in the bows.'

'Old man?'

'Churchill.'

Müller stared at the Englishman, hardly able to believe him.

'There must be something big on in the States,' Nobby

continued conspiratorially, but Müller scarcely heard his next few words. Everything had become clear. The notices in Dutch, the special ramps, the rumours about Queen Wilhelmina—they were just a clever plan to disguise the most important target of all. Only one doubt remained in Müller's mind.

'Why on earth is Churchill sailing on a ship carrying Jerry prisoners?' he asked. 'They're tough nuts, you know.'

Nobby scoffed. 'They might be, but have you seen those marines? They're the best troops in the world. Even so they won't be needed because even if the news leaked out that Winston was on board, the Jerries would refuse to believe it. They'd think we were stupid, carrying the prime minister with such a dangerous lot.'

Müller shook his head. 'I think Churchill's taking a big risk. Even if there's no danger from his being actually on board there are still a lot of U-boats between here and New York.'

'They've got to catch us first,' Nobby said proudly.

Müller studied his beer, trying to come to terms with the information he had just received. He only noticed that Nobby was going back on duty when he was halfway to the door. Thankful to be left alone he found it hard to believe the strange twist of fortune which had placed the British prime minister aboard the ship SKL planned to capture. Müller's mind went back over Padilla's briefing. At no time had he mentioned the possibility of the British war leadership sailing in the ship, nor had there been any specific instructions how to deal with such a contingency. The news might well come as a great surprise to the German High Command. The possibilities for the operation were now immense. One action alone could have devastating repercussions—the assassination of Winston Churchill.

Yet he was nagged by doubts. He could scarcely decide to kill Churchill without the approval of the High Command or, he realised, that of the Führer himself. Higher politics were a mystery to Müller, and he was uneasy about how the Nazi leadership would react. By acting alone he would be entering unfamiliar territory, threatened by events he only vaguely understood.

His mind went to the radio hidden in the bows. To contact Berlin would be far too dangerous: the British would be able to intercept his signal and so be alerted to the presence of an agent on board.

The best chance of success was to keep radio silence and to execute Operation Iceman as near as originally instructed. If it were successful then Churchill would become his prisoner, while at the same time he would have carried out his orders to the letter. Once the operation began he would contact Berlin; the decision over what to do with Churchill would be theirs.

Müller pushed his glass away, relieved to have reached a decision. He knew that Jacobsen would still be expecting him, but there was one errand he had to run first. In the new situation on board he might be forced to risk detection by British Intelligence and contact Berlin, yet it would be impossible to transmit from the bow chamber. He had to move the radio to a new hiding place, one that he knew would enable him to send a clear radio message. A lifeboat would be ideal: the radio could be carried to the boat deck in his carpenter's bag.

There was no time to lose. He would use the general commotion of sailing to start moving the equipment.

Quickly Müller made his way along C Deck and cut down the companionways towards the bows. There was a great deal of activity on all decks, but nobody took much notice of Müller in his carpenter's apron, and he progressed through the hull encountering fewer and fewer members of the crew. By the time he reached his hiding-place in the bow sweat was pouring from his body. He hauled back the stiff watertight door and ducked low into the stuffy triangular chamber. He switched on the low-powered light and scrambled across to where he had hidden his equipment. The sacking was undisturbed.

With great care Müller lifted out the amplifier, placing it at the bottom of his toolbag, and carefully replaced the sacking. Then he walked to the door, checking that nothing could be seen before he switched off the light.

Bending low, he crawled out of the small compartment, but before he could slam the door behind him his eyes fell on two stained tennis shoes in the shadows less than a yard away. At once Müller recognised their yellowing canvas and frayed rubber.

'What the hell are you doing here, Jacobsen?' he began, looking up at the powerful figure standing over him.

'Just stay where you are,' Jacobsen replied quietly, the poor light throwing his strong jaw into relief. Müller tried to raise himself to his full height, but with a metallic click the blade of a flick knife shot out from Jacobsen's hand.

'You're going to tell me what's so interesting in there,' he said, pointing to the tool bag, his face like a mask.

Müller gave a wry smile. 'There's no mystery. I'll show you. But why the knife? Are you going to keep me on my knees like this all night?'

The American's eyes glowered with the same expression Müller had seen when he had cursed Jacobsen's clumsiness.

'I've had my suspicions about you, Larsen—if that's your real name. I don't like the smell of you. And what I smell is Nazi.'

'You're talking nonsense,' Müller said evenly. 'Now, why don't you let me get up?'

Jacobsen appeared to waver, and it was the moment Müller had watched for. His right leg was bent beneath him, the muscles taut; with a dancer's control he kicked out at the big man's groin. Jacobsen winced with pain and momentarily his right arm dropped. Müller moved again, launching himself from the hips; with a brutal shock to his spine and neck, his forehead met Jacobsen's chin.

The carpenter fell to the ground, the knife slithering from his hand. Müller stood looking down into the dazed eyes, feeling almost sorry for Jacobsen, but pushing all sympathy from his mind. He bent down to pick up the knife, but his fingers never reached the ivory handle. To his amazement Jacobsen's powerful hands gripped his right ankle and his workmate's shoulder thrust against his thigh. The next moment, Müller's vertebrae felt as if they were being shattered into a dozen pieces as his spine hit the bulkhead. A fraction later and the back of his head landed against the steel wall. The world blurred and dimly Müller made out the shape of Jacobsen's face close to him. Pain seared through

Müller's throat and temples as strong fingers tightened on his windpipe.

He tried to move to his left, so that his hand could grab the knife, but Jacobsen shifted his weight and brought his right knee down sharply, pinning Müller's wrist to the floor. The German could see Jacobsen clearly now, and from his dark stare knew that his one-time workmate was determined to kill him. His own head was bursting, and he tried desperately to think. With a supreme effort he twisted sideways and felt Jacobsen's weight shift. With a sudden arching of his back Müller toppled the heavy man aside. Jacobsen fell heavily on to his shoulders, his head striking the deck behind him.

Breathlessly Müller picked up the knife. Pain still racked his throat and he felt no remorse. With almost surgical precision he thrust the blade deep into Jacobsen's chest. The carpenter's eyes opened an instant to stare at Müller, bewildered and afraid. For a moment he lifted his chest clear of the floor. A large patch of blood spread across his chequered shirt and he fell back with a gasp.

Müller stared down at the body. He had not reckoned on killing Jacobsen like this. How was he going to cover it up? He caught his breath, certain he could hear footsteps echoing further along the dark corridor. Only a distant hum of machinery . . . somehow he *had* to move the massive corpse. But where?

He began to search the narrow area in the bows. Perhaps he could push Jacobsen into the bow chamber? He began to heave him towards the door when he changed his mind. The small space might be inspected, and any enquiry could only lead to Müller.

In the distance he thought he heard another footfall and again he held his breath, straining to interpret any distant sound. His muscles tensed, his ears detecting the unmistakable buzz of voices. He had only a few minutes, and desperately tried to think of a place to hide the dead carpenter. Suddenly it came to him. From his early recce of the ship he remembered a small chamber on the deck immediately above. A notice on the outside proclaimed it to be a danger area and entry was prohibited. Müller had not been inside but from the chamber's position in the hull he guessed that it housed the *Queen Mary*'s massive chains and hawsers when they were wound inboard. He glanced at the ladder only six feet away, and knew that it would bring him to the cable room door.

Once again he listened for any sounds, and was now certain that the footsteps were drawing closer. Quickly he pulled Jacobsen's lifeless trunk into a sitting position, the knife still buried in his chest, then hauled the body on to his shoulders. Some of Jacobsen's blood, he noticed, had congealed on his wrist. Then, using his experience of climbing the perpendicular ladders of U-boats, he placed his hand on a rung and began to climb, slowly, to the deck above. A minute later he raised his head cautiously above the steel floor. The heavy door was closed, the area all around deserted. He hauled Jacobsen through the hatch and yanked at the steel door, praying that it would open. For a moment it refused to give, then it duly swung back, groaning, and the smell of the seabed filled Müller's nostrils in a rush.

His eyes spied the gigantic chain, coiled like a serpent, some ten feet in front of him. Its links were each the size of a man's body and ran upwards to a chute in the ceiling: the *Queen Mary*'s anchor chain. From somewhere above, Müller heard a distant rumble and Nobby's words spoken only a short time before came into his mind—the ship was preparing to sail. Already powerful capstans were beginning to haul the forty-six-ton starboard anchor from the seabed, and Müller could hardly believe his good fortune when he realised that the heavy anchor chain would soon fill the room.

With renewed energy, he dragged Jacobsen across the wet floor and dumped him on to the pile of links, wondering how long he would have to wait before the chain began to move. Suddenly the room shuddered and with a deafening roar the anchor chain began to fall link by link from the conduit. Müller ducked to avoid injury and watched from the door as first Jacobsen's battered shoes, then his blood-stained denims and chequered shirt disappeared under the cascade of steel. His sightless eyes stared back at Müller a few moments more, then the tousled head disappeared from

220

sight, leaving only one strong, calloused hand reaching out from under the massive links. Then it too was buried, and Müller was left alone.

Chapter 22

It was just after eight o'clock in the morning and the pavements were thronged with Londoners on their way to work.

Tracey O'Brien stepped out of the Tube station on the Embankment and set off towards the *Sentinel* offices in Tudor Street, a busy newspaper centre just behind Fleet Street. Only forty minutes earlier she had arrived at Euston from Glasgow and had decided to go straight to work.

She turned into the Georgian courtyards and alleyways of the Inner Temple, the honeyed brick and bright spring windowboxes cheering her before she passed into the sombre canyon of Tudor Street. The bureau was on the first floor and the cleaner had just finished, so that for once the place was refreshingly tidy. Chuck Mason's secretary, Sally, had already arrived and was standing over her typewriter, completing her make-up with the aid of a small mirror.

'Welcome home,' she said brightly. 'How was Bonnie Scotland?'

'Fine—if you want to meet ten thousand love-sick GIs.'

Sally stowed away her lipstick. 'What a wonderful prospect!'

'Where's Chuck?' Tracey asked.

'He went to an early press conference at the US Army HQ in Berkeley Square. You know how he hates that, first thing in the morning.'

Tracey duly commiserated, then reached forward for a copy of the *Daily Express* among the various papers heaped on her desk, to begin her morning routine of scanning the columns for material. She worked quickly through the rest before gratefully sipping the coffee Sally had placed before her.

'Here's today's batch of mail,' Sally said, handing her a pile of letters.

They were mostly public relations handouts and press invitations, many of which Tracey dumped in the wastepaper basket. Then she came across a small buff envelope marked 'Personal'. It was in James Alloway's handwriting.

The note inside was friendly but curiously restrained: a simple apology for being unable to attend Tracey's cocktail party in two days' time. His duties were taking him away from London for the next week or so, the note said.

She felt disappointed that the letter had not shown more sign of affection, but she knew Alloway well enough by now just to curse his incurable British understatement.

With a sigh she put the letter back in the envelope and pulled out a notebook from her handbag. It was almost nine o'clock and she wanted to draft the material she had gathered in Scotland before Chuck returned.

She fed paper into her Remington and typed out the heading: *Allied Summit Soon?*

Checking with the notes she had taken aboard the ship she began her story.

'In the highest circles a meeting between Churchill and Roosevelt is now regarded as a matter of utmost urgency to plan the final strategic steps to destroy the Axis.'

She knew that she had to tread carefully because the government censor would remove any reference he believed of military significance, and might well forbid the story altogether. So she touched deftly on the possibility of differences between the British and Americans, and concluded the piece with a veiled forecast that there would be dramatic events in the near future which would raise British morale.

With her draft completed Tracey sat back and was making the odd correction when Chuck Mason arrived, puffing after the climb upstairs. He beamed at Tracey.

'Thank heavens you're back. The world's falling apart today.'

'Why? Some big story?'

He slipped off his jacket, his white shirt rolling over his waistband.

'Just the usual army PR stuff, this time about new military appointments. I won't bore you with it, although I suppose it has to go into the paper.'

He peered over Tracey's shoulder at her copy. 'So what have you got for me, honey-child?'

She handed him her story. The bureau chief's expression became serious as he glanced through her copy.

'Hey! What is all this?'

'Something I discovered in Scotland,' Tracey answered, trying not to sound smug.

Briefly she told Chuck about the ramps, of the tremendous amount of work being carried out on board for what appeared to be a major conference. 'And let's face it, Chuck, there's only one Very Important Person who would justify having ramps built all over the ship. The President of the United States.'

Tracey also told him that Queen Wilhelmina might be travelling aboard the ship, but dismissed this as a deliberate red herring planted by the authorities.

Chuck paid careful attention, and Sally stopped work to listen. 'In my view, Chuck,' Tracey concluded, 'Roosevelt and all his top staff will be coming here on about twentieth May. And I've got that on good authority.'

'What do you mean you have it on good authority?' Chuck demanded.

Tracey suppressed a triumphant smile.

'One of the American officers permanently on board told me.' Briefly, she recounted her conversation with the American lieutenant.

Chuck shook his head in amazement.

'Then this guy's either a first-class security risk or he's planting a cover story.'

Tracey was surprised. Perhaps Chuck was suffering from an attack of sour grapes. 'I considered him a reliable source,' she answered loftily.

Chuck thought for a moment, then read through Tracey's copy for a second time.

'Well, it's a good story, and you've written it well. Even the censor might pass it. I'll push it through to him by noon.' He moved towards his own desk, then stopped and looked at her thoughtfully. 'Of course, there's one way you could really check out the story . . . you could tactfully ask your boyfriend, Squadron Leader Alloway, if there's anything in it.'

Tracey was silent. It was not something she wanted to do. She thought of the restrained tone of Alloway's letter: perhaps she had already been an embarrassment to him.

'Sorry, Chuck,' she said. 'No can do. Anyway, he's away on business.'

'How long for?'

'A couple of weeks.'

'Just long enough to get to New York and back,' Chuck mused.

A twin-engined Junkers 86P dropped down from the early morning sky and landed at a camouflaged Luftwaffe base in northern Holland. Before she had even finished taxiing a ground crew were running across the tarmac ready to unload her reconnaissance camera.

Two hours later, in his office in Berlin, Boehm scanned the developed pictures. They showed the Clyde Estuary earlier that morning.

'She's sailed,' he announced abruptly to his staff, and left at once for the Operations Room ten storeys below.

As soon as he entered the large underground chamber he walked over to Admiral Forster, Chief of Naval Operations, who was standing before a vast chart of the Atlantic. Forster was a short, robust man with a deserved reputation for efficiency, and his face beamed when Boehm told him his news.

'Good. That means she must have been at sea for about fourteen hours, which will put her on an arc somewhere north-west of Ireland.' Stepping closer to the map Forster rapidly gave Boehm a résumé of the latest dispositions of all U-boats which could be a par of a vast net, coming finally to two small clusters of pins south-west of the Denmark Strait.

'Those are your two special battle groups—Hartstein and Sieg. They will be on station tonight.'

Boehm could see that the twelve boats had been well positioned, capable of striking over a vast expanse of ocean. Mentally he began to estimate the time it would take for the *Queen Mary* to come within the Black Gap where Hartstein's group would be ready to strike—as soon as he was directed on to the liner's position.

He looked at the chronometer above the Atlantic chart.

'If the *Queen Mary* maintains her average speed of twenty-eight knots she should be in the Black Gap within sixty hours,' he said to Forster. 'Then it will depend on Iceman.'

Müller tapped on the staff captain's door and did his best to appear diffident as he entered the room. It was essential to avoid any prolonged investigation into Jacobsen's disappearance which might occur if the British discovered it for themselves.

The staff captain glanced up. 'Well, who might you be?' he asked, clearly irritated.

'Larsen, sir. Carpenter. I shipped aboard in New York, sir, if you remember.'

'Oh yes. You are one of the two emergency carpenters. Whatever it is you want, make it snappy. I have to get these papers finished.'

'It's about Jacobsen, sir. My mate. He shipped aboard in New York too, sir, but he's disappeared.' Now the officer was interested.

'What do you mean, disappeared?'

Quickly Müller explained how his mate had failed to turn up for work on the ramps, and had not been seen since the liner set sail twelve hours earlier.

'Are you trying to tell me that you think Jacobsen has jumped ship?'

Müller nodded, rather shamefacedly.

'It's not that I wanted to squeal on anybody, sir, but he did talk about wanting to go ashore to see a relative in Glasgow. And I don't want him to get into trouble—I mean, he might be arrested or something.'

The staff captain was annoyed. 'He'll get into trouble all right, when the police pick him up.'

'I think he was under a strain, sir. He's not used to the sea and a message from you might make the situation easier when they do find him . . .' Müller ventured.

'Message from me! He'll get no bloody help from me. But thanks for letting me know, Larsen. We'll find him. Don't you worry.'

The staff captain dismissed Müller, who closed the door, relieved that he had not been more closely questioned.

He headed for the swimming pool, considering his second gamble that day.

The *Queen Mary* had been under way for ten hours, and he had to make contact with the prisoners. The first contact would be crucial. Not only would a clumsy attempt to gain their confidence raise suspicion; it would also waste valuable time.

Müller had already decided who the most effective contact might be and, carrying his tool bag, he made for the swimming pool and Major Preuss.

There were two pools aboard the *Queen Mary*, and Müller had established that Preuss and his fellow POWs were billeted in the smaller Tourist pool. It was on F Deck, deep inside the ship, and he paused a moment to collect himself before pushing through the swing doors. Inside he saw that the tiled interior of the bath had been filled with bunks. They formed a honeycomb structure with narrow pathways running between the tiers.

Canadian guards patrolled the sides of the pool, armed only with batons. In the close atmosphere they had discarded their battledress blouses in favour of shirt sleeves, and through an open door at the side of the pool Müller could see their rifles stacked near their beds. One of the Canadians spotted him at once and waved him towards the sergeant's room, which had once been the attendant's cubicle in the left-hand corner of the pool. It was garishly decorated with pin-ups inherited from the Americans. The sergeant was engrossed in a copy of *Picturegoer*, which he dropped with a yawn as Müller appeared.

'And what can I do for you?'

'I've been sent down to do some repairs.' Müller held out a scrap of paper on which he had prepared an official-looking list. 'It's from the staff captain.'

The sergeant studied it for a moment, his feet still propped on the desk. 'Don't tell me you're going to do all this work yourself?'

Müller grinned. 'Not a chance. We're normally assigned a fatigue party of about half a dozen men. If you've got anyone experienced in woodwork . . .'

The sergeant put his feet down and straightened his cap.

'You mean you've got to work with those bastards in the pool? You'll have to watch yourself. They're all Nazis for a start, and they'd string you up if they could!'

Müller shrugged. 'They're probably so bored they'll be glad to have something to do.'

The NCO stood up and walked towards the door, giving Müller a curious look.

'What are you, Dutch or something?'

'Norwegian.'

'They're going to love you then. Come on, let's see what we can do. I reckon it can't do any harm to keep the buggers occupied.'

The NCO led Müller to the edge of the swimming bath. Several prisoners looked up quizzically from their bunks, reminding Müller of animals in a zoo.

'Who's that bloke with the blond hair?' Müller asked, pointing to a thickset young captain sitting talking to several men around a packing case in the middle of the pool.

'That's Schmidt. Second in command. It's a Nazi bastard called Preuss who's in charge.'

'Where's he?'

'Probably on his bunk reading *Mein Kampf*. Come on.'

The sergeant gripped the handrail and climbed backwards down the steps into the pool. They squeezed along a narrow path between two rows of bunks. One or two men poked their heads out in irritation at being disturbed, and Schmidt broke off his conversation to look contemptuously at Müller and the sergeant. His small bright eyes remained on Müller's face.

'Captain Schmidt,' the sergeant began, 'this man's been

227

sent on official orders to carry out any necessary repairs in your quarters.'

'You mean the British are going to make us comfortable?' Schmidt commented ironically. 'Wonders will never cease.'

'He will undertake only major repairs,' the NCO countered.

'Then he will be busy. Half the bunks seem to be collapsing. The Americans who were on this ship must have lived like pigs.'

'It would help if you could provide me with three or four men,' Müller said.

Schmidt stared at him. A small group of officers had gathered around.

'And who the hell are you? A damn carpenter asking a German officer to help you do your job. You'll be telling me to sweep the floor next.'

Müller stood his ground. It had been some time since he had been bawled out by a German officer, but he knew the type well.

'It will merely help me to do the job faster,' he answered.

'Look, Captain,' the NCO broke in, 'this man's here on official orders and can ask for any help that's necessary. Do I have to get the commandant? I thought you might have welcomed a chance to make your berths more comfortable.'

Schmidt was unmoved, but Müller heard a quiet voice over his shoulder.

'Quite right, Sergeant. If the carpenter has orders he must carry them out. Is that not so, Captain Schmidt?'

Müller swivelled round; the lean figure of Major Preuss was standing just two feet behind him.

'Some of our bunks are in a terrible state,' Preuss continued in a business-like tone. 'Captain Schmidt, allocate four officers to help this man.'

The captain's attitude changed completely and, ignoring Müller, he immediately shouted out the names of the officers who were to help with the work.

One was a tough young Luftwaffe officer with pale, unblinking eyes, and two others were junior army lieutenants. The fourth man was very different. He was an older Kriegsmarine lieutenant, whose brown hair was flecked with grey. He bore a shrapnel wound on his cheek, and studied Müller with quiet authority. Müller was outranked by all these men, but it did not worry him; in becoming an agent he felt that he had stepped outside the normal hierarchy of military ranks, and was an instrument of the High Command.

'You could build a cathedral with these men,' Preuss declared, and Müller led the group in search of damaged bunks and woodwork. For the next hour they sweated in the close atmosphere of the pool, watched idly by the guards. Lack of space forced them to haul damaged frames up on to the slipwalk along the bath. Several other prisoners joined in, eager at having something to do at last. Müller had an excellent vantage position on the side of the pool, and he began to build up a picture of the whole area. Preuss, he noticed, had taken the bunk in the bottom left-hand corner of the pool, where the vertical side of the swimming bath prevented anybody watching him. Two junior officers occupied the positions above him, acting as his immediate staff. One of them always seemed within sight or earshot of Preuss.

Several bunks were made serviceable and the Canadian guards idly watched the prisoners help Müller to shift damaged beams back into position. Then Müller climbed down into the pool. His arms ached with fatigue and he found himself longing for a cool beer in the Pig and Whistle. Tossing his hammer and screwdriver into an open tool bag, he looked round to speak to his German helpers, but to his surprise they were nowhere to be seen. Instead the slender figure of Preuss blocked his path. Behind him stood Schmidt. The officers who had been his workmates appeared from the other direction. Now there was no sign of their earlier bonhomie; instead they watched Müller carefully, clearly waiting for orders.

Müller looked around but the side of the pool prevented him seeing the guards. Preuss took a pace forward. In the dim lighting darkness filled his deep eye-sockets.

'What's going on?' Müller asked sharply, his back against the tiles.

'You know very well,' Preuss replied. 'We cannot tolerate enemy agents. For the last hour we have been observing

229

you; as you have been observing us. I must compliment you on your training.' Laconically Preuss went on, 'My officers tell me that your conversation shows a great deal of fascination about how many men we have here, their military units, their backgrounds. It all sounds so innocent, but it isn't, is it?' He paused, his eyes burning into Müller. 'Who are you?'

Müller stared back, wary of Preuss's next move. A foot-long piece of wood was in Schmidt's hand, its top spiked with nails. He also saw out of the corner of his eye the young lieutenant take up his claw-hammer, eager to use it as a weapon.

'I don't think you understand the situation, Herr Major,' Müller began, but his voice was drowned by the strains of the Flying Dutchman overture, played on an old gramophone on a nearby bunk. The guards would not hear his cries. Müller moved towards his toolbag, hoping to grab a chisel, but the bull-like lieutenant kicked it out of his reach. He felt helpless, and stupid at having set the Germans against him, but his mind remained clear. He threw back his shoulders and his laughter mingled strangely with the chords of Wagner. Irritation swept Preuss's face, while the other prisoners exchanged uncertain glances.

'I am sorry to laugh, Herr Major,' Müller declared in German. 'You are right, I am an agent, but I am not serving the Allies. I am serving the Reich. Allow me to introduce myself, at least by my code name.' Müller drew himself to attention. 'Obersteuermann Iceman, Kriegsmarine.'

The other Germans seemed perplexed, but Preuss was sceptical. 'Iceman, eh? What was your ship?'

'A U-boat, U-1543. Based at Lorient.'

'A fine performance,' the major replied lightly. 'But we shall soon see whether you are telling the truth.'

He turned and whispered a few words over his shoulder to Schmidt, who promptly marched off. Then he indicated that Müller was to follow him, two other officers bringing up the rear. They threaded their way between the cramped bunks, the Canadian guards watching them abstractedly, suspecting nothing, doubtless still thinking that Müller was engaged on repairs. The group halted at Preuss's bunk in the far corner of the pool. It seemed remarkably private. A small coffee table, purloined from a stateroom, stood to one side.

Preuss parked himself on his haunches on a box behind it, telling Müller to draw up an empty beer crate.

'Herr Major? You sent for me.'

A Luftwaffe officer pushed his way between Müller's former workmates and saluted. He was about thirty and wore steel-rimmed spectacles over a ruddy peasant face. Preuss explained to Müller, 'Captain Schiller was in command of the flak batteries at Lorient before he was posted to Africa.'

He turned to the newcomer. 'Interrogate him, Schiller. Ask him about every alley and every brothel in Lorient. Ask him everything you can remember.'

Müller felt his unease growing. It had been more than three months since he was in Lorient. The questions came fast. What were the names of the main German units at the naval base? What was the street running along the quay? Where were the Brittany rest camps where the U-boat crews relaxed?

Schiller probed repeatedly, questioning him about bars, cafés, the layout of the docks, the big air raids; but Müller's answers flowed easily. Eventually Preuss stopped the questions and sat studying his hands.

'Very good, Iceman,' he said eventually. 'But you could have been fed that much information by the French Resistance. There is, however, one place where there are no Resistance groups. In Kiel, your training base.'

He searched Müller's face for a hint of anxiety before summoning the Kriegsmarine lieutenant who had been in the carpentry group.

'Leutnant List, you know Kiel and all the main bases— see whether our Obersteuermann's knowledge compares with yours.'

Once again the interrogation started, with List deliberately asking difficult technical questions to trap Müller. At the end List seemed impressed with Müller's answers and turned to the major.

'This man is genuine. Even more, I believe I know him.'

Müller was surprised by his admission as the lieutenant continued, 'Were you in the fourth Lorient flotilla?'

Müller said he was.

'And what was the name of your flotilla officer?'

'Captain Rheinhardt.'

'*Sehr gut!*'

Suddenly the lieutenant took Müller's hand and shook it warmly. But Preuss still looked sceptical. 'So, if you are a U-boat man, what on earth are you doing on this ship?'

'I joined her in New York, and have special orders—to seize the liner.'

Even Preuss registered surprise at Müller's statement, and a smile of disbelief spread across his features.

'Oh, is that all?'

Müller was beginning to lose patience with the SS man, and thrust his chin to within a few inches of Preuss's face.

'I tell you I have my orders, and you are expressly commanded by the Führer to assist me in every way.'

Preuss returned an even stare, though visibly impressed.

'And what is to happen to the ship once she is captured? Is she to be scuttled?'

Müller shook his head. 'The *Queen Mary* is to be taken to St Nazaire.'

Preuss grinned. 'A lovely idea. But the British won't sit idly by.'

'I know, that's the last thing they'll do. But first they will have to decide whether to attack their own ship. After that it will be left to the Luftwaffe and Kriegsmarine.'

Preuss raised thin eyebrows. 'And what do you want of me?'

'You have fifty men under your command; tough and experienced in combat. I need them to form the spearhead of the assault. To seize the key objectives—the armoury, bridge and radio room. Above all, to release the other prisoners.'

Preuss gave Müller another rare smile. 'You make it sound very attractive. But what are we to use for weapons? Did the Kriegsmarine think of that?'

'There is an armoury on B Deck. Our first priority will be to seize it. After that your men can be armed.'

'And who is to command this operation?'

Müller shook his head. 'I cannot command your troops,

232

and certainly not the main body, but the plan I have outlined must be followed in every detail. Now, Major Preuss, you must help me to contact the officer commanding the rest of the prisoners. We have little time.'

'Leave it to me. We all eat together in the main canteen. That will be in half an hour's time.'

'I want you to tell the senior officer to make sure there is serious damage to the bunks in Cabin D 187. His men can see to it that it looks like the effects of a storm.'

Preuss agreed, then, staring unblinkingly at Müller, he asked, 'When do we go into action?'

'Within forty-eight hours.'

Chapter 23

Pat Collins, Anna Rabin's friend, was dreading the task ahead of her. She was standing in the marbled vault of the New York Police morgue trying to avoid staring at the covered trolley across the room.

'I'm sorry to put you through all this,' Lieutenant Patrick Riley declared, an expression of sympathy on his bluff features. He steered the dumpy girl across the tiled floor and with a practised hand pulled back the rubber sheeting on the trolley.

'It's her—Anna,' Pat whispered.

'Sure?'

She made herself look again at the taut white skin and nodded. Riley quickly covered the body and escorted the girl away, conscious she was fighting to contain her tears. They took the lift to his office three floors above.

Gratefully Pat accepted a chair. Riley shouted down the corridor for coffee.

'I can't understand,' she whispered. 'What happened?'

'We found her in the East River last night. Reckon she'd been there some days.'

Pat lifted her head. 'But why?'

An obliging sergeant had brought in the coffee. Riley poured her out a cup. 'I was hoping you could help us find the answer.'

'I'll do my best.'

Riley opened the thin file in front of him. A few lines described the uneventful life of Anna Rabin. He drew a note-pad towards him.

'What sort of girl was she?'

'A very shy, gentle person. I guess she didn't have many friends—apart from me and the girls from the store.'

'And men friends?'

Pat folded her plump arms over her tight-fitting black jumper.

'Only one, ever. His name was Olaf Larsen. A Norwegian seaman.'

Riley looked at her, then glanced at the forensic report from the laboratory. Tests had shown that Anna Rabin was about three months pregnant; death had been caused by drowning. There were no marks on her body suggesting foul play.

'Was it Larsen's baby she was carrying?' Riley asked.

Pat nodded unhappily.

'Where can we find Larsen?'

'You can't. He was sunk on his last voyage. The shipping authorities posted him missing, presumed dead.'

Riley pursed his lips. Anna's motive for suicide was becoming apparent. He looked at Pat's large, round eyes. 'How did Anna take Larsen's death?'

'Take his death?' Pat echoed with a bewildered expression. 'She never accepted it. Anna believed that Larsen was still alive. She never stopped looking for him.'

Pat told him of the enquiries her friend had made at the Norwegian consulate and her long trip to Norfolk. 'Surely the Navy people in Norfolk convinced her that Larsen was dead?' Riley insisted.

'No. She telephoned me when she got back to New York. Anna was very excited because she'd discovered a survivor from the ship.'

Riley was immediately interested. 'A survivor?'

'Yes. It was odd, because she said his name was Larsen

too. Anna was determined to trace him, to try and find out whether the man she loved was still alive.'

Riley regarded Pat with a puzzled expression. 'You say this man's name was Larsen, too?'

'Yes, *Olaf* Larsen. Even the same Christian name. But Anna told me it's a common name in Norway.'

'Must be,' Riley muttered. 'But did Anna find him?'

'I don't know. The last I heard from her was the day she left the store to start looking.'

Riley seemed to be thinking aloud. 'Anna's landlady didn't notice any strange men visiting her. We checked.'

'She was a terrible old witch,' Pat scoffed. 'Anna would never let her find out anything.'

The lieutenant nodded sympathetically and looked down at the file; then he studied Pat for a moment. 'There is just one last question I would like to ask. Was Anna pleased to be having Larsen's baby? The child of her own Olaf Larsen, that is.'

Pat Collins answered without hesitation. 'It was the greatest thing that ever happened to her. She never stopped talking about it.'

Riley thanked her courteously for her help and ushered Pat out of the office.

When he came back to his desk he turned through the pages on the file and pondered Pat's words. Then he made his decision. It would not be easy to track down the mysterious survivor, and a time-consuming manhunt would hardly make him popular. Many of his colleagues would already have closed Anna's case as an obvious suicide, but . . . Riley thought of her sad, lifeless features. She was not a girl to kill herself with new life inside her. The detective picked up the phone and spoke incisively.

'Get me the War Shipping Administration in Norfolk, Virginia.'

In a stiffening south-westerly breeze, the *Queen Mary*'s grey bows dipped into the Atlantic swell as she forged steadily towards New York. The sea hissed past her camouflaged hull and foamed into a broad wake across the surface of the ocean.

In the cluttered offices on Main Deck, coffee cups slid sideways and papers slipped to the floor as the liner kept up a steady twenty-nine knots. Some of the members of Churchill's team were looking decidedly sick—but as yet nobody had failed to turn up for duty.

Müller hardly felt the rolling of the ship as he descended the broad aft staircase towards D Deck where the mass of the prisoners, over nine hundred of them, were accommodated. As he arrived at the entrance to the POW area he reported to a guard room that had once been one of the larger cabins in the tourist-class area, at the head of the long corridor running fore and aft. A burly Canadian lieutenant rose from behind a table and stretched out a massive palm for Müller's ID card. He took his time examining it and Müller began to feel uneasy.

'You want to do some repairs in D 187, you say. I didn't know that there was any damage in that cabin.'

Müller prayed that Preuss's message had got through and that the prisoners had prepared the way for him by making it look as if D 187 had suffered badly on the voyage over.

'It was reported after the storm some days ago,' Müller explained. 'I don't think you were on board then.'

The lieutenant looked up uncertainly and reached for the phone. 'Maybe, but I'd better check.'

Müller's heart raced. It was exactly what had to be avoided. 'It's the senior chippie you want,' he cut in, 'and he's working in the foc'sle. You won't get him until lunch break.'

The lieutenant was undecided.

'In that case I'd better try the staff captain.'

'If you bother him he'll blow your balls off, and mine too!' Müller sighed, and leaned confidentially across the table. 'Look, I just want to get on with this job and get out. It'll only take an hour. Still, if you insist, I'll go off for a beer and come back when you've checked up, but nobody's going to be very pleased. Believe me, I know this ship.'

The Canadian shrugged. 'Well, all right, if it's only a couple of hours.'

He handed back Müller's ID card. 'But you'd better be careful with those Krauts. I don't want a dead chippy on my hands . . .'

The lieutenant buttoned up his battledress and, leaving the office in charge of an NCO, took Müller towards the prisoners' accommodation. Hundreds of Germans were housed in the small cabins flanking the corridor. They were crowded four or five to a room, sleeping on temporary bunks and using a single washbasin. Occasionally the lieutenant would put his head round the door of a cabin, addressing the men inside in bad German, and Müller glimpsed the canvas bunks folded back against the wall, allowing the inmates just sufficient space for reading or playing cards. The thick layer of grey camouflage paint over the portholes stopped any light, turning the area into a densely populated catacomb.

Once or twice the lieutenant stopped to exchange a few words with one of his troops patrolling the area. Halfway along the passageway he suddenly turned left along a smaller corridor and pulled up at the door of D 187. Inside, four German officers were sitting around the cabin. They seemed slightly older than the men in the swimming pool. On the bulkhead behind them Müller could see that a set of bunks had been sheared away. The prisoners had done their work well.

'My God, it must have been some storm,' the Canadian declared.

'It was given emergency repair and must have come away during the night.'

'It certainly did,' one of the Germans said, rubbing his shoulder. 'I was in it.'

The lieutenant explained that Müller was going to carry out repairs, then left him to it. Once he had departed one of the officers, who had been watching indifferently, pulled his hands out of his pockets and stepped forward. He was aged about thirty and his field-grey tunic was patched in several places, but neatly pressed. For a moment or two he studied Müller, then spoke.

'I am Captain von Albrecht,' he said. 'We've been expecting you. Come with me.'

The occupants of the cabin watched in silence as Müller followed the stiff-backed officer across the passageway, where he tapped on the cabin door opposite. With a brusque wave of his hand he directed Müller to enter. Beneath a blacked-out porthole Colonel von Stoltz was sitting bolt upright at a narrow table, scratching away with a fountain pen. Von Albrecht saluted. 'This is the man Preuss said would be coming, Herr Colonel.'

Müller drew himself to attention. 'Obersteuermann Iceman, Kriegsmarine. Heil Hitler!'

Von Stoltz shifted his gaze towards Müller. The deep-set eyes were sceptical. 'Preuss told us about you. What are you doing aboard this ship?'

Müller shot a wary glance at the captain, but the colonel reassured him. 'You can speak in front of von Albrecht.'

Müller told him why he was aboard and outlined the SKL plan. As he spoke he studied the colonel's face for any sign of reaction, but von Stoltz sat expressionless. When Müller had finished, the colonel put his fingers together and let his eyes wander across the cabin.

'Well, well. An extraordinary scheme. But we cannot put our heads into a British trap, you know.'

Müller was taken aback. 'But I have been specifically ordered to carry out this operation. Unfortunately I cannot contact SKL by radio and seek any proof you demand. It is too risky.'

Von Stoltz went on as if Müller had not spoken. 'You have talked with Major Preuss—is he in favour of this scheme?'

'I thought so.'

Von Stoltz's brow furrowed. 'Assuming that all you say is true and that this plan has been ordered with the sanction of the Führer himself, I still find it hard to accept. The risks, above all. There are a large number of highly trained guards on board, while the ship has extensive anti-aircraft armament. It could be turned on our men—they would be slaughtered.'

The thought had also worried Müller, but idle conversation with the gunners in the Pig and Whistle had taught him that most of the Oerlikons could not be turned inboard.

'The flak armament can be taken care of, Colonel,' he answered simply.

'Do you seriously think it possible to seize a ship of this size with unarmed men?'

'There is an armoury on board which can be seized,' Müller countered.

The colonel sat silent behind his desk, and Müller wondered what he was thinking. Was he considering the morale of his own men, whether they were able to undertake such a bold operation?

Captain von Albrecht was clearly concerned with the same problem, for he now spoke. 'The men would carry out the plan, Colonel—if you were to order it.'

Von Stoltz still only nodded quietly. Müller felt anger welling up inside him. 'My orders are clear, Colonel,' he said sharply. 'If you are unable to help me I shall have to carry on without your support. Major Preuss will—'

'Preuss!' the colonel spat out. 'The SS may feel that they are a law unto themselves, but I command every German in this ship, not Preuss.'

'Not if his orders come from a higher authority,' Müller replied.

Von Stoltz gazed at him coldly. 'I am not accustomed to receiving orders from an Obersteuermann in the Kriegsmarine. The men on this ship are *my* responsibility. I will not see hundreds of them shot to pieces for some fanatical scheme dreamt up by Naval Headquarters in Berlin, and cleverly sold to the Führer.'

The prospect of a damaging rift between the colonel and Preuss worried Müller even more than von Stoltz's reaction. Only hours remained before the deadline for Operation Iceman to begin. He realised that he would have to play his final card. 'Colonel,' he said evenly, 'I have my orders and shall carry them out, with or without your support. We still have a chance of pulling off a staggering coup, diverting the ship to St Nazaire.'

'You will never make it. Even if you overwhelm the guards the British would have no hesitation in destroying the ship.'

'I think not, Colonel.'

Von Stoltz looked at Müller in surprise. 'And why not?'

'Because the stakes are far higher than you or even Berlin are aware. There is something very special about this ship. She is carrying Winston Churchill and his Chiefs of Staff and some of the most important members of his government.'

He paused, conscious of the colonel and von Albrecht staring at him incredulously. 'The whole of the Main Deck has been turned into a war headquarters, with communications rooms in direct contact with London and Washington. Gentlemen, the nerve centre of Britain's war machine is just four decks above us.'

Von Stoltz was on his feet.

'Churchill aboard this ship?' he repeated in disbelief.

'It makes sense, Colonel,' Von Albrecht remarked thoughtfully. 'Remember the curfew just after we came on board when nobody was allowed to move, and we were confined to cabins.'

'That was when Churchill came aboard,' Müller added, and moved to reinforce his argument. 'Think, Colonel. At one blow we could win a victory a thousand times greater than we have achieved so far. The most dangerous enemy of the Reich is within your reach.' He looked up at the cabin ceiling. 'Just four decks above. Without him Britain would collapse.'

Von Stoltz exchanged glances with von Albrecht and when he spoke again his voice was a whisper.

'And Berlin knows nothing about this?'

'I've not attempted to contact them. It would be too dangerous.'

The colonel lowered his heavy frame into the chair and considered Müller a moment before speaking.

'Then we do not know what Berlin's orders would be. It might be to sink the ship at all costs, regardless of the prisoners on board.' He paused. 'What is Preuss's view?'

'He doesn't know,' Müller replied. 'I haven't told him Churchill is on board.'

'Why not?'

'Because my orders are to bring this ship back to St Nazaire, and that is what I intend to do, with Churchill and all his advisers aboard. Just imagine the effect on our people's morale, and the shock to the enemy. It could even bring the war to an end. But there is a danger that Preuss would not see it that way. Quite frankly, I believe that the major would regard it as his top priority to kill Churchill at all costs.'

'Prejudicing the wider, far more important scheme?' von Albrecht queried.

Müller nodded.

'In that case you acted wisely,' von Stoltz remarked. 'And indeed we have no choice. The prize is so great it outweighs all other considerations, especially the risks to ourselves. I don't expect Preuss to see that if Churchill were killed, the true victory, the bitter humiliation of the British, would be lost.'

He took a silver case out of his hip pocket, selected a cigarette and slowly lit it. When he had finished he addressed Müller in the practised tones of authority. 'I must know all the details of your plans. Preuss will be answerable to me. On no account will Churchill and his entourage be harmed: they are to become our prisoners. Those are my strict orders.'

'And when shall I tell Preuss about Churchill?'

'You don't—at least, not until you have to.'

'God help the Americans. They won't know what's hit them,' Alloway thought to himself as he reflected on the intense detail with which the British were preparing their case for the forthcoming conference. He was sitting at his desk in the stateroom assigned to the Military Secretariat. Oblivious of the noise of typewriters around him, he had begun drafting a message to London reporting on the main decisions taken in the meetings that day. Since early morning Churchill and his advisers had been in continuous session, and from the outset of the voyage Alloway himself had been kept busy organising background briefs from the hundreds of files and memoranda brought on board by the Military Secretary. General Ismay appeared to be giving him increasingly important tasks to carry out, and he felt a growing confidence that, in spite of being a fairly recent recruit, he could come up to the demanding standards set by the Defence Office.

It was well after eight o'clock when he finished his report and took it to the cipher office, a short distance along the passageway. A team of Wren officers were sitting shoulder to shoulder at a long trestle table, thumbing through code books and translating piles of signals sent down from the radio room above.

'What have you got for me, Squadron Leader?' the Wren officer in charge asked. She was a lady who amply filled her navy-blue uniform and who had the generally forbidding air of a schoolmistress.

'A signal for the Cabinet Office. Pencil Number Twenty-seven. Category Immediate.' He handed her his report. Without glancing at it she called over a young third officer with neatly bobbed fair hair. The girl gave Alloway a smile and he glanced appreciatively at her slim figure before he felt the senior Wren's disapproving eyes watching them.

'Get this away as soon as you can, Robbins,' she boomed. Alloway watched as the girl slipped gracefully back to her seat.

'Is that all?' the schoolmistress asked drily. Alloway mumbled that it was, and thanked her. He was on his way out of the cipher room when the telephone rang on the senior Wren's desk. 'It's for you, Squadron Leader,' she announced, handing over the phone as if on unwilling loan.

It was the general. 'I'm with the PM at the moment, and I want you to join me. There's an urgent signal to be drafted.' Alloway acknowledged the summons and replaced the receiver, cursing under his breath. It looked as if he would miss his dinner. Again. He walked out of the room, conscious that the bright blue eyes of Wren Robbins were following him.

Outside cabin M 66 Inspector Thompson, Churchill's personal detective, gave him a friendly nod. Within, the stateroom was luxuriously appointed. Its walls were covered with an ivory-white sycamore veneer, which seemed to shimmer in the light. A large tapestry depicting the warm colours of the English countryside hung on the far wall, above a sofa covered in deep brown velvet. The prime minister was leaning back in an armchair in the middle of the room, a glass of cognac in his hand. Senior staff were grouped around him, enjoying pre-dinner drinks. In an armchair opposite Churchill sat General Brooke, while directly behind him was General Ismay. At the far end of the suite stood Beaverbrook, his head bowed. He was obviously doing little to conceal his boredom. The reason became clear. Churchill was expounding on the problems of fighting the Japanese in Burma. Alloway made his way silently towards Ismay, aware that it would be fatal to interrupt the flow of words. 'Going into swampy jungles to fight the Japanese is like going into the water to catch a shark,' the prime minister rumbled. 'It's better to entice him into a trap and catch him on a hook then demolish him with axes after hauling him out on to dry land . . .'

Churchill finally finished, and the military secretary seized his chance. 'Prime Minister, I would like to get away the signal you mentioned about security in Whitehall.'

Churchill swallowed some more cognac. His eyes settled on Alloway. 'Of course, of course. I don't want Whitehall going to sleep while we are away.'

Alloway drew out a notebook ready for Churchill's words. They were not long in coming. 'I want you to send a message to the secretary of the War Cabinet in London, kindly reminding him that it is imperative that every member of the government should abide strictly to agreed security procedures. There has been a certain laxness in some—'

The prime minister did not finish the sentence. Admiral Pound had entered, a deep frown on his face.

'Forgive me for interrupting, Prime Minister, but we have just received a signal from the Admiralty War Room. According to Intelligence intercepts there is a U-boat some thirty miles ahead of us and Western Approaches have ordered the master to make a diversion.'

Churchill seemed unimpressed. 'Surely we can outrun a U-boat.'

'I think the risks of a torpedo attack are too high,' Pound insisted.

'How much time will it add to our journey?'

'At least another day, and we will be beyond immediate air cover and surface escort; but I think it is the proper decision to take.'

'Very well,' Churchill conceded. He turned to Ismay. 'Draft a message to the president. Tell him we expect to be slightly late.'

It was early evening in New York, and Lieutenant Patrick Riley of the city Police Department was looking at a large official envelope he had received from Norfolk, Virginia. He ripped it open and emptied the contents on to his desk. A photograph immediately caught his eye. It showed a typically Nordic face, with a strong jawline and evenly moulded bone structure. The clear eyes were set well apart and stared frankly out of the picture. So this is our elusive Olaf Larsen, he told himself. Riley was surprised by the long hair, but then he recalled that the picture had been taken shortly after the man had been discharged from hospital.

There were several lines of information typed beneath the photograph, with more details on an accompanying sheet: Larsen's country of origin, date of birth and the shipping companies for whom he had worked. There was one other document in the envelope, a small buff card. It too bore Larsen's photograph, and was the visa automatically issued to foreign merchant seamen entering the United States.

Riley turned the card over in his hand before picking up the telephone. He asked for the New York office of the Immigration Department. After some delay in finding the right section he made an appointment to see a senior executive officer in half an hour. Then, packing the file in a briefcase, he set out to take the subway downtown.

The official who received him seemed annoyed at having to delay his lunch break. He was a dry, elderly man, who peered humourlessly over the top of his spectacles.

'What's the man's name again?'

'Olaf Larsen. He's a merchant seaman. Norwegian.'

'Give me a couple of minutes.'

He left Riley alone in the office and returned shortly with a large official card which he slapped in front of the detective. The words across the top read 'Olaf Larsen, Nationality Norwegian', and there was a small photograph pasted at the right-hand corner. Riley carefully set the Norfolk documents alongside the immigration card. All the details corresponded, including the visa number and the date of its first issue: only the pictures were of different men.

'Is that the guy you wanted?' the executive asked, nodding at the immigration card.

'Not quite,' Riley answered with a faint smile.

He asked the bemused executive for a copy of Larsen's documents. The man jibbed, and began to explain that such a request would have to go through official channels, but Riley was no longer listening. He had picked up the phone and was asking for the FBI. He knew that somehow he had to find Larsen, although he could be anywhere—perhaps on an ocean thousands of miles away, possibly even in Britain. Already the detective sensed that the search could take on an importance far beyond his own patch in New York Police Homicide Department.

Alloway walked along the Main Deck where, even now, many of the staff were still at work, preparing papers and briefings for the next day. He bade goodnight to the marine guard and stepped outside on to the deck, hoping that the cold air would revive him and blow away the stench of Havana smoke from his clothes. It was pitch dark, and he walked carefully over to the rail, listening to the hiss of the sea racing past. For a moment he imagined the massive black shape of the *Tirpitz* looming on the horizon. If ever the battleship found the *Queen Mary* and opened fire he wondered how he would behave. It would be terrifying to be trapped on a ship being pounded to bits by those massive guns.

With feelings of bitterness he recognised his own powerlessness. He would not be called up to man the guns. Even if the enemy boarded the liner he would only be capable of feeble resistance: his wounds made certain of that. He looked over the rail at the dark sea below, and knew that if the order came to abandon ship his damaged body would not allow him to survive. It had not always been like this, but he had to face the truth—he was no longer an active combatant. Gazing down at the waters beneath him he tried to console himself that it was exciting, working close to Churchill—and certainly it had been a stroke of luck getting into the Defence Office. But he had nevertheless become what the men of his squadron patronisingly called 'a chairborne warrior'.

He remembered the stares of Londoners whenever he limped across a road, and wondered idly how the young Wren who seemed attracted to him would react if ever she saw his mutilated thigh. Tracey had understood, as Tracey would, and the memory returned of the evening when they had first made love . . . he realised suddenly how much he wanted to see her.

He shivered. There was a bottle of whisky in his cabin. He made his way down to B Deck, bidding the marine sentry goodnight. On the lower deck the lights had been dimmed, leaving large areas of the corridor in darkness. The line of cabin doors seemed endless, and he began to feel irritated that his room was so far away. He would have to be the only fool awake at such an hour.

Suddenly he realised that a shadowy figure was coming towards him; about twenty yards ahead. The man crossed quickly through a pool of light on the left-hand side of the passageway. There was something purposeful about his movements that made Alloway apprehensive. The man passed into a patch of darkness again and Alloway's stomach tightened as he saw that their paths would meet under the next lamp. Moving towards the light he could hear the soft tread of the man's feet. Ten feet away he emerged into the light. His trousers were faded blue denims and the brass tip of a carpenter's rule peeped out from the breast pocket of his grey shirt. Alloway peered at the stranger's face and with a start he realised that he had seen the blond hair, the well-moulded cheeks and intelligent brow before. The man half nodded in greeting and there was a look of familiarity in the glittering blue eyes.

They passed each other without speaking. A moment later Alloway turned, but the stranger had already moved beyond the patch of light, and his soft footsteps receded into the darkness.

Chapter 24

At seven o'clock next morning the atmosphere in the seamen's mess on D Deck was warm and convivial. Members of the *Queen Mary*'s crew sat at the long benches eating enormous breakfasts or lingering over final mugs of tea before the day's work began.

Müller finished his egg and bacon, barely listening to the conversation around him. He was still tired after moving the last component of the transmitter to his new hiding-place, a lifeboat on Sun Deck. Its steel hull contained a number of lockers, ideal places to conceal the plastic explosive as well as the radio equipment.

Nobby's bony fingers prodded him in the ribs. 'You're quiet this morning, Olaf. No wonder, the way you roam around at nights!'

So Nobby had noticed his absence from the crew cabin in the early hours of the morning. 'I wish I could sleep as well as you do,' Müller retorted quickly.

'That's the trouble when you come from the land of the midnight sun,' another member of the crew joked, and the conversation took another turn. Müller glanced at his watch: in twenty minutes the sergeant in charge of the guard at the swimming pool would be finishing night duty, and Müller wanted to make him a closer acquaintance. He cleared away his dishes and left. Arriving at the pool with his tools, he was pleased to see that the sergeant was still on duty. He gave Müller a friendly greeting.

'You're early. Not finished yet?'

'Just a bit more. Trying to make our guests feel comfortable.' Müller fastened on his carpenter's apron and glanced at the office beyond, where he glimpsed several sten guns stacked against the far wall.

'If I get all the work done by the time we reach New York I get a bonus.'

'Lucky bastard,' the sergeant returned enviously.

Müller grinned. 'I get a few perks, I suppose. I could fix you a bottle of Johnny Walker if you're interested.'

'Really? You're on.'

'Thirty bob all right? Black market prices, I'm afraid.'

'Sure. I don't mind paying for the right stuff.' The sergeant offered him a cigarette. 'Do you want some help from the Jerries today?'

'You can leave it to me,' Müller replied, taking the cigarette and slipping it into his apron pocket. 'Believe it or not Preuss himself said he wanted to help. Must be getting bored.'

'That's a laugh.'

Müller left his new friend and clambered down the steep ladder into the pool. He sauntered casually to the last tier of bunks, where Preuss was leaning against an upright. He granted Müller a frosty good morning.

'There's a lot on today. Fancy giving me a hand?'

The major shrugged.

Müller unpacked his tools and chatted about the work to be done. After some minutes he observed that the sergeant had been relieved by a young subaltern, who clattered round the pool in a cursory inspection before disappearing into the attendant's room. Three privates were posted on guard duty, and from time to time they strolled along the slipwalks like police constables. They seemed unaware of the close attention being paid to them by Preuss's look-outs, a pair of young officers perched on top of a tier of bunks, ostensibly playing chess.

When he was sure that no guards were in the vicinity Müller knelt on the boarded floor and rummaged in his tool bag, drawing out an old tobacco tin. Watched intently by Preuss, he prised off the lid, to reveal a layer of one-inch screws. He dug his fingers into the screws and pulled out a slip of paper, which he handed to Preuss.

'I've sketched a plan of the ship. It sets out the key targets to be seized by your men and also the fastest way of getting to them.'

Preuss glanced at the paper. The armoury, bridge, radio and engine rooms were all circled and clearly numbered.

'The first step,' Müller continued, 'will be to disarm the guards here in the swimming pool and seize their weapons. They have quite a little arsenal.' He nodded in the direction of the large room which had once been a gymnasium. On his first visit to the pool Müller had observed that half a dozen Canadian troops were billeted there, with enough weapons to equip an assault party.

'I've been careful to get into the sergeant's good books,' Müller went on, 'because I've discovered that he'll be on duty tomorrow morning, when the operation starts. I shall come down here and create a diversion that will give you a chance to go into action.'

Preuss listened impassively as Müller outlined his scheme for overcoming the guards, commenting with a grin, 'We'll lock them up in their own prison.' The major motioned towards the changing cubicles across the pool. 'Those little cells can be made distinctly uncomfortable.'

Conscious that they might be under observation, Müller picked up a piece of timber and began to mark it for cutting, whilst Preuss pretended to hold it for him.

As he leaned over the wood Müller said in a low voice, 'The whole operation will start here in this swimming pool, Major. I can't emphasise enough the importance of your men succeeding. Our two primary objectives will be to seize the armoury and release the thousand men under Colonel von Stoltz.'

Preuss glanced down at the sketch-map, spread out beneath the piece of timber, and Müller pointed to the heavy black line drawn round the weapons store in the bar on B Deck.

'I've marked the fastest route through the four decks to the armoury,' Müller said. 'You will have the advantage of surprise, and should reach it in five minutes. It's vital that we keep the initiative and act before the British can organise their defences. Once we release von Stoltz's men we shall have almost as many as the British, but they still have the fire-power. You should lead the attack on the armoury yourself.'

'But what about releasing the bulk of our forces?'

'Whilst you are attacking the armoury I will guide a second section through the ship to D Deck to release the main body of prisoners. We can use weapons seized from the guards here. Once the main body of von Stoltz's men have been released you are to send down as many arms and as much ammunition as you possibly can from the British reserves.'

Suddenly Müller noticed that Preuss was looking at the look-outs placed on the bunk above. One of the chess players had begun to whistle: a guard was moving within earshot. Quickly he finished marking the piece of wood and picked up a saw, while Preuss began to unscrew a splintered rail on one of the bunks nearby. Grinning cheerfully at the Canadian as he wandered past, Müller started to saw through the timber. 'Keep them at it,' the soldier said cheerfully to Müller, who grinned back. When he had gone Preuss came across. For a moment Müller made him wait, then deliberately put down the cut pieces of wood. He looked straight at Preuss. 'Zero hour is at two o'clock tomorrow morning. That is SKL's deadline.' The monk-like head half bowed in acknowledgment, and Müller continued, 'It's important that you give this information to von Stoltz as quickly as possible so that his men are ready. Soon it will be exercise time, so tell him the zero hour and pass the message that I shall be briefing him in two hours' time.'

'How will you know that I have managed to contact him?'

'I shall be on the Promenade Deck, overlooking the Exercise Deck. You can show me that the message has been passed by joining the PE party. Turn towards the stern, raise your arms above your head and sway your trunk three times.'

'Do you have to turn me into a chorus girl?' Preuss asked, finally unscrewing the rail.

Müller smiled and handed him a new piece to replace it. 'Who knows? You might make a good one. And there aren't many women on this ship.' He watched Preuss working for a moment, then added, 'But whatever you do you must give me the signal. We need all of von Stoltz's nine hundred men if we are to take this ship.'

Preuss swung round to face him. 'I will get the message through to the colonel, Obersteuermann. All these plans sound admirable, but I hope that you know what you're doing.'

'What do you mean?' Müller hissed, trying to keep his voice low.

Preuss looked blankly at him and answered in a reasonable voice. 'I am sure you are an excellent U-boat coxswain. You must know everything there is to know about fighting at sea, about torpedoes, periscope attacks, that sort of thing. But you have never led men in close combat, with the enemy determined to kill you only feet away. Paper plans tend to be forgotten then.'

Preuss's apparent lack of confidence in him was disconcerting, but Müller recognised the truth of the major's words. Perhaps more worryingly, he was convinced more than ever that the major might take matters into his own hands once the operation started.

'Herr Major, I know that I cannot command your men in action: it would be foolish for me to expect otherwise. But I have orders from Naval HQ to seize this ship according to a definite plan, and that I shall do.' He moved closer to Preuss. 'Remember, my orders have been sanctioned by the Führer himself.'

His companion drove home another screw and bared his teeth in a half smile. 'You explain yourself most clearly. But when the shooting starts it will be very different, I can assure you. Who will take the decisions when things go wrong?'

'Colonel von Stoltz, as senior officer on board. There can only be one man in command of such a complex operation, and that is the colonel.'

Preuss's mouth tightened, then with a slight frown he turned back to the sketch.

'And when we have obtained our first objectives, what then?'

Müller began to rummage for a chisel with which to split another damaged rail. 'Assault groups from von Stoltz's men will fan out through the ship, to take the wireless room, to stop the British calling for support, the engine room and the bridge. Engineers will be sent into the engine room to ensure that all machinery continues to function, and once we have captured the bridge the ship will be turned on to a course for St Nazaire.'

'Can we expect much resistance?' Preuss asked casually.

'Most of the troops on board are low-grade fighting men, who are here to guard you and your fellow prisoners. The Canadians are thinking only of getting home and back into bed with their wives and girlfriends. Other than that, there are about fifty RAF aircrew cadets who might give some trouble, but no match for experienced infantrymen.'

'We shall go through them like a knife through butter,' Preuss said coldly.

'Maybe, but there is just one group who might give us serious trouble. There's a detachment of Royal Marine Commandos on board.'

Preuss looked serious. 'How many?'

'Perhaps fifty, even a hundred. I think they are being sent on a training course in America.'

'You don't think they are here for another reason—because your plan has been blown?'

Müller shook his head. 'There's no sign of that.'

'Where do we find them?'

'On the Main Deck.'

Preuss frowned. 'Main Deck? Why the Main Deck? I thought that was for top-level passengers, not fighting troops.'

Müller worked on in silence a moment, trying to think how he could divert Preuss's unwelcome questions. He wanted to wait until von Stoltz was free to take command before telling the SS man about Churchill's presence on board.

Müller grinned. 'You should know, Major. First-rate

fighting troops enjoy the pleasures of luxury accommodation from time to time.'

Müller heard a whistle from the watchkeepers above and looked towards the ceramic edge of the swimming bath. Two guards were marching slowly in their direction from the far end. He had already been talking to Preuss for some time and to avoid suspicion he would have to move out of the pool on to another job. Yet he would not be able to talk to Preuss again until moments before zero hour. The two Canadians were only twenty yards away now, with another couple almost parallel to them on the other side of the pool. Suddenly the place seemed alive with troops.

Preuss's eyes darted expectantly to Müller as he bent to throw tools into his bag, signalling his intention to leave.

'Remember,' Müller whispered urgently to him, 'you *must* contact von Stoltz—it doesn't matter how. I shall be waiting for your signal during the exercise period in the bows. If you fail, it will be a disaster.'

Müller stood up and shouldered his bag as the Canadians drew abreast of him. One of them looked down.

'Fed up already, mister?'

Müller grinned. 'I'm off to dinner. You won't get me down here again. If there's any more damage they can sleep on the floor.'

Preuss squatted on his bunk and quietly watched Müller leave.

A short while later Müller dug into his lunch of sausages and chips on the crew's mess deck. Around him the seamen were still full of gossip about Churchill being on board.

'And did you see those Wrens?' one of the young lads asked across the sauce bottles. 'Gorgeous birds. Black nylons and all that. I could screw one of those.'

Nobby, spreading margarine thickly on a slice of bread, stopped and turned towards him.

'What do you mean? You could screw one of the Wrens? That's the last thing you would do. Those ladies, and they are ladies, are under top security guard all the time. And that

Major Summers—the one with the little black tash—he'd shoot your balls off if you went near them.'

There was a guffaw from the men round the table, and Müller gently probed Nobby for any more information.

'I wonder what it's like up there on the Main Deck? Must be a fantastic sight.'

'It is. Mr Jackson, the senior steward, told me. They've got phones and telex machines everywhere. Maps, charts, the lot. Mr Jackson's looking after Churchill. Says there's a special dining room where all the work is done. He's cursing, though, because their dinners go on right into the night. Must be fantastic—eavesdropping on Winnie and all his top brass. They say that Professor Lindemann is there, the scientist.'

'He was born a Jerry, you know . . .' a burly seaman pronounced authoritatively from the end of the table.

Müller smiled to himself. Perhaps the Führer would make a special example of Professor Lindemann when they brought him back to Germany . . .

He glanced at the clock, and downed the rest of his tea. In a few minutes it would be exercise time for the prisoners.

He swung his legs over the bench to leave, but Nobby held him back a moment.

'Oh, by the way, mate. The first officer has got some little job he wants you to do . . . putting up some shelves, I think it is.'

'Let me know when he wants to see me.'

'Okay. I'm going back on duty, I'll ask him. But for Christ's sake, if he wants to see you, don't be late. He's a nut for punctuality. Been known to put men in the brig for being late.'

'Sounds like Captain Bligh . . .' someone said, and there was a laugh as Müller headed for the door.

It was just after one-thirty when Müller reached the bows and leaned over the rail above the well deck. The large area below was thronged with prisoners, and the whispering noise of a hundred conversations rose above the sound of the sea. Two machine guns had been set up in the bows, and their crews watched the Germans calmly.

There was a stiff breeze and many of the POWs had done their best to wrap up against the cold ocean air. Some wore long military overcoats, caps pulled down almost to their ears. Others had turned up the collars of their leather panzer jackets or had buttoned tunics to the neck. In the middle of the well deck, however, a group of hardier prisoners relished the Spartan conditions and had lined up in two squads ready for PT. Some wore singlets while others were brave enough to strip to the waist. Here and there a man had been lucky enough to have scrounged a pair of army shorts. Müller smiled to himself as he watched them begin their exercises, thinking how typically Teutonic the scene had become.

The sun appeared from behind a cloud bank and flooded the deck. A group of prisoners, chatting near one of the life-rafts, suddenly parted to make way for von Stoltz, who walked unhurriedly across the teak boards towards a patch of warmth in the far corner. His adjutant and staff followed.

'A lot of them, aren't there?' It was Nobby Clark. Müller had not seen him come on deck, but now he leaned on the rail next to him, rolling a cigarette. He wetted the paper with a flick of his tongue, then squeezed the cylinder together. 'They should be happy about going to the States. No rationing and lots of pretty girls.'

The words acted like an unexpected door to Müller's memory. He found himself thinking of the true Olaf Larsen, leaning next to him, a smile on his face as he joked about Müller being able to live off the fat of the land as a prisoner, if ever they were rescued. Müller looked at Nobby's leathery face and sensed a similarity with the Norwegian's wry humour and the same expansive goodwill.

'Still, they say that all's fair in love and war, don't they?' Nobby laughed. 'And that's bloody well true as far as those buggers are concerned. He drew on his cigarette before announcing, 'The first officer wants to see you—that job I told you about.'

Müller nodded, half listening, and turned back to comb the ranks of the POWs for Preuss. He was nowhere to be seen. Müller could feel the worry growing within him.

'How long are they allowed to exercise?' he asked Nobby casually, his eyes on the lines of men now swinging their arms rhythmically from side to side.

'Only about twenty minutes. They come up in groups.'

Christ, Müller thought. Preuss might be allowed on deck at a different time to von Stoltz. If that were so his message would never get through.

Nobby was pulling at his sleeve.

'Here, come on, Olaf. I've been sent to get you.'

The little man was beginning to irritate Müller.

'Get me? What for?'

'Well, you're a bloody chippy, aren't you? The first officer wants you. He's God, you know, and he's got some job he wants you to do.'

'Can't he wait a minute or two?' Müller said.

'He's off duty in a few minutes and told me to bring you up right away.'

Nobby detected Müller's sudden tension. 'There's no problem, is there?'

Müller again swept his eyes over the deck. To his dismay von Stoltz was standing up, pulling his greatcoat round his shoulders, preparing to leave. Where the hell was Preuss? The thought crossed Müller's mind that the SS man might have decided to abandon the whole operation as too risky. Or von Stoltz might be suspicious.

The prisoners began to leave the deck. When Nobby spoke again, this time more insistently, Müller almost pushed him away.

'Come on, Olaf, you'll get me into hot water. The first officer can be a right bastard.'

Müller threw Nobby a sidelong glance and pointed to his stomach. 'Sorry, mate, but I've been feeling a bit sick. Just wanted some air. Can't he wait for a minute or two?'

Nobby looked askance. 'What is it? Some bug? You seemed all right earlier.' Nobby's grey features began to redden and Müller was surprised at the seaman's strength when he gripped his arm and wheeled him around. His jaw was stubborn.

'What the hell is this all about? For Christ's sake, tear your eyes away from the deck for a minute. I put a word in

256

for you with the first officer because he wanted a job done. Now you're going to drop me in it . . .'

Müller stepped back from the rail, still aware that Preuss had not appeared. Von Stoltz was certain to go below at any moment.

'I'm sorry,' he replied, 'but I really have been feeling a bit queasy. It just suddenly happened. Can't you give me a couple of minutes?'

Nobby's eyes were suspicious now, and drifted from Müller to the deck below. 'Have you been working a fiddle or something with those Jerries? Flogging them cigarettes?'

Müller stretched out a hand beseechingly. 'Now would I do a thing like that?' He turned and waved his arm over the well deck. 'Look at them. They haven't got two pennies to rub together.'

Nobby followed Müller's gaze, and Müller seized the chance to scan the deck again for Preuss. At last he saw him immediately below the rail, but von Stoltz had gone. Had they been able to speak to each other? If not, how on earth could he re-jig Operation Iceman? The colonel would not be expecting a briefing, and would never have time to organise his men.

Nobby turned from the rail, a look of disgust on his face. 'I really don't understand you, Larsen. What shall I tell the first officer—that you won't come up, even though you've got nothing on?'

Müller turned away from the rail. He did not want to turn the little man into an enemy. Nobby was shrewd, and might well start to look at Müller in a new light—as Jacobsen had done. Yet how could he risk the operation?

'All right, Nobby, I'm coming,' he said with a sigh, and took a last look over the rail. He almost laughed aloud with relief. A new squad of prisoners had lined up for PT, a blond-haired instructor stretching his arms out before them. They moved rhythmically in unison—except for one man. In the last rank on the far right Preuss was in short sleeves, his arms held above his head. Slowly he swung his torso, once, twice, three times. Müller grinned at Nobby. 'C'mon, mate, I'm not that terrible. To tell you the truth, I got pissed last night and I've got a god-awful hangover.'

He pulled away from the rail and clapped the Englishman on the shoulder.

'Now, what does number one want?'

'You'll find out soon enough,' said Nobby, turning from him without a smile.

Chapter 25

Tracey O'Brien strolled along St John's Wood High Street in carefree mood. She had finished early for the day. It was a pleasant sunny afternoon and she stopped outside a small greengrocer's, alive with spring flowers. The proprietor, a shabby man in his late forties, came out to serve her, eyeing her admiringly. She bought a bunch of yellow irises, thanked him, and carried on towards her flat. How pleasant it would have been to have enjoyed a quiet dinner with James! What was he doing now? He hadn't written to her since that hasty note, but that wasn't surprising in wartime. Just so long as he had not been sent on a dangerous assignment . . .

She entered the dark Victorian building and stepped into the lift. Had James been there he would have been standing close to her, as he had the night they returned from the Wigmore Hall. Those quiet, intelligent eyes would have been looking down at hers. 'So, up we go to another of those splendid American dinners. What are you making this time? Baked ham? Sweet corn?'

'I am indeed,' she imagined herself answering.

'I've brought you this,' he would say, flourishing a fine bottle of claret. 'From the PM's personal wine cellar.' And then, conspiratorially, 'Only the most trusted members of the Secretariat are allowed down there.'

The lift came to a halt at the third floor and Tracey imagined James's arm around her waist, steering her gently along the corridor. The warmth of his hand pressed through the thin cotton of her dress on to her back. The apartment door was ahead, and she was fumbling for her key, conscious of his body against hers.

'Good evening, Miss O'Brien.'

This time it was not James's voice she heard. Two men were standing in the shadows at the far end of the landing. Tracey stood holding her key, feeling foolish at being caught out in her reverie. The men walked towards her. The younger of the two was well built, in his early thirties. He was dressed in a crumpled blue suit, the knot of his tie fastened small and tight. His shirt collar was damp with sweat and his pallid face was topped by straw-coloured hair already beginning to thin.

His colleague was about fifty, and clearly the more senior of the pair. He was short and dapper, and advanced with quick, purposeful steps. He held a brown trilby in his right hand, like a courtier; an umbrella was slung over his wrist. His brown hopsack suit was showing signs of wear but his brogues were highly polished and his grey hair was well groomed. Tracey regarded him with a journalist's eye, even now noticing the neat grey moustache and odd eyebrows, which curled upwards at the corners, giving him a momentarily comic appearance.

'Miss O'Brien, we would like you to come along with us. To help us with our enquiries.' The older man's tone was courteous.

'Enquiries? Who *are* you?' she demanded, instinctively taking a step backwards and holding her flowers as if to ward off evil spirits.

He pulled at his moustache. 'I really don't want to discuss it here, Miss O'Brien,' he said, more brusquely. 'We are Intelligence officers. That should be enough.'

'But what's going on? Are you arresting me? If you are, I shall phone my embassy. I do have that right.'

'Of course. Only we have spoken to your embassy already. It's our normal procedure.'

He drew out a buff card about the size of a small envelope, and Tracey was reassured to see the royal coat of arms on the cover. Inside there was an identity photograph of the man before her and a short, typed statement introducing her to Major Holden, member of the Special Investigations Department, Home Office. Beneath she read the signature of Herbert Morrison, Home Secretary.

'Thank you, Major Holden,' she said politely, handing back the card.

He gave a faint smile and introduced her to his companion, whom he referred to simply as 'Dawkins'.

'May I at least ring my paper before we leave?' Tracey asked, moving towards her flat, key still in her hand.

The major shook his head. 'I understand your feelings, Miss O'Brien, but we would prefer you not to talk to any newspaper at this stage.'

'Why not?'

'It's not convenient,' the younger man cut in sharply. Tracey began to protest, but Holden cut her short.

'As I say, I do realise how you feel, Miss O'Brien. If it helps in any way I have no objection to you telephoning Major Van Kleef who, I believe, is a friend of yours. You can do that from my office. In the meantime if you wish to collect anything from your flat . . .'

The mention of Van Kleef's name took Tracey by surprise, but though meant to reassure her it merely fed her anger. What had these men been doing, probing into her private life? What made her so interesting to them that they had been going round interviewing her personal friends? She asked herself what right they had to find out how she spent her time and where she went. And the answer, she knew, was they had all the rights they needed. That small buff card represented the total power of the State to act as it deemed necessary in time of war.

Major Holden pointed to the door and suggested agreeably that Tracey should leave her flowers in her flat. As she turned the lock she felt the younger man's pale eyes watching her like a fish. Although both men automatically followed her into the flat she made no attempt to invite them to sit down, but left them standing in the middle of the lounge whilst she took her time putting the irises in water. Then she picked up a white cardigan and announced herself ready to leave.

Outside, the sun had gone in. She pulled on her cardigan, tugging it closely round her shoulders as Holden led her towards a black Wolseley parked across the road.

The car swung out of St John's Wood Road and turned right, heading for South London. She had been placed in the back, next to Holden, her view blocked by the broad back of Dawkins behind the wheel. The predominant smell was of stale tobacco and leather.

As they passed through the traffic Major Holden made one or two sporadic attempts at conversation, commenting on the weather, bomb damage, the shortages in the shops; but Tracey was distant in her replies. She deeply distrusted both men, and had developed a distaste for the suave charm of the major. Dawkins rarely spoke, but drove directly towards Lambeth Bridge, where they turned right along the Albert Embankment. Staring at the classic view of London across the river, Tracey found it hard to believe that she had allowed herself to be taken to an unknown destination by two men she had never met before.

The Wolseley sped past the fresh spring foliage of Clapham Common until eventually Dawkins drew up outside a rambling Victorian house on its north side. A stocky man opened the front door. Tracey followed her inquisitors into a large hall, and Holden opened the door of what appeared to be a large drawing room, with bay windows overlooking a leafy front garden. A plush three-piece suite stood in front of a cast-iron fireplace, with a marble mantelpiece. On the walls there were one or two gloomy landscapes in the style of Landseer. The carpets were beginning to wear, and it had plainly been some time since the room had been dusted.

Holden walked over to a leather-topped mahogany table by the window and waved Tracey to a straight-backed chair next to the table on the far side. He himself settled in an armchair, and as the evening sunlight picked out the grey in his hair Tracey was reminded of nothing so much as a shrewd headmaster. About to address a recalcitrant pupil?

She undid her cardigan, feeling that the room was airless, and watched Holden lean forward and draw a cardboard file from one of his trays. She glanced around for Dawkins and discovered that he was standing quietly by the door.

'You can ring Major Van Kleef now, if you wish.' Holden pushed the phone towards her.

Tracey immediately dialled the number of the US Army Headquarters, and breathed a sigh of relief when Dutch's voice came on the line. 'Hi, Tracey.'

'Dutch, do you know what I'm ringing about? I'm with two strange men somewhere in South London.'

There was an embarrassed pause before Van Kleef answered. 'Yeah, I guess so.'

'What's going on? Am I under arrest or something? They say they're special investigators. Who are they? And what the hell am I supposed to have done?'

'Now don't go jumping to any wrong conclusions,' Van Kleef said quickly. 'The two gentlemen with you are officers of MI5. I can vouch for them personally. They just want you to help them on a delicate investigation. That's all, Tracey.'

'But Dutch, can anything happen to me here . . .?'

'Tracey, take it easy,' Dutch said reassuringly. 'I'll keep an eye on you. You can trust me.'

'Yes, okay,' she said quietly, the anger in her dying away as quickly as it had begun. There seemed nothing else she could say. She put the phone down, aware of the awkwardness in Van Kleef's voice.

She turned to Major Holden, who had been staring idly out of the window.

'Could you please tell me what this is all about?'

'I am afraid we have to ask *you* to help *us* by answering a few questions.'

'But how can I help you?'

He considered her thoughtfully from under his bushy eyebrows for a moment, then walked away from the window and stood in front of his desk. He picked up the file and studied the papers as if Tracey were not there, then with a deft movement untied the cord on the file's spike and lifted out a sheet of paper. When his large brown eyes switched to Tracey, she began to feel afraid.

'Now, you are a good journalist, I gather, Miss O'Brien. And I am sure you have a very good memory. Can you remember the news story you wrote on twenty-ninth April this year for the *Sentinel*?'

Tracey's mind whirled. The end of April: what had that been? The trip with James, or had it been a story at the US embassy? She struggled for an answer, anxious not to commit herself.

'Come now, Miss O'Brien. You remember it, surely,' Holden insisted. 'I would if I were a journalist. It appears to have been something of a scoop.'

Holden squared his shoulders and held up the paper before his eyes. A news cutting was pasted in the middle of the sheet. He began to read from it in measured tones.

'"It can now be confidently forecast that important meetings between the president and prime minister are about to take place. Already there have been rumours of disagreements about the main thrust of the Allied efforts . . ."'

Tracey shifted in her chair. So MI5 had been checking into her sources. Probably her story had been far too accurate. If so, that was too bad; it had all been cleared through official channels.

Holden continued reading. '"Frequent meetings between the two leaders of the Alliance have been a feature of the war effort, and there is every sign that only the mutual respect of the two world figures can reconcile major strategic plans."'

He dropped the paper on the table and surveyed Tracey evenly, his polished brogues swinging idly.

'That's very interesting stuff, isn't it, Miss O'Brien? Especially for the enemy.'

Tracey made up her mind. She felt totally sure of herself. Holden had put his foot in it, dragging her here like a criminal, denying her the right to phone her office. He was going to pay for the trouble he had caused. Her grey eyes flashed.

'Now look. You may be MI5 but you can't accuse me of leaking information. That story was passed by the censor. I find your whole attitude deeply offensive, and I demand an explanation . . .'

Holden lifted up his hand beseechingly. 'Miss O'Brien, let's not get into arguments about freedom of the press. It's much too tedious in wartime.' He sighed. 'Yes, the censor did see your story and yes, he did pass it, with a few important changes. Then he informed us.'

Tracey rose to her feet. 'Why have you brought me here then? I've done nothing wrong.'

Holden slipped off the table and walked behind her. 'Miss O'Brien, please sit down. This will get us nowhere. Believe me, we have ample powers to deal with you.' Tracey resumed her seat. The major continued. 'You wrote your story very well, and passed it through the proper channels. There's no question about that. What we are interested to know is how you came by such information.'

He gave her a faint smile but Tracey felt her confidence seep away. Were they investigating her connection with James? As if to answer her question Holden turned over a page in the file and said, 'We have been keeping you under observation, so to speak. And of course we are very interested in your circle of friends. One in particular.'

'Who?' Tracey asked, dreading the answer.

'Squadron Leader James Alloway, of course. A highly regarded man at Downing Street.'

'James is nothing to do with my professional activities.'

'We shall see.'

There was a tap at the door and the thickset young man who had let them into the house entered the room with a tray laden with a teapot and cups. Holden watched him set it down in front of him.

'I'm sure you would like some tea?' he said courteously.

She looked at the teapot suspiciously. 'No, thank you.'

Holden's eyebrows rose, making him look for a moment all the more like a music-hall comic.

'We are not running the white slave trade, Miss O'Brien.'

He insisted on pouring her a cup and placed it steaming before her, but she still refused to touch it.

As he sipped his own tea she studied his complacent features and wondered what his next move would be. Her anger rising, she decided on counter-attack. 'If you have kept me under observation then you will know that your suspicion is misplaced. I might remind you again that I am an American citizen and an accredited war correspondent.'

The major nodded. 'Indeed. We are aware of that. After all, we are on the same side, aren't we?'

There was a pause. Tracey began to feel that things were falling into perspective. 'Look, if that article was a security risk then I am deeply sorry. I don't want to embarrass the government in time of war.'

For a moment Holden pursed his lips thoughtfully, then turned over another piece of paper.

'Miss O'Brien, it's not your article on twenty-ninth April that worries us, but it did encourage us to take a look at your other work. After all, we do this quite regularly, especially with the neutral correspondents in London.'

Tracey frowned. 'I'm not a damned neutral—'

'Of course not,' Holden interrupted soothingly. 'Although it has to be said that your father was a leading isolationist.'

His words angered Tracey even more. She leaned forward, pushing her hair from her forehead. 'That is nothing to do with my attitudes. Your research should have told you that, at least.'

The major ignored her protests and silently turned the pages in the file, taking out a sheet marked with a red asterisk.

'We have some very good cryptographers in Britain,' Holden remarked drily. 'Strange, eccentric people who can find all sorts of buried meanings in the simplest of messages. Many cables and messages sent out of the country by neutrals are examined by them. We asked them to look at your articles.'

Tracey smoothed her dress and sat back in her chair, looking at the darkening trees outside.

Holden spoke again. 'Do you recall the article you wrote for the *Sentinel* on thirtieth March? Surely you do? It was on the inoffensive subject of Woolton Pie?'

'Yes,' she said uncertainly.

'Woolton Pie. Only it turned out to be a far more interesting subject than that.'

He handed her the sheet to which a news clipping from the *Sentinel* had been attached. It was already turning yellow. She scanned it eagerly, and frowned when she perceived that certain groups of words had been ringed in blue crayon.

'But what does it mean?' she asked.

'I think you know what it means. Turn over the page.'

Slowly she read the devastating words: ' "*Queen Mary* to ship GIs east, prisoners west, soon." But I didn't send that. I wouldn't have sent that. No—'

She began to feel sick.

In New York another woman was being questioned, also by declared agents of the State. Within hours of Lieutenant Riley's call FBI investigators had begun checking out shipping companies, maritime administration records, seamen's clubs, and the crewing lists of all vessels leaving the East Coast ports.

When it became clear that the man they were seeking could also be on board one of the thousands of merchant ships sailing in distant waters the local chief of FBI operations in New York had exploded at the impossible task Riley had imposed on his department. The lieutenant had been told in no uncertain terms that his request for such a vast hunt bordered on the irresponsible, and a definite limit had been placed on the number of days it would continue.

Only a few hours remained when, shortly before six p.m. on 7 May, a footsore FBI agent named Hammond had arrived at the War Shipping Administration building close to Pier 90. One by one he interrogated the staff, showing them a photograph of a clean-shaven Norwegian. At last he came to a friendly-faced woman in her early thirties. She peered at the photograph through tortoiseshell spectacles before saying warmly, 'Why, I've seen him before!'

'When?' the agent asked wearily.

It was the tenth time somebody had claimed to have seen Larsen before; each time, following hours of industrious checking, they had been proved mistaken. The woman looked more closely at the picture. 'Oh yes,' she beamed. 'No doubt about it. He came in here about two weeks ago. A charming man.' She described how the Norwegian had come into the office. Suddenly her face clouded. 'Why, has he done anything wrong? I wouldn't want to get him into trouble.'

'We're just trying to find him, that's all,' the agent said.

'He was a nice man, but it was such a pity about his family. I remember now he had a pregnant wife in Scotland, you know. That's why he asked me if I could get him aboard the *Queen Mary*.'

Six men sat before Colonel von Stoltz in his tiny cabin, and listened attentively. They had all been carefully chosen by their commander to lead the prisoners on D Deck into action. Major Erik Mecklen in his late twenties was in the front row, his arms folded across his chest. Behind him were three experienced infantry officers, one of whom, Bucholz, still wore an Afrika Korps cap. The two other men were engineers. Captain von Albrecht, the colonel's aide, stood close to the door where he could be in easy contact with watchkeepers posted outside.

From time to time the men's eyes moved to the sketch drawing of the *Queen Mary* that Müller had prepared and which now lay on the table before them. The Main Deck had been heavily outlined in black crayon.

'That is where we shall find Churchill,' the colonel said, and the other officers murmured in agreement. 'And it is our mission, and I repeat *our* mission, to capture the whole of the Main Deck intact. It is full of priceless information and you must move with great speed, the enemy must have no chance to destroy their papers.'

'When do we expect to come up against the Royal Marines?' Mecklen asked.

'Zero hour plus fifteen minutes,' von Stoltz replied. 'By then Major Preuss will be holding the armoury with an advance party. He has only fifty men available in the swimming pool, and the first assault group will be kept to only a handful of men so that it can move fast and avoid attention. A second, larger group of fifteen men accompanied by the special agent code-named "Iceman" will advance from the swimming pool to make contact with us, and overwhelm the guard.'

267

Von Stoltz paused, considered the sketch once more then said, 'Then the main assault will be up to you. The nine hundred men on this deck will be split into six action groups, and each of you will be assigned to command one of them. Major Mecklen will lead the biggest group in an attack on the primary objective—the Main Deck.'

There was a silence as the officers absorbed the information they had been given, then, at von Stoltz's invitation, von Albrecht gave further details of the allocation of men to various units, communications procedures through runners and how captured weapons were to be distributed.

'And when we have control of the ship, what then?' an infantryman asked.

'All civilians will be placed in the main restaurant under armed guard,' von Albrecht declared. 'British troops and service personnel will be imprisoned on this deck in our accommodation. Any crew member not obeying orders will be shot. Women and children will be confined to their cabins.' Von Albrecht continued to explain in detail how the ship would be run by the Germans, even down to the management of the kitchens.

The meeting was drawing to a close when von Stoltz thanked his aide and spoke confidentially to his men.

'This is a difficult operation, gentlemen. I want it carried out with the utmost efficiency. But there is one consideration above all. We must take Churchill alive. I make no secret that in the heat of the action some groups may be tempted to take independent action, and will try to kill as many of the British leaders as they can. Such a course can only be a last resort and carried out on my specific orders.'

The colonel paused a moment, knowing what his men were thinking.

'That directive applies to Major Preuss and his men as much as it does to you. Disobedience will be severely and summarily dealt with.'

In the ship's cinema on the Promenade Deck HMS *Victory* bore down under full sail towards the French line at Trafalgar. There were growls of approval from the prime minister. Beaverbrook too chuckled as he watched the British broadsides smash into the French rigging and cascades of water deluge the French sailors. Masts fell amid the roar of the cannon while Nelson stood serene on the quarterdeck. Alloway sat in the back row enjoying the prime minister's favourite film, *Lady Hamilton*, but a quick glance at his watch reminded him of his duties. There would be incoming signals at the cipher office, and he had to check a long despatch on the Middle East. He hurried along to the Main Deck.

'Good film, I suppose? It's been quite busy,' the Wren duty supervisor said, her head bent over a long signal. 'I was just about to send for you. A top priority signal went down for the general some time ago. It was for his eyes only.'

Alloway nodded, aware that signals were often of such a secret nature that they could only be read by the person to whom they were transmitted. He had begun to read through the long Middle East despatch when Major Summers entered the small office. Alloway was surprised to see him, but asked cheerfully, 'Been inspecting the guards?'

Summers stood erect, coolly observing Alloway.

'General Ismay wants to see you at once.'

His clipped tones jarred, and the Wren supervisor glanced up anxiously as Alloway followed the major to the general's office. Ismay was sorting out papers and seemed paler than usual. He immediately stopped working and studied Alloway for a moment, marshalling his thoughts. Summers hovered in the background. 'Shall I go, sir? he asked.

'No, you'd better stay.' Ismay leaned forward and handed Alloway a slip of paper. 'What do you make of this?'

It was a terse message from MI5 to Ismay:

'*For Your Eyes Only.*
Strongly advise you suspend James Alloway from all duties. He is a contact of Tracey O'Brien, suspected enemy agent.'

It was signed by the deputy head of MI5. Alloway could not take in the words at first. Then the full meaning of the message bore in on him.

'I just don't understand it, sir.'

'But you do know this woman?' Ismay's expression was grave.

'Yes, sir. We are close friends.'

'Lovers?'

'Yes, sir; lovers,' Alloway replied, conscious of Summers behind him.

The general seemed to relax and there was a sympathetic look in his eyes. 'You see what a terrible position this puts you in?'

'Of course,' Alloway said firmly. 'Although I find it hard to believe that MI5 is right. I believe they are acting on circumstantial evidence, and they have drawn the wrong conclusions.'

'But this girl is the daughter of Henry O'Brien?' the general protested. 'A bloody isolationist, a sworn enemy of this country.'

'Yes, sir.'

'Well, it's hardly wise of you to be on such close terms with someone like her,' the general commented with irritation. 'Have you told her anything of importance that you can recall?'

Alloway flushed with indignation. 'No, sir. Nothing.'

'Nothing about this trip, for example? That would be too bad.'

Alloway's mind went back to the times they had spent together. To her grey eyes, her mane of auburn hair. Had she been betraying him? He choked back a feeling of sickness.

'There must be a terrible error,' he persisted limply. But the general's questions came thick and fast. How long had he known her? Where had he taken her, to whom had she been introduced? As he answered Alloway felt doubts rising in his own mind. He recollected their first lunch, at the Connaught, and the way she had continually seemed to push for information: MI5 could be right.

At last Ismay stopped, rose to his feet and poured himself a whisky. He offered Alloway a glass.

'I really don't think she's a spy, sir,' Alloway ventured. 'There must be some balls-up by MI5. It has been known.'

'I grant you that,' Ismay replied. 'Damn it, you're one of my most valuable men, Alloway. I would have thought you had displayed your loyalty pretty convincingly against the Luftwaffe.' He put his glass down wearily. 'But there will still have to be an investigation. No doubt it will start in New York—and I shall have to suspend you from any work you are doing until you are cleared. You could hardly be in a more sensitive area. You had better stay in your cabin until we reach New York, where you can help MI5, the FBI or whoever get to the bottom of this.' The general's face softened, and he went back to his chair. 'I'm sorry, James.'

Summers opened the door and escorted him back to his cabin. Once they were on their own Summers no longer seemed his Puritan self. He looked at Alloway with sympathy as he slumped on his bunk.

'I'm sorry too, Alloway. I'm sure it will be cleared up.'

'It had bloody well better be. Stupid bastards, MI5.'

'Of course, the prime minister has been told. We had to do that. You'll have Inspector Thompson and the security officers down here soon. If I were you, I'd reserve my defence until we reach New York.' The major moved to the door. 'It's all right, this will be unlocked. But don't do anything silly.'

Alloway managed a smile. On squadron operations he had shot three German fighters out of the sky and had flown forty missions over enemy territory. He would not 'do anything silly'.

After Summers had gone he began to try to face the appalling damage he had done to himself through his friendship with Tracey. He was certain that he had not told her anything that would be a security leak, but MI5 were powerful and clever enough to use any circumstantial evidence to ruin him if need be. He wondered what had happened to her, how she was being treated and, as he went over their conversations together, he tried to recall any moment when Tracey had appeared to be other than an attractive young journalist. She was ambitious, and determined, but he loved her candour and forthright attitudes towards the world. No, he was certain MI5 had made a disastrous error.

Several hundred miles north-west of the *Queen Mary*'s position Captain Werner Hartstein took a last look round the horizon. The ocean was pitch black, broken only by the white bow wave of U-1264. To north and south he knew that the other U-boat captains in his group were likewise scanning the empty sea, yet even if they sighted an enemy battle fleet they were forbidden to attack it. Once again Hartstein wondered what his sealed orders contained and could only imagine that it must be a very special target!

'I'm going below,' he told his number one, and slid down the steep ladder to the control room. Once there, he walked across to the hydrophone operator, sitting at his listening post.

'Any signs of life?'

'Just a few whales, Captain.'

'Keep me posted.' Hartstein moved to the radio booth. Inside, the telegraphist was listening for any signals beamed at Hartstein's group, but nothing had been received for almost twenty hours. The telegraphist lifted off an earphone. 'Nothing new, sir,' he reported. 'But there's tremendous radio traffic between HQ and the wolf packs farther west.'

Hartstein nodded dispiritedly. He knew that there was a major convoy battle going on, with perhaps forty boats involved, and he had to sit idly by waiting for orders. Aware of his own frustration he walked into the wardroom and slid behind the narrow table. The chief engineer put his head round the corner.

'Any news?'

'Nothing. It's black as ink out there. Not a sign of life.' Hartstein drew out a bottle of schnapps from a locker and filled the engineer's glass, offering him a dark Sumatra cigar.

'What's going on, Skipper?' the chief asked through a blue haze.

Hartstein shrugged. 'Whatever it is, it must be pretty big to keep us out of that little fight off Newfoundland. Here we are with perhaps the best battle group in the Kriegsmarine, armed with the latest Zauenkönig torpedoes, and we aren't even allowed to attack an enemy ship unless specifically ordered to do so. I suppose all will be revealed when we open the sealed orders.'

'The ways of U-Boat Command are mysterious to behold,' the chief commented. 'But if ever we have a chance to use the Zauenkönig that will shake the British. It might be worth waiting for.'

Hartstein agreed, and remembered the torpedo tests in the Baltic where the new weapon had tracked down a target boat however much it twisted and turned. He poured himself another schnapps.

'God knows why HQ are keeping us on station like this. It's three days now.'

'It'll be just our luck for a battle wagon to come over the horizon. What are you going to do then?'

Hartstein laughed drily. 'Obey orders like a good officer, and let it steam by.'

There was a tap on the wardroom door and the yeoman of signals looked into the room. 'A message from U-Boat Command.'

Hartstein's spirits rose as he took the signal log, hoping that it was the directive to open the sealed orders—or at least instructions to join the battle farther west. To his surprise the message was quite different.

'What have we got to do now?' the chief asked.

Hartstein read aloud from the signal. ' "Proceed three hundred and fifty miles, south-south-east, with complete group. Group Sieg will be positioned two hundred miles north west of you." '

Hartstein pulled himself to his feet and stomped out of the wardroom to consult the small chart table in the control room. The reason for the new position mystified him, and he was unaware of the painful guesswork taking place in Headquarters, thousands of miles away, where it had been decided to move his group south, ready to intercept the *Queen Mary*.

In a few minutes Hartstein had worked out the new course and gave his orders to the engine room.

'Full ahead both. Steer starboard thirty.'

With a shudder the MAN diesels picked up speed and U-1264 turned her prow towards the south, closing the gap with her prey.

Chapter 26

It was almost midnight. Müller lay on his bunk, his eyes on the small reading lamp next to Nobby's bed. All the other men in the cabin were asleep, but the Cockney was absorbed in a detective novel. Müller began to sweat. Under his bedclothes he was wearing his navy-blue jersey and dark denims. He wondered how the other Germans were faring several decks below, whether they had managed to keep their preparations secret: one blabber-mouth could destroy the entire operation.

Again he looked across at Nobby, curled up on his bed. It had been a strange evening, drinking in the Pig and Whistle, and Müller regretted that he would soon be fighting the men he could still call his friends and shipmates. One or two of them had commented on his silence, and asked whether he might not be sickening for something. He found himself wondering how they would react once the truth was discovered. Nobby in particular would be appalled. The Englishman turned over a page and glanced up.

'What's the matter, mate? Can't you sleep?'

'I could if your light was off,' Müller complained lightly.

Nobby grinned. 'Okay. Two more pages to the end of this chapter, then out it goes.'

He was as good as his word, and soon the room was plunged into darkness.

Two decks above, Major Summers was sleeping soundly. At first his eyelids did not move when the Royal Marine lieutenant threw open his cabin door. Once a sumptuous suite for film stars, Summers's room was now furnished austerely with a phone and filing cabinet. The only concession to comfort was a large lamp next to the bed.

Without hesitation the lieutenant immediately reached for the lamp, switched it on, and began to shake Summers's shoulder. The major's eyes opened and were still clearing of sleep when the lieutenant announced, 'An urgent signal, sir. From Washington.' Summers sat bolt upright and took the paper from his subordinate's hand. He quickly read:

'FBI reports suspected enemy serving aboard Queen Mary *under name of Olaf Larsen. Working in capacity of ship's carpenter. Assumed nationality Norwegian. Age 28. Hair fair. Six feet one, 170 pounds. Action soonest. Extra cover being sent via Admiralty.*
USN, USAAF.'

It was signed by the FBI.

'Christ,' Summers said, swinging his legs over the side of the bed and reaching for his trousers. 'A Jerry agent on board. This is going to make us popular. Put all our units on alert at once. Double the guard on the prime minister, but for Christ's sake don't make a fuss about it.' He prepared himself to break the unpalatable news to General Ismay.

It was well after two a.m. when Müller left his bunk and cautiously made his way up the aft staircase to the Boat Deck. He checked to see whether the upperworks were deserted then, as noiselessly as he could, crept towards the lifeboat in which he had installed the radio transmitter.

He reached the boat, pushed his tool bag gently over the side and hauled himself over the gunwale. He carefully unpacked his tool bag and took out six packets of yellow plastic. These he lay side by side beneath the thwarts in the boat's stern, where nobody could see them. All his equipment was now in the lifeboat, including the Smith and Wesson, which he checked to ensure was dry and fully loaded.

There was little he could do now, except hope that the prisoners were quietly assembling below, ready to carry out their orders. He found that he had developed a growing dislike of Preuss, but at least the major could be relied upon to execute his part of the operation efficiently.

At fifteen minutes to zero hour he crawled across the thwarts to the transmitter. His palms were damp and for a moment he fiddled nervously with the last valve until it slotted firmly into place. The set was ready; it was time at last to signal Headquarters.

He looked around the confined space under the awning, and the memory of Larsen's strong hands pulling him over the side came back to him. It took him some effort to realise that it had happened just over two months before—he felt he had lived a lifetime since then. With relief he realised that he could now cast aside the identity of Olaf Larsen, and become once again a member of a regular fighting service. His eyes caught the small locker in the lifeboat, and he remembered the cognac that had warmed him as he lay exhausted on the boards of the *Empire Rose*'s lifeboat. He could never face an ordeal like that again. Operation Iceman had to succeed.

He reached forward and delicately raised the radio key on the transmitter, then resolutely tapped out, '*Iceman—Iceman—Iceman.*'

After a brief pause he tapped: '*QM Central Atlantic. Churchill aboard. Repeat. Churchill aboard. Operation begins.*'

Once again he repeated the signal until he felt sure that the Kriegsmarine radio masts in western France and Holland had received it and fixed the *Queen Mary*'s position. Then he stowed the radio away. He had timed it perfectly: five minutes to three.

He clambered into the lifeboat's stern and pulled open the small locker which contained emergency rations. Inside he felt the distinctive shape of a Johnny Walker bottle that he had hidden there. With the whisky under his arm, he climbed out of the lifeboat and made his way towards the aft lift which would take him to the swimming pool. There was a narrow circle of light outside the entrance to the pool and he could see two soldiers chatting quietly in front of the doors. Each was armed with a Lee-Enfield rifle. The younger one, a thin lad who could have been no more than nineteen, lounged against the wall, the top button of his battledress undone. His colleague, a short, bow-legged man almost twenty years his senior, was talking. He stopped as Müller emerged into the light and turned his pale face towards him.

'It's all right. Only me, Olaf Larsen,' Müller said, hoping that they recognised him from his stints in the pool. 'I've brought something for the sergeant. There's nobody around, is there? No officers?'

The young soldier stopped leaning against the wall. 'Officers?' he crowed. 'At this time of night? You must be joking.' His eyes spotted the whisky bottle and he gave a knowing grin, but the older man merely looked suspicious. When he spoke it was with a strong Welsh accent. 'Strange, you walking around in the middle of the night. What's it you want?'

'To tell the truth,' he said conspiratorially, putting his hand on the man's shoulder and breathing out whisky fumes, 'I've lost a packet at cards and thought I might refill the coffers by a little trading.' He waved the bottle. The Welshman turned away with a disdainful expression. 'That's the trouble with you Norwegians, you drink too much.'

Müller towered over the Welshman, who obviously had no intention of being helpful. He had not expected to be thwarted by such a stickler for the rules, and began to wonder what to do next. The young soldier was only three feet away. He could probably kill both of them, but it would be risky: they might cry out and alert the entire guard.

He glanced over the Welshman's shoulder at the frosted glass doors. Inside Preuss and his men would be waiting tensely for the operation to begin. If he did not appear soon they might be tempted to jump the gun.

He turned and gave the young soldier a wink, before addressing the Welshman.

'You know, the sergeant's going to be furious if you don't let me through.' He looked sombre. 'I wouldn't like to be in your shoes in the morning, Taffy.'

The Welshman's mouth was set in an uncompromising line.

'Tell you what,' Müller ventured. 'Let me through and I'll ask him to give you a drink.'

'Never touch the stuff,' the Welshman retorted, his nose wrinkling with disgust, but as Müller anticipated the younger soldier brushed past him, pushing back his shoulder strap.

'Come on, Taff. Don't be such a spoil-sport. You may not like the stuff but I wouldn't mind a swig. This bloke's all right—he comes down here to work every day.'

The Welshman's pale eyes darted from the young soldier to Müller then, to Müller's relief, the forbidding set of his mouth relaxed a fraction.

'All right. You can go through. But don't drop us in it.'

Müller grinned, patted the young soldier on the shoulder and pushed open the doors.

The lofty ceiling of the pool was in darkness. Only the slip walk was illuminated, by one or two lamps set low in the ceramic walls. There was no sign of life from the bunks in the centre of the bath, and the door to the gymnasium was closed. A bright shaft of light shone from the half-open door of the sergeant's office. Gripping the neck of the whisky bottle, Müller strode forward, certain that Preuss was watching his every move from his bunk.

Two sentries were on duty on the long slip walks down the side of the pool, and Müller stopped when one of them approached him from the far end. There was nothing to fear: the soldier knew Müller's face, and gestured for him to go ahead.

With a loud knock Müller pushed open the office door. The NCO was sitting at a table, working busily on a duty roster watched balefully by two privates drinking tea on a bench against the wall, some twenty feet away. A poster with a girl in a bathing costume advertising a swimming gala was pinned above their heads. Müller's eyes brightened when he spied in the far left-hand corner a neat stack of rifles and six sten guns.

The sergeant put down his pen and looked up. 'Blimey, talk about burning the candle at both ends.'

Müller held out the bottle. 'I've brought you a present.' The sergeant's eyes widened appreciatively.

'Just what I need.'

He took the bottle from Müller's hand and his stubby fingers began to strip away the paper round the cork, eyed enviously by the two privates.

'What about a drop over here then, Sarge?' one of them said, sticking out his large mug, but the sergeant ignored his call and began to look around for glasses.

'How much do I owe you?'

'Thirty bob,' Müller answered, slipping his hand into his pocket and gripping the butt of the Smith and Wesson. He kept half an eye on the two men at the end of the room as the sergeant began to fumble in the breast pocket of his khaki blouse. When he looked up he found he was staring straight into the muzzle of Müller's gun.

'What the bloody hell—?'

'Over there, fast,' Müller ordered. He stepped back to cover the two privates, who were staring at him open-mouthed. One made a clumsy attempt to grab his rifle.

'*Nein*. Stay as you are.'

The sergeant pushed back his chair, eyes blazing.

'You're a right bastard. I never knew . . .'

The NCO's next move was to reach out quickly for the whisky bottle on the table. But Müller had anticipated the reaction and with a swift movement chopped down with his hand, hitting the sergeant's neck an inch above his khaki collar. With a sigh the NCO sagged to the ground, his feet kicking out at the table. Miraculously the bottle of Scotch still stood upright, but an open bottle of ink rolled on to its side and a blue-black stream poured down on to the soldier's head. The two privates at first sat stunned, then one of them tried to get to his feet.

'Stand still or I will kill you,' Müller barked.

The soldier paled and slumped back, and Müller was relieved that the man was too cowed to shout for help. If any of the privates did so, he would shoot them at once.

He ordered the soldiers to stand facing the wall.

'Place your hands on your heads.'

The two men sheepishly did as they were told. Still covering them with his gun, Müller moved towards the door and edged it open about six inches. The nearest guard was on the left-hand side of the slip walk, about thirty yards away, well out of earshot of anything happening in the attendant's room. Müller waited until he was a little closer then called softly.

'If you want a quick drink there's one in here for you.' He pointed to the other soldier whom he could just see emerging from the shadow on the far side of the pool. 'Bring your mate with you.'

The soldier caught his colleague's attention with a low whistle and pointed in the direction of the attendant's room, motioning with his hand that there was a drink going. Then he started to walk quickly towards the sergeant's room.

Müller stared into the dark well of the pool behind the two men. Now was the time that Preuss had to make his move, but there was no sign of life from the nest of bunks. The first guard would soon reach the attendant's room, and Müller felt for the trigger of his automatic, then stopped when he spied a movement behind the khaki figures. At last, shadowy forms swarmed over each side of the pool and silently advanced on the two guards from behind. Müller managed to distinguish two separate groups of POWs each side of the pool before the soldier nearest him let out a choked cry. A prisoner had crooked his arm round the man's throat. The man on the other slip walk half-turned, grabbing his rifle, but it was too late, another massive German fell on him and brought him to the ground.

The slender figure of Preuss emerged into the light. Stepping nonchalantly over the prostrate body of the first guard, he moved purposefully towards the attendant's room; the bulky figure of Schmidt was at his shoulder.

Preuss's eyes blinked in the bright light of the sergeant's office, and he glanced curiously at the NCO lying on the floor, his hair tinted strangely blue by the pool of ink. The major strode past the body and inspected the two privates. There was a new confidence about Preuss, who had discarded his Wehrmacht tunic for a dark jumper. Not a hair was out of place on his head, and his hands were clasped behind his straight back as if on parade.

'It seems that you have everything under control.' He pointed to the guns in the corner. 'A very useful bag.'

He spoke to Schmidt. 'Get these weapons distributed to A Squad as fast as you can. We have to take the gymnasium before any of the fools wake up.'

Schmidt nodded and waved at two Germans to come into the room and start moving the weapons. Müller watched them for a moment, then glanced at Preuss.

'Major, there are two men guarding the main doors. I want to deal with them now. Please give me three of your men and tell them to wait just inside the entrance for my orders.'

Preuss agreed and Müller turned on his heel, leaving the major to supervise the movement of the weapons.

The German prisoners had by now all climbed out of the pool, and stood in two squads of twenty-five men on each slip walk. The lights were still dimmed, in order not to attract attention from outside, and the men stood in silence, waiting for orders. They were mostly dressed in dark shirts and jerseys, though some still wore their field-grey tunics. Müller could see that they had done their best to arm themselves with wooden batons, chair legs, bottles, kitchen knives—anything they could lay their hands on. One man on the far side had even fashioned a noose from an army belt and strands of electric cable.

Weapons were already being passed to selected men in the nearest squad of prisoners, and Müller watched them eagerly examine the rifles, expertly pushing back bolts and testing their weight and size. Schmidt interrupted them to pick three men who came across to Müller for briefing. Meanwhile, Preuss emerged from the attendant's room, a Sten gun under his arm, and began quietly briefing the Germans on the far side for the seizure of the gymnasium, where the rest of the guards were sleeping.

It impressed Müller how fifty men were able to organise themselves in virtual silence and he led his own small squad towards the swing doors at the pool's entrance. He told them in hushed tones to wait just inside, ready for the enemy who would be coming through, then he pocketed his automatic and slipped outside.

Neither of the two guards showed any signs of suspicion, and the young soldier greeted Müller like a long-lost friend, although the Welshman merely cast him a disapproving look.

'What about a little party then, Larsen?' the young man suggested.

Müller managed a grin. 'The sergeant wants you. Reckon he's got something for you . . .'

The older guard began to protest, but Müller broke in.

'Don't blame me. You know what the sergeant's like. If he wants company . . .'

The young soldier did not wait for a reply but pushed his way through the swing doors. It seemed almost a pleasure to be alone with the Welshman, and Müller fixed his eyes on the self-satisfied face, then slowly drew his Smith and Wesson. The sight of the gun transfixed Taffy, who seemed to fall into a trance as Müller seized him by the shoulder and bundled him through the door, where the Germans were waiting.

When he got back inside the pool, Müller watched the two guards being marched off to the cell-like cubicles and noticed that the squads were making ready to move. One of them was in position outside the attendant's room, while the other had advanced towards the entrance.

Preuss was nowhere to be seen at first, but he suddenly emerged from the gymnasium followed by a line of dishevelled and pyjama-clad Canadians. They stared around, blinking in bewilderment, plainly overawed by the way in which the prisoners had taken control. With hands clasped on their heads, they were shepherded towards the cubicles by three Germans armed with rifles. Preuss kept one of the soldiers back, a tall, skinny boy, still in his teens whom he pushed into the attendant's office, beckoning Müller to come.

Müller strode across and Preuss ushered him into the room, kicking the door closed behind them with his heel. The gangling young soldier stood before them, his night-clothes hanging on him, and his bony fingers clasped on top of a thatch of fair hair. An ugly weal marked his cheek, and Müller noticed that the prisoner was shivering.

Preuss looked up to the private, casting an accusing look at Müller.

'I want you to listen carefully to what this man has to say,' he said before addressing the young soldier in a clear voice.

'Just repeat what you said when we kicked you on to the floor in the gymnasium.'

The young man stared back defiantly and said nothing. Preuss raised the barrel of the Sten gun he was carrying and pressed it against the man's temple.

'I said that you would not get far against the Royal Marines on board,' the prisoner stammered.

'Yes, and what else?' the major prompted.

'And that you would never get to Winston Churchill. They would kill you all first before you reached the Main Deck.'

The soldier looked apprehensively at the SS man, expecting him to pull the trigger, but Preuss lowered the gun and kicked him.

'Get out.'

The soldier scurried out and Preuss slammed the door after him, so that he and Müller were alone.

'What the hell is going on, Müller?' Preuss demanded coldly. 'You've been wandering round this ship, you must have known that Churchill was on board.'

Müller assented.

'Then why the secret?'

'I don't have to answer that,' Muller retorted.

'Berlin must have given you orders what to do. But we seem to be operating in the dark.'

'Berlin does not know that Churchill is aboard. He arrived only two days ago, and I've been unable to contact my HQ. Does that satisfy you?'

Preuss had begun to cool down. 'This discovery changes the entire nature of the operation. We must now concentrate on eliminating Churchill. Nothing else matters. It is far more important than some loony scheme to capture the ship.'

'We must keep to the plan,' Müller insisted sharply.

'Damn the plan,' Preuss said vehemently. 'A special assassination group should be formed now from my best men. I will lead it.'

'No,' Müller countered emphatically. 'That is forbidden.'

'By whom?'

'Colonel von Stoltz.'

'Then he knows Churchill is on board?'

'Of course. I have told him as senior officer.'

Preuss let out his breath sharply, and stared angrily at Müller. 'We've got to look at this whole plan again,' he snapped.

'The decision is made. Von Stoltz is in command. Churchill, together with all his underlings, is to be seized and held in close confinement until we reach St Nazaire. That is the plan.'

'Idiots,' Preuss spat out. 'If you are wrong, you will regret this.'

Müller suddenly grew alarmed at Preuss's attitude, and thought for a moment that the major might try to shoot him. But he realised that there was little the SS man could do for the moment—he depended on Müller to find his way round the ship and link up with von Stoltz.

After a moment's pause Preuss swung on his heel and opened the door, saying over his shoulder, 'If anything goes wrong with your damned Operation Iceman, Obersteuermann, I shall kill Churchill and then you . . .'

Müller turned Preuss's words over in his mind before he went outside. He did not wish the men to sense that there had been a raging argument between them. It was unlucky that Preuss had discovered the true facts about Churchill before Müller had had a chance to tell him, but there was nothing to be surprised about in the major's reaction. Müller knew that if Preuss tried to kill him, he would be ready.

When he stepped outside the attendant's room Müller saw that there had been a good haul of automatic weapons from the gymnasium and ten Germans had changed into captured British khaki. A moment later Preuss too emerged from the gym as a rather unlikely British NCO, his monk-like head topped by a forage cap, its badge gleaming in the dim light.

Preuss formed up his new detachment of ostensibly British troops, inspecting them closely, jerking down webbing belts and pointing to clumsily fastened gaiters. Müller glanced at his watch, and wondered why Preuss had to go through such a ritual. At last the major spoke to Müller.

'We are ready to move,' he declared. 'That is, if you are ready. I am taking the first five men to attack the armoury. The others are for you and Schmidt.'

Müller looked round at the other prisoners, grasping their bottles and chair legs. Preuss answered the question in his mind. 'They've been divided into a back-up force for the armoury, and a group for your attack on D Deck.'

Müller was relieved to have the help of an experienced officer like Schmidt and he checked his watch a further time.

'It's time to move, Major. Best of luck.'

Preuss nodded impassively and turned for the door. Müller shouted after him, 'By the way, if there's any snag I have a radio in the last lifeboat on the starboard side. Rendezvous there.'

'For the last-ditch stand, you mean?' Preuss said with a cynical smile. 'I don't think that will be necessary.'

Then he led his five men through the swing doors in single file, like a British patrol.

Around the pool the back-up force squatted and made themselves comfortable, while Müller stood waiting just inside the door until Schmidt had organised his group of prisoners into a squad, and placed his men in British uniform around them, so that they would appear to be guards. His mind drifted to the nine hundred men under von Stoltz's command: battle-seasoned veterans waiting to be armed. If he could reach D Deck and release them without any enemy resistance, the *Queen Mary* was as good as taken. Then he would cope with Preuss.

Chapter 27

'How the *hell* did a German agent get on board?' Ismay stood in his paisley dressing gown, the FBI signal in his hand. The other men hastily summoned to his cabin looked around them uncomfortably. Summers fingered his service revolver. Inspector Thompson and the special branch sergeant shifted on their straight-backed chairs: with their jackets pulled over the tops of pyjamas, both men could have been scarecrows. The staff captain and the colonel commanding the Canadian troops stood respectfully at the back of the room, slightly overawed by the presence of the Chief of the Imperial General Staff.

'He came aboard in New York, so our security arrangements in Scotland can hardly be blamed,' Thompson commented.

Ismay's face was sombre. 'This might be tied up with Alloway. God help him if it is.'

'We don't know that, sir,' said Summers.

'Where is he?' Brooke asked.

'He's been relieved of duty.'

'He's not under arrest?'

Ismay shook his head. 'I didn't think it necessary. But I have a nasty feeling I may have been wrong.'

'We've got to find this agent quickly,' General Brooke said. He looked round the room before adding, 'I also think we must keep this news away from the prime minister for as long as possible. If he finds out there's an agent on board he will take a personal hand in the search, and everything will be hopelessly disrupted. Strengthen the bodyguards around him, but make it unobtrusive.'

'All my men are already on alert,' Summers chipped in.

Colonel James McNeil, commanding the Canadian guards on board, coughed. He was a large man and when he spoke it was in measured tones giving the impression that everything was well under control and that he had been a police officer in civilian life. 'I have not placed my men on alert, sir. We could easily cause a commotion and frighten away the man we want to catch.'

Both Ismay and Inspector Thompson nodded in approval.

'This is a big ship,' the Canadian explained. 'If our man gets wind that we are after him it will be the devil's own job finding him.'

'What do we know about this agent?' Ismay asked.

The staff captain moved into the pool of light thrown from the military secretary's desk. He had a large green file in his hand, listing everybody on board. 'A carpenter by trade, sir. He came aboard in New York. He's quartered in the for'ard crew cabin on C Deck.'

'Do you have a photograph of him?'

'I'm afraid not, sir. He's not strictly a member of the crew, but I remember him coming to see me in New York, trying to join the ship as a seaman. Said he had a wife expecting a baby in Scotland.'

'And you turned him down?'

'Yes, but he got on board under the auspices of the Americans.'

'We'll go into that later,' Ismay said irritably. 'What does he look like?'

'He's a big, broad chap, aged mid to late twenties. Short blond hair, blue eyes, fair skin.'

'Typical German,' Thompson scoffed. 'He should be no problem to pick up.'

'What we need to know is why he is on this ship.' It was Brooke who spoke.

Ismay rubbed his unshaven chin. 'I agree. It looks to me as if German Intelligence have got wind of the prime minister's trip. They could be planning something particularly nasty— an attempt on his life.'

'I think an assassination attempt highly unlikely,' Thompson interjected gruffly. His hangdog face seemed to lengthen. 'The prime minister only decided to travel aboard the *Queen Mary* after the ship left New York, so this man can hardly have been infiltrated aboard to kill him—unless the Germans are clairvoyant.'

'Or took a long shot,' the Canadian added.

'That doesn't sound very likely,' Thompson continued. 'I believe he could be a saboteur, trying to sink the ship with the best part of an American division on board. If so he has been presented with a monumental piece of luck—the PM on board.'

Ismay pulled his dressing gown round his shoulders and spoke thoughtfully. 'My instinct is that it's none of these things. If it's not a plan to murder the PM and the rest of us then I think it could be connected with the prisoners. Remember, we have a thousand of them on the lower decks, many of them fanatical Nazis. If a trained agent could find a way of overcoming one of the guard posts and releasing them then all hell would break loose, especially if he managed to arm them.'

'Arm them?' Summers asked with a puzzled expression. 'How?'

'He could have a cache of weapons on board. After all, if our security is so lax that he can get aboard scot free, why shouldn't he have an arsenal hidden away somewhere in this vast ship? And he may not be working alone. There could be other agents among the crew.'

The Canadian colonel shook his head.

'Even if he had his own task force, Larsen would still have to get past my men.'

'There's always the element of surprise, Colonel,' Brooke said quietly. 'And we can be sure that the enemy will have planned everything thoroughly.'

The Canadian pursed his lips. 'You may be right, sir, but personally I can't see Larsen getting access to the prisoners' accommodation.'

'In my view he has already,' the staff captain remarked gloomily, and everyone in the room stared at him as he continued. 'Larsen said he was a trained carpenter, and we have never had any reason to think otherwise until now. So he's had the run of the ship to do his work.'

Ismay swore under his breath and Brooke rose to his feet. 'Then that's it. General Ismay is right. We could be facing a full-scale rising.'

'The question is, has Larsen been able to get hold of any

weapons?' Ismay said, but Brooke was already addressing Summers. 'You are to take whatever steps are necessary to safeguard security. Protect all strategic points and above all the life of the prime minister. And for heaven's sake, pick up Larsen immediately.'

The armoury smelt of linseed and machine oil, emanating from the stacked weapons. The duty corporal enjoyed the workshop atmosphere and sat perched on a stool behind the curved bar, humming to himself. He had begun to reassemble a Lee-Enfield rifle he had been cleaning. Six Bren guns were lined up along the floor, and there was a row of Stens on the shelf behind him, shelves which had previously held spirits and aperitifs. Around the room green ammunition cases were piled to the pink ceiling, and the sensuous shapes of mermaids painted on the walls peeped between the steel boxes. One of the two sentries on duty outside opened the door. 'What about tea? Shall I brew up?'

'It's about time,' the corporal shouted back, and the man entered, putting down his rifle and making for the kettle. His banter with the NCO was interrupted by the telephone ringing. The corporal picked up the ivory handset on the bar.

The platoon commander's voice bristled down the line.

'Corporal Jackson. There's an emergency alert. The armoury doors are to be kept locked. That's an order. Nobody is to be allowed in without express authorisation from me. Understood?'

'Yes, sir.'

'Set up a Bren immediately to cover the door, and keep a constant eye open for anybody suspicious. A section of men are on their way to reinforce you.'

'What's it all about, sir?'

'There's an enemy agent on board, and he might make for the armoury.'

'Yes, sir.'

The corporal put down the phone with a look of astonishment. 'What is it, Corp?' the private asked, looking up from the kettle.

'Some cock-and-bull story about a Jerry attack on the

armoury, in the middle of the Atlantic. That takes a bit of beating.'

The second sentry put his head round the door. 'There are some blokes coming, Corp.'

The NCO slipped off the bar stool, and grabbing a Sten gun walked over to the double doors. A detachment of troops was approaching along the corridor. Instinctively, the corporal's hand tightened on the barrel of the Sten, but he relaxed when he saw the khaki uniforms.

'Reinforcements,' he announced cheerfully. 'Brew up for them too.'

He stepped forward to greet the new troops. 'We've been expecting you. Just had the CO on the line. There's supposed to be a Jerry agent on board. We've got to set up a Bren to cover the entrance.'

The news that the British had been placed on alert came as a blow to Preuss as he stood listening in his captured uniform. Somehow he managed to control his true reaction. 'An agent on board? I didn't know that.' He tried to disguise his accent, but there was a puzzled expression on the corporal's face.

'We are Czechs,' Preuss explained hurriedly. 'We've been sent to relieve you.'

'Relieve us? We haven't been told anything about that.' The corporal stared hard at Preuss's men. One of them wore a pair of baggy trousers which hung loosely at the knees, and a webbing belt that seemed too large for him. Another, standing just inside the doors, had a pair of ill-fitting gaiters whose buckles had swivelled round the wrong way. The Englishman was used to the slack appearance of some Allied units serving with the British army, but this detachment worried him. They were not even wearing the customary Czechoslovakia shoulder flashes, borne by all Czech units, but sported the crimson patch of a Canadian infantry regiment.

The NCO edged back against the bar and placed his elbows casually on the counter behind him. Aware that Preuss was observing him, he made no move towards the ammunition case that stood just beyond the counter. A private entered the room, carrying a steaming kettle, and Preuss turned to watch him.

'Now that you're here, why don't you have a cuppa?' the corporal suggested cheerfully. The private poured the boiling water into a chipped enamel pot in the far corner of the bar. Preuss continued watching him. The NCO casually pushed his left hand back over the counter until his fingers touched the metal case. They felt nervously for the catch, found it and flipped it open. Gently the corporal lifted the lid, probing inside for the steel jacket of a hand grenade.

Preuss swung round, the khaki forage cap perched oddly in the middle of his head.

'Good try, Corporal,' he said mockingly, and pushed the snub-nosed barrel of his Sten gun into the Englishman's chest. He jerked his head towards the mirror at the end of the bar, which gave a clear view of the ammunition case.

'I found your little effort quite commendable.'

The private stood transfixed, holding the kettle, which he almost dropped in astonishment when one of Preuss's men pointed his weapon at him. The second British soldier was already covered by another German from behind the door. Preuss indicated a tangle of rope and cord in the corner which had been used to secure the ammunition cases.

'Tie these men up,' he ordered. 'Get them out of the way behind the bar.' Then he immediately despatched one of his men to summon the follow-up party, ordering the German in the baggy uniform to set up a Bren gun to cover the corridor.

A third man seized a trolley parked in the corner and pulled it across the bar. Together with the remaining members of the squad, he began to load it rapidly with ammunition.

Alloway was sitting on his bunk, staring glumly at a half-empty bottle of whisky. It had been impossible to sleep, and he cursed the stupidity of the military mind for thinking him a traitor. The mere idea had appeared absurd yet, true or false, it seemed painfully certain that the very fact of the charge meant that his career was in ruins. He stood up, eager for fresh air. He had shunned the mess and had been cloistered all day in the small room. He pulled on his squadron leader's tunic then suddenly stiffened. His ears detected the guttural tones of German being spoken in the corridor outside. Cautiously, he walked to the door and opened it a few inches. Staring through the narrow gap, he made out the tall figure of a sergeant whose shoulder flashes were those of a Canadian infantry regiment. Alloway began to wonder whether he had been mistaken in hearing Teutonic voices until the soldier half turned, then to his astonishment he found himself looking at the pallid complexion and sharp features of the Nazi officer who had instigated the riot at Tregaron Camp—Major Preuss. As the figure moved into the light Alloway was certain that it was the man he had grappled with in the POW hut. Preuss was supervising two of his men in loading a trolley. It was stacked with several large ammunition boxes, and Alloway distinguished several weapons on top. The major gave a last check, then said in German, 'All right, get these weapons to von Stoltz's quarters as fast as you can.'

Ducking back out of sight, Alloway kept his eyes on the men as they trundled the arms past his cabin. There were enough weapons on the trolley to equip twenty men.

Once they had gone he eased the door wider and peered towards the bar. The mahogany doors were open and Preuss was addressing the three Germans left behind. From the other direction he heard the thump of running feet, and just managed to pull the door to again before a dozen German POWs clumped past. He leaned against the door, his muscles tense, and tried to calm his rapid breathing.

The Germans had clearly broken out and seized the armoury, and there was going to be serious trouble in other parts of the ship. His gaze fell on the telephone standing on the table next to the bottle of whisky. For all the Scotch he had drunk, the sight of Preuss and the other prisoners had instantly cleared his mind: he had to contact Summers to report what was happening.

He picked up the phone by his bed. At first the operator did not answer. The earpiece hummed, and there seemed to be some sort of jam on the switchboard.

He looked up quickly towards the door. There was a sound of scuffling and other doors being opened farther along the corridor. A man's voice shouted in English, there were shots and a woman screamed. The Germans must be breaking into the passenger cabins. Anxiously watching the door, he dialled Summers's number again.

'Alloway?' Summers's voice at last.

'Summers? Look, I haven't much time. The prisoners have broken out. They've occupied the bar on B Deck where the weapons are kept and are seizing passengers.'

To Alloway's amazement the major was silent. It occurred to him that Summers must still be suspicious of him—perhaps believed he was lying. When he spoke again there was a controlled anger in his voice. 'Listen to me, Summers. I don't care whether you trust me or not: that's your bloody business. All I can say is that the armoury with all its weapons and ammunition has been seized by a dozen Germans. I'm certain that the man in command is Major Preuss. He's a nasty piece of work, one of the trouble-makers at Tregaron POW camp in Wales. He's already started to turn the armoury into a strongpoint. He's got plenty of weapons, and he's shifted a trolley load of arms to von Stoltz, the commander of the rest of the prisoners.'

Summers was silent for a moment, digesting the information. 'Sorry, Alloway. You say there are a dozen Germans down there?'

'Possibly fifteen.'

'How long ago did the trolley leave?'

'About two minutes.'

'We'll intercept it.'

'You might have a job identifying them. The Germans pushing the trolley are wearing Canadian uniforms.'

'That won't help them,' Summers said. 'We'll scour all decks. When we find the Germans we shall shoot them. They can forget the Geneva Convention.'

Summers's final words were drowned by the sound of splitting wood and the thud of rifle butts as the Germans drew closer.

'The Jerries are clearing all the cabins along this deck ready for action. God alone knows what's happened to the other passengers. They will be here any moment, Summers. Get here fast.'

There was a crash from the cabin next door and the sound of voices as a passenger was hauled out of bed.

Alloway put down the receiver and looked desperately round the room. In the far corner, next to the porthole, was a narrow wardrobe where Alloway had hung his spare RAF uniform, together with the lightweight suits and jackets he hoped to wear when off duty in America. He yanked the door open. The cupboard was four feet above the floor and seemed too small to hide a grown man, but there was nowhere else. A terrible splintering of wood and the sound of boots came from outside: Alloway could wait no longer. He hauled himself into a sitting position, then swung his legs into the cupboard. Pushing aside the suits, he pressed through the line of clothes and jammed himself against the back of the cupboard. His legs nearly touched his chin, and he winced with pain from his damaged right leg. Carefully, he slid the hangers back into position then pulled the door closed. It shut with a loud click. The small stuffy space smelled of mothballs and dry-cleaned clothes. His nose itched as it rubbed against a flannel suit only an inch away and his leg rapidly grew numb. The wardrobe was stifling. For a moment he almost panicked in the darkness, but he was soon distracted by the sound of the cabin door being thrown open. There was the sound of a single soldier's boots crossing the room. Another pair of boots. Then a brutal thud jarred him and there was a tinkle of breaking glass. The Germans were smashing up his cabin.

A gruff voice spoke, inches away, just the other side of the wardrobe door. '*Niemand hier.*'

A reply came from the far side of the cabin, but Alloway could not make out the words. Then the latch on the wardrobe door clicked and light flooded into the small cupboard.

Instinctively he clutched his knees and pressed down his head. Thick fingers moved the jackets and he glimpsed a high cheekbone, fleshy lips, and a field-grey tunic buttoned up to the neck. He clenched his fist, ready to lash out. If the

294

man pushed the clothes away from the farthest end he would surely be discovered.

Then another voice spoke in German and the wardrobe door was slammed shut. There was a brief interchange, and the soldiers left. Alloway let out a deep breath in the darkness. For several minutes he stayed stock still, before his fingers reached out and he felt for the catch on the door. Taking a thin pencil from his top pocket he pushed open the catch. Impatiently he pulled the suits and shirts aside and air flowed back into his lungs. As he clambered into the cabin it was as if he were climbing out of a cockpit once again. If Preuss was ready for action, so was he.

In the emergency command post set up in his cabin on the Main Deck, Summers put down the phone. He had just briefed General Ismay on the situation. Colonel McNeill stood next to him, arms folded and a revolver sticking out of his hip holster.

'If they manage to get those arms through to von Stoltz we're in trouble,' said Summers.

McNeill nodded grimly.

'I've alerted my units on D Deck and I'm mustering all reserve detachments. They should be ready to move in fifteen minutes.'

'Too late,' Summers exclaimed. 'We've got to stop that trolley-load of arms getting through *now*.' He strode across to the large drawing of the *Queen Mary* pinned to the far wall.

'There's one way we might be able to do it,' he said. 'If we can close all the watertight bulkheads we will be able to seal the ship into sections. The entire operation can be carried out from the bridge and nobody will be able to move from one part of the ship to another.'

McNeill stepped forward, protesting.

'If you close the watertight doors my reserve detachments will never be able to reinforce the guards on von Stoltz's men. The whole ship will be isolated into compartments.'

The major's grey eyes were unmoved.

'Sorry, Colonel, but it's the only way we can stop

them. Those arms must be damned near von Stoltz by now. We must bar the way. If not, God knows what will happen.'

'I understand. But don't you see that you will be condemning some of the passengers to being hostages of the Germans? There will be no way we can rescue them. They may even be murdered.'

Summers turned towards the Canadian, who saw that the marine's fist was tightly clenched.

'We'll have to risk that. My top priority is the safety of the prime minister. If necessary I shall sacrifice the rest of the ship to protect him.'

McNeill was silent as Summers grimly picked up the phone and asked for the bridge.

Chapter 28

Müller marched at the head of the column approaching D Deck. Four Germans in British battledress flanked the party, while Schmidt was at Müller's shoulder. To any observer it appeared that a party of POWs was being moved through the ship under escort.

The advance from the swimming pool had gone smoothly. Although the group had passed several members of the ship's crew and a detachment of troops, there had been no signs of suspicion. Müller wondered how long their luck could hold.

Ahead he could see a line of troops drawn up across the small concourse outside the cabin-cum-guardhouse. They were standing a yard apart, with a second line behind them. Beyond, the corridor into the POWs' quarters disappeared into the darkness.

Schmidt nudged Müller. 'See what I see?'

Müller nodded. He too had observed the funnelled barrel of a Bren gun, positioned on its tripod in the middle of the line.

'Christ! They've been placed on alert,' Schmidt whispered.

'Keep moving. We'll try to bluff it out.'

'When we get within ten yards we can rush them,' Schmidt suggested.

Müller agreed and kept his eyes firmly on the cordon ahead. Now the Bren gunners were no longer on their haunches but had taken up firing position on their bellies. The other troops brought their arms to the ready. Twenty yards of corridor separated the two groups, and Müller was counting every inch.

'Okay. Hold it there. The officer in charge to advance and identify his unit.'

The voice came from a stocky commander stationed behind the second line of troops. Müller shouted in English for the detachment to halt, hoping that the distance was too great for the Canadians to see who was giving orders. The next move was the problem. Schmidt could hardly be sent forward as a British NCO: his poor English would never pass muster. Müller had to play for time.

'We are from the First Battalion, Czech Volunteers,' he shouted. 'We've been ordered to bring a party of prisoners down here from the swimming pool. Haven't you been told?'

There was a pause before the Canadian replied. 'I'll check with the CO. In the meantime I want the officer in charge to advance and identify himself.'

There was the click of a Bren magazine being slipped into place. Müller sensed that the unarmed Germans were looking around for cover.

'We could pull back,' Schmidt whispered. 'I'll give covering fire.'

Müller glanced over his shoulder. They were perfect targets but the corridor behind seemed empty. Yet if he sanctioned a withdrawal, would he ever be able to release von Stoltz's men? The decision was made for him. There was a deep rumble and, twenty-five feet away, a massive steel door swung across the corridor. It fitted snugly into

297

place, sealing the passageway completely. There could be no retreat.

Müller glanced apprehensively at the Canadian guards.

'I'll try to bluff them once more,' he said quickly, knowing that it was their only chance of avoiding heavy casualties. 'Hurry because—' His words were drowned in a tremendous shout from in front of them.

In the corridor behind the guards a dense mass of prisoners was charging down on the Canadians out of the darkness. They carried clubs fashioned from broken furniture and stanchions torn from their bunks. The Canadian commander half turned, only for a prisoner to catch him with a terrible blow on the side of the head. In the front rank Mecklen, the panzer commander, lashed out with a steel bar. Beside him another German kicked the tripod of the Bren gun sideways. Shots rang out and a prisoner fell to the ground, bringing down three or four others. Müller waited no longer. He shouted an order and his squad surged forward. Their help was scarcely needed. Those Canadians who were uninjured were being lined up against the wall by Mecklen. One man's battledress had been torn, another's face was puffing up with bruises. Others were less fortunate and were lying bleeding and unconscious on the deck.

Mecklen stood surveying the battleground, his face wreathed in triumph. 'Well, I think we saved you just in time,' he smiled at Müller.

Schmidt overheard the remark. 'We could have looked after ourselves.'

'Yes, all the way to the graveyard.' Mecklen turned and began issuing orders for a barricade to be built across the concourse from furniture and filing cabinets taken from the guardhouse.

He also despatched a Bren party down the corridor to the end of the prisoners' quarters, where the main stairway for'ard began its ascent to the upper levels of the liner. Like a broad thoroughfare, it passed through the restaurant and upper decks and could be used by the British to send in troops to regain control of D Deck. Mecklen was already ɑware of this danger and was ordering the bulk of his forces in that direction. Müller paid little attention to these movements; he wanted to find von Stoltz. Shouldering past the long lines of POWs being assembled in action groups he found the colonel at the foot of the main staircase. Von Stoltz was immaculately dressed and completely unruffled. He peered towards the deck above, then glanced at Müller.

'You've arrived on time, Obersteuermann. That's excellent.'

'Yes, sir, but there's been a setback.'

'Setback?'

'The British are on alert. They have closed all watertight doors. We can only move in strength up the main stairway. We must attack *now*.'

The colonel drew the sketch of the *Queen Mary* out of his pocket and, as if summoned by telepathy, his senior officers gathered round him for an impromptu conference. Müller stood at his elbow.

'But what about the arms from Preuss?' von Stoltz demanded.

Müller pointed at the drawing. 'They can't get through.'

'In that case we have only one chance. We must attack up the main staircase immediately while the British are off balance.'

Von Stoltz turned to Mecklen. 'Draw up your assault force, placing whatever armed men you have at the head of the column. The rest will follow. It's the only chance we have, but it might work. We should overwhelm them by weight of numbers.'

Müller listened anxiously.

'What about Preuss? And our other objectives?' he asked. 'We still have a chance of seizing the bridge and controlling the ship, as the plan dictates, if we can infiltrate a group of men to the upper decks.' He waved his arm towards the end of the corridor. 'Next to the guardhouse there is a small room which was used by stewards. It has a service lift, which could move a party of men to the kitchen. From there they could try to reach the bridge.' The colonel listened closely as Müller continued. 'At the same time we could send another group down the main stairway to seize the engine room.

Then we might be able to bring the ship on to a new course for St Nazaire.'

'There will be plenty of action on the staircase to distract the enemy,' Bucholdt added grimly.

Von Stoltz nodded in agreement. Müller could take Schmidt's detachment. Wishing them luck, he sent them on their way.

There was an atmosphere of growing excitement among the prisoners as Müller moved back along the corridor towards the service room. When he entered he saw that its walls were lined with shelves and cupboards, and it was packed with mess tins and serving dishes. The dumb waiter was a small box-like lift, open on one side and operated by a rope which hung next to it.

Müller's instinct was to climb inside himself, but he had second thoughts. He knew that the success of Operation Iceman rested on his shoulders, and if he were hauled up through the decks he might suddenly find himself staring down an enemy gun barrel. Schmidt would have to go first. He turned and looked at the captain's bulky figure, still in British battledress.

'In you go,' Müller said. 'I'll haul you.'

On the main staircase Mecklen placed himself at the head of the column of prisoners. He gripped the Canadian officer's revolver and glanced at his men. They were armed with rifles and Sten guns. Behind came the Bren gun party and then, in groups of twenty, the rest of the prisoners.

With a wave of his arm, Mecklen moved forward: three hundred men began their advance on the Main Deck.

Three levels above, on C Deck, Major Summers stood staring down the staircase. He glanced at the faces of his marines who were waiting patiently, green berets pulled tight over their foreheads. They stood half hidden in the entrance to the main restaurant, or lay with their weapons ready behind upturned dining tables placed across the top of the stairs.

There was a nervous cough behind him, and Summers glared at the small party of seamen standing pale-faced near the far wall. Two of them were unwinding a firehose from a hydrant, three others were standing ready to handle the water line. They appeared to steady themselves under Summers's gaze. He switched his attention back to the stairs, furious that the Germans had managed to overwhelm the guards on D Deck. He thanked heaven that he had closed the watertight doors in time.

The sergeant lying on the ground next to a Bren gun peered up. 'I think I can hear something, sir.'

Summers took a few steps forward to the edge of the stairs, peering over the top of an upturned table. He stared at the landing twenty feet below, and the first stair of the flight descending deeper into the ship. Far below, he heard the sound of feet. He moved calmly to his position behind the Bren gunner. The clatter of hundreds of feet grew louder. The marines hunched low, bringing their automatic weapons to the ready. 'Remember, men, if they get through us they get to Winnie.'

There was a cry from the corporal. 'Blimey, sir. Look at them. Worse than Arsenal supporters.'

He pointed below, where Summers saw a phalanx of men advancing up the stairs, like a medieval army, waving sticks and batons. They were moving rapidly, the shock-headed figure of Mecklen at their head, brandishing a revolver.

Summers raised his arm, then barked at the seamen, 'Hose party forward. Turn on the mains.'

The water cracked out of the spout. The Germans were only thirty feet away. Its fierce pressure cut into the front ranks of prisoners, bowling them over and cannoning them into the men coming behind. The noise was deafening, with the unarmed prisoners shouting abuse at the British and hurling bottles, staves—anything they could lay their hands on. Even a boot came flying through the air. But it was hopeless trying to make headway against the powerful jet of water. Mecklen, his hair plastered to his head, waved his men back, and they retired round the bend in the stairs, taking their injured men with them. Summers ceased firing.

'Turn off the hose,' he ordered. 'But stay awake.' He began to ponder on his next move, but his thoughts were soon interrupted by the staccato sound of a Bren gun. Shots smashed into the wooden tables and the marines ducked instinctively. Behind them two seamen doubled up in agony. 'They've got a bloody Bren, sir,' the corporal shouted. 'We won't be able to work the firehose with that around.'

Summers had hit the deck and crawled across the floor on his belly to look through the chink between two tables placed side by side. When the gun fired again he detected the flash from the funnelled barrel which poked out from the corner of the landing, where the next flight of stairs descended below. The marines returned fire, but Summers had read Mecklen's next move. Taking two steps at a time, Mecklen and his men came racing up the left-hand side of the stairs. All six were firing from the hip. At once an arc of fire from the British guns curled towards the Germans. Hot steel tore into their legs and stomachs. Mecklen himself reached as far as the top of the stairs, stumbled, then fell. Around him other prisoners skidded on the wet surface as the bullets brought them down. Three Germans managed to withdraw, one badly wounded, but bodies littered the stairs. Only the Bren gun kept firing.

'There's only one answer for that bloody thing,' the corporal said to Summers, tapping the hand grenade on his belt. The major nodded.

The trajectory was timed perfectly. The grenade bounced once, like a ball, then pitched into the corner, rolling to a halt a few inches from the stairs. A split second later there was a loud explosion and the Bren gunner was hurled into the air.

Summers ordered his men to cease firing. There was an uncanny silence. One German was nursing his head in his hands, badly wounded in the neck, another was crawling painfully towards his own lines. Bottles, steel bars and batons were everywhere. Mecklen was sprawled, head downwards, his legs covered in blood.

Summers stepped over the crude barricade and began slowly to descend the stairs. He waved his revolver at his men and they immediately jumped up to follow him. Twenty marines in full battle gear spread out evenly behind their commander. A second wave followed.

On the landing Summers waited for the first rank of his men to draw level before he edged round the corner. Then he shouted, loud enough for the Germans to hear him, 'Colonel von Stoltz. I am Major Summers, commander of the security forces on this ship. Your men are unarmed and we have overwhelming firepower. If you want to avoid needless casualties please order your men to return to quarters. The wounded will be looked after.'

There was a low murmur from the Germans. Edging round the corner of the landing Summers stared down at the deck below. Just twenty feet away, separated by the broad stairway, hundreds of drawn faces were staring up at him. One or two prisoners had weapons but they did not bring them to bear on the major as he came down towards them. The marines fanned out behind him, several men dropping instinctively on to one knee to cover the Germans.

Summers stopped, his feet astride. 'I call on you, Colonel von Stoltz, to order your men back to their quarters. There is no way in which they can take control of this ship. If you persist there will be a massacre.'

The faces below glared back angrily, and there was commotion in the front rank at the foot of the stairs. Summers shouted out again, 'Any prisoner who moves will be shot.'

There was a movement among the men at the rear of the crowd. Heads turned expectantly and prisoners jumped to attention as von Stoltz passed through the mass of his men. The front rank parted and the colonel marched out on to the bloodstained deck. Shoulders square, he stood in front of Summers and deliberately appraised the enemy positions as if he were judging a pre-war exercise. Then his eyes met Summers's, and he seemed to recognise that one word from the British officer would indeed produce a massacre in the German ranks.

When at last von Stoltz spoke his voice was firm. 'Very well, Major. There is nothing that I can do now except save the lives of my men. We are unarmed, as you can see.'

He turned his broad back on the British and addressed the strained faces before him.

'All ranks return to quarters and await further orders. It was not our day.'

Von Stoltz swung to face Summers once more, but said nothing. He simply clicked his heels, gave a curt bow and made his way back to his cabin.

Summers watched his marines shepherding the Germans back to their compound and his mind turned to the other parts of the ship which must be on the enemy's target list. He realised that von Stoltz's effort may have disguised a series of far more dangerous threats. Preuss still controlled the armoury, and was capable of inflicting tremendous damage with the weapons he now possessed. Equally serious, there had been no sign of the highly trained agent Larsen who might, at that moment, be preparing to attack the prime minister's quarters on the Main Deck. Unaware that Müller's squad was in fact advancing on the bridge, the major hastened to regroup his men. The next phase of the battle was going to be tougher still.

Chapter 29

Müller could hear the firing on the main staircase as he sat hunched in the dumb waiter. He fought down fears that he might be trapped; the creaking of the rope and the steady, slow ascent reassured him. A chink of light above his head indicated that the lift was coming to a room on the deck above. It was deserted and very similar to the one below. The small cubicle continued on its way upwards, into darkness again. For a few seconds it stopped, lurched another eighteen inches, then Müller found himself staring into the anxious, sweat-lined face of Schmidt.

The small room in which he found himself seemed crowded with the other four men of the detachment. Two stood by the door, guns at the ready. The others were still panting with the effort of having hauled Müller up the shaft.

'What's outside?' Müller asked.

'A damn great kitchen,' Schmidt answered. Müller edged open the door. Gleaming steamers and boilers lined one wall, while a massive gas range dominated the middle of the kitchen. More significantly some dozen cooks were sweating at their work.

Müller closed the door. 'We can't get out through there. Too many of them.'

'We don't need to,' said Schmidt, pointing to two more lift shafts next to the one which brought them from D Deck. On the shaft nearest the door a small printed notice announced that the lift served the Sun and Sports Decks.

The wireless office was on the Sun Deck, and the wheelhouse could also be reached from there. Müller gathered his men around him. Schmidt and a young Luftwaffe lieutenant were directed to attack the wireless office, whilst Müller himself would lead the attempt on the bridge with another Kriegsmarine lieutenant named Uhlmann. That would leave the remaining member of the detachment behind to haul the others aloft. Müller picked the fifth man, a tall, well-built officer for this job: apart from Schmidt he was the strongest man in the group.

'All right, let's go,' Müller said. 'And this time I'll be first in the box.'

Alloway's cabin had been almost totally wrecked. The bathroom door was riddled with bullet holes, while drawers had been pulled out and their contents strewn on the floor. He crossed to the main door, which hung on a single hinge, and pulled it open. To his left, where the corridor debouched on to a staircase landing, stood five POWs. They were all heavily armed.

They were preparing to defend the cabins each side of the passageway as strongpoints. Holes had been smashed in the stout doors to provide loopholes for automatic weapons. In the corridor itself, just ahead of the cabins, a crude barricade made of bedsteads and wardrobes had also been erected some ten yards from the stairs. A Bren gunner was positioned in the middle. All the other cabin doors were closed and Alloway wondered what had become of the passengers: they had probably been locked into one of the larger cabins.

In the opposite direction, some twenty yards away, the bar doors leading to the armoury were wide open, a squad of six Germans lined up outside. Each man carried an automatic weapon, and one, a lanky, fair-haired subaltern, a steel ammunition box. A seventh was humping a case of grenades from inside the armoury. As Alloway watched, he put down the load and started to issue grenades to the squad.

Suddenly the men stiffened as a slender figure emerged from the armoury. Preuss again. Although Alloway's German was not good enough to understand every expression, it soon became clear as the major addressed his men that he was uncertain about what had happened on D Deck and whether or not the arms he had sent had got through to von Stoltz. It struck Alloway that Preuss was none too sorry about developments on other decks. 'Complicated plans are useless,' Preuss was saying. 'Our job is to find Churchill and kill him. That is the greatest act we can do for the Reich.' The men expressed strong agreement; for a moment Alloway even thought that they were going to clap their commander on the back.

'We shall be in two groups,' the major continued. 'There's a small stairway farther along this deck which will bring us on to the Promenade Deck. From there we can attack Churchill's cabin from above.' Preuss tapped a hand grenade hanging on his shoulder. Alloway could not catch the German's remarks, which were greeted by a guffaw from the men around him, but it seemed to be some insulting threat to Churchill.

Alloway was now thoroughly alarmed at the deadly threat to Churchill but as he listened it struck him that Preuss was taking a deliberate risk in leaving only a handful of men to occupy B Deck. This became even more apparent when the major declared, 'We shall leave Captain Schultz to guard the armoury and the prisoners there. With his weight, I'm not sure he could keep up with us! It's a long climb to the Promenade Deck.'

A plump figure, which Alloway took to be Schultz, clicked

his heels in unoffended acknowledgment. There was a further guffaw from the squad.

Preuss's tone suddenly sharpened. 'We leave in five minutes.'

Alloway drew back into his cabin. He had to act at once. At first he could not see the telephone anywhere. Perhaps the Germans had ripped it out during their search of the cabin? At last he spied the earphone lying on the floor in the corner, its cable still attached to the base some feet away. He picked it up and pressed rapidly on the crossbar. No reply from the operator. He tried again. At first it seemed as if the line were dead, then he heard—'Who's speaking?' It was the rough North Country voice of the signaller.

'Squadron Leader Alloway, Defence Officer. Put me through to Major Summers at once.'

It was an operator who had taken many messages from Alloway during the working sessions on the Main Deck, and he responded immediately. 'Hang on, Mr Alloway.'

There was a click and then McNeill's broad Canadian drawl.

'Where the hell have you been, Alloway? We'd given you up for lost.'

'Hiding in my cabin. The whole of B Deck has been occupied by the bloody Germans.'

'There's all hell breaking loose on D Deck too. Summers is down there with his marines.'

Alloway cut in impatiently. 'Listen, Colonel, I spotted Preuss outside the armoury on B Deck. He's just briefed his men for an assault on Churchill's quarters.'

'Christ!'

'He plans to get to the Main Deck by climbing the last stairway on B Deck—I think, from what I could follow— he's going to try to kill the whole leadership.'

'We'll be ready,' McNeill growled. Over the line Alloway could hear McNeill rattling out orders to his adjutant, moving more troops to the Main Deck, and sealing off the sternmost stairway.

He kept his eyes on the door. Not that he could do much if one of Preuss's men came in. He could feel his bad leg throbbing like a piston.

McNeill's voice came back on the line. 'Stay on B Deck. We need you there.'

'Listen, McNeill,' Alloway interjected. 'We can recapture the weapons store if we try. Preuss has left himself wide open. He's only got one man there.' In a few hurried words he explained where the Germans were positioned. 'If you can mount an attack down the aft stairway, even if it's only a diversion, I can try for the bar, and defend it. There are three of our chaps, prisoners, in there, who can help.'

There was a pause as McNeill pondered the suggestion. 'You'll be taking a big risk,' he said finally. 'They're in quite strong defensive positions. Even Summers's marines may have a job getting to you.'

'Maybe. But I'm going to try.'

McNeill was incisive. 'Right. We'll attack in ten minutes.'

Alloway put the phone down, feeling jubilant. At last something positive, and against Preuss too. He edged his way across the room and peered outside. Preuss's squad had gone, and there was no sign of any guard outside the bar. He could not see inside. At the other end of the corridor the Germans were still watching the stairs. The whole scene seemed ludicrously calm. Alloway glanced at his watch. In just over seven minutes it would all change . . .

He glanced left towards the fortified cabins and the barricade. To his alarm one of the POWs, a tall, broad-shouldered lieutenant, was advancing along the passageway, a Sten gun slung over his shoulder. Alloway darted inside. His eyes lit on his umbrella and he hastily picked it up. It would hardly give him much chance against a sub-machine gun, but at least he could use it bayonet-style. The steady tread of the man's feet got nearer and Alloway pressed himself behind the door, tensing his muscles. The feet were outside now. His hands gripped the umbrella, one in front of the other grasping it like a rifle. But the German went on walking, his footsteps fading in the direction of the bar.

After a few moments Alloway peered out again. The tall officer had disappeared, but not for long. There was the sound of voices and a moment later he emerged from the armoury with the pot-bellied Schultz. Between them the two men began lugging an ammunition case towards the barricade. Schultz's face was already bright red, and Alloway could tell the exact position of the pair by the noise of his laboured breathing. He waited till they had moved well past his room, then looked cautiously outside.

He checked his watch: two minutes till McNeill's attack, but for the moment nobody was guarding the armoury. Alloway decided to seize his chance. Checking that there were no Germans looking in his direction, he stepped into the corridor and moved swiftly towards the open door of the bar. He paused to glance over his shoulder. The two Germans stood at the barricade, and the other POWs were too interested in their arrival to notice Alloway.

He turned and walked inside, half expecting to confront a German; but the room was deserted. There were large gaps in the piles of ammunition boxes and weapon racks where the Germans had helped themselves. A solitary Bren stood on the floor and Alloway was thankful to see a row of Stens behind the bar. There were no signs of the British prisoners, however. Then he leaned over the bar. Three pale faces looked up at him apprehensively. All three khaki-clad figures jammed behind the counter were bound hand and foot. The soldier farthest to the right, a corporal, had a purple bruise on the side of his head, but his eyes were alert. The other two, both in their late teens, were too petrified to speak.

'Blimey, what are you doing here?' the soldier with the injured face asked, staring at Alloway's RAF uniform.

'What the bloody hell do you think? We've got to get the Jerries out of this place.'

The soldier brightened. 'Can we help?'

Alloway nodded and crossed the bar to pick up one of a pile of bayonets resting in the corner. As he did so he noticed Schultz's tunic hanging behind the bar. With luck the German would not suddenly return. As quickly as he could Alloway hacked through the tight cords round the NCO's wrists, and as soon as they were free tossed him the bayonet.

'Get yourself and the others free. Then move the Bren over to the door.' He moved back to the door, grabbing a Sten gun from the rack. Schultz was coming back now and was only twenty yards away. For a moment Alloway wondered what to do. The German made a plump target, but if he opened fire the enemy would immediately be alerted. Whispering to the others to be quiet, Alloway slipped behind the door.

Schultz's feet drew nearer and Alloway thought he could hear him humming. At last the rotund figure came into the room. As he passed, Alloway brought the Sten gun down on the back of his head. With a cry, the captain fell to his knees, stretching out a hand towards the stack of bayonets. Alloway hit him again, twice more, until he collapsed motionless.

Alloway peered down the corridor and swore. Schultz's cry had alarmed the men farther along. Two Germans were already doubling towards the open doors. Without hesitating for a moment Alloway jumped out into the corridor and felt the Sten gun kick into his stomach as he loosed off a burst of fire. Both Germans were taken by surprise. One immediately fell headlong, while the other hurled himself into a cabin, kicking open the door. Farther back another POW began to advance, weaving from door to door. Alloway dived for cover as a savage burst of machine-gun fire scythed along the corridor, spattering the entrance to the bar.

'Get the bloody Bren into action,' he shouted at the corporal, who was already dragging it across the floor. He pulled one side of the double doors and helped the soldier position the gun. One of the privates rammed a magazine home. The Germans were twenty yards away when the Bren opened up. Alloway shouted for everybody to keep their heads down, just before the enemy returned a fusillade of shots which scorched the woodwork and ripped into the walls. For a moment he feared that one of the ammunition boxes or, worse, a box of grenades, would take a direct hit and blow the place apart. But they remained untouched.

Where the hell was McNeill? The enemy were highly trained in infantry tactics and he could not hold them off for long.

He leaned beside the open door, staring down the corridor, waiting. Suddenly there was a tremendous burst of firing from its far end and a cloud of smoke billowed from the landing. Shadowy figures began to emerge, pouring a steady stream of fire at the Germans. McNeill's men had arrived. The Germans at the barricade opened up with automatic fire and several of the attackers fell. Then a soldier lobbed a grenade and the barricade disintegrated, jagged pieces of furniture hurtling along the corridor.

One by one the Germans began dodging back towards the armoury, moving from cabin to cabin. There were only three or four of them and the first were only yards away when Alloway yelled, 'Open fire'. At once the corporal lying on the ground pressed the trigger and the Bren gun raked the cabins. With McNeill's men attacking from the barricade the Germans were caught in a cross-fire.

Sweat dripped off Alloway as he wearily slammed home another magazine. Only two Germans seemed to be left standing and they moved into position ready to attack, desperate to regain control of the armoury. A stream of automatic fire streaked from the left of the corridor as the enemy opened up. Alloway ducked as bullets struck the steel sides of the ammunition cases. One of the privates was hit, and the next moment the Bren gun ceased firing as the corporal slumped forward. Alloway pushed him aside and, dropping on to his belly, felt for the trigger. He could see the two POWs racing towards him. His finger pressed the sliver of metal and the gun kicked into his shoulder. At the last moment the two Germans tried to escape the devastating fire but, only feet away, they crumpled to the ground. The arm of one was raised as he fell and Alloway was dimly aware of an object like a ball dropping towards him out of the smoke. It rolled along the ground, past the door and towards the ammunition cases. In desperation he lashed out at it with his right leg, kicking it into the corridor. A second later he felt as if the world was collapsing as the grenade exploded.

Müller dropped out of the service lift, landing on all fours like a cat. He scrambled to his feet, gun in hand. The room was empty and dark. He reached inside the lift, pulling out a Thompson sub-machine gun. Then he tugged the rope twice and there was a responding creak as the lift began to disappear down the shaft, ready to collect Schmidt and the rest of the group.

Müller began to explore. The room was about thirty feet long, and had a shabby abandoned air. The atmosphere was stale and musty. The shaft was at the far end of what appeared to be a long counter and there were doors at each end of the room which he assumed were used by waiters serving peacetime diners on deck. Cupboards and refrigerators lined one wall, all of them locked. Müller crossed over to the left-hand door and opened it. Fresh sea air wafted into his nostrils.

He slipped outside on to the Sports Deck. After the darkness of the lift shaft and the confined atmosphere below decks he immediately began to feel more relaxed. He found himself in a sheltered area beneath the first of the huge raked funnels. One or two iron tables still remained there, the only indication that the area had been a popular open-air restaurant.

He walked cautiously across the deck. Only twenty yards away, on the starboard side, an Oerlikon battery pointed at the sky, its crew watching the dark sea. There was already a pink hint of dawn in the eastern sky.

Müller wondered how the struggle was developing below. Something had obviously gone very badly wrong. But how? Who had tipped the British off about Operation Iceman? And where was Preuss?

Müller returned to the service room just as the lift rumbled into view. Schmidt was packed uncomfortably into the square box, his large frame bent double, and had to be helped out. Together they mounted a careful watch until the other two men arrived. Then Müller outlined the position of the Oerlikon anti-aircraft batteries on the Sports Deck and the main stairways to other parts of the ship. Finally he picked up his Thompson sub-machine gun, and said, 'Let's go. Best of luck, everybody. If you are in trouble make for the last lifeboat on the starboard side.'

He led the way outside, and they moved through the tables, skirting the starboard Oerlikon battery, and using the shadow of the huge funnel. On the other side of the open-air restaurant the two groups separated, Schmidt heading towards the staircase descending to the Sun Deck, where the wireless room was situated.

For the first time Müller took a close look at his companion, Lieutenant Uhlmann. He had the fresh complexion of a schoolboy, and was scarcely in his twenties. Although his physique was not powerful he was very agile, and his intelligent eyes watched Müller, waiting for orders.

'For'ard there's an entrance to the wheelhouse,' Müller whispered, as he led the way past a massive ventilator. They crept cautiously along the port side, and had just dodged behind another large ventilator when a patrol of four marines passed within a few feet. As soon as they had disappeared Müller slipped out and led the way across a disused badminton court. Ahead lay the bulk of the wheelhouse.

A guard was standing outside the small door leading into the structure, and Müller whispered over his shoulder. Uhlmann came at the guard from behind and stifled his cries before letting him fall gently to the ground, a knife in his back.

Müller was impressed by the young man's coolness and together they pulled the sentry's body out of sight behind some life-rafts. Then Müller tried the door.

To his relief it was unlocked. Inside a narrow corridor led to another door at the far end—the entrance to the wheelhouse. Two other doors opened to the right, where Müller guessed that the ship's officers had cabins.

He darted towards the far end with Uhlmann behind, keeping watch on the cabins. When he reached the wheelhouse entrance Müller paused a moment to collect himself, going over in his mind the layout of the bridge from his sketch maps. Then in one quick movement he whipped open the door and moved inside with Uhlmann at his heels.

Startled faces turned towards them. It was dimly lit but Müller could distinguish three officers, two of whom were watching the sea ahead. Behind them stood the first officer, whose eyes widened as he saw the Thompson sub-machine gun.

Uhlmann covered the left-hand side of the wheelhouse, where there was another officer, watching the hooded radar screen. A seaman on duty at the far end of the wheelhouse began to move.

'*Nein*,' Uhlmann shouted, and the man immediately stopped when he saw the sub-machine gun trained on his chest. Müller's eyes, however, were on the quartermaster gripping the wheel. His grey face was thrown into relief by the shielded light shining upwards from the binnacle housing the compass. Müller was very familiar with those features: Nobby's.

There was a look of bewilderment on the Englishman's face as he saw Müller's gun. 'What the hell are you doing here?'

Müller gave a wry grin. 'My job, Nobby.'

The other man's face screwed up in anger. 'You've been a Jerry all along?'

'I told you, I've been doing my duty.'

'Just carrying out orders?'

Müller ignored him. He had to get the *Queen Mary* on to her new course for France. 'Steer course south-south-east *now*.'

Nobby hesitated and looked at the first officer who disregarded Müller's gun barrel and protested in a loud voice. 'The quartermaster will only take orders from me. Hold to the present course, Quartermaster.'

'Ay, ay, sir,' Nobby acknowledged.

The rest of the men looked on in silence, and Müller wondered how they would react if he shot Nobby. He did not want to kill him, but all trust and bonhomie between them had disappeared, and the little man was an obstacle. If it was the only way for Operation Iceman to survive . . .

'Why don't you give up?' the first officer asked in a reasoned tone. 'Even if you shoot us all you know you won't succeed. How can you on such a ship this size? Whoever sent you must have been crazy . . .'

Another officer joined in, speaking from the radar screen. 'Your attack on the engine room failed. There's a lot of dead men down there. Nobody will obey your orders.'

'I don't want your advice,' Müller spat out. 'Get this ship on to a course steering south-south-east at once, or I will not be responsible for the consequences.'

In the half light he saw Nobby move only when it was too late. The Cockney's hands left the steering wheel, and he twisted his agile frame towards Müller, his right arm whipping up to his shoulder. Müller instinctively ducked, and he heard a grunt over his shoulder. He glanced round quickly. A patch of blood was already widening on Uhlmann's shirt, where the haft of Nobby's sheath knife protruded from his chest. The lieutenant staggered forward, but somehow kept the snub nose of the Sten gun pointing at the others on the bridge. Müller wheeled round furiously looking for Nobby and was just in time to catch two officers advancing on him. He pulled the trigger, and there was a spurt of flame.

One man stumbled to the deck, but the rest of the watch dived for cover behind the binnacle and engine room telegraph. Determinedly Müller peered round for Nobby and spied the small figure creeping behind the steering column. He felt no compunction about killing him now and had raised his Thompson machine gun when Uhlmann spoke hoarsely.

'Get out of here. The marines will be coming in at any moment. I'll cover for you.'

Müller was shocked by the young man's ashen face, then realised that he was right. He could not afford to take vengeance against Nobby, much as he might want to. There was no time. Operation Iceman still had a slender chance of success, and it rested on him.

Uhlmann pushed him feebly towards the door. 'Get out. *Get out!*'

After a moment's hesitation Müller threw a last look at Nobby, then dashed down the corridor.

Outside it was almost light now, and he moved cautiously towards the stern, hiding in the narrow space between the Carley floats and superstructure. A clatter of boots came from ahead and he pressed himself against the cork sides of a life-raft as a detachment of marines doubled past a few feet away. If they were on their way to the bridge, they would be too late, Müller thought. By now Uhlmann would have bled to death.

The attacks on the bridge and engine room had failed, and

Müller knew the British were still in total command of the ship. Operation Iceman had almost collapsed and his only hope was that Preuss might still be at large and capable of improvising some new operation. Bitterly Müller realised that he had failed.

He crossed over to the starboard side of the liner in the shadow of the funnel. The row of lifeboats seemed endless, but eventually he stood beneath the last one in the line. The teak deck planks stretched emptily away in each direction. Using the tiller and stern post as cover, Müller hauled himself upwards.

He put his foot on to the seat close to the tiller and climbed into the lifeboat. As he did so a strong hand gripped his ankle and pulled him down into the bottom of the boat. He half fell, colliding with another body in the darkness. Before he could scramble to his feet a gun barrel was pressed into the tender flesh beneath his ear.

Chapter 30

Torchlight stabbed Müller's eyes, and a voice which he immediately identified as Schmidt's spoke gruffly near his right shoulder.

'It's all right. It's the Iceman.'

A bottle was pressed into Müller's hands and the beam was switched off. 'Welcome aboard,' Schmidt said lightly.

Müller took a grateful swig. It was cognac, from the boat's emergency stores. The burning liquid relaxed him. Stiffness left his muscles and his eyes began to adjust to the darkness. Four men were crouched in the bottom boards of the boat. Schmidt sat close to him.

'What happened in the wireless room?' Müller asked. 'Did you knock it out?'

The captain laughed grimly. 'There were a dozen marines waiting. We couldn't get anywhere near the place. Lieutenant Braun took a bullet straight through the temple. I got out.'

Müller patted him on the shoulder, hiding his dismay that the British would now be able to transmit calls for help to every Allied ship and plane within reach. With Churchill on board, they would send the whole Royal Navy. He eased his way past Schmidt, knowing that he had to signal Kriegsmarine HQ at once, to give them the grim news of failure. He recognised the next man as one of Preuss's subalterns from the swimming pool. He was very young and sat with his head cradled in his arms. 'Are you wounded?' Müller asked solicitously.

'No. But I can't understand how we could get so near to Churchill, just a few yards from his cabin, and yet screw it up. It's unbelievable . . .'

Müller scrambled round him towards the lifeboat's bows. The third man blocked his way but made no attempt to move, so Müller slid across to the starboard side of the boat where he could pass. From this angle he could see that the POW was winding bandages round the bare chest of another wounded man, propped up in the bottom of the boat, his narrow back turned towards the stern. Müller waited until the dressing had been fastened, then asked how he was. The head swivelled towards Müller, the dark eyes furious.

'I'll survive, Iceman. I've been through bigger balls-ups than this.'

It was Preuss. Carefully the attendant POW put his hands under Preuss's arms and lifted him gently into a more comfortable position. The major's chest rose and fell rapidly, but his eyes flashed in the half-light beneath the tarpaulin.

'Well, coxswain, it was a shambles, wasn't it? Don't say I didn't warn you.'

Müller rested uncomfortably on his haunches, his face level with the major's. 'The British were on alert,' he replied. 'Somebody must have given away the operation.'

'Whoever it was did a good job. That was the only thing properly executed. As soon as we appeared on the Promenade

Deck the British opened up on us. They knew exactly where we were.' His head lolled towards his men. 'We are the only survivors and lucky at that.' A note of sarcasm crept into his voice. 'What about Colonel von Stoltz? What happened on D Deck?'

'I don't know,' Müller answered. 'He was trying to take the Main Deck by direct assault. The British were ready there too . . . It looks as if we're the only ones who can still do anything.'

Preuss's face was racked with pain as he tried to laugh. 'What can we do now? Let's face it, coxswain, we've missed the biggest chance of our lives.'

'Operation Iceman is not over yet, Major,' Müller replied.

'Whatever you are planning, you should do it now. The British will be combing the whole ship.' Preuss's words followed Müller as he moved towards the bow. The other men in the boat stared while he rummaged beneath the first seat. The radio set was still in position, the high explosives lying neatly beside it.

He pulled the set on to the boards between his feet and checked that the aerial was still connected. Then he switched on, and after a quick check of its tuning tapped the key, repeating his call sign. '*Iceman—Iceman—Iceman.*'

With the others listening in silence he signalled Berlin. 'Plan to seize ship aborted. Sink the *Queen Mary*. Sink the *Queen Mary*.'

Alloway stood in the Operations Room on the Main Deck, waiting for Summers to arrive. Around him staff officers moved quietly and efficiently taking telephone calls, passing on directives and marking the position of units throughout the ship on a large drawing of the *Queen Mary*. In the centre of the room McNeill was supervising operations. He amicably offered Alloway a chair in front of Summers's desk.

Alloway sat down, gently fingering the ugly bruise on his right cheek. His nose felt twice its normal size, and he was sure his whole face presented a terrible sight. He was grateful to the ship's surgeon who had treated him expertly, and fixed a piece of plaster over the neatly stitched cut on his left cheek. His injuries, he knew, could have been far worse. He had only the haziest recollection of the last moments before the grenade exploded. The soldiers who had defended the armoury with him had suffered terribly, and before he left the sick bay, now crowded with British, Canadians and Germans, he had visited the corporal who had manned the Bren gun, to find him lying pale and unconscious on a small cot. Next to him one of the privates sat upright in bed, his leg suspended in a sling. The third man had already died.

McNeill turned from the operations chart and instructed an orderly to bring Alloway a mug of tea. He stood over him a moment, his bluff Canadian features crossed in a broad smile.

'It's a good job you learnt to kick a football, mister. You wouldn't be here otherwise.'

'I always thought I was pretty lousy at the game.'

'Benefits of a good education,' McNeill rejoined and turned away to brief an adjutant. The mug of tea arrived, strong and sweet. Alloway gulped it appreciatively. He began to think more clearly. Why had he been summoned to Summers's operations room? He could still not forget the major's reserved tone of voice when he reported Preuss's actions on B Deck. He tried to tell himself that he was wrong to feel uneasy. He was the equal of Summers, after all.

At that moment Summers marched into the room. He greeted Alloway in a matter-of-fact voice, drawing up the chair on the other side of the desk. Carbon from the smoke canisters had rimmed his eyes, giving them a strangely theatrical appearance against the pallor of his skin. There was a bruise too on his square jaw, his uniform was stained, and there was a neat triangular tear on his shoulder.

In spite of these signs of struggle the fighting seemed to have acted like an injection of adrenaline on Summers. His eyes sparkled and he surveyed Alloway as if he were on parade.

'You look as if you've been in a prize fight.'

'I have,' Alloway replied drily.

'It was damn close. D'you know that there could have been a terrible loss of life, what with the PM's party and all the other passengers on board?' Summers went on, as if he were talking about a horse race. 'Fortunately we got wind of what Jerry was planning just in time. A few minutes later and they would have taken over the whole bloody ship. Imagine that!'

Alloway could have laughed at Summers's realisation that he might have ended up a POW himself.

The major looked across the table from under his thick brows.

'Your intelligence was crucial. If you hadn't told us that Preuss was planning to attack the Main Deck and assassinate the PM, we might have lost the day. The consequences would have been unthinkable.'

Alloway gave a shrug. 'Thank God I could speak German. Although, no doubt, that makes me a security risk in some people's minds . . .'

Colonel McNeill had come across from the wall chart and stood next to the desk, his arms folded. Alloway sensed that he enjoyed the jibe.

'I don't understand all that MI5 stuff,' Summers went on. 'But I can't ignore what I'm told. Nor would you. I expect you are wondering why I sent for you.'

Alloway's face was aching, but he remained silent.

'Well, I'm prepared to stick my neck out and forget MI5's suspicions because I think you can help us.'

'That's good of you,' Alloway said, straight-faced. The major would never have deigned to ask him for a favour unless he were in a difficult spot. Now he had the gall to pretend that he was risking his career to help Alloway.

Summers shot a glance at McNeill, then leaned back in his chair, hands gripping the arms. 'We're back in control of the ship now. Order has been restored on D Deck, and the POWs in the swimming pool are under heavy guard. We have checked all the Germans and we've had a body count, but a handful of prisoners are still missing.' He paused before he added, 'One of them is Preuss.'

'He might have jumped overboard,' McNeill commented.

'In the middle of the Atlantic? There are no rafts or boats missing.'

'Then if Preuss is still on board,' Alloway said, 'you must find him at once. He's very dangerous.'

'Exactly,' Summers concluded, and leaned across the table. 'You know Preuss well?'

'What do you mean?' Alloway protested, still suspicious.

'Perhaps I should make myself clear. You had a confrontation with Preuss at Tregaron POW camp, and again last night. You must know his character as well as any of us. What will he do next?'

Alloway thought for a moment. 'So long as he draws breath and is within striking distance of the PM, he'll try to kill him—and anybody else who gets in his way. Preuss is a Nazi and will regard the defeat of the attempt to capture the ship as a mixture of bad luck and botched planning. It will merely serve to make him more determined than ever to show the invincibility of his version of the master race.'

Summers's face was serious, and McNeill unfolded his arms.

The major put his fingers together. 'I'm sure you're right. Preuss will strike again. Nobody is safe until we find him, but there's another difficulty. We'll need your help to track him down.'

Alloway was suddenly angry. Summers was asking him to draw on his knowledge and experience of Preuss but made no offer to raise the cloud of suspicion over Alloway's own head.

'You should be able to find Preuss easily enough,' he declared coldly. 'He doesn't know the ship.'

'It's not so easy. Preuss isn't acting alone. The POWs didn't jack up this little show unaided. An agent was infiltrated on board in New York. As far as we know he's still on the ship.'

Alloway was taken aback. He had imagined that the rising had been planned by the POWs themselves. Now it seemed the ship was in far greater danger. An agent would almost certainly be equipped with radio, and might have explosives too. More sinister was the implication that German Intelligence had planned the operation. Perhaps the POW rising was merely a diversion. Perhaps it was meant to fail, and another, more ominous development was about to take its place.

Summers had reached for a metal filing tray, and began

reading aloud from a sheet of paper. He was describing a man believed to be an enemy agent, and his words began to conjure up a disconcerting image in Alloway's mind. However, it was only when the major added the words 'short blond hair' that Alloway recalled the pool of light on B Deck, and the unknown figure passing him in the small hours of the morning.

Strangely it came as no surprise that the man was a Nazi agent. It was as if he knew already, and he realised that he had seen those well-sculpted features on yet an earlier occasion: not masquerading as a ship's carpenter, but gazing out from the conning tower of a U-boat. It was the same face that had stared out proudly from the centre spread of the Nazi propaganda magazine *Signal* and Alloway remembered where he had seen it—in the flat belonging to Tracey O'Brien.

He pushed back his chair. 'I want to see General Ismay— now,' he declared to a surprised Summers.

'What do you want to say to him?' the major asked officiously.

'That's my affair. Personal. I want to see General Ismay.'

'That depends on whether he wants to see you.'

McNeill leaned forward, picked up the phone and gave it to Summers. 'Why don't you ask the general if he's free? Alloway has obviously got something important to tell him.' Summers looked at him, and slowly nodded.

Ten minutes later Alloway was ushered into Ismay's cabin by his adjutant, Summers bringing up the rear. The Military Secretary was standing by his desk reading a memorandum, but immediately put it down as they entered. The adjutant was dismissed and Ismay's pug-like features wrinkled as he appraised Alloway's battered face.

'My God, you've been in the wars, Alloway.'

'I'm feeling fine, sir,' he countered, anxious to get on with the meeting. It was essential for the general to understand that Larsen was from the U-boat arm. That meant that the entire operation was being planned by the Kriegsmarine. It could mean a sudden new threat.

'Major Summers has told me of the tremendous things you did down on D Deck. Very plucky, Alloway. Most commendable. This won't be forgotten.'

322

Alloway sensed the general's embarrassment and again cursed the stupidity of MI5.

'There's something I want to tell you, sir.'

The general's eyes were attentive.

'I must say first that I am in no way connected with enemy Intelligence. I am not a security risk.' He heard his voice rising fractionally. 'I hope that you at least believe this, sir, if nobody else, and I intend to clear my name of any kind of suspicion at the first opportunity.'

The general inclined his head and Summers shifted awkwardly.

'Thank you, Alloway,' Ismay replied civilly. 'I am sure you will be out of this trouble in no time. Was that all you wanted to tell me?'

'No, sir. I think that Larsen, the agent infiltrated on board this ship, is a member of the Kriegsmarine. Indeed, sir, he was in the U-boat arm, probably a chief petty officer.'

The general's brow puckered. 'But how do you know this?'

Briefly Alloway described the magazines, although he was careful not to mention Tracey's name, saying rather that he had seen them at a Cabinet Office meeting. Then he told of passing Larsen on B Deck.

The general rubbed his chin and walked over to the port-hole. He seemed sceptical.

'Remember, sir. I am a lawyer by profession, used to evidence. I am sure Larsen is a U-boat man.'

'What do you make of this, Summers?'

'If the Squadron Leader is right then we could be facing a Kriegsmarine attempt on this ship, something far beyond just Larsen's involvement.'

'Yes,' the general said reflectively. 'Call a meeting of the security people on board, and for goodness sake make sure that the Main Deck is well guarded. I will speak to the first sea lord.'

The general turned to thank Alloway, but Alloway spoke first, having thought carefully what to say. 'I have a request to make, sir, before I leave.'

'Well?' the general said sympathetically.

'I want my job back.'

The general sat slowly down in his chair, then studied the top of his desk. 'Alloway, you have been an excellent officer. I have never had any reason to be dissatisfied with your work. I miss your efforts sorely, but I cannot overrule the security people. Some very strange things have happened on this voyage, you must admit, and they will all be investigated thoroughly. I am sure you have nothing to fear, but I dare not risk crossing the security services.'

Alloway clenched his teeth, aware that if he spoke he might regret his words.

The general's eyes were sorrowful. 'I will signal MI5 in London and demand more information. Especially what they have found out about the young woman, Tracey O'Brien.'

Alloway nodded. He hated to think of what Tracey would have been going through, but he too had to know the truth.

'In the meantime, Alloway,' the general continued, in a conciliatory tone, 'I am sure Major Summers will be grateful for any assistance you can give him in finding this man Larsen. See what you can do.'

Chapter 31

The quiet inside the lifeboat was broken only by the sound of Preuss's uneven breathing. Müller stood up awkwardly, head bowed beneath the tarpaulin. Schmidt was crouched behind him, with one of Preuss's men in front. Each man pressed two packets of plastic explosives to his body, and between them they fastened the thick bandage from the lifeboat's first aid kit around his midriff.

'Don't make it too tight, or I'll never get the damned stuff out when I want it,' Müller whispered.

Schmidt nodded and adjusted the dressing to hold the explosives like an improvised pouch. Müller made sure that the packets were secure, then stuffed four detonators into his pocket, finally pushing the Smith and Wesson into his belt.

It was hot under the canvas and he was aware of the other men watching him closely. He was grateful to be leaving the lifeboat, in spite of the risks outside. To be cooped up made him uneasy, strangely sealed off from the outside world.

In his mind he went over the details of the operation he had to carry out. He checked the explosives once more to see that they were securely in place, then began to clamber towards the stern.

Preuss's eyes followed his clumsy movements, and when he spoke his voice was now much weaker, hoarse. He nodded towards Schmidt and the other prisoners.

'Why leave these men here? Whatever you have been ordered to do they could give you covering fire—perhaps create a diversion.'

Müller shook his head. 'I have a better chance of getting through on my own, Major. I know this ship well.' He put a foot on the stern seat, and began to move back the canvas. 'If the British find you, it will be futile to resist. You need medical attention badly. If you are found, give yourselves up.'

'The others can do as they wish,' Preuss replied laconically. 'Whatever happens I shall fight.'

His hand patted the Sten gun next to him while the others murmured agreement. The major's dark eyes blazed. 'I think you're crazy,' he went on, directing his words at Müller. 'You should take these men with you and kill Churchill.'

'We've been over all that before,' Müller sighed. 'The British will have turned the Main D Deck into a fortress.'

'So what's your brilliant plan?' Preuss asked mockingly.

'That concerns me alone,' Müller rejoined. 'What I can tell you is that we're likely to be attacked by U-boats at any moment.'

'So that's what your message was about,' Preuss commented. 'Churchill might die after all, and we'll drown with him.'

325

'Except that we are in a lifeboat,' Schmidt remarked lightly. 'That's some consolation.'

Looking down on the small group from the stern seat, it dawned on Müller that they were worried about what they should do if the ship were torpedoed.

He glanced around the hull. 'When the ship sinks you can easily get away. It's simple enough to launch this thing. If I am successful the ship will begin to lose way before she is attacked. That will be your chance to launch the lifeboat.'

'How?' Schmidt asked sullenly. 'I've never had the privilege of boat drill. It's not usually given to prisoners.'

'There are levers on the davits which raise and lower the lifeboats,' Müller answered. 'The two fittest men should jump on to the deck and use them to launch the boat regardless of the enemy. It will only take a few seconds for the boat to reach the water, and whoever mans the davit can slip down the ropes into the boat. It won't be easy, but it's your only chance.'

'But we'll be swamped if the ship is moving,' Preuss said thoughtfully.

'You've just got a chance if you start your engine before you hit the water.'

There was nothing more to be said. Müller placed his hand on the tarpaulin and wished them luck. Preuss acknowledged him with a tired wave of his arm, while Schmidt pulled himself to his feet to help Müller over the gunwhale.

'We may not have done so well,' the big German said, 'but thanks, Iceman. At least you got us out of that damned pool. Let's hope we meet on the Reeperbahn one day.'

Müller dropped softly on to the deck, which was now swathed in the grey light of dawn. Several groups of soldiers were on patrol and farther forward a party of marines was searching the lifeboats, but the davit and its tackle provided Müller with cover. Towards the stern there seemed to be no guards on duty, only a party of deck-hands washing down the teak planks and beyond them, some twenty yards distant on the port side, two men of an Oerlikon crew sat by their slender-barrelled weapon. Müller was aware that he might just have been visible to them, but luckily their heads were turned away, watching the sea.

Precious minutes were passing but he forced himself to wait behind the rudder until the cleaning party had moved farther across the deck. It would be dangerous to pass close to seamen who might remember him from the mess deck or the bar of the Pig and Whistle.

Eventually he dare wait no longer, and stepped out from behind the boat. At first he pretended to examine the lifeboat for safety, cocking his head expertly towards the stern, then started to walk towards the far end of the deck, half expecting a summons from behind ordering him to halt. None came. Keeping his eyes straight ahead, he drew level with the cleaning party, and at the edge of his vision detected a pale face turned momentarily towards him, but there was no gesture of recognition. Then he was on the ladder, moving quickly towards the Promenade Deck and Main Deck beyond, where he knew that troops would be guarding the entrance to Churchill's quarters. When he stepped off the ladder he counted four men in all, grouped round the double doors opening on to the deck. They seemed tired after the long night's action and two of them were leaning wearily against the superstructure, while another had a bandage around his right hand. Müller passed them over twenty yards away, and prayed that he was too distant to be identified. If challenged he would open fire, aiming for the wounded man first. He walked on, conscious of their eyes on him, but none of the soldiers stirred, doubtless accepting him as a member of the ship's company.

When he reached the stern he began to breathe more easily, and spied the hatch opening on to the crew's stairway. Gratefully he stepped inside, thankful for the cover. It was only five flights to F Deck. His rubber soles made scarcely any noise, but he was halfway down when he heard the clump of boots and the sound of voices rising towards him from around a bend in the stairway ahead. He held his breath, his heart pounding. There was hardly room for two men to pass on the stairs. His fingers released the safety catch on the Smith and Wesson, and he silently back-tracked to the landing above. A heavy door led from it and he pushed through it, checking the empty passageway ahead. A short distance away there was a linen store and he prayed that no stewards would suddenly appear, laden with sheets and pillow cases.

Poised behind the solid door Müller listened intently for the approaching party. The ring of their boots on the steel treads grew louder and he detected the bosun's rolling Hampshire vowels giving directions to the men behind him. Pressing himself against the wall, Müller waited for them to pass, but to his dismay the feet halted. Gruffly the bosun asked whether anybody had searched the passageway and there was a mumbled reply which Müller failed to catch. The door began to swing back and he pressed his spine hard against the wall behind him. The bosun's bull-like head poked inside the passage and peered along the corridor and, after a loud sniff, pulled back without seeing Müller, barely a foot away. Then the footsteps departed and the party continued its climb.

Müller let out a gulp of air. As soon as quiet had returned he raced down the remaining flights to F Deck, which lay just above the liner's rudder.

The lighting was dimmer at this level, and he began to wonder whether SKL was mistaken in sending him into the bowels of the ship. Then he saw it—just ten yards away towards the bows, an oblong hatch edged in brass. Blessing SKL for the accuracy of their intelligence, he dropped to his knees. The brass rings in the cover cut into his flesh as he heaved the hatch upwards. Before him a short ladder descended into the compartment and he slid down it as if he were on U-1543, into a chamber only six foot high. There was a strong smell of engine oil and dimly he made out an instrument panel to his left and reached for a light switch. Müller found himself looking at a gleaming complex of pipes and machinery—the *Queen Mary*'s hydraulic steering gear.

For a moment he stood gazing at the machinery in admiration. It was beautifully made, and stretched some twenty feet in each direction. To his left the dials and meters of an instrument panel rose behind three large motors, set in line abreast. They powered two ramrods which ran parallel for fifteen feet, like buffers in a railway terminus, until they bedded in two cylinders. The astonishingly gentle movement of the ramrods acted on a massive bearing which sat on top of the steel pin securing the *Queen Mary*'s 150-ton rudder to her hull.

Müller could see that it would take a massive charge to damage the rudderhead, but SKL's experts again impressed him with their inside knowledge. They had instructed him to seek out a small four-foot-long steel bar which controlled the action of the hydraulics. Müller followed the line of the pipes until he found the slender arm poised above the main control valve. As he watched, it moved slightly to the left in response to the quartermaster's movements on the bridge nine decks above. This was his target.

He hauled off his jersey, then with the fingers of his right hand felt for the ragged end of the adhesive tape around his waist. When he ripped it off, it was as if his skin was being torn away, leaving ugly red weals across his stomach. He had sweated so much that the plastic explosive stuck to his skin and had to be pulled away. The yellowish slabs were still moist and warm as he began to press them around the metal control bar.

The *Queen Mary*'s bridge seemed crowded. The liner's master, Captain Stewart, stood by the wheel, his stolid figure wrapped in a duffle coat. In the far corner a Royal Naval commander, sent up by Admiral Pound to maintain a link with the liner's bridge, scanned the waters ahead, watching for the first sign of approaching escorts.

Nobody felt the explosion in the liner's stern. It was the quartermaster who detected the first sign of trouble. Staring at the compass platform with a puzzled expression, he frowned at the officer of the watch standing next to him.

'She's not responding to helm, sir.'

The captain raised his beak-like nose and walked across to the binnacle like a parent going to deal with a way-ward child. He studied the needle, then issued a series of terse orders to the quartermaster who acknowledged the instructions smartly, each time swinging the wheel to a new course. But the compass remained set in exactly the same position.

Stewart exchanged a glance with the first officer as the deck began to move and the liner started to heel over in a twenty-nine-knot turn.

'Half ahead!' The four engine-room telegraphs rang on each side of the wheel as the officers of the watch pulled them to the new position.

'We're still turning, sir,' the quartermaster announced.

'Slow ahead starboard. Half ahead port.' The captain's face was expressionless.

The ship's speed dropped and the deck slowly levelled. 'She's coming round, sir. Holding course.'

'What the hell's happened?' Stewart asked sharply.

The first officer was already on the phone to the engine room.

'Your steering gear has been damaged,' the Navy commander declared. 'Could be a torpedo hit.'

'Come on, get those damage reports,' the captain urged, and his officers busied themselves contacting parts of the ship by phone and voice tube.

'All secure for'ard, sir,' a junior officer cried.

'Engine room secure, sir,' the first officer added.

'Get the engineers down to the steering chamber fast,' Stewart ordered. He strode over to the phone and spoke directly to the engine room.

'Hello, Chief. Captain speaking. We've got some sort of trouble with the steering gear. Get someone down there right away.'

A broad Glaswegian voice acknowledged, and the captain swung round on the naval commander.

'I think you had better report our problem to Admiral Pound. Tell him I'm only able to maintain a speed of six knots without going round in circles or placing undue strain on the engines.'

Before the naval commander could reply the telephone rang, and the first officer's lean features seemed to grow even longer as he answered it.

'Captain Stewart, it's the prime minister. He wants to know what's happened.'

The *Queen Mary*'s master took the receiver, and after listening a few moments calmly described the situation.

330

'We can hold course, sir, but we can't keep up twenty-nine knots. Not until we sort it out.'

He put down the phone thoughtfully and walked across to the compass.

'Maintain present course and speed as best you can.'

Some minutes later the engineer sent to survey the damage reported to the bridge.

'Can you do anything?' Stewart asked, his brow furrowed.

'Well, we'll have to try to straighten out the coupling somehow. I hope we can do that without dismounting the whole column.'

'How long will it take?'

'I don't know, sir. It could be a couple of hours, could be five minutes. I don't know until we get started.'

'Get on with it then, as fast as you can,' Stewart replied. He glanced impassively at the rest of the watch. The first officer's face seemed even more lugubrious, the commander simply thoughtful.

'We shall just have to steam along like an old tramp steamer and wait for the U-boats.' Stewart placed his hands behind his back. 'Let's hope your escorts are not too long in arriving, Commander.'

Kapitanleutnant Hartstein listened to the throb of U-1264's main diesels and restrained himself from asking his chief to coax even more power from the over-worked engines. He had pushed the engineers as hard as he dared, and knew that they were doing all they could.

Spray broke over the boat's prow and swept the conning tower, deluging Hartstein, but he hardly noticed. His eyes were fixed on the horizon.

Ever since the long-awaited signal had arrived to open his sealed orders he had been a changed man. Snatching only a few hours' sleep, he had urged his chief to force U-1264 through the waters at all possible speed towards the reported position of the *Queen Mary*.

Every man aboard was aware that the mighty prize which had eluded them a few short months before off the coast of Africa was once more within their grasp. The radio operator sat listening for any new position from HQ, and in the bow chambers the torpedo men were loading the gleaming Zauenkönigs, waiting for the order to prime them.

'Ship bearing fine on the starboard bow.'

The for'ard watchkeeper pointed across the brightening waves and Hartstein moved quickly across to the starboard bridge parapet. He combed the faint line of the horizon, then stopped. Against the sky he could make out the slightly darker shape of a vessel. He pushed his battered white cap on to the back of his head.

'Bring her to starboard twenty. Full ahead both.'

The tension rose as the crew exchanged knowing glances and the U-boat rumbled into higher gear.

The number one climbed on to the bridge. 'Well, is it our famous lady?'

Hartstein scratched his stubbled chin. 'I'll bet my last Havana it is. Anything on the sonar?'

The number one spoke down the voice tube and a report came back from the hydrophone operator.

'Very distant echo, sir. Sounds like engines.'

They butted onwards into the easterly swell, with Hartstein staring across the water, his shirt open at the neck, his face shining with the elation of the hunt.

'This is it, Number One. I feel it in my bones.'

'There is one thing, Captain,' his number one said quietly. 'Where is the rest of the group?'

'Coming up behind us,' Hartstein replied. He glared back at his junior. 'But we shall be first on the scene, and we will have the first shot.'

'Shouldn't we send a signal to concentrate?'

Hartstein moved to the rear of the bridge, out of earshot of the watchkeepers. The number one followed him.

'We shall concentrate soon enough. We deserve first crack.'

The watchkeeper reported over his shoulder. 'She's only making a few knots, Captain. I can't even see a bow wave.'

'That's unusual. Normally she steams flat out,' the number one commented. 'Something must have happened on board.'

Hartstein was silent, impressed to see that as Headquarters had promised the target would be travelling at less than half her normal speed. From his sealed orders he knew that the ship was carrying German prisoners and that the Zauenkönig torpedoes would lead to heavy losses. He feared the possible effect on his crew's morale if they discovered thousands of their countrymen struggling in the sea. Their spirit would suffer and he would try to pick up as many German survivors as possible, but he could not expect to save more than a handful. Grimly he accepted that he might never be a popular commander with his crew again; but the great ship had to be sunk.

'Maybe she has some engineering breakdown. Or it could be a trap,' his number one was saying.

'Trap? What do you mean?'

'She's carrying about fifty ack-ack guns, Captain, and a six-inch. If we approach too close on the surface she could riddle our hull.'

'I've thought of that,' Hartstein replied sharply. 'Sound diving stations.'

The klaxon sounded and the watchkeepers on the bridge slid one by one down the conning tower. Hartstein waited until the last, his eyes still on the distant hull.

U-1264's bows were already well under the water and the sea was swirling around the conning tower before Hartstein swung his legs over the hatch. In fifteen minutes, he told himself, he would be surfacing to a very different scene. And his reputation as the Reich's top U-boat ace, greater even than Prien and Kretschmer, would be secure.

Müller panted as he lay on top of a large life-raft nine feet above the Sun Deck. The ship's alarms had ceased to ring, and the guns' crews were closed up for action on the Oerlikon batteries. The stern had been sealed off, look-outs doubled and armed patrols now passed along the deck. He felt a strange sense of satisfaction at having caused such a commotion, and was even more jubilant that his luck was holding so well. In the general alarm nobody had noticed him retracing his steps to the upper deck. He glanced at the boat opposite, which contained Preuss's group.

The detachment examining the lifeboats had worked halfway along the starboard side of the ship, and were nosing about in one of the midship boats, still some forty yards away. But the ship was noticeably slowing down and it was time Preuss started to move. He wondered whether to try dodging across the teak planks below to make contact with the others, but dismissed it as too risky. He also admitted to himself that he did not want to join up with Preuss and enter the lifeboat. Somehow he knew that he would never find the strength to survive another ordeal in a lifeboat. In any event, he still had work to do.

To his left another squad of troops—six heavily armed marines and a junior officer—were approaching from the bows. At their head, walking with a pronounced limp, was a dark-haired young man incongruously dressed in RAF uniform. It was too far away to see his face, but Müller recognised the awkward gait. It was the same halting stride of the man he had encountered on B Deck at one that morning. His fingers tightened on his Smith and Wesson.

To his relief there were now signs of movement in the lifeboat opposite. The canvas cover had been rolled back and, oblivious to any danger around them, Preuss's two lieutenants jumped on to the deck. Schmidt's head poked over the gunwale near the stern, and the big man pointed to the davits. So far, the party advancing along the deck had not noticed anything unusual. They were still some distance away, and Preuss's two men were half hidden by the davits. Even so, it seemed an eternity as they fiddled with ropes and stays. Finally the Germans took up position, one at each end of the boat, and, on a curt nod from Schmidt, jerked back the levers. There was a squeal of pulleys, rope scorched through the eyes of the davits, and the boat lurched towards the sea.

Müller glimpsed the pale features of Preuss propped in the stern, clinging to the tiller. Next to him Schmidt yanked desperately at the cord to start the boat's engine. There was no answering sound. He tried again, throwing his full weight against the cord. With only ten feet to go before they hit the sea the engine coughed once, then burst into life in a cloud of acrid smoke.

Farther along the deck the RAF officer had broken into a shambling run and the marines were doubling forward, weapons at the ready. The two POWs still on board did not waste another second, but grabbed the ropes from the empty davits and leaped over the side. The man who had been manning the aft davit hung perilously a moment, then his grip loosened and he plunged headlong into the sea. Müller knew he would never survive the razor-sharp rivets and barnacles along the liner's sides, and anyway, the bow wave would drag him under. The second POW was luckier and fell untidily into the bows of the lifeboat, just as it struck the sea in a great cloud of spray. Water streamed on board and, still attached to the davit at the bow, the lifeboat's hull reared at a crazy angle. Schmidt yelled at the young man who had tumbled aboard, and he tugged desperately at the bowline. It was enough. The boat dropped clear, to be almost submerged as it fell away from the liner's hull. Müller prayed that Schmidt and Preuss had the sense to keep the boat head-on to the sea. As he watched, a solid green wave swept across them, but the lifeboat's propellers were biting and a bedraggled Schmidt emerged to take the tiller; the boat was under control.

Below, the first marine had arrived at the empty davits. He knelt on the deck where the lifeboat had been and immediately loosed off a magazine from his Sten gun, but the range was already too great, and his shots splashed harmlessly into the sea. The rest of the squad took up firing positions as they arrived, but the lifeboat was now level with the liner's stern, and bobbing like a toy in the *Queen Mary*'s wake. It was an impossible target.

Müller heard the breathless voice of the RAF officer below. 'We've missed them! We've bloody well missed them!'

'That's all right, sir,' said a marine standing at the officer's side. 'The ack-ack guns will blow them out of the water.'

Hartstein's periscope was filled by 81,000 tons of ship. Crouched in the attack position in U-1264's conning tower, he permitted himself a final examination of the famous hull. The slender barrels of the Oerlikons were just visible on the upperworks and he wondered what agonised decisions were being taken on the *Queen Mary*'s bridge. For a while he stared at the line of windows along the main deck, covered with grey paint. In one of them Churchill and his top advisers might be meeting, deciding their future moves against the Reich. It was a perfect target, the biggest ship, the most important enemy. He had already placed the U-boat's cameraman on stand-by, knowing that the propaganda effect of the sinking would be worth a thousand victories in the field.

Once the ship was hit he had decided that he would surface and risk the *Queen Mary*'s armament. There would be chaos on board her as the ship settled and thousands of passengers and crew tried to get away. His principal duty, according to his orders, would be to find Churchill, whether in the sea or in a lifeboat, and to take him aboard U-1264. A list of further top personnel to be picked up had been transmitted to him and to the other commanders in his group. All the British leaders were to be taken directly back to Lorient as prisoners. All other British would be abandoned to the mercies of the Atlantic.

He glaced at his watch. The rest of his group would be arriving on station within thirty minutes. He was still determined to strike first. They would be just in time to help round up the survivors and to ambush any Allied escorts, which HQ had warned were racing to the *Queen Mary*'s position.

'Stand by forward tubes,' he shouted. 'Prepare to fire one and two.' Suddenly through the lens of the periscope he observed a splash along the liner's hull, almost at the stern. A torpedo attack? Perhaps one of the other boats in his group had arrived and attacked first, damn them! That would be intolerable. He hastened to issue his directions for the attack.

'Prepare to fire one and two,' he repeated.

'One and two tubes ready for firing,' the bow chamber affirmed.

Hartstein took a last look, then slowly squeezed the firing trigger.

'Torpedoes running,' came the shout, and the crew, cramped at their action stations, held their breath. With a surge of compressed air the two Zauenkönig torpedoes streaked from U-1264's prow. In their blunt noses delicately balanced acoustic detectors immediately registered the regular beat of propellers reverberating through the water column. They transmitted their intelligence to the torpedoes' guidance systems and the weapons locked on to their target.

In the silent control room, the hydrophone operators strained for the first sound of contact. Hartstein listened, chin on chest, to the number one's voice reading from his stopwatch, counting down the time to impact.

The lifeboat rounded the *Queen Mary*'s stern and pitched in her wake. Preuss levered himself up and peered over the gunwale at her hull.

'Hold the boat steady. Keep her dead astern of the liner,' he said hoarsely to Schmidt who sat behind him clutching the tiller. 'If we do that, they won't be able to bring all their guns to bear.'

Schmidt acknowledged Preuss's orders. Although the major was now breathing with great difficulty he was still in command. He had just finished speaking when two Oerlikons on the liner's superstructure opened fire. Their first shots curved gracefully over the top of the lifeboat, slicing into the sea beyond. Then the gunners found their range and heavy cannon shells cut through the water alongside the steel hull.

'Keep your head down,' Schmidt yelled, and yanked on the tiller, pulling the boat hard to starboard, shipping water into the hull. The lieutenant in the bows began to bale frantically, and the boat tossed dangerously, but the next burst from the Oerlikons streaked harmlessly overhead.

'We can't keep this up for long,' Schmidt yelled, and throttled down on the engine. Again the staccato chatter began from the liner, and the cannon shells came slicing across the sea. Schmidt pulled over the tiller but shots pierced the hull, and there was a splintering of wood as another blew apart the emergency locker.

Schmidt pushed his weight against the tiller again and opened up the throttle. The engine roared and the propeller churned the sea.

Forty yards from the lifeboat's hull the delicate sensors

in the nose of U-1264's first Zauenkönig quivered and transmitted a signal to its fin-like rudder. Streaking forward at thirty knots the torpedo cut beneath the lifeboat's keel. A trigger clicked in the Zauenkönig's second chamber, and in a glistening column of water a ton of explosive ignited. The second torpedo exploded moments later, ensuring that nobody could survive in that small patch of the ocean.

The explosions reverberated through the layers of water and brought wild cheering aboard U-1264. Only Hartstein was unmoved. His eyes stayed pressed to the periscope, and from his grim expression his crew knew that something had gone terribly wrong. The enthusiastic back-slapping stopped, the cheering died down. Hartstein watched the great columns of water subside. The *Queen Mary* sailed on unharmed. But now her bow wave was higher, the white wake was churning astern and her speed had begun to pick up. By the time he had reloaded, Hartstein knew that she would have reached twenty-nine knots.

Chapter 32

There was a drone of aircraft engines and a grey US Navy Liberator circled over the *Queen Mary* before flying out on a long leg over the ocean, searching for U-boats. Standing on the Sun Deck, watching the distant shapes of the escorts against the evening sky, Alloway found the noise comforting. The events of the morning seemed far off now, and he found it difficult to believe that the dramatic attempt on the *Queen Mary* had ever happened. Since the U-boat attack a massive screen had been thrown round the ship. Escorts had arrived in strength, ready to protect her all the way to Pier 90. On D Deck and in the swimming pool the Germans were subdued, counting the cost of their failure to capture the ship. The departure of Preuss in particular had demoralised them, while von Stoltz seemed totally uninterested in making trouble.

The atmosphere on board was far more relaxed, and although the hunt for Larsen continued it was at a leisurely pace. Summers, McNeill and other security experts were convinced that the agent had been blown to pieces in the lifeboat. There was general agreement that three men were seen in the boat, and a fourth had fallen into the sea. This was believed to be the Norwegian.

Alloway still felt uneasy about Larsen's whereabouts and was not yet convinced that he had met a watery death. He turned and walked back towards the Main Deck. Many people greeted him, but although his face was no longer swollen he felt distinctly embarrassed by the discolouring bruises.

He now had a small cabin on the Main Deck, since his own had been so damaged in the fighting, but he still felt angered by the MI5 investigations. Bitterly he noted that General Ismay had taken no steps to offer him back his job.

He unlocked his cabin door and sat down at the writing table in the corner. All afternoon he had been busy with a report for Summers on the attack on the armoury and Preuss's escape in the lifeboat. He began to read over the paragraphs he had drafted, but found it hard to concentrate. His mind wandered to Tracey. How on earth had she become involved with MI5? She had always been frank with him, and he still found it hard to believe that she was an agent. He would have given anything to have had her with him now. He resolved, then and there, that if ever they survived he would take her with him on a transatlantic crossing, champagne and all.

There was a knock at the door, and when he opened it he found a marine orderly outside.

'General Ismay's compliments, sir, and he would like to see you.'

He screwed his fountain pen together and straightened his tunic. He really had no desire to see the general and felt that their relationship was now hopelessly estranged by the misunderstandings and distrust over the security investigation.

He walked along the Main Deck to the general's office, and when he entered found him in the middle of being briefed by Summers, who was giving him the latest report on the POWs and the whereabouts of Larsen.

The general waved Alloway to an armchair in the corner of his room, and came over to join him with Summers. They sat around as if they were in a club and Ismay called for his adjutant, who entered from another room with a bottle of whisky and glasses.

Alloway studied his superior's leathery skin, but Ismay's expression was impassive. Suddenly he said, 'Do you think this agent, Larsen, is still on board?'

'He could be, sir. There's no proof at all that he has gone, and he was able to conceal himself very effectively before.'

The general nodded, then looked across at Summers.

'Well, that's a job for the security people. They must find him. There's a war to fight and a tremendous amount of work to be done before we reach New York.'

To Alloway's surprise, Ismay suddenly turned and raised his glass in his direction.

'Pleased to have you back, James. I had a signal from MI5 this morning. You are completely in the clear.' To his delight Alloway realised that the general was taking him back into his department.

'And Tracey O'Brien?' he asked nervously.

'Your young woman friend as well.' The general chuckled. 'I was always confident that it would happen.' Summers raised his glass to join in the toast, grinning at Alloway.

Still he could not relax. 'I just don't understand what happened, sir . . .'

Ismay stroked his moustache. 'MI5 were apparently not so stupid as we thought. There was indeed a security leak on the *Sentinel*. Somebody had been sending out coded messages in news stories. An old trick, I might add. Most of them were under the name of your friend, Miss O'Brien. But it was not that simple. It emerged that the girl was completely innocent; all her stories were being sub-edited by her bureau chief in London, and he was planting coded information into her articles. They picked him up yesterday.'

Alloway thought of the paunchy figure of Chuck Mason. How could he implicate Tracey in his operation? But there was no time to look for an answer. The general had already drained his Scotch and was talking to him about the papers he required for the next Chiefs of Staff meeting in an hour's time. It was as if nothing had ever happened.

The night air was cold and Müller's limbs were painfully stiff. He had been in the life-raft all day, hidden by its bulky cork sides. He had been able to stretch his limbs, but had to remain on his back most of the time to avoid being seen from below.

Throughout the day troops had crossed and recrossed the deck below, and he had had to keep a wary eye open for search parties. Usually they walked straight past the life-raft, which was on top of a stack. Once, a more efficient marine sergeant had insisted on climbing up the side of the stack to look inside the top one, and Müller, covered by the rubber sheet which survivors used at sea, had held his breath. The man had felt aimlessly around, then climbed down again.

The loss of Preuss's group had depressed him. He had clearly seen the explosions in the *Queen Mary*'s wake and cursed the U-boats for getting so close but not succeeding. The dark sky seemed to reflect the hopelessness of his operation. The effort had been vast, yet it had all foundered.

He realised suddenly that Preuss had been right. He should have thrown aside the elaborate SKL plan and gone all out to kill Churchill. That would have really shown them that personal initiative could do more than fleets and armies.

He chuckled softly to himself. Perhaps Operation Iceman could succeed after all. The Reich's greatest naval victory: Obersteuermann Ulrich Müller, formerly U-1543, would kill Churchill single-handed.

All day he had thought of the ship, of the alternative and possibilities for getting near Churchill, and as the sun had gone down a plan had formed in his mind. It was eight o'clock, and he remembered from the gossip in the

341

Pig and Whistle that the prime minister dined at eight-thirty.

'I think it is time for an aperitif.' The prime minister looked over the top of his glasses and beamed at his advisers. It had been a long meeting in his suite on the final tactics for the meeting with Roosevelt. Alloway looked at his notes, delighted to be back working with the Defence Office. Everybody in the room had been very friendly towards him, with no mention whatsoever of his injuries, or of why he had been relieved of his duties.

The Chiefs of Staff gathered up their papers and General Ismay scribbled a draft of a message to London, which he handed to his young assistant. Alloway studied the familiar handwriting, then started to make his way to the cipher office. Over his shoulder the prime minister was launching into an analysis of the strategic situation, heavy with reference to Nelson and Bonaparte. Alloway regretted having to miss what promised to be a fascinating monologue. In that moment he realised how fortunate he was to be serving so close to Churchill. At some stage the war would finally end and he would climb out of uniform to return to the legal career which he loved. When that happened, the experience of working in the Defence Office would stand him in very good stead, so long as the story of his being suspected of treason never leaked out. He had the reassurance of being cleared by MI5, but nasty stories had a tendency to stick. Tracey at least would understand what it had meant to be under suspicion, and he resolved to tell her everything that had happened to him on his return from America. She too had suffered, and it should bind them closer together. In any event she was too much of a journalist ever to stop asking questions.

The prime minister's private dining room offered the shortest route to the cipher office, and as Alloway crossed it he could not fail to be impressed by the splendour of the table which had been laid for dinner. The *Queen Mary*'s chief steward had seized the opportunity to restore some of the pre-war standards of service. A dozen places had been set with a fine display of silver bearing the Cunard markings.

To judge by the array of cutlery the fare was going to be rather more luxurious than the wartime ration. At least six courses would be served, accompanied by a fine range of wines, to be drunk from long-stemmed glasses and crystal goblets. It was all deeply impressive, but what fascinated Alloway most of all was the fine spray of carnations placed in a silver vase at the centre of the table. Just what kind of foresight was involved to guarantee such fresh blooms in the middle of a grey North Atlantic?

With a wistful feeling that he would have enjoyed being a guest at such a dinner, Alloway placed his hand on the door knob leading to the corridor beyond.

As he turned it a slight rumbling seemed to come from the other side. The noise should have warned him, but when he pulled back the door he cannoned straight into a serving trolley laden with drinks. The white-jacketed steward who was pushing it was still half concealed in the dim light of the corridor. On top of the trolley was an array of bottles, including the prime minister's favourite Pol Roger champagne and Hine cognac, while at the very front stood a large silver dish of canapés covered by a white cloth. Plates and shining cutlery were piled next to it. There was a wetness on the back of Alloway's hand, and he saw that a bottle of claret had been knocked over in the collision. It had gushed to the floor, splashing over his sleeve on the way. As he looked down at the mess, the steward muttered an apology and offered him a napkin to dab off the worst of the wine. Distractedly Alloway had begun to thank him when he noticed that, in reaching forward, the steward had exposed a shirt cuff. It too was stained, and Alloway could tell from the stiffness of the dried liquid that it was not claret. He was looking at blood.

Alloway looked up quickly to meet two clear blue eyes, observing him with a hint of mockery. Instantly he identified the broad cheekbones, glistening fair hair and thick eyebrows of the U-boat man whose photograph he had seen three weeks before in *Signal* magazine. It was also the face of the dark stranger who had passed him in the corridor at one o'clock that morning.

From the steward's half smile Alloway immediately knew

that the German recognised him too, knew him to be his enemy. The white sleeve was reaching now for the silver dish. Instinctively Alloway swept down with his left hand. The pain left him surprisingly untouched as he knocked the dish flying. It spun a moment in the light before striking the wall in front of him. There was a shower of petit fours, cocktail sausages and puff pastry. A vol-au-vent splattered against the wood panelling. In the middle of the mess a heavier object lay spinning: a Smith and Wesson revolver glistening with caviare.

It took only a split second for Müller to recover his balance and reach forward along the length of the trolley, hands grabbing for the Englishman's throat. There was no hatred on his face, only an inner certainty that he would get his man. Yet Müller had misjudged his move. The trolley rolled forward under his weight and he stumbled, half falling on to his stomach. His shoulder connected with a jug of cream which splashed over his face like shaving lather, and for a moment Alloway imagined that they were both taking part in some crazy slapstick comedy. Then realising Müller was off balance, he raised his right arm, bringing the flat of his hand down on the German's neck. But Müller rolled expertly to his left, so that Alloway's hand bounced harmlessly on the trolley's surface, knocking aside more plates and bottles.

Alloway tried to retreat into the dining room, but Müller was crouched on the right-hand side of the trolley; with a fierce shove he pushed it at Alloway's legs, pinning him to the wall of the corridor. A stab of pain went through Alloway's thighs and his damaged leg began to crumple. Summoning all his remaining power Alloway kicked out at Müller's crotch with his injured limb. But the U-boat man grinned—the squadron leader was an amateur after the men he had faced in the bars of Brest and Lorient. Müller moved sideways, taking the blow on the thigh, then clamped his right hand on to Alloway's ankle, giving it a savage wrench. Alloway almost fainted with the pain. It was as if his hip was being torn from its socket. He fell to the ground and at once Müller's right knee pinned him like a steam hammer. His head swam and the vertebrae in his neck seemed to be coming apart as his skull was forced against the doorpost. He managed to turn enough to glimpse a flash of glass in Müller's right hand: the German was about to plunge a broken Hock bottle deep into his exposed neck. In panic, he twisted his head violently, and the jagged glass speared his right shoulder, narrowly missing his exposed jugular. Now Müller pressed with his left hand, forcing Alloway's face to the ground. Cognac fumes seeped into his nose—somewhere Churchill's brandy must have been spilt—and he felt as if he were suffocating. He winced as Müller pulled out the improvised dagger and waited for the next blow. The fatal one. But it never came. Instead Alloway felt as if his rib cage was being flattened. Blood poured over his shoulder, warm and sticky past his ear. In that moment of panic he thought he had been savagely wounded, but then the weight was pulled off him and he breathed again. Choking, he pulled himself to a sitting position and looked round ready to face Müller.

To his surprise the German was stretched out on the floor, one leg twisted awkwardly over the other. Above him, feet apart, a stone-faced Major Summers held his service revolver by the barrel. There was blood on the butt where he had brought it down on Müller's skull.

Suddenly there were troops everywhere, and a sergeant was kneeling at his side, carefully examining the place where the glass had ripped into his uniform tunic.

'You all right, Alloway? It seems as if you've found our agent. We knew he had talents, but never suspected that he could pass as a steward as well as a chippy.'

Alloway managed a slow grin and sipped gratefully at a glass of Scotch and water which the NCO was pressing to his lips.

'We'll have to get you to the medic, fast,' Summers declared.

'I'll survive,' Alloway replied, feeling angry at being treated like a wounded man. He watched Summers turn Müller over with his boot, studying the bruised face. The German's eyes were closed and there was blood on his temple.

'Get this Kraut out of here,' Summers ordered contemptuously. 'Put him in the sick bay and place a two-man guard on him. Round the clock. Look after him. We've got a lot of talking to do.'

Two marines dragged Müller along the corridor by his feet. Somebody ordered Alloway a stretcher. Another marine started to wheel the shattered trolley away and he idly watched it go. Miraculously two claret bottles still stood erect on the bottom shelf, although the top was a shambles. He smiled at the German's thoroughness at having placed two large boxes of Havana cigars next to the wine. Müller had been ready to offer the prime minister his favourite brand of cigars before he killed him! Yet the joke was on the coxswain. The boxes were marked as American King Edwards, whereas Churchill unfailingly smoked— suddenly Alloway's expression changed and he struggled awkwardly to his feet. Summers stopped talking and the marines stared at him anxiously. Shouldering them all aside he somehow made his way to the trolley, gathered up the boxes and, half hopping, half trotting, made off down the corridor. Past bewildered Wrens and officers, an angry brigadier, then at last the door and the ocean breeze . . . With his lungs burning with the effort Alloway reached the rail and hurled the two boxes over the side. A small, bewildered crowd gathered round him, observing him with apprehensive respect as if he had taken leave of his senses, but he ignored them and stared out at the sea. Somebody ventured the suggestion that he must be concussed, and he was beginning to wonder himself when there was a dull boom thirty yards aft, followed by a cascade of water. An explosion rocked the hull.

Müller's head throbbed as he lay in his narrow cell, half closing his eyes to blot out the weak light above. It had been almost two hours since his interrogation by the domineering marine major. That had been followed by a succession of Intelligence officers who had each tried their own techniques to break him down, but he felt proud that he had frustrated them. So far at least. No doubt they would try again once the ship reached New York. The FBI had a reputation for dealing with prisoners.

He tried to turn his mind to more optimistic thoughts, but

felt sick and depressed. His right arm seemed to be burning, and he was certain that the doctors had allowed some fragmented glass to remain in his flesh, probably on orders.

It was bad to feel so broken; now that he was a prisoner he would never again reach that peak of fitness and fighting efficiency that he achieved in Mexico. It could all have been so different if he had never gone there. He was not an agent, had never really been, and he detested what his uncle had forced him into, the sad absurdity of his efforts.

It would have been better if he had gone the same way as Larsen. He suddenly felt chilly and recalled the strong, capable hands pulling him out of the water.

It was airless in the cell. The atmosphere possessed a strange decaying smell, like rotten vegetation or old timber. It was like the atmosphere in the small chamber in the bows which had been his hideout on board. Ironically it was very close to his present cell—as was the chain locker where Jacobsen had been buried in his steel grave.

The measured words of Major Summers rang in his ears, his cold insistence that Müller would be executed. He wondered what he would have to face—exposure in a court, then a firing squad—or was it an electric chair? He braced himself against the fear which had begun to grip him.

There was something ignoble, humiliating about execution. It would be like dying a criminal. Patriotism, love of the fatherland would be far from anybody's thoughts. He hoped they would treat him reasonably at the end.

On 11 May 1943 the *Queen Mary* anchored off Staten Island and lay within sight of the skyscrapers of Manhattan. A boat came alongside with the slight figure of Harry Hopkins, the president's personal aide, who welcomed the British party. The prime minister was soon taken ashore and immediately entrained for Washington.

At 2.30 the following afternoon Roosevelt, Churchill and their attendant Chiefs of Staff met in the White House. After a welcome by the president, who told the meeting that in the pursuit of victory, 'Nothing that could be brought to bear should be allowed to stand idle', Churchill addressed the meeting.

According to the records he 'recalled the striking change which had taken place in the situation since he had last sat by the president's desk and had heard the news of the fall of Tobruk'.

He went on to remark that there might have to be adjustments in strategy now that North Africa had fallen and the invasion of Sicily was on the horizon . . .

The Trident conference had begun.

For the next twelve days all aspects of Allied strategy were argued and examined. On some issues there was complete and immediate unanimity, on others, such as Far Eastern strategy and the invasion of Italy, there was passionate debate. Meeting three or four times a day, the staffs toiled towards agreement, whilst Churchill and Roosevelt renewed their close contact, relaxing at the weekend at Shangri La, the president's retreat in the Catoctin Hills.

By the morning of 25 May the Trident discussions had come to an end, and a joint declaration on strategy was signed. Churchill was disappointed that his scheme for the invasion of Italy had not been endorsed, but his main purpose had been achieved: the Americans had undertaken to defeat Nazi Germany first, before turning their full might against Japan. With some satisfaction the prime minister cabled home news that 'an agreement most satisfactory to our Chiefs of Staff was being reached over the whole strategic field'.

The Allies were in good shape for the final thrust to victory.

Winston Churchill took off the next morning in a flying boat bound for Algiers, where he was to meet General Eisenhower. The remainder of the British mission wearily packed their files to travel home from New York aboard the *Queen Mary*.

After the hectic days of the conference James Alloway managed to spend two days looking round the city, but he was soon to be back in North America as a regular member of Churchill's secretariat for the Quebec Conference in August. He also travelled to the summit meetings in Tehran, Cairo and Yalta.

On his return to London, Alloway continued to see Tracey O'Brien, but the affair did not last. In 1944 she returned to the United States as Washington correspondent of the *Sentinel*, and on her father's death in 1948 became editor-in-chief and sole proprietor of the paper.

MI5's files on Squadron Leader James Alloway are still kept in the Ministry of Defence registry.

The pendulum was beginning to swing decisively against the Axis powers when Ulrich Müller was brought to trial on Governor's Island in the late summer of 1943. Evidence was produced by the prosecuting attorney that Ulrich Müller had murdered Abraham Nathaniel Jacobsen. He was found guilty and sentenced to death by electrocution. No evidence was offered on any other charge.

On 3 September 1943 the sentence was carried out.

CHRIS MULLIN

A VERY BRITISH COUP

It is March 1989 and Britain has a new Government. Ex-steelworker Harry Perkins has led his far-left Labour Party to victory on a manifesto which includes withdrawal from NATO, nuclear disarmament and the removal of all U.S. bases from Britain. Horrified, the British Establishment musters its forces and as senior civil servants, press barons and the City conspire to bring him down, Perkins finds hmself embroiled in a battle for survival. Can Pekins and his elected Government hold out or is the Establishment bound to win what turns out to be a very British coup . . . ?

'His narrative rattles along with speed and great credibility, not least because of his accurate and detailed backgrounds, from a nuclear power station to the interior of No. 11 Downing Street.'

Alan Hamilton, *The Times*

'A spiffing read . . . calculated to grip blue-rinsed Conservative ladies and make Socialist eyes pop.'

Matthew Coady, *The People*

Post·A·Book

A Royal Mail service in association with the Book Marketing Council & The Booksellers Association.

Post-A-Book is a Post Office trademark.

STUART JACKMAN

SANDCATCHER

Something was brewing in the Empty Quarter of Saudi Arabia. Something Military Intelligence in Cairo wanted to pin-point and contain. Something to do with Abu Marak, a renegade sheik who was terrorising the Bedu tribes and whose actions threatened the security of the Middle East. And it was up to four men from the RAF Desert Patrol Group to sort out the mess. For three of them it was to be a straightforward, if dangerous, mission. But for Sergeant Tom Race it was something much more . . .

Here is a microcosm of war: its horror, its sacrifice and a moving climax which you will never forget.

'A tremendously thrilling tale'
Manchester Evening News

CORONET BOOKS

ALSO AVAILABLE FROM CORONET BOOKS